THE DROP OF A HAT

HAT TRICK

THE DROP OF A HAT

**LUKE CHMILENKO
AND
G. D. PENMAN**

Podium

This book is dedicated to all you low level monsters out there—getting none of the respect you deserve and dropping three gold pieces when you die.

All rights reserved. No part of this publication may be reproduced, stored in a retrieval system, or transmitted in any form or by any means electronic, mechanical, photocopying, recording, or otherwise without prior written permission from Podium Publishing.

This is a work of fiction. Names, characters, places, and incidents are either products of the author's imagination or used fictitiously. Any resemblance to actual events, locales, or persons, living, dead, or undead, is entirely coincidental.

Copyright © 2023 by Luke Chmilenko and G. D. Penman

Cover design by Mansik Yang and STK Kreations

ISBN: 978-1-0394-4278-8

Published in 2023 by Podium Publishing, ULC
www.podiumaudio.com

THE DROP OF A HAT

CHAPTER ONE

CONCERNING KOBOLDS

In a hole in the ground, there lived a kobold.

This was not a fully furnished and tastefully decorated hole in the ground with all of the modern appliances such as doors or walls. Rather, it was the muddy gap between two half-rotten tree roots that the soil had simply forgotten to fill in.

It was not the sort of place that a cohort of adventurers might gather at the behest of a wise wizard to discuss where their grand quest might take them. They likely wouldn't have even visited for the purposes of pest control, given that it was much more economical to farm and fatten up rats to produce "kobold" tails when they were requested in exchange for a quest reward.

Now when I told you that in this hole lived a kobold, I may have been slightly underselling things.

There was, at the lowest level, a bountiful feast of invertebrates for those with a taste for the crunchy things in life. Then, slightly above that on the food chain, kobolds. It should be said that kobolds are not generally known to be solitary creatures. A singular kobold tends to have the sort of life expectancy usually only known to creatures that awaken from a pond and frantically fornicate to produce the next generation before nature realizes she has forgotten to furnish them with the necessary organs to eat anything.

The plural of kobold is kobolds. The singular is prey. They are born in vast litters of blind, wriggling pink pellets and seek to maintain that quantity of warm bodies pressed in around them throughout their lives, whether for their comfort in a cold world, or to serve as armor. Protection in numbers taken to its natural extreme.

But what is a kobold?

The answer to this question is not one that I had often considered in my old life. To me, they were barely a footnote in the annals of history. But if you were to ask others, you may have come across a wide variety of answers. A farmer, for instance, will tell you that they are tantamount to a plague, eating anything that isn't nailed down. Which is not to say that they won't also attempt to eat anything that is nailed down, only that they tend to have less success doing so.

If you were to ask one of the charmingly deranged people that make a study of monstrous creatures, then you'd be told that they were Bipedal Muroidomorphs. Which will of course mean absolutely nothing to anyone who has not submerged themselves so thoroughly in academia that they are liable to get decompression sickness if they ever make an attempt at returning to reality.

Perhaps the best person to ask would be those who are most familiar with the creatures, adventurers! If you were to ask an adventurer what a kobold was, they would tell you, half a copper each, but bulk discounts apply.

Observe, the kobold. It looks as though someone has taken a rat, inflicted some unpleasant skin diseases upon it, grown it to the height of a dwarf, and then forced it to walk upon its hind legs.

Given the fuzzy cuteness associated with many rodents, we should probably make some amendments to your mental picture. Strip away the fur and replace it with the kind of wrinkly skin that would make a scrotum consider investing in a better skincare routine. From there it is only a matter of exaggerating the aforementioned skin conditions and inflicting a smorgasbord of nervous tics.

All of this, unfortunately, ignores the kobold's most distinctive feature. Its smell.

You could use it to strip paint and clear sinuses at a range of fifteen feet. There are elements of decaying meat, spoiled milk, excrement, and more to be found, and it is also important to note, for clarity of your mental image, that this is not some natural trait like a skunk might wield in its own defense. To a kobold, hygiene is something that happens to other people.

With all of this in mind, let us examine our kobold in particular. Currently lying, sleeping, amidst a heap of its kin. Most of its surface was caked in such a layer of dried-on muck that it would require a fast-flowing river or a chisel to discover its natural coloration. At present, it was making the most of its current fetal position to suck on the blunted end of its well-chewed tail.

In the language of the kobolds, which is barely a language at all, this kobold was named Ig. Were you to scrub aggressively at the areas of a kobold that nobody in their right mind would have any interest in, then you might discover that Ig was a male kobold. If Ig were to discover this, it is unlikely that he would know what to do with that information. Like hygiene, matters of romance and procreation were entirely alien to kobold-kind. They tend to reproduce primarily through accidental collision while attempting to find a more comfortable spot in the kobold heap to sleep.

What makes this kobold special? What is it about him, surrounded on all sides by equally grotesque specimens, that draws our attention? Why is he the one kobold in this entire hole that we care about in the slightest?

Because he needed the bathroom.

Were he to relieve himself in his current position, then he would become rather unpopular among those sleeping on the lower layers of the pile, though he would likely improve their cleanliness significantly. But Ig, he was better than that. He was a kobold of some dignity, by the rock-bottom standards of kobolds. He was not some freshly laid pink morsel, he was an adult, almost a year and a half old. When he needed to piss, he could go outside and find a tree.

So, half-asleep, and still absently gumming at his tail-tip, he began to wriggle his way out. Passing by parents, aunts, uncles, cousins, sisters, and brothers, with several of those titles typically attached to each individual kobold, in his journey towards the trickle of cold air coming down from the forest above. He could not smell the freshness of the air, as his nose had shut down out of self-defense many hours ago, but he could feel the breeze.

As he emerged from his hole in the ground, it was with no small amount of nervous energy. There were not many things in this world of ours that a kobold could not consider a predator. Owls, foxes, wolves, they'd all make a meal of a kobold. A decent-sized rabbit could likely give Ig a run for his money if it came to a straight-up fight.

Kobolds did have opposable thumbs, which allow their hands to do many of the terrible things that human hands do, and some have supposed that it is simply their lack of will to do harm that renders them so helpless. After closer examination of the kobold psyche, I can assure you that it is not some inherent benevolence. It is incompetence. There is no task in this universe so simple that a kobold cannot find some way to bugger it up.

Case in point, after tentatively creeping from his hole in the ground, Ig scuttled through the dew-damp undergrowth to the side of the river, squatted down, and urinated on his own feet.

Cursing and grumbling as much as any living creature without an actual language can, he made his way past the other midden heaps of his people to the river where they fetched their drinking water and gave his feet a quick splash in the shallows after making sure that the vicious and well-fed pike that sometimes took kobold toes was nowhere about.

To those of you concerned about the fact that the kobold waste product was flowing directly into their drinking water, I can assure you, there is a good reason that the kobold's life expectancy is typically measured in days. It is a miracle that they still exist, given how intent they seem to be about wiping themselves out through sheer stupidity.

After paddling his feet in the stream, Ig turned slowly to take in the world. This forest was all that he had ever known of it. Safe as things got for kobolds, thanks to its great distance from civilization, or anything of value that civilized people might want to fight over. This was a borderland, the outer edge of every map, the middle of nowhere. Nothing ever changed here, nothing ever happened here, and that was for the best, because change did not bode well for kobolds.

They might have been bizarrely resilient, capable of existing in almost any climate, but the one thing that they were not resilient to was other monsters. Even the lowliest goblin could have come through and made these hopeless creatures subservient to it, and from there it was always a short distance to ritual sacrifices or cannon fodder. Neither of which did much to extend the already miniscule lifespan of the kobold.

Yet something had changed. Something small enough that nobody else would ever have seen it, but that someone who lived every moment of their life within a single square mile of their grotty little hole in the ground would notice despite having the attention span of a ferret on stimulants.

There was something in the trees on the far side of the river.

At first, Ig did what came naturally to him, which was making a valiant attempt at pissing himself again before realizing that his bladder was already empty, and then running as fast as possible back towards his muddy little hole in the ground.

Kobolds are not particularly fast, nor known for their stamina, so he made it about halfway back before becoming winded. At which point he flung himself face-first into the long grass and remained as still as possible. Stopping to catch his breath, and also absently wondering why whatever it was that he'd seen hadn't already eaten him.

After several minutes of shivering in terror and setting all the dry spring grass around him rattling like a maraca, it slowly dawned upon Ig that he may not have been facing the final moments of his rather meager life.

He emerged from the long grass that he had taken for a shelter, nose poking out to lead the way, and discovered to his immense surprise that nothing was in fact chasing him. Given that this was the first time in his life that nothing was chasing him, this came as something of a shock to Ig, and his surprised condition probably informs many of the decisions that followed after.

His beady little eyes narrowed as he set his brain, such as it was, to the task of deciphering what he had seen, and why he was not currently being murdered. It was the harshest mental challenge that he had ever encountered. A tension headache began to spread from somewhere between his eyes, to encompass his entire scalp. He scratched himself in a place that I shall not mention in polite company, and then waddled back over towards the river to see if he could spot whatever he'd assumed was planning to murder him.

Kobolds have the brains of prey. Just as surely as they have bodies designed for much the same purpose. Which is to say, their intellect is a wire, pulled incredibly taut, ready to strum at the faintest brush of danger, sending them scrambling for safety. In the place where a thinking creature might have had those parts of the brain reserved for art, poetry, and culture, the kobold had a flight or fight instinct that would put the twitchiest vole to shame. It robs them of any ability to concentrate, as their attention is constantly divided between a million little noises that just might be threats. It robs them of the ability to think with any acuity, because thinking big thoughts takes a very long time when you are designed exclusively to function on a scale of split seconds.

Back by the river, which he once again dutifully checked for the risky pike, Ig waded over to the far side to see what he could see. It was not quite the farthest that he had ever gone from the hole that he called home—that honor went to the patch of mushrooms that he and his siblings had discovered to the south and consumed in one long, orgiastic afternoon of bizarre hallucinations, visions that for Ig involved an unknown creature that he would in later life learn was an aardvark—but it was still farther than he really felt comfortable traveling.

Yet there was a siren call to the flash of color that he had seen in these otherwise drab woods. Gray and brown were the predominant colors here, even at the height of summer. Even Ig and his siblings tended towards gray and brown, from lichen and mud. To see something that was not only blue, but a rich royal blue, was enough to make the few hairs that grew on the back of his neck stand on end.

Excitement was not an emotion that was familiar to Ig.

He knew hungry. He knew itchy. He also knew afraid. He was very familiar with afraid, in fact. Some might say it was his primary state of being, with all others only occasionally passing through. But excitement, that was as alien as this flash of blue in the drab of the woods.

Overwhelmed with excitement, Ig did something that hitherto this point he most likely would have considered to be outrageously bold. Something that neither he, nor any right-thinking kobold, would ever attempt. He opened his mouth and squeaked.

It was a tiny sound. Light as the faintest flirtation of a grasshopper and twice as shrill. A sound that anywhere else would have been entirely unremarkable, and that here in the forest even would have been unremarkable, but for the fact that it came from the mouth of a kobold.

Nobody answered him. Not even the blue thing in the tree.

It still hadn't moved. Still hadn't made a sound of its own. If it were some sort of ambush predator in a battle of wits with Ig, it clearly had him outclassed. If it were a plant that he was unfamiliar with then in all honesty it still probably had him outclassed in wits. Yet he could not resist it. Even though his whole body prickled with barely contained terror, he came closer and closer to the tree. To the broken-off branch. To the thing hanging there from the broken-off branch. Some sort of circle with a triangle protruding out the middle of it. A thing completely unfamiliar to his gaze. What you or I, dear reader, would know as a hat.

And what a hat it was. Such finery had never been seen in those desolate lands. It was a rich royal blue as deep as the fiercest of oceans or the calmest of night skies. The embroidery upon it was a masterwork of golden thread, outlining the positions of the stars to those with the knowledge to decipher its glyphs. In all of the world there has never and shall never be a more attractive and well-put-together hat than that very hat, that Ig found hanging from the branch of a tree.

He threw a pine cone at it.

The pine cone missed. Aiming may not have been Ig's forte, but what he lacked in strength of arm or hand-eye coordination he more than made up for with being willing to do the same thankless task over and over again without pause. Nor was he missing pine cones. The forest floor was littered with them. Not to mention that a fair few of his missed throws rebounded back off the tree to land by his feet and be thrown all over again.

So passed a goodly portion of Ig's morning. He had found something rare and beautiful in his little slice of the world, and he fully intended to pelt it with a pine cone if it was the last thing that he did.

Fear that it might be the last thing that he did, did of course creep into Ig as he stood there, tossing cones. His mind, ever in a turmoil, heard the echoes of his cones falling as approaching footsteps. Every creak of the trees was a bow being drawn back. Every twig snapping was a colossal carnivore connivingly creeping closer.

Yet still he persisted, not because he was brave, but because it hadn't quite occurred to him yet that he might have been safer were he not standing out in the open, throwing pine cones around.

Ig was not considered to be the most intelligent of kobolds by his kin. In the grand ranking of things, scaling down from the oldest mother-aunt, who knew which mushrooms were safe to eat, vaguely, all the way down to the tiny mewling pink things that dropped out of them every so often and grew into kobolds, Ig's intellect would probably be placed somewhere between the dry moss that they sometimes slept on and the mud it was used to protect them from. All of which is to say, he was not the brightest of boys. Even for a kobold.

Despite this failing, and a multitude more, there is something to be said for persistence. Though the task was clearly beyond him, though he lacked the skills and capabilities required to complete it, though every moment attempting to complete it put him into ever greater danger of being set upon by one of the myriad creatures of the forest that meant him harm, Ig persisted in throwing his pine cones until finally, surprising him as much as anyone else, one hit home.

The rim, where it was struck, bent a little out of shape. The silk lining, where it was hooked on the bark, suffered a minute tear to its stitching. But most importantly of all, the feeble throw of his tiny noodle arms managed to dislodge the hat from the branch on which it had been hanging for an indeterminate length of time.

Dashing forward, he snatched up his prize in his grubby little hands. Delighted and excited and staining the rather fine blue fabric with hands that had touched both mud and river recently. He spun around, holding the hat, as though to show off his prize to all who were gathered there, realized that he was alone, and let out a deflated sigh.

Then, finally, he turned his full and undivided attention to the hat, for the whole half a second that he was actually capable of maintaining attention. He looked at it and saw that it was beautiful and wonderful and strange. Then he heard a bird in some distant bough drop a twig, and he was off scampering back towards the river and the hole beyond.

The hat dangled in Ig's grip, flapping in the wind as he put on a brief turn of speed. It became bedraggled and sodden as he crossed through the river, forgetting it was in his hand, and paying far more attention to the possibility of pike. He was, in fact, almost all of the way back to his little den in the middle of absolutely nowhere when he seemed to realize that he was safe and sound and had something in his hand.

He wrung the water from the hat, mangling it more than a little and rearranging the cosmos as described in its embroidery in catastrophic and apocalyptic ways before flapping it in front of himself a few times to try and straighten it out again. The hat would never be quite the same again after this treatment, but holding grudges against creatures that aren't technically sapient seems something of a waste of time.

Regardless, it seemed that some singular brain cell in his head was sparking. Sending signals throughout his shrunken skull. The same joke that every living being with a head has ever made when confronted with something that looks like it might fit on that head. He lifted up the hat and placed it on his head.

Finally.

CHAPTER TWO

CONCERNING WIZARDS

The very moment that the hat touched down upon Ig's grime-encrusted scalp, sentience returned to me. It was not that I was lacking in intelligence while my being was confined to the hat, you must understand—all of the potential for my usual intellectual acuity was there; I simply lacked the physical structure required to think thoughts. Now that I had a brain attached, I was able to push some part of myself down into it and use its admittedly meager processing power to think again.

My first thought, directed at the vile little creature beneath me, was, *Don't you bloody dare.*

He had been reaching up to pluck the hat off his head again from the moment that he heard my voice. But it seemed that when I directed the full puissance of my will at him, he was incapable of movement. He stopped dead, swaying slightly from his abruptly arrested movement, clawed little grippers just inches from my rim.

Do not touch that hat. Do not move a muscle. I need a moment to gather my thoughts.

As you can imagine, I had quite a few thoughts to gather. The first and foremost of these being "Why am I a hat?"

To the best of my recollection, I had never been a hat before that moment. So far as I was aware, I was Absalom Scryne, the greatest and most puissant wizard that the world had ever known. Becoming a piece of apparel was quite a step down.

I will not say that I was absent any memories, because in truth, every single one of them had been stowed away neatly in the vast mind palace that I typically keep between my ears. Accessing the full breadth of them was not immediately possible, what with me having to shunt the parts of my mind that I was currently using to think, and prevent the kobold from moving, out of his wretched little brain if I wanted to look at them. Hardly ideal, given the sensory void I was cast into whenever I was not settled upon someone's brow.

So it was that I made some suppositions, that I might confirm or disprove at a later time. The first of which was that, while my body was currently absent, there could be no denying that I was possessed of the mind of Absalom Scryne, and given that was the most important part of Absalom Scryne, I therefore was Absalom Scryne, current conical shape notwithstanding.

This in turn suggested one of two potential reasons for my current predicament. The first: that someone had finally succeeded in assassinating me, presumably so that they might introduce themselves in every future conversation as the greatest and most puissant wizard that the world had ever known without me contesting their claim. The second: someone had managed to get through all of the myriad layers of arcane protection that I laid upon myself day and night, and successfully afflicted me with some sort of spell of baleful polymorph, transforming my physical form into that of a hat.

Either of these was tantamount to murder, and as the murdered party, I felt sufficiently aggrieved at the current situation that I desired either vengeance or justice. Whichever of those came in the form of a fireball cast directly at whoever was responsible, for preference.

While I was thinking all of these rather rapid-fire thoughts, Ig was also experiencing something new. The gray bulb that rested behind his eyes, that had previously been used predominantly for the cooling of his blood, now buzzed with activity.

As it turned out, kobolds are in fact capable of thought, they are simply unaccustomed to it. At some point in the development of their species, they discovered that thinking was a non-essential function, and the brain became a vestigial organ. But now, now that the old gray matter had been shocked to life, our dear Ig rapidly became capable of feats that hitherto would have been impossible for him. Things like going to the toilet without getting wet feet and forming whole syllables.

"What?!"

That was practically a twelve-hour soliloquy on the nature of life in kobold terms.

Just wait a moment, rodent. I am trying to think, something that would be markedly easier if you hadn't emptied your skull of any workable equipment.

"What?!"

At least he was consistent.

I am attempting to ascertain how I came to be here, and how I am going to depart with all haste. The more that you interrupt, the longer that process will take.

Ig paused to consider this, weighing his next words carefully.

"What?!"

You would not have thought it possible for a hat, devoid of a head of its own, to develop a headache, but I could already feel a twitching in my stitching that surely would have been a tension headache if I were more properly corporeal. I ignored Ig, as I suspected I would many times in the immediate future, and turned my borrowed mind to planning.

Judging from the position of the sun, I was able to determine the time of day and year. Judging by the local flora, it was easy enough to determine that I remained upon the same continent as I had dwelled on in life. Thinking on the distinct possibility that I was deceased may have sent me into some sort of existential spiral, so I sidestepped it entirely to continue focusing on the practical matter of returning home and inflicting explosive violence upon those who had usurped my place in the Great College.

I have a plan.

Ig waited with bated breath to hear it. Or perhaps he always breathed through his mouth. I was doing my best not to judge.

You shall take me to the magical city of Arpanpholigon, to the Great College where I studied the highest Art, and there you shall assist me in identifying whosoever condemned me to my current state.

There was a long—one might even say dramatic—pause and then Ig replied to my entreaty. "No!"

I assure you that you will.

"Nope." A variation on the single-word answers! His intellect must have been developing at a prodigious rate thanks to my influence.

Are you aware that I am a wizard, young kobold?

Ig answered more cautiously this time. In exactly the same manner as before. "No."

Are you aware of what wizards do to young kobolds that defy them?

At this point I was prepared to flood the creature's mind with horrifying images of the awful torments that magic could inflict on the body and the mind. However, he was ahead of me by miles. While his rational mind moved at a pace that would have made snails traveling behind it in single file shout abuse and complaints, his imagination when it came to all of the awful things that could happen to him moved so fast that it broke the speed of sound. He had conceived of a dozen awful punishments that I might inflict before I had been able to consider a single one, and his were markedly more gruesome than I could ever have come up with. Ig was doing my work for me.

"No . . ." Digging deep into his newly developing vocabulary, Ig sought out a second word to supplement the first. ". . . please?"

The fact that he was already at the pleading stage boded well for their ongoing negotiations. The fact that he was paralyzed from the neck down probably helped with that.

You need not fear me, Ig the Kobold. I shall be the best friend that you have ever had . . .

As I was preparing my sales pitch as to why helping me would be immensely beneficial to this disgusting creature, I was startled to realize that he had already sunk into contemplation. Well, I say sunk. That implies that there was more than a puddle's worth of depth to his mind. Regardless, he seemed to be considering my offer before I had even made it.

"Never have friend."

I was about to make a plethora of comments regarding the root cause of this absence, most likely relating it back to the fact that his personal hygiene was not questionable. For it to be questionable, there would have had to have been some doubt about it. Nobody in a quarter mile could have had any doubts regarding his cleanliness.

But instead, I restrained myself and let him think this through. Let him think that we would be friends, if it meant that he would obey me. Just as I had set aside all thoughts of my own mortality, or lack thereof, I set aside all consideration of the full number of people that I personally would have considered a friend through the years. It was not relevant to the current conversation, or the manipulation that I was attempting, so I pushed it aside.

"No."

No?

Ig shook his little head from side to side, almost dislodging me. "No want go. No want far away. No."

For a moment, I was so stunned at the rapid growth of his intellect that I released my control over his body. His hands, already en route to my rim, continued as though there had been no interruption, but it seemed that dear Ig had enough time for his immediate terror to abate, so after twisting me around a little to be more comfortable atop his ears, he let go.

There would of course be a reward for your aid.

Greed is an alien concept to kobolds. For there to be greed, there must be plenty. Without plenty, there is no disparity, only survival. Despite this, kobolds do have a drive for acquisition. Scavenging, one might say. What they lacked, unfortunately for my attempts at negotiation, was any abstract idea of what they might want until it was directly in front of them. For instance, say you were to offer a kobold a gold piece. They might want it because it was a shiny thing, but if they were hungry, and discovered that the gold was not edible, they would discard it as useless.

Here I was, offering this . . . Ig, the greatest of gifts, and he could not comprehend why any might desire it.

"Food?"

I . . . Yes. I can assure you that you will be well fed so long as you are my . . . friend.

Clearly, he was a savvy negotiator, for no sooner had I accepted his terms, he was already pushing for more. "More food?"

As much food as it takes to fill your little stomach up to bursting point.

He let out a little yelp, somewhat akin to a ferret being trod upon. "No burst!"

As much food as it takes to fill your little stomach up to just before bursting point?

Ig nodded affirmatively at the mental image of a distended stomach that I was pushing down into his brain. Glimpses of the many delicious meals that I had consumed throughout my years, and banquet after banquet in honor of my supreme wizarding triumphs. Works that would strain even the complexity-addicted minds of my peers to their breaking point.

Ig was still nodding. "Me like food."

It was a statement of such profundity that I was, for a moment, deprived of my own faculties. A moment in which Ig began to wade his way back across the river towards that place that he called home.

With all of the mind control, new wardrobe choices, and excitement that he had encountered, the more practical matters that usually occupied Ig's mind had slipped into the background. He did not see the dark shadow cutting through the water. He did not realize the significance of the v-shaped waves lapping back from the rear dorsal fin of the pike as it rose up from the depths to open its jaws wide and consume him. Yet for all that this would have spelled doom for any other kobold in the world—or at the very least a 50 percent reduction in the cost of boots—Ig was not alone. I was there with him. Present and accounted for, but incapable of seizing control of his body and leaping him out of the way, incapable of casting any of the innumerable incantations that I knew which would render this pike into sashimi, due to my current lack of mouth, incapable of doing anything helpful at all as the pike sloshed towards him, and my odds of ever getting home and learning the truth dwindled with every passing moment.

This would not stand.

Though it may have seemed that all of my prodigious intellect had been turned to the task of convincing a moronic kobold to do my bidding, it may surprise you to hear that the greater part of my mind had actually been focused on more arcane matters, understanding the nature of my predicament, and how it was that my consciousness had been confined to this pointed hat.

Magic gathers where it is used. It accumulates, and builds up, and while there are several well-documented ways in which excess magic vents itself, one of the most fundamental rules of magic is that it expresses itself in ways that are arcane, mysterious, and confusing. For instance, the fact that excess Quintessence gathered in one spot will often manifest in the form of a living creature, typically a small white fluffy rabbit, is well-documented. They are forever appearing under wizard's hats. Yet no rabbit had formed beneath me.

Quite the opposite, in fact. Rather than entrapping the excess Quintessence that had been leaking forth from my scalp when I cast my spells and rituals, it seemed that same immaterial had instead infused the fabric. Instead of creating new life, it had bestowed upon an inanimate object some degree of life, and when my incredible mind vacated its fleshy tomb, it inevitably would have been drawn to it. There would have been a resonance between the magic still held in my mind, and the magic that had been infused into this hat, which would have drawn it up and in.

Which meant two things. The first, that I had a small pool of Quintessence to draw upon, and the second, that it was extremely unlikely that I had been polymorphed into a hat rather than having my consciousness transferred into it by an accident, postmortem.

It was the pool that had become relevant in this stream, however. Without words to shape that power, it was next to useless, and compared to the arcane might that I had cultivated over long decades, the amount at my beck and call now was frankly pathetic, but the first magic that anyone learns is low magic. The direct application of Quintessence to move physical objects. It was, being the first thing that every young wizard learned, the most useless thing that they learned too. The efficiency of the magic was awful; you'd spend ten times the amount of Quintessence to perform a task that could more readily be done with a simple spell. Or, more often, by hand.

Yet here, devoid of spells and hands, I reached for that most basic of magic and bopped the pike on its nose.

What the pike thought was happening, I could not say, though it practically flipped itself over trying to get away from the sudden and unexpected contact. Maybe it had concerns that it had swum into some invisible wall, or that it was being haunted by the ghost of a crucian carp. I could not tell you.

All that mattered was that Ig was safe and I could continue riding atop without any unnecessary hobbling and hoping knocking me loose of my perch.

Well, that wasn't all that mattered, obviously. There were a great many far more important things afoot than the safety of a kobold's foot, not the least of which being the rapid depletion of Quintessence stored within my fabric. Low magic is the least efficient of magic, and so that tiny expulsion of force had drained my reserves in a way that a far more complex and impressive piece of arcanum would not. In short, I would not be able to pull that particular trick out of my . . . self again until I found a way to restore what had been lost.

None of which I could convey to my new servant, as he was too busy blubbering in gratitude for my rescue. Or at least, I assume that was what he was trying to do. It was a little difficult to parse his words when he was trying to speak too quickly. They all tended to flow together into a stream of squeaking.

Yes, yes. There are many benefits to being the friend of a wizard. Let's not lose our focus now.

"You save me!" Ig let out a squeal that could probably be heard for miles.

Please stop your blubbering. Of course I saved you, we're friends . . . aren't we?

For a moment I was concerned that I may have overplayed my hand, as Ig went stiff and rigid beneath me. It was rather unbelievable really, the idea that I, one of the greatest magical minds of all time, would befriend a creature that usually ranks somewhere between pond-weed and vermin on the social ladder. Surely, he must have realized that, and was about to fling me from his scalp into the river to be torn apart by the very pike I had just snooted.

But no, it seemed that was not the case. With quaking hands, Ig tentatively stroked my rim. "Thank. Friend."

He was truly as smart as he looked.

That is only the beginning of the things that I can give to you, my friend. Next time, it will be you that casts the spell to turn the monster away. For you, my dear creature, shall now be my apprentice.

Had I a face rather than a conical protrusion, I likely would have struggled to keep it straight as I said all of that to him. The idea that a kobold could learn magic was preposterous. Even among civilized races it required an unparalleled intellect and dedication that was beyond the vast majority of the populace, yet the truth of the matter was that until I could find a more suitable creature to be worn by, this Ig would be my sole means of transport, protection, and sustenance.

I could not cultivate a fresh reservoir of Quintessence to restore what I had spent—that required a living body and a brain—but if I could somehow drill the absolute basics of magic into this creature, he would doubtless allow me to siphon off whatever I needed for my own restoration. Not to mention how much easier it would be to return to Arpanpholigon with a little magic on our side.

Given that my bodyguard currently couldn't cross a river without almost dying, it seemed to be almost a necessity, and I could comfort myself with the thought that the moment I was no longer upon Ig's head, he would doubtless return to his previous, mindless self. Incapable of using what he had been taught for any nefarious purposes.

Though what nefarious purposes a kobold might use basic magic for currently eluded even my prodigious mind. Uniting his burrow in worship of his new power perhaps? Conjuring food rather than going out to fetch it? The sky may have been the limit when it came to what magic could do, but kobolds tend to be accustomed to a much lower ceiling.

While I had been pondering all of this, Ig had remained in motion, still scrambling his way back towards that hole he called home. Some of his kin had emerged into the gray dawn light, looking every bit as pitiful and flea-bitten as him, but while they took note of the new stylish headwear that Ig was sporting, its significance clearly eluded them. They went about their usual business of digging for grubs in the mud, consuming the grubs, and expelling the grubs from their other end as though today were a day like any other.

Ig moved to join them initially. But some portion of my disgust at the squishing sounds that he made as he mashed them with his teeth must have passed down into him, because it seemed that he could not maintain his appetite for long.

Sated to some degree, it seemed that he was now making ready to say his goodbye to friends, family, and all that he had ever known, because he proceeded back to the hole in the ground that he called home.

Do not fear, dear friend. You will be able to return here once our quest is through. To return a hero and a wizard will doubtless be incredibly impressive to . . . whoever it is here that you'd like to impress.

Ig cocked his head to the side, and I slipped a little in the direction of his ear. "Quest?"

Yes, our quest. To return me to the city of magic. With rewards of food?

I was tilted in the opposite direction as Ig considered this. "No. No going."

I beg your pardon? I thought that we had an arrangement. We are friends. Aren't we, Ig? Don't friends help each other?

"Not going. Sleep time."

Sleep time. I was momentarily stunned.

"Night night." With that, Ig scrambled back into the pile of kobolds that occupied the majority of the muddy floor, tucked the end of his tail into his mouth and almost immediately lost consciousness. Leaving me alone once more in my own head, or hat, as the case may be, to stew.

CHAPTER THREE

CROSSING THE SAME RIVER TWICE

Much like his attempts to engage with the culinary delights of the underfilth, it seemed that Ig's attempt to return to napping in a heap of his foul-smelling kin was doomed to similar short life. He was uncomfortable. Tossing and turning fitfully and receiving several kicks and groans from the others in the pile for his troubles.

For my part, I had mostly been using this time to grow accustomed to sensing the world through a kobold. Admittedly, his eyes were currently closed, leaving me only his other senses to toy with, but to my surprise it turned out all of his other senses were remarkably acute in comparison to his rather shortsighted view of the world. With those little twitching ears that kept nudging my rim I could hear everything that was happening within the burrow, all the little grunts, farts, and wheezes of kobold-kind pressed in around me, but also the gentle, frantic strumming of their hearts. I could hear the bugs crawling, the wind passing by the outside of the entrance to the hole, the distant calls of birds, and even the faint scritching of those of his kin still hunting for fodder outside. Kobolds may have been prey, but they were very well adapted to the role. It would have been a wonder that anything could take them by surprise given the quality of their hearing, were it not for their inability to understand what the majority of the sounds signified.

All of which paled in comparison to the amazing nose of a kobold. I will admit that I was extremely reluctant to engage with that particular sense given the overwhelming intensity of kobold stink surrounding me, but as I made tentative overtures to the pointed nose of Ig, I also made a startling discovery. Yes, everything in here reeked to high heaven, but from amidst that miasma I could pick out individual notes. I could tell which of the kobolds had crossed the river by the faint hint of its crisp scent. I could tell which trees they had used as back-scratching posts from the sharpness of the sap left on them in traces. To a human, these creatures were merely filthy, but to a kobold, each one of them wore a map of all the places that it had been and done. Given sufficient study, I likely could have deciphered who had eaten what, when and where they had done so, and whether it was likely that there was anything left over that I might go and scavenge later. Fruits and grubs, berries and dry leaves, tadpoles and grass, all of them were there if you knew to sniff for them. The patina of filth upon each kobold was their history, and to another kobold it could be read as easily as I might parse a tome.

Ig twitched in his sleep once more, and then his eyes opened. I was immediately treated to a close-up view of the least pretty end of a kobold, pressed close to my borrowed eyeballs. The truly remarkable thing about kobolds was not that they survived despite all the odds, it was that they survived despite themselves. Any humans sleeping in this arrangement would have had to deal with endless infections and bruises.

For a moment, Ig did not move at all. Fidgeting on the spot without going anywhere. Then, finally, after what seemed like a long deliberation, he extricated himself from the heap, moved over onto a mostly clear patch of mud and sank down again. Deliberately pressing his eyes shut against the sensation of the cool soil beneath him.

If you can't sleep, then might I suggest a brisk jog to tire you out? Perhaps a quick jaunt in the direction of Arpanpholigon? He made a little grumbling noise and curled tighter around himself. The little grumble was not acceptance. Drat.

I cannot say that I knew a great deal about kobolds' inner worlds, but this seemed like an unusual behavior. Isolating himself from the pack. Lying on the ground instead of the apparently comfortable-to-kobolds heap. After a few minutes more, he stirred again, grumbling.

Even if you could just start taking me in the right direction, I'll hitch a ride with someone else if needs must. Even though it would of course break my heart to leave such a dear friend behind.

"No. No go." Despite his eyes being screwed firmly shut, Ig was still quite awake, it seemed.

All the food you could ever want. Supreme magical powers. Excitement and adventure.

I'm pretty sure I had him up until that last moment. Excitement and adventure seemed to have been the moment that he started freaking out. Perhaps to a creature so highly strung, excitement and terror were too synonymous. Perhaps adventures were understood by kobolds to be a prelude to their slaughter by those who undertook such things. Regardless, my kobold was up and gnawing nervously at the end of his tail before the words had so much as filtered down into his head.

"No going nowhere. This home." He looked around him then, at the squalor in which he lived, and I finally understood what was happening. "This my home?"

When he could not think, could not comprehend the horror of where he lived, and the life that he lived, it was comfortable enough for him, but now that the cogs of his brain had begun turning, a degree of awareness must have been creeping in. Just as I, as a thinking creature, viewed his home with equal parts horror and revulsion, so too had his inflated intellect begun to interpret matters in the same light. To wit, he saw for the first time what everyone else saw when they looked at kobolds and their hovel-holes. He saw, he understood, he was repulsed.

He had to climb over the mound of bodies to make his frantic escape, each one of them grunting and wheezing in dismay as his feet dug into their flesh. The crust of filth coating them crackled underfoot as they writhed. Oh, how they writhed.

Leaping free of his kin, Ig scrambled up the tunnel to the exit between the roots, gasping for the fresh air that awaited him. Desperate to be anywhere else. He emerged into the morning light and then collapsed into a far smaller heap of kobold than the one he had just escaped. "Why? Why feel this?"

Alas, my dear companion, it seems that as your faculties grow, so do your tastes for the finer things in life.

"Why no sleep? Why . . . feel bad?"

I am afraid that, like all other sentient creatures, you have just become aware of the genuinely vile nature of flesh. All stickiness and fluids. You're better off as far away from it as possible.

He looked around him with bleary eyes. Some of his kinfolk were digging in the mud with their bare hands, searching for worms to eat. Some were simply wandering aimlessly and mindlessly, in the manner that Ig himself had been exploring before his discovery of me. Looking at them now, he could see them as I saw them, as barely more than beasts. It must have been downright unsettling to realize that he himself had been little more than that until he was blessed with self-awareness.

"Take back."

That was unexpected. This idiotic creature was truly full of surprises. *I beg your pardon?*

"Make me again."

I was so taken aback by the request that, instead of conjuring up some fresh lie about how I'd be able to make him himself again on return to the Great College, I blurted out, *I can't*.

"Please?"

Who could have predicted that a kobold would become intelligent enough to develop manners and then use them to beg for a return to his earlier state?

I am terribly sorry, my friend, but even were you to rid yourself of me, the changes that you have already undergone will not fade so easily. Your once atrophied mind has begun to function once more, and I could not make it stop by doing anything short of ending your life.

"Don't want think. Don't want know things." He seemed to struggle for the words to convey what he actually wanted from me. "Make Ig kobold again."

But can't you see how wondrous this turn of events is? You have achieved a degree of enlightenment hitherto unseen by your kind. You could be a king among them, or an ambassador for your people to the rest of the world. Just one sentient kobold might be sufficient to sway the tide of public opinion about your species. You could be their savior!

There were tears pooling in Ig's eyes. Were he any other sort of creature, I would doubtless have felt some sympathy for him, but unfortunately he remained a kobold, and as such, the only way he would ever have puppy-dog eyes was if he were to pluck them from an itinerant hound. "No want king. No want change. Want sleep and foods and sleep."

I assure you that despite whatever gains you may have made in the upstairs department, you remain kobold in body. Sleep and food shall almost inevitably remain a feature of your ongoing survival.

There was a frantic edge to his wavering voice as he seized me by the rim. "Make me same again."

My dearest friend, I cannot.

"Me will throw you away. Me is doing it!"

Were he not so pitiful, I likely would have taken such a threat more seriously and made moves to prevent him from pulling me off, but I was so busy feeling empathy for the oversized rodent that I didn't even realize that he was pulling me off his head until all the lovely sensory data that had been feeding into me from that diseased little brain of his were suddenly torn away, and my hat-shaped self was flung like a frisbee to land by the foot of a tree.

For a time I was returned to the awful limbo of having thoughts but nowhere to think them. A darkness more profound than night and deeper than death. An absence of being that went beyond sleep and on into the great nothingness beyond the edge of creation. An awful purgatory that I could not even begin planning to escape without a brain of my own.

Some time later, and I could not honestly tell you how long but for the fall of night and the rise of the stars and moon, I was placed back on Ig's head.

His memories came on in a flood. The hours of slow degeneration as he returned to being a shadow of his former self. Striving for the utter mindlessness that he had damned me to by throwing me off. He had failed to become himself again. He had failed to become as mindless as the rest of his kobold clan, and the disgust that he felt with himself had only grown, until finally, depressed and defeated, he returned to retrieve me and place me atop his head.

"You can fix?"

The very idea of it was abhorrent. Taking a thinking creature and stripping it of its ability to think? Monstrous. Yet if that was Ig's truest desire, then who was I to stand in his way?

If you will return me to the College of Arpanpholigon then in return, I shall research the means by which you might be returned to your former state of ignorant bliss. If that is truly your desire.

"You fix me. I take you. Deal?"

I was struck then with the terrible awareness that he was holding up one of his grimy little paws to shake my hand, despite my being a hat. Whether this oversight on his part was due to the degeneration he had suffered without me serving as a beacon of enlightenment or if he would remain approximately this intelligent for the duration of our venture was yet to be discovered.

That is a deal that I shall hold you to, my dear friend.

He glanced longingly back to his hole in the ground one final time, then nodded. "Which way we go?"

The first step of our journey together was back to the river, where I convinced the grotesquery that was to be my home for the foreseeable future to bathe himself. I explained that this was part of the ritual to initiate him into the fraternal order of wizards, but in truth, judging by the aromas of bodily odor that I had encountered among those students lucky enough to study at the same institution where I was gainfully employed, cleanliness was not adjacent to arcane might. However, while the students may have had someone in their dormitories willing to creep in by night and douse them with buckets of ice-cold water until they learned the purpose of the communal bathing area, Ig had not had the benefit of such help. I was all that he had in the world, and if that meant I had to bully him into wading out deep into the water and scrubbing at himself in the moonlight, then that was precisely what I would do. I told myself that it was because his rather ripe aroma would attract unwanted attention during our travels, and in part that was true, but a far larger part of why we were conducting the "ritual of scrubbing thoroughly behind our ears so that we might hear the secret whispers of magic" was that I could smell him through his own nose, and I wasn't entirely sure how much more of it I could endure.

The pike that had been so startled by our last passage seemed to recall what had happened to it and kept its distance. As it should. I was, after all, a most puissant wizard, even if I did currently have a rim and some tasteful astronomical embroidery.

The net result of Ig's diligent ritual was a creature that looked even more like a drowned rat than usual standing on the riverbank, shivering in the dark of night. There was a piebald quality to the patches of natural color upon Ig's skin that I would never have noticed if he were not scrubbed clean, and very briefly, before the cold of the night caused a hasty retraction, I was distressed to have his alleged sex confirmed by a downward glance.

We would have to fashion him some clothes as soon as we were able, if only to prevent the incessant chattering of teeth. But for now, he was looking as good as I could make him, which admittedly was not very good at all. At least the smell was gone. For now.

While he had been distracted with his ablutions, and I had been cursing the lack of available soap, I had not been entirely idle. Using the glimpses of the sky that Ig's rather dim eyes had granted me, I had studied the position of the celestial bodies above us and calculated not only the direction in which we would need to travel, but also the distance. I chose in that moment not to convey that distance to Ig, because it was . . . it was a lot. Even on the swiftest of steeds coursing along the smoothest of roads, we would have been weeks off from civilization of any sort. I was forced at last to contend with the truth that I had been trying to deny, even to myself. We were in the Badlands.

On each map of the continent, there are some areas not fully filled out. Cartographers may be braver than the usual breed of academic, but even they have their limits, and the fact that none had chosen to come here might have spoken to the great distances involved, the lack of interest in the area, or, more likely, the massive number of wandering monsters that we were liable to encounter out here.

The bad part of the Badlands was not a description of the geography, which to my eye seemed perfectly serviceable, but a reference to the creatures that dwelled here.

Even adventurers didn't head out this far very often. Not when there were lucrative contracts clearing goblins away from farmlands or exchanging a few hours of lackluster labor in the field of flying lizard extermination for the hand of a princess. Why on earth would there be any quest to come out here? Nobody lived here. What did it matter if monstrous beasts roamed the lands if nobody lived here? The monstrous beasts could have it.

Well, the population of the Badlands had now increased by one fairly significant somebody. Me. And that meant that it would have to be navigated safely without the use of any map. Not that I could imagine there was a handy library around here where I might peruse one. I would have to rely on my wits to keep us alive. My wits, and Ig's natural strength. Wait, no. He didn't have any of that. His natural . . . speed? By the nine hecks, I was in real trouble if I ever had to rely on Ig for anything beyond basic transportation. He could barely even accomplish that, tripping over every tree root he encountered on the way to the river.

We head north, my friend. North by northeast.

Ig nodded sagely, then asked a quick clarifying question. "What that?"

North! The direction of the constellation of Marius.

He gazed up at the sky at that direction then, again, quickly clarified my statement. "What that?"

I will admit that I was beginning to grow exasperated by this point. *The direction from which the cold winds blow?*

"What that?"

Should have seen that coming really.

With a surge of effort, I dragged one of his limp and dangling arms up and pointed it in the correct direction. *That way.*

"Oh!" Ig nodded again. "Why no say?"

Reconsidering my reserves of Quintessence, I wondered if I might have just enough left in me to explode this infuriating creature's head before I was depleted. North, as it turned out, was in the opposite direction. Back past the kobold warren.

Ig waded out into the river one last time, slipping on every smooth rock and stubbing his toes on every rough one. If I had hoped to rely upon stealth to see us through our journey, I had the sense that hope was soon to be tarnished by reality. Ig crossing a stream sounded something akin to a very well-shaken cocktail.

Setting out on such a grand journey, I felt it was my duty as the resident wizard and mentor to make some sort of grandiose statement that Ig might reflect upon. *The philosophers say that you never cross the same river twice.*

Ig seemed to consider this as he emerged onto the bank and started plodding northwards. "Just did."

Ah, we crossed the same land, but the water had moved on.

He glanced back towards the river, confused. "Was still there."

That was different water, my friend. Running from farther upstream.

"Looked same." His beady little eyes narrowed as he considered the possibility that someone had made off with his river.

Perhaps you can just trust me when I tell you that it was not the same water, and that the water you encountered earlier is likely many miles away now.

Ig nodded. "Me walking fast."

That isn't . . .

I managed to strangle that sentence off before I said something that might have offended my new ally. *Yes. Well done. Making excellent time. Keep up the good work and we shall be in Arpanpholigon before you can blink.*

With very deliberate movements, he closed and opened his eyes. Almost theatrically. "Me blinked."

Within the hat that was the sum of my parts, I was internally screaming. If you have never heard the screams of a hat, consider yourself to be lucky, for it is a truly terrible and anguished sound.

Aloud, or, as aloud as I was capable of communicating, I said, *I was not speaking literally, my friend.*

"No." Ig nodded sagely once more. "Was speaking in my head."

If this was the shape of the days to come, then the sensible option would of course have been to expend the very last vestiges of my power on incinerating him from the inside out, and allow myself to fall, burnt out and useless, to the carpet of dry leaves below us. It would have been more humane. Yet I was not prepared to admit defeat just yet.

Ig was nothing if not pliable, I simply had to give him better direction. *Why don't we walk in quiet contemplation for a while.*

"What me contemplate?"

On reflection, asking a creature that had until this day been incapable of any rational thought to contemplate quietly probably had been a mistake on my part. There was no need to take that out on Ig. Even if it would be supremely satisfying to do so.

Putting one foot in front of the other without falling over.

Another accepting nod from Ig, and we were on our merry way in blessed silence. I had found a worthy task that would occupy his full attentions and leave me to my downward spiral of despair in peace.

If only it could have stayed that quiet.

CHAPTER FOUR

AN EDUCATION IN ENCHANTMENT

Ig marched on through the night, as we followed game trails through forest so dense that even were it daytime, I doubt we would have seen much light. This was untouched land, untamed and ungoverned. There would be no woodsmen or charcoal burners out here to provide us with direction. No little old lady's cottages that definitely didn't belong to a witch. Nothing. Just us and the beasts.

To Ig's credit, he got us a goodly distance before exhaustion began to seep into him, graying the periphery of his vision and sapping him of what little coordination he had. In truth, we very well may have been heading north almost all the way through the night before he came to a rest on a fallen tree to catch his breath.

I think perhaps it would be best to take a little break from walking.

Ig yawned out. "Me like sleep."

If I pushed this horrid little creature to the verge of death within a day of our meeting, then he wasn't liable to be able to carry me the full distance, so I was forced to reckon with his physical limitations once more. *And you have most assuredly earned it, my little friend. Let us seek out somewhere secure for you to rest.*

Casting his eyes to a pile of dry leaves beside the log, Ig looked for a treacherous moment as though he might simply flump over, but to his credit, he managed to resist. Something that was for the best, in no small part, due to the hissing and rustling that his ears had picked up from that heap of leaves, which his shriveled walnut of a brain hadn't quite managed to parse probably meant some sort of murderous serpent.

That tree over there looks sturdy enough to support you. Why not climb up to the lowest bough and settle there for the night?

Ig peered up at the tree, then down at his paws, then up at the tree once more. "Me not know how to climb. Teach?"

Regrettably, this was an area in which I lacked expertise. My lifestyle had always been somewhat sedentary, even in the halcyon days of my youth. I was categorized as an "indoor kid" by my peers, and while they engaged in their roughhousing and tree climbing, the closest that I came was scrambling up a ladder attached to a bookshelf to retrieve an out-of-reach tome.

Which was to say, I'd hoped that Ig knew how to do it.

Perhaps we should seek out some sort of . . . shelter then. A cave, or hollow?

As it turned out, caves are not actually all that common in woodlands. All of the legends and tales that I had absorbed through the years, which plopped them down like tents wherever they were required for heroes of old to take shelter or experience moments of contemplation, seemed to have misled me somewhat about the geological realities. An hour or so later, when it became apparent that the earth wasn't going to helpfully open up and swallow us, we settled for huddling under the upturned roots of a toppled tree.

Ig was, by this point, beginning to slur his words somewhat, having spent a life engaged in little more than napping interrupted by sporadic eating up until this point. "Spleepy."

Then rest, my dear scabrous friend, while I watch over you.

He required very little prompting indeed, tucking his tail into his mouth to get it out of the way as he wandered in little circles looking for a comfortable patch, before finally slumping down onto what must have been the lumpiest stretch of ground available. It had a sharp rock poking up, performing a minor chiropractic operation on his hunched spine; it had a tree root that seemed quite intent on masquerading as one of his intestines; there was even a conveniently placed piece of lichen dangling down to tickle right beside his ear. Needless to say, he was out like a light within moments, and I was left alone with my thoughts and the vague impressions of kobold dreams.

There was a hoot of an owl somewhere up above us, the rustling as various invertebrates went about their business, a slight tickle as some spider wandered across Ig's snout. Apparently, the spider was just big enough to register such a creature as terrain rather than a snack, which was something of a relief. I already had to protect the imbecile from everything bigger than him; I didn't like my odds if everything smaller than him was also seeking his destruction.

With the blissful silence of the night and no chance of Ig overhearing, I needed to formulate a plan. The original concept of having him traipse back to Arpanpholigon was all well and good, but the land between here and there were known as the Badlands not because of how incredibly pleasant and welcoming they were. He was going to encounter trouble. He was going to get brutally murdered. I was going to end up as some orc's poop sock. This was an unacceptable outcome.

The obvious solution would be to make an immediate leap from the head of Ig onto someone infinitely more competent, which was to say, literally anyone else. However, given the quality of people we were liable to encounter out here in the wilderness, this still came with significant risk of poop-sockery.

Monsters, outcasts, adventurers, none of them had the proper respect for a fine piece of headwear, and unless I was placed upon a head, I was trapped in a senseless void, bereft of all sense of time and place. Which I did not much fancy experiencing ever again.

So, assuming that I did not, by luck, happen upon the sort of person who became an adventurer despite being incredibly well-liked and normal, I was going to be stuck with Ig for the foreseeable future.

This was not ideal, but neither was it unworkable. He may have been the most watery, pathetic little lump of clay that any potter had ever spun, but with a master craftsman handling him, there could be no doubt he would become at least admirably competent in our travels. After all, he would have Absalom Scryne as his teacher, the greatest and wisest of all wizards.

While he dozed and a millipede made its industrious way up his nostril, I formulated a lesson plan.

WAKE UP!

By my estimation, we were now well into the early hours of the morning, there was a slight increase in temperature that could not be explained away by Ig wetting himself in the night, and there was a distinct increase in tweeting birds. Besides, I had finished my plans for Ig's education several hours ago and now I was extremely bored. If you had told me in my youth that a time would come that the awful burden of sleep would no longer be laid upon me each night, I would have been delighted. Just think of all the extra time that I would have for my studies! Yet now, here I was, sleepless as a stone yet deprived of either books or eyeballs to make use of the time.

To his credit, it seemed that the anxiety-ridden kobold was not slow to rise. Quite the opposite in fact. He heard my voice screaming in his head and shot from horizontal to vertical with such force that his head collided directly with the decaying roots overhead, showering him in soil. Typically this would have been a source of some dry amusement for me, but unfortunately, I was upon that very head.

My point got bent out of shape, I was showered in mud, something sticky that I hoped was sap became stuck to my broad rim. It was the gravest indignity that I had ever suffered in my life, short of my presumed murder, and I had none to blame but myself.

"Weh? Where?" Ig spun in circles, looking for the source of danger. "Weh? What?!"

It is morning.

"No," he said, surprisingly firmly. "Wake-up time not dark."

The dawn chorus has sounded, the sun rises in the . . .

The rude little rodent cut me off. "Dark is sleepy time."

I was so surprised by that particular display of spine that I didn't even threaten to fill his with molten lead. Instead I elected to cajole him ever so gently. *Once the sun has risen, we must be on our way, and before then I mean to impart upon you ancient and powerful secrets of magic.*

He cast a somewhat desperate look back to the world's most uncomfortable patch of dirt. "But spleep."

Would you rather have supreme cosmic power with which to remake all of reality, or another ten minutes snoozing in the mud?

He had to think about it. And not for a short period of time. By the time that he actually made a decision, the red sun rising was beginning to shine through the woods to the east. "Magics."

It seemed that his priorities weren't entirely skewed. I could recall several young men from my dormitory during my student years who had been faced with that very same choice and selected the incorrect course, which had resulted in their expulsion from the school and forcible polymorph into newts. I would not have newted Ig, of course. A newt's head would have been even smaller than a kobold's shriveled cranium.

Ig set about his morning ablutions in a bush while I did my best to pay no attention and prepared my speech. When he was finally done, and we had begun ambling in what I hoped was the correct direction, I began.

There is no force in the cosmos more pervasive and mysterious as magic. It is . . .

"What pervasive mean?"

Ah. Right. Kobold vocabulary. I may need to tone my own down slightly.

Pervasive means spread widely throughout an area.

After a moment of considering this, Ig nodded, then followed up with, "What mysterious mean?"

It was going to be a very long morning.

Several hours later, we had made it through my introductory spiel, abbreviated and patchworked repeatedly as I tried to avoid any words that were unfamiliar to Ig, which was, unfortunately, most of them. Still, his vocabulary was improving if nothing else, and I could almost feel the crusty raisin inside of his skull beginning to pulse with new life.

Finally he managed to hold on to the main points that I was instilling in him. Magic big. Magic powerful. Magic hard to control. It was the sort of lesson that most students of magic already grasped instinctually before they got to formal education, as a result of having the slightest bloody awareness of what was going on in the world around them. Ig did not benefit from that awareness, nor any sort of informal education on the subject, or indeed on any subject. Were my new form shorn of its rim, with all of its embroidery picked out and a large D painted upon the remaining cone, I would have become a more appropriate hat for this particular dunce of a student.

He was not stupid. To be stupid he would have to ascend through several untouched layers of intellect that he could not even comprehend, let alone reach. Each moment that we spoke, I could practically feel myself becoming dumber. As though he were infectious.

Still, with that most basic lesson imparted, and a hearty lunch of what I was pretty confident were not poisonous mushrooms consumed, we moved on to the practical lesson of the day.

To perform any act of magic requires Quintessence.

"What squint-sense mean?"

Strangling him would leave me stranded in the middle of the forest. It would not be helpful to me. It would run counter to my plans. I had to remember that. Also, I had no hands to strangle with.

Quintessence is the element of magic. All of creation is formed from combinations of elements, and Quintessence is the one that accounts for the existence of arcana, both naturally occurring and cultivated.

Ig nodded as though he understood what any of that meant, and I endeavored not to scream. I pushed on quickly. *To perform any spell, you need Quintessence. To get Quintessence, you must either find a source saturated in it, or you must gather the ambient Quintessence from the world around you.*

"What ambient . . ."

Save all questions for the end, please.

He plodded on a little farther while I braced myself for more of his witless inquisition, but it did not come. He was saving all questions for the end. Assuming he could remember any of the questions by the end. Perhaps this wasn't actually the best method for teaching, but it did get us through the material quicker.

Quintessence is all around us, permeating all things. It is the raw stuff of creation, which we, through magic, can manipulate to produce our desired effect. Some philosophers argue that it predates all other things, and reality is but a conjuring, but we have no evidence as to whence it came or when. What matters to you is that it does exist, and that you need it to perform the High Art.

"So how I get?"

Nothing could be simpler, my dear friend. Quintessence is naturally drawn to the living; it gathers around us. All that we need do is absorb it into our being. Once we have done so, we shall form a reserve, or reservoir, of Quintessence within ourselves that we can draw upon when we cast our spells. There is a natural hollow within the energies of all living things into which that Quintessence gathers, and as you gradually gather more, that spiritual sac shall expand, allowing you to store greater and greater . . . My apologies, I am getting ahead of myself.

"So how I zorb?"

Asking all of the right questions, dear Ig!

Was I desperately clinging to any faint hope that every moment of this process wasn't going to be agony? Perhaps.

In my training I was taught to meditate, to clear my mind entirely of all thoughts and to simply feel for the presence of Quintessence around me. In your case, I suspect we can skip past the meditation. Close your eyes for a moment and let me guide you.

Allowing my awareness to slip out of my hat and into Ig's body—a thoroughly unpleasant experience, I can assure you—I made an attempt to strike a balance whereby the both of us were in control at the same time and as such could both experience what his body was exposed to. With all the skill of a practiced old hand, I reached my will out beyond the confines of his body, felt the Quintessence already gathered there, and drew it inside.

For me, at the height of my powers, this process was more or less automatic. I gathered Quintessence the way that lesser mortals drew breath, and it accumulated within my body in such vast amounts that a paper cut was liable to let loose a tidal wave of arcane power.

Had a mosquito ever ascended through the clouds to the tower that I had made my home, settled upon my skin, and taken a drink, then it would have proceeded to simultaneously implode, explode, and plode—the rare state when the catastrophic destruction is neither going outwards or inwards, but remaining in the same place while still occurring. It would also have gone through the five stages of grief, the three phases of matter, and an entire bestiary's worth of polymorphic flux before dying in a spectacular manner.

This was not the case with Ig. I had expected some sort of mild euphoria to set in as he felt the power coursing through his veins for the first time, perhaps some mild cackling and megalomania, as were common, but instead he started to make little yipping sounds that I realized after a moment were sounds of pain. Confused, I turned my senses, such as they were, inward, only to discover that the reservoir into which this miniscule amount of power was being gathered was not the convenient little waterskin, just awaiting filling, that a human student would have had at the ready, but instead a pathetic little twist of spirit that looked like a worm that had been left to bake in the sun for a period not exceeding three months.

As the Quintessence flowed into this desiccated mollusk, it was being brutally stretched to accommodate the new power. Ig was in yipping agony as his very soul was torn apart to make way for the accumulating power. Typically not something that would have concerned me, but if he ripped open in a plosion of arcane power, I'd be back to square one.

So I stopped drawing in power and he walked into a tree, because apparently when I'd told him to shut his eyes, I hadn't specified that he should stop walking while doing so.

Right, that was not the ideal outcome.

"Why hurty!?"

I do apologize, it was meant to be a painless process, I had simply underestimated the quantity of . . .

"Me give up. Not doing no more. No more hurt."

It was an accident; I can assure you that drawing upon Quintessence is usually an entirely painless process. In fact, many find it to be quite pleasurable . . .

"You no say it hurt."

I was not aware that it would cause you any discomfort or distress, otherwise I would not have proceeded as I did.

That wasn't entirely true, but he didn't need to know that I'd willingly put him through perpetual torture if it meant getting home in one piece. Such things are not shared in polite conversation. Regardless of how irritating the kobold side of the conversation may have been up until this point.

He seemed to be calming down now, his heart slowing from the rampaging thrum that I could feel vibrating all the way up my length to more regular vibrations, more akin to the beating of a hummingbird's wings. Yet despite his panic and his pain and everything else, I could not help but notice that the Quintessence remained within him. The tiny worm of his reservoir expanded out into a bloated grub with the sudden influx, straining, but not bursting. It was barely enough Quintessence to perform a single act of the most mundane low magic, but it was a start.

That will be enough for now, I think. Perhaps we can try again later.

"Nope." His eyes narrowed as he tried to straighten out his snout with his hands. It was not broken, merely bruised and slightly moss-stained. "No trying again later because me give up because hurty."

Screaming would not be productive. Nor would belittling the opinion of my dear companion just because he had a level of experience of the world more commonly held by slime molds. Pointing out the vast degree of suffering that he was going to endure at the hands of the first creature we came upon if we did not have the power of magic on our side, compared to the mild discomfort he had just experienced, would also have been somewhat counterproductive, as it might very well encourage him to turn tail and sprint back to his burrow, abandoning the cruel hat that had led him astray to its awful fate.

As placidly as I could muster, I told him, *We can discuss that later, also.*

His tail lashed behind him, but he did not argue. I supposed that for a creature with an attention span like Ig, kicking a problem down the road to deal with later was somewhat akin to blinking it entirely out of existence. The level of constant anxiety that he lived in despite having little to no ability to think about the future was frankly remarkable.

We trudged on for a while, with Ig simmering with resentment at the slight soul-searing I had accidentally inflicted on him, and my own mind occupied with the best way to convince him that the solution to this discomfort was actually to cram more Quintessence into his body until he became useful to me. I may have been able to rewrite the cosmos with my brilliant mind, but tricking a kobold into doing something uncomfortable was apparently beyond me at this point. It would have been embarrassing if there had been anyone to see my shame. But as the only observer was too oblivious to even understand it, I was in the clear.

CHAPTER FIVE

THE LAW OF LAGOMORPH MATERIALIZATION

His stomach began to rumble within a few moments of us setting off, and with that mounting awareness of hunger came a very welcome distraction from his bitterness towards me. I could not actually recall the last time that he had eaten, unless you counted the millipede, but it had entered via his nose rather than mouth, so that probably didn't count as eating per se.

This presented me with both a concern and an opportunity. The concern, that I was going to have to waste a portion of each day helping this imbecile scavenge for scraps, and that I would then have to endure the experience of consuming handfuls of still-living insects. The opportunity, to show him that the Quintessence that had been somewhat uncomfortable to acquire could provide him with immediate and notable benefits. He had wanted food as his reward for accompanying me on this journey, and it was time for him to reap the rewards of his labors.

While he wandered along, glancing about for any particularly crunchy-looking beetles on the trunks of nearby trees, I turned my own attentions higher. From what I knew of kobolds, they were omnivorous. Not by choice, but simply because they were so incompetent that they had to settle for literally anything that wasn't nailed down. As such, if I could locate a fruit tree, this day might have been about to take a turn for the better.

Shockingly enough, the wilderness beyond the reaches of all civilization was not furnished with a full orchard, lush and ready for us, but nature does have a wonderful way of throwing random nonsense into places where you would not expect it. Something that anyone who has spent any time out in nature can attest to. I, of course, was not one of those people, but some of my fellow students who had been born into more rural environs had provided me with ample stories of unexpected snakes in boots and the like.

To me, living my comfortable life in the city, nature was something that happened to other people, unfortunate people who had lacked the good sense to walk somewhere nature wasn't happening, but I had not been deaf to their stories and had taken from them the required lesson. Wild places were chaotic, and that could be both advantageous and lethal in equal measure.

And from chaos was born my first true victory of the day. A plum tree, or, more accurately for this particular crop at this point in time, a prune tree.

Shall we stop for some lunch?

Ig was delighted by the prospect and immediately squatted down to begin digging for worms. He was still diligently digging when I nudged his chin upwards a touch with a little flex of control. The moment that his eyes locked upon the withered plum dangling from a branch, his pupils dilated and he began to salivate wildly. For him, a simple piece of fruit, even one so pathetic as the ones on display here, was such a treat that just the sight of it was already sending him into paroxysms of delight.

That had been easier than I'd anticipated.

He abandoned his burrowing and made a run for the tree, leaping with all of his might for the delectable treat. He fell somewhat short. Presumably because the fruit was hanging from a branch about ten feet up from the ground, he was about two feet tall, and he had the kind of musculature usually associated with sufferers of some sort of wasting sickness.

Yet despite this, he was not dissuaded. He jumped again, and again. Each little hop coming no closer to the prize, and in fact rising slightly less every time as he became tired.

The final few jumps were less the mighty leaps that he may have envisioned and more flops. On the last one, I wasn't entirely convinced that his feet actually left the ground and he wasn't just aggressively reaching.

Finally, despondent and sad, he sank down onto his haunches and I pretended to take an interest at last.

Oh, did you want that plum?

He let out a low moan. "Yes."

That plum all the way up there where you can't reach it.

"Yes!" He was practically sobbing at this point, I almost felt bad for him.

If only there were some way to pluck it from that high branch and bring it down here where you could eat it.

"Me tried!" His whining was starting to grate on me by this point, but I endured, as this desperation was precisely what I was banking on.

If only you had some sort of magic that would let you affect the world around you. Some reserve of power within you that you could unleash to pluck the plum from the tree.

He sat in miserable silence for what felt like a solid minute before the two brain cells bouncing around inside his skull collided.

"Me could magic it down!"

Finally.

You are entirely right, my friend. If only I had thought to suggest it to you.

All of his prior misery and trepidation had now been washed away. He was ready to learn. And all it had taken was the considerably smaller reward of a sweet treat. I really should have borne in mind who I was trying to train instead of promising him awesome cosmic power.

"You teach now. How get?"

Of all the magics available to we practitioners of the High Art, the lowest is the direct application of Quintessence to the world around us. It is the most wasteful and squanderous use of Quintessence to fling it unrefined by rite or ritual back into the world to exert force upon objects.

"How do?" Ig was back to hopping up and down again, presumably from excitement. "How do?"

Feel the reservoir of power inside you, touch it with your awareness, feel the way that it seeks to escape, to be set loose. You can loose it, whenever you so choose—in fact it is by far more difficult to contain it once those floodgates open.

"Me can feel it!"

Of course he could bloody feel it, didn't I just say that?

Now, before loosing it, be ready to slam those gates shut once more lest the excess be spent without direction.

"Me am ready! Me am ready to be wizard!"

His excitement bordered upon endearing, but at present it was liable to cause more trouble than it was worth.

The final thing that you need before unleashing your power is focus. You must concentrate entirely upon the plum. Look at the plum, know where it is, know where you mean to direct your Quintessence.

And just like that, our progress hit against a brick wall once more. Ig had the attention span of a kobold, which is to say, his ability to focus was very much like a fish's ability to breathe air, or fly, or ride a horse. Each one was perhaps possible for a fraction of a moment, but all would have been quite impossible for our piscine example to achieve deliberately.

His eyes locked on to the plum, then there was a rustle in the leaves, then there was a brush of air over his tail as the wind passed by, then there was a gurgle in his stomach because he was hungry, then that bush over there looked a little bit menacing, then a cloud drifted into the periphery of his vision and startled him, then I withdrew from his awareness because the constant jolting was giving me motion sickness.

No. This will not do, my boy. You must empty your head of all distractions and focus exclusively upon the place you wish to direct your magic, otherwise the power will be unleashed in a manner you had not planned.

If I had thought that he lacked focus before, the introduction of consequences to his actions sent him into a spiral. He yelped out, "What that mean?"

Too much doom, not enough positive reinforcement. *It means that you must bring the sole target of your low magic into focus or you shall invariably fail.*

In an uncharacteristic display of focus, he did manage to hold on to the one stray thought bouncing around in his skull. "But what not planned thing?"

Pray that you never discover what happens when concentrated Quintessence is left to its own devices.

There, that should have been vague enough not to raise any alarm bells.

Ig had begun to sweat. All of the progress that we had made in terms of his aroma were being rapidly undone by the day's activities. At least I could console myself with the fact that it was a cold sweat.

Now focus!

To Ig's credit, he did try. He tried with all of his might, eyes on the prize, mind drawn back like an arrow with an admittedly blunt head. If he could have unleashed his Quintessence in that one moment then he very well may have succeeded, but in the instant it took him to use the power held within him, his concentration wavered. There was a bird chirping in a distant tree. There was a rustle, this time from within the ominous bush. The cloud that had caught his attention earlier was now overhead and looked a little darker than the ones around it, so might have been some sort of bird of prey just about to swoop down and get him.

How any kobold makes it through the day with this base level of absolute terror is completely beyond me.

Regardless, he had raised his hand, unleashed his power, completely failed to stop the full wash of Quintessence leaving him, and instead of it being focused upon the one thing that it was meant to be heading towards, it instead burst out and did what came naturally to it.

There have been a great many theories presented upon the laws of magic, and in particular the first of those laws: the Law of Lagomorph Materialization. I could present to you these myriad theories here and now to little or no avail, or I can present you with the viewpoint that I subscribe to, and as such, the one that is the most likely to be correct.

Quintessence, in addition to being the element governing magic, is also the elemental force governing life. It is drawn to living things, permeates their bodies, and gives druids the impression that their obsession with trees has some significance. Therefore, when a spell is miscast, and there is an overflow of excess Quintessence, it spontaneously generates life, and not only life, but the most lifey life to ever live. A creature that is devoted with all of its being to the rapid propagation of more life. Ergo, a rabbit.

In keeping with the second law of magic, the Law of Comedic Timing, such creatures will typically be created out of sight of both the caster and any bystanders, typically in whatever place would prove to be the most embarrassing to the wizard in question. Normally appearing underneath the caster's hat, but sometimes in some other nearby location.

I will admit that my preferred explanation for the Law of Lagomorph Materialization does not account for the inexplicable appearance of knotted strings of handkerchiefs in pockets. That one remains a mystery.

Regardless of my academic opinions, the facts of the matter were simple. Ig had buggered up the most basic rudimentary magic imaginable, and now we were going to pay the long-eared piper.

It was not a large bunny, because Ig did not have a great deal of Quintessence at his disposal, but it was a pure white coloration that made it stand out perfectly clearly in the rather drab brown of the forest. It was practically glowing.

The rabbit came lopping out from behind the tree where Ig had so desperately tried to acquire a plum, twitched its little pink nose, and then hopped on about a foot more before the rustling in the ominous bush resolved itself into a blur of dark motion.

Ig, eyes wide with wonder at the sudden appearance of a creature even more defenseless than himself, had only the briefest of times to appreciate the new life that he had brought into the world before the forest panther was upon it, and arterial spray was misting all over him.

"Bun?"

RUN!

And run he did, as fast as his little kobold legs could carry him. Pumping those little stompers so quick that even I was surprised at the turn of speed that he was putting on.

The common forest panther, or *Panthera Ohbuggerhesaftrus* in Archaic, was not a common sight in the areas surrounding civilization, due to civilization tending to be opposed to things like being mauled to death every time that you step outside, and in favor of lovely fur coats. Yet if you were to travel a few miles away from every sentient creature on the planet into the wild places of the world, you would soon encounter them, eating things like rabbits, deer, farmer's children, and, of course, kobolds. How a creature with a sense of smell so honed it could detect blood from three miles away managed to stomach chowing down on a kobold escapes me, but I have always assumed that it is akin to the one person in a tavern who insists upon eating a pickled egg to show off in front of their friends.

Regardless, it was all sleek muscle and ear tufts, and it was bounding after Ig with all haste. Perhaps it had been drawn away from the smaller snack of the rabbit by his sudden sprinting. Perhaps if Ig had simply stood still, it would have consumed the rabbit and left the far more filling meal quivering in terror a few feet away entirely alone. And perhaps I'm a farmer's flat-cap.

"Me am going to die! My am going to be eaten and die!" It seemed that even running full speed, he still had enough air to spare for whining.

You must gather more Quintessence, Ig! You must use low magic to strike out at the beast and scare it off!

"Me can't!" he blubbed, ducking under a low-slung branch and only keeping me atop his head by grabbing for me before I was entirely knocked off.

I suppose that if Ig were to be eaten, I would simply fall off, just as that branch would have knocked me down. I would have had to wait for a time, until some new creature wandered along and got me stuck on its head. But who could say how long that would take? No. I needed this kobold to survive, which meant that this kobold needed to become the world's first kobold wizard. Preferably before the cat on our heels caught up to him.

There were tears streaming down his cheeks, raining back into the panther's face. "Me not know how!"

Draw in the Quintessence!

And would you believe it, with the impetus of impending death chasing him down, he closed his eyes, opened his mind, and drew the Quintessence in. Like he'd been doing it his whole life. I suppose that having a master wizard in your head teaching you how to perform the most basic acts of magic was actually quite helpful in getting over the initial hump of the learning curve.

Once more it was scarcely enough Quintessence to comment on, the sort of magic that I'd spend on tying my shoelaces back at home, but for him it was a vast improvement, almost twice what he'd managed the first time.

Bravo, my dear apprentice! Now you just need to concentrate on the panther right behind us and let the Quintessence flow free once more.

He did not. Rather, he went on running. His stamina was already beginning to lag, his steps more often stumbles; every tree root in the forest seemed to be snatching for his ankles.

Focus, and release!

Still absolutely nothing happening in the magic department. Quite a lot happening in the leg department still, some things that were a little concerning going on with the plumbing, but we could always find a stream to wash him off again later—but as far as magic went, absolutely nothing.

Ig, you must cast.

"Can't." He panted. "See it."

That was a reasonable concern. He could not turn his head around to view the pursuing beast without invariably taking a tumble, by which point whatever magic he could bring to bear would be moot, due to the terrible slicing claws ripping his guts open.

There was no shortage of other sensory information informing him of precisely where the panther was to be found. He could hear the soft thumping of its padded paws as it hurried after him. Feel the few wiry hairs that poked out of the back of his neck standing on end from where its gaze lay upon him. Smell the sickly metallic tang of blood on its breath. I could tell precisely where it was using that information, but Ig, it seemed, was in too much of a panic.

Cast anyway. Don't worry about focus. Just cast like your life depends upon it!

The Quintessence that he had gathered squirted out of him, rather like an octopus leaving behind ink to mask its escape, but while the best hugger in the ocean had only a shroud of darkness left in its wake, Ig's magic left something else behind entirely. Bunnies.

Two rabbits appeared with the first attempt, hopping out from inside a nearby log, and even without Ig looking, I knew that the panther must have been tempted to stop running and eat them instead. That is the wonderful thing about nature—as chaotic as it is on the whole, on an individual level, most animals are imminently predictable. They will choose whatever is easiest. They will not scale the walls of a city to reach the chickens roosting inside when they could just go find some wild birds. They will not chase a kobold for miles if there are perfectly plump coneys just waiting to be munched down.

Not that Ig was going to make it for miles. It already felt as though his heart might explode at any moment. His legs may as well have been lead for all the lift that he was getting from them, and so far as I could tell, we had traveled approximately twelve feet since he began his frantic sprint.

We ran on for but a moment before it became clear that those new bunnies had survived the crucible of their creation.

Again!

But Ig, he was faltering. What little strength he had left in his body was waning, and the dubious amount of arcane potential that he'd shown had already exhausted him mentally. He was a goner, done for, kaput. I considered my own reserves of Quintessence and realized that to cast even low magic in his aid would likely serve only to see to it that I died with Ig.

He ran on a few more steps as I tried to ponder out the best way to ask him to throw me onto a high branch where the cat that was about to slaughter him was unlikely to use me as a litter tray, when the unexpected occurred. Ig reached out once more, drawing in all of the Quintessence that his body could hold, which was, admittedly, not much, and he cast it all out in one great sputtering gout.

There was no little white ball of fluff and adorability this time around, but a lop-eared monster that a dwarf could have ridden into battle. And in keeping with the second law of magic, this stupendous beast was created not anywhere sensible, but instead atop one of the branches above us.

With a cracking of wood and the whistling of a falling star, the big brown rabbit fell.

It would have made a more than ample meal for the panther, had it landed in its path, but it was not destined for such a fate. Instead it came down directly upon the poor cat's back, drawing from its snarling lips the kind of yowl that it would have required a good tail stomp, or a mild inconvenience, to draw from one of its domesticated cousins.

The panther attempted to simultaneously chase after Ig, leap into the air in surprise, twist around and attack its own back, and freak out about all of the above. What it succeeded in doing instead was making itself into some kind of feline pretzel. Twisting and contorting frantically to try and rid itself of the unexpected back bunny, while also keeping its head in the hunt.

Needless to say, it was unsuccessful. It tripped over its own ass, tumbled end over end, and collided face-first with a tree while Ig jogged on.

As the panther lay there in a knot, regretting its life choices and attempting to work out which of its four legs was which, the large brown rabbit extricated itself from the crash and ambled off, as though it were running slightly late for a game of darts with people it didn't much like. Unhurried, but still going somewhere.

Ig continued moving as fast as his little legs would carry him, even after we were long out of sight of the panther.

I believe that we are headed slightly off course at present. You may want to adjust your . . .

"Going home." Ig panted. "Cat try . . . eat me."

I must admit that I had a sneaking suspicion that his courage would not hold out, a suspicion that had only been growing the longer that I spent in his company and head. Where other people might have had thoughts, kobolds had an extremely well-developed sense of self preservation. That is not to say that they were cowardly, although they most certainly were, but also that they were built to flee at the slightest provocation. There would have been days, when Ig was not under some degree of control from a piece of majestic headwear, when he might see a bumblebee in the distance and go cower underground for the remainder of the day. The threatening cloud that he had encountered earlier? He most likely would have sped off in the direction of the nearest bolt-hole and stayed there until the wind had carried it off. Kobolds did not last long if they were courageous, because all that they had to back their courage up with were muscles like elastic bands and the kind of personalities usually reserved for tiny inbred dogs that you keep in your handbag.

Luckily enough, I had foreseen this turn of events and planned accordingly.

And which way, pray tell, is home?

Ig lumbered on a few more steps before coming to a grinding halt. His mouth opened, then closed, then opened once more. He reached up with a hind leg to scratch behind his ear as though he might kick his memory into action with enough recurrent whacks. I was in his head. I knew that he couldn't remember which direction we had come from. I was banking on the fact that he couldn't remember which direction we had come from.

Oh, my dear friend, I would never have asked you to take me if I had known that you would have been in any danger, I am so sorry. I will gladly accompany you back home right now, if you will just tell me which direction it is in.

More mouth flapping occurred. Spreading out into some rather frantic arm flapping also. It was safe to say that Ig was in a bit of a flap in general. "Me . . . me forgot?!"

Oh no! How could you possibly forget which way is home? Wherever will you go now? Will you wander aimlessly through the Badlands, awaiting some monstrous fate? Or, if you prefer, I could guide you . . .

"Yes!" Ig cried. "You big smart! You know way home!"

I felt ever so slightly like a bear hunter, hearing a spring trap twanging off in the distance. *Of course, my dear boy. I should be delighted to guide you there.*

"Thank," Ig warbled. "Thank!"

Under my direction, Ig turned around, sought out the sun in the sky, and set out course with precision. The fact that I was directing him towards my home in Arpanpholigon rather than his home in a hole would presumably come up at some point, but by then I could simply feign confusion. After all, he had said "home" without specifying whose.

CHAPTER SIX

A BRUSH WITH DANGER

By the evening of our second day's travels, I was beginning to suspect that the dangers of the so-called Badlands had been greatly overemphasized. We had encountered a single large cat, this much was true, but beyond that, the flora and fauna of this allegedly dangerous place seemed to have been almost entirely benign.

Even the terrain, which I had heard variously described as treacherous, bizarre, and impassable seemed to mostly consist of thickets at its worst, and I could not help but wonder if the people who had been giving those various descriptions had ever actually been here, or if they were spinning a tale of woe in the hopes that someone might attempt to drown it with liquor.

I would of course never disparage the noble profession of "adventurer" with the implication that every single last one of them was so blatant a liar as to make me doubt that a single quest had ever actually been completed. Nor would I insinuate that the vast majority of their dungeon-delving adventures were less glamorous and more grave-robbery. All that I am saying is that perhaps were the truth to be a solid and granular thing rather than an ideal, then we should put every single adventurer in the world through a colossal mortar and pestle to grind them down to mulch in the search for even a single speck of it. Even if truth did not become solid, perhaps that would be the best course of action.

Of course, Ig saw the world through the eyes of an adventurer, in his own way. Every cheeping bird was actually a cockatrice approaching from a great distance at high speeds. Every change of the wind was actually the sudden inhalation of a great red dragon, readying to roast us with the outward breath. Every time that he stubbed his toe on a rock covered in leaves, it was a deadly trap that had been laid by some ancient enemy.

At least Ig had the excuse of stupidity to explain away his understanding of the world; adventurers just had an addiction to attention. And gold.

Regardless, while he was entering twitching paroxysms of absolute terror every twelve seconds or so, I was feeling quite relaxed as night began to fall. As relaxed as one can be when starched into a point.

No small part of my relaxation was based in the fact that Ig had begun to collect Quintessence entirely unaided. In most likelihood, he didn't even know that he was doing it at this point. There was a vacuum where the Quintessence that he had used in his rabbit-summoning escapades had departed from and the natural flow of the elements was moving to fill it. And while the reserves of power available to him would accomplish little more than plucking a long-forgotten plum from a tree if unleashed, the fact that he was continuing to draw more in meant that I could begin to draw some out, ever so subtly suffusing my hat form with the power that was preserving my consciousness. Not so much that Ig would ever notice, but enough to ensure that I was not going to dwindle down into oblivion.

As far as life as a hat went, this was as good as it had been so far, so I was doing my best to enjoy it.

So of course when night was beginning to fall and we came upon something that looked like it might possibly have once been some sort of hunting lodge before nature reclaimed it, wedged into the lee of a hillock, I was feeling relaxed enough to suggest that we might take a look inside, perhaps use it as our shelter for the night. Were there any wild animals inside, Ig could now competently drop a rabbit for them three times out of four, and we would be able to scamper off without too much trouble. Hopefully.

I considered the risk-to-reward ratio of a night spent under an actual roof, without the danger of an owl mistaking Ig for something more palatable. An itinerant badger was a fairly small danger to face by comparison.

Yet when he scurried up to what had once most assuredly been a window frame, judging by the mossy stone lintel still holding off the encroaching slump, there was no animal within. Quite the opposite actually.

Civilization!

Within this old, worn-down heap of a house in the middle of the woods, there was furniture. Real furniture, old and worn by all means, perhaps even patched and repaired a little too much, and built to far too large a scale for Ig, but not decayed at all. Not only that, but there were pictures hanging on the wall, paintings, art. Art meant culture, and culture meant sentience. Something that had been in short supply thus far in my journey.

There was someone living here, someone sapient. I would be able to get off this accursed kobold and onto the head of someone with a halfway-to-usable brain. I'd be able to train them in magic in the course of a couple of days, whip up a teleportation spell, and reek unholy vengeance upon my killer. Finally things were starting to go my way.

Ig's eyes narrowed. "Me no like this."

Of course he didn't.

And what, pray tell, is wrong with the current situation.

"Look human." He was whispering, hilariously enough after his attempts at stealth while moving through the undergrowth had been akin to a rampaging bull's progress through a glass factory. "Humans like stabby us."

Ah, but you forget, my dear Ig, that you are no mere kobold anymore, you are a wizard! Whoever we meet here will treat you with the awe that is suited to wizards, not the disdain with which your kind have been so long showered.

He seemed disgruntled by that particular turn of phrase. "Me already wash in river!"

I consoled myself with the fact that I would not have to endure such idiocy for much longer. After all, if there were any justice in the world, whosoever we discovered within this building might very well murder Ig on sight before plucking me off his cold, dead scalp.

We should proceed with caution and good manners. Approach the door and knock.

"Nope."

He was becoming entirely too accustomed to denying me. But at least neither one of us would have to endure that for much longer.

Do as I say and your rightful reward shall be delivered unto you even quicker than either one of us might have hoped.

Tentatively, terrified and quaking, he raised his little paw up to knock on the door. I could feel his terror, but by this point in the day he had twice been scared into a sprint by the sight of his own shadow so it was a little difficult to take seriously.

Knock on the door, Ig.

He tapped it. Barely brushed it with his knuckles really. Then he took off running towards a bush that was growing up from the ramshackle hut's foundations and leapt inside, making considerably more noise than either the pathetic little tap or a full and hearty knock would have accomplished.

"Nobody home," he whispered. "We go now."

Yet despite his ineffectual attempts to get out of it, there was movement from within the building. A creaking of old floorboards that were unmistakably footsteps, trudging over to the front door.

Against what in a more intelligent creature might have been called his better judgment, Ig pushed his snout out of the bush to take a peek.

The door to the cabin swung open and a towering figure ducked its way out, getting slapped in the face by dangling ivy all the same. Despite Ig's fears, we had not discovered a human being all the way out here in the middle of nowhere. We had instead discovered an ogre.

Now I must admit, that made considerably more sense than a human being so far from all the rest of humankind. It threw up a great many questions about why an ogre might have had all the hallmarks of culture, when they were allegedly a brutish and mindless species, considered by most to be second only to kobolds themselves in terms of intellect. But of course, while a kobold was a diminutive rat-lizard-dog, an ogre was eight feet of solid slabs of muscle peering out of beady, piggy little eyes at the world with the kind of malice one usually only saw in budget proposal meetings at the university.

This particular ogre was no less muscular or malevolent-looking than all of the rest, but there were certain elements to his attire that struck me as incongruous with my assumptions. For instance, rather than wearing untanned furs, leathers, and scraps of bones, this ogre appeared to be wearing a shirt of white cloth, stained with a wide variety of different colors. It had started life many sizes too small for the ogre and showed signs of darning and patching all across it where the flexing of his stupendously oversized muscles as he went about his daily business had torn it apart at the seams.

In shape, an ogre could generously be described as human-ish, though given its bulk, comparison to bulls and boulders often featured heavily.

Atop this ogre's head there was a flattened lump where one might have expected hair on a human. A soggy-looking bundle of cloth that, on closer examination, might very well have turned out to be some sort of dead animal or perhaps a fungal growth. For now, it gave the general impression of a beret. An appearance that was exacerbated by his attempts at a mustache. Hair did grow on an ogre's face, but it was typically wiry and patchy, restrained not only to the lip and jawline, but appearing more or less at random. In the case of this ogre, there were a great many scars occupying most of the places where hair had previously grown, as though his attempts to shave had been made with a butcher's cleaver that was none too sharp. All except for his lip, where the tangle of fur had been waxed and teased out into a sort of upward curvature.

He was a truly hideous sight, and I now regretted asking Ig to knock. Even though an ogre body would definitely carry me through the Badlands with considerably less danger, there was an infinitely increased danger that he might tear me apart simply for existing and scatter my threads to the wind.

Stay very, very quiet.

There are of course two facts about kobolds that we now know all too well for having spent so much time in their company. They are incredibly nervous, and incredibly aromatic in all of the worst ways. And as the ogre cast his gaze around the little garden outside of his house, Ig's nervous stomach got the better of him, unleashing a whistling toot that was almost musical. A horn of doom sounding.

The ogre's head snapped around to face us, and a grin appeared upon his face that could be described in a variety of different ways: gap-toothed, terrifying, maniacal. It is probably a requirement to mention something about halitosis potent enough to stun at fifteen yards too. The combination of blind terror and that surprisingly meaty aroma brought Ig up short of his usual wild capering sprint, and the beast was upon us, massive sausage fingers delicately pinching Ig by the scruff of his neck and plucking him from the bushes. Lifting him up until he was level with the monster's eyes. Eyes so beady that up close they seemed to be peering out at us from amidst a vast ocean of face, stretching from horizon to horizon.

"Wot's this then?"

And I had thought the breath was bad at a distance of some paces. Poor Ig practically wilted in the face of such overwhelming aromatic superiority, the stench of his own milky sweat knocked from the top spot with ease. He'd bathed at some point in the near past; he couldn't compete with a full lifetime of meals wedged between teeth.

To his credit, Ig did try to speak through his terror. I just wouldn't let him. I could not envision any possible combination of words coming out of his mouth that might make the situation any better, and so I clamped his little snout shut.

"Spy?" The ogre leaned in closer still, until Ig's captor became a cyclops in his blurred vision. "No. Not sneaky 'nuff."

Ig began to shiver and quake in the mighty monster's grip, trying to speak, or simply terrified, who could say.

"Buyer?" He jerked Ig upside down and shook him abruptly, almost dislodging me from my place. "No. Not money 'nuff."

In a truly surprising burst of will, Ig managed to overpower the clamp that I had placed upon his jaws and said, "Me am not any those things, me am . . ."

But it was too late, the ogre had already come to his own conclusion. "That leaves critic."

There are probably few words in the guttural tongue of the ogre that do not sound like some sort of cuss. Even saying hello to your neighbor in that language more or less directly translates into a string of insults along the theme of "you stay over there, you nasty, disgusting thing I have to put up with having next to me." Yet even in a language so clotted with slurs and insults for everyone and everything, I had never come across a word used by an ogre with such venom as this ogre said the word *critic*. As though it were lower than the lowest of worms, something to be reviled and loathed. Something worthy of destroying simply to make the world a better place by removing it from it.

Kicking the incompetent Ig out of the captain's chair, I seized control of Ig's mouth. "Not a critic! Uh, the opposite of a critic. The furthest thing from a critic."

Both Ig and the ogre were confused. Which bought me the precious moment that I needed to think up what the exact opposite thing to a critic was.

"I'm a fan."

I didn't know precisely what would occur once the ogre had processed that, but it bought us another moment of life, which was all anyone can really hope for. In that moment, I took stock of all that I had available to me to resolve the situation.

One kobold, slightly used.

One hat, stylish and sapient.

Zero point seventeen micro-thaums of stored Quintessence, sufficient for an archmage to shape into a spell and slay an ogre, utterly useless to Ig, who might have just about been able to pat it gently with such miniscule amounts of power.

That was it, that was all that we had. We were doomed.

The ogre's face split into a grin so wide that I feared it would consume my entire world. "You know Vaughn Gouge's work?"

Ig's head began to shake before I seized control and made it vigorously nod instead.

"Yous is welcome then!" He carried Ig with him, tucked under his arm like a rolled rug, and gestured grandly as we entered the rundown shack. "Welcomes to my studio!"

It was in fact a pretty good approximation of an artist's studio, although perhaps composed by someone who had only ever heard them described. The thick layer of filth coating everything was very much in keeping with every artist's hovel that I'd ever laid eyes on, as was the rather slapdash approach to rooms. Every internal wall of what had probably once been a rather quaint cottage had been smashed through to make more room for the activities that Vaughn undertook here. They had not been removed with any sort of expertise or care for the effect that such removal would have upon the structural integrity of the building, and as such there were several gaps in the external walls currently being pried wider open by tree roots. The thatch roof, which had long ago gone to rot, was currently sagging down towards us in a half dozen places, where it wasn't outright leaking soil. There were a few pieces of furniture dotted around the place, almost as decoration rather than as anything of use, with the vast majority of space instead being turned over to the various stretched canvases on which Vaughn had been inflicting his work.

"Dis is the new stuff. Thems in the city, they didn't understand my vision."

I cannot claim to be an artist, nor to truly understand painting, collage, or whatever that smearing was, but I have always been of the opinion that if I look upon a work of art and do not know what I am meant to be seeing, then the artist has failed in their duty. In much the same way that if I were to cast a spell and it had no effect, I would be considered to have failed. Perhaps this comes from my background using illustrations as educational aids, perhaps I am simply too literal minded.

I will readily admit that it is entirely possible that for someone else, the definition of art is entirely different, and that what sparks joy and delight in one mind is a sour poison to another. However, I could not conceive of any world in which the creations laid out before me were judged to have merit. Perhaps because of the inclusion of all the severed ears nailed to the boards.

Ig made a little squeak of horror as he understood what he was looking at, and Vaughn took it as acclaim. "Dis is my new phase. I calls it happy new ears."

Doubtless there was some symbolism inherent in the severed ears that I, as a non-artist, could not decipher, but I couldn't help but feel like each of the abstract pieces that they were dotted across would have been improved by not having a decaying piece of skin and cartilage rotting slowly down them.

"Wot you think? Better than stuff back in the city, yeah? When them lot wouldn't let me keep the gizzards in?"

Ig was still speechless, but I cannot claim that I was much better off. "I have never seen anything like it."

Luckily enough, Vaughn was sufficiently convinced of his own greatness that such a statement was interpreted as a compliment. "Next one is gonna be my masterpiece, just need some new materials."

Everywhere that Ig's eyes turned as they rolled in abject terror brought with it the sight of a new art piece. The lumbering ogre had finally placed us down to observe his works in the awed silence that he assumed it was provoking, but there was no hope of outrunning a creature whose stride was greater than Ig's height. A creature that wasn't also half-starved and exhausted from a day of fleeing certain death.

There was indeed a single blank canvas in the center of the charnel house, a wooden frame of what had presumably once been a deer's skin, tanned and stretched and bleached to as close as paper as could be achieved by an ogre's skills.

Both Ig and I had been so preoccupied with the horrors of the art that we had briefly stopped paying attention to the artist, but now Ig's breath caught in his throat as he realized that the ogre was crouched low beside him, peering underneath my rim to examine the sides of his head. "Reckon what I really need is littler ears. Delicate like. So them art-school folks stop saying stuff like 'brutalist.' Gotta get a pair of little cute ones."

Ig's little cute ears twitched nervously as the ogre's breath tickled over them.

"Yous said you was a fan, hows would you like it if yous could be a part of the art? Yous could be like . . . my patron, and when folks looked at my masterpiece, they'd look at the little brass thingy beside it in the gallery and see you helped."

I will admit that some portion of Ig's terror may have bled into me a little, so that when I tried to demur it came out sputtering and stuttering. "You can't . . . I mean to say . . . I'm not worthy to be a part of your . . ."

A pair of thick, pigment-stained fingers pinched hold of one of Ig's ears before Vaughn whispered in. "Yous would be doing me a big favor."

I had been expecting a knife. Perhaps some sort of axe, or butcher's cleaver, but Vaughn was an ogre, despite his pretentious nature, and as a people, they were not inclined to use anything sophisticated when brute force would suffice. He began to pull.

Ig's own voice came through then, in a pained yelp. "No! No!"

"Yous right." Vaughn sighed. "That's never going to work."

For one blissful moment relief washed through us, then he caught hold of Ig's other ear. Vaughn grinned, lost in his artistic fervor. "Need leverage!"

He rose to his full, intimidating height, lifting poor little Ig from the floor by his tight and painful grasp upon his ears, readying the vast muscles across a torso that could have been described as barrel-like only if one were taking into consideration those vast barrels that monks sometimes decide to spend their lives inside. The ones that were built to house enough beer to render whole townships unconscious.

Vaughn rolled his shoulders, then started to pull.

CHAPTER SEVEN

THE INCORRIGIBLES

There is a time in every wizard's life when he wishes that he could tear off his own ears.

For me, this was during a particularly strenuous time in my studies at the University of Arpanpholigon, when I was attempting for the first time to manufacture a spell that would continually gather ambient Quintessence to reinforce itself, and thus become a permanent fixture rather than a temporary effect. Curses and enchanted items require this sort of careful planning and manipulation to generate the desired effect without constantly drawing upon the reserves of the caster throughout all of eternity. The formulas required to draw in precisely the correct amount of Quintessence, to store excess for times of drought, and to maintain a balance so as not to overload the structures of the spell are intensely complex, and every different spell created with permanence in mind requires minute adjustments to the seventh decimal place based upon things like the moon phase when the spell is cast, the presence of other elements in proximity to the initial Quintessence being expended, and a million other tiny minutiae.

While I was attempting to calculate all of this—thus ensuring my acceptance into the next school year and that if all else failed in academia I would always have a fallback career in the crafting of magical lanterns—my roommate was attempting to learn how to play the lute.

What precisely had possessed him to take up the study of an instrument at that moment in time now escapes me, though I believe that there was a local barmaid with a predilection for bards who had caught his eye.

If he had simply wanted her attention, then his current skill level with the lute would have been immediately useful, as it was certainly attention-getting when someone seemed to be strangling a cat as loudly as possible behind you, but if he was looking for some kind of deeper connection than despairing stares then he definitely needed to make considerable improvements to his playing.

Polite requests that he practice elsewhere had been stymied by the many complaints already filed about him strumming in communal areas, and everyone else on the dormitory floor had become proficient in noise-cancelling spells well ahead of time, leaving me, the class valedictorian, as the sole sufferer of this young man's lustful plucking.

While the matter was finally resolved after I had discerned the correct formulae to make the lute strings slice off his fingers, in the preceding time, as I was attempting to study, I most certainly desired to tear off my own ears and toss them away.

Which brings us back to now, when I was discovering for myself exactly what such an act would feel like. It hurt. The ears weren't even off yet, and it was the worst pain that I or Ig had ever experienced.

So certain was Ig of his own demise in that moment that his entire life flashed before his eyes. A dank hole in the ground. Bugs. Various excretions. An endless loop of the same mindless nothing played out over the years until finally he laid eyes upon me. He could have gone on doing nothing forever quite happily if it hadn't been for my intervention, and I felt some small pang of sorrow to have dragged him into this situation.

Of course, if he'd done something more useful with his life, like studying magic, then he wouldn't be having his ears yanked off. So really, the blame lay entirely on him for wasting all that time.

As for me, I had a rather unpleasant future of my own to look forward to after Ig died of ear-trauma-related blood loss. I would be a piece of scrap cloth, used to mop up after this ridiculous ogre's attempts at artistic expression.

The soul of the ogre had been expressed since the dawn of history by clubbing things to death, and I had no idea what awful quirk of biology had imbued this particular ogre with a desire to make paintings instead, but at least his fundamental nature could rest assured that he was still going about making art in as bloody and horrid a way as was possible.

Death was coming, any moment now, one ear or the other would go pop, and the blood would start flowing and Ig would expire.

Then suddenly the pressure stopped. Ig dropped to the floor. Both ears must have come off at once, oh no. The poor, stupid little rodent. Yet . . . despite his sudden loss of ears, he was practically deafened by all of the screaming and roaring that was going on. Sprinting for the questionable safety of a heap of discarded paint tubes, Ig leapt and slid out of sight before immediately swiveling around to poke his snout out and take in the scene unfolding before him.

To the eyes of a kobold, it was a clash of titans. The vicious ogre swept his fist with awful fury, and power enough to shatter bones with but a single touch, but the brave warrior woman who faced him deflected the blow with her shield and repaid it in turn, driving the curved blade of her falchion down into the mass of meat that composed Vaughn's body.

He let out a roar of agony, then set out to return the pain with interest, snatching up his blank canvas, easel and all, and bringing it crashing down over the woman's blonde locks.

She crumpled beneath the blow, and all hope that Ig and I might have had of escape disappeared in an instant. Yet Vaughn did not go on pummeling her into paste, or even attempt to pluck off her ears. He stopped, upright and perplexed at the new feathers that had sprouted from his chest. For an instant I cast my mind out to seek the wizard that was failing in his attempt to turn this ogre into a turkey, only to realize my mistake as another two arrows hammered into Vaughn's guts.

Now hope sprung anew in Ig's little heart, and I desperately tried to convince him that now was actually the very best time to leave this little heap and escape through one of the holes in the walls while everyone was busy. Ig, by comparison, was quite convinced that staying perfectly still was actually the best tactic, as he was small and useless and nobody would bother looking for him.

Usually, I'd agree, but I had already recognized the work being done before me, the kind of thing undertaken only by the very worst of the worst in civilized society. Adventurers.

The arrows continued to find their mark in Vaughn's torso as the warrior woman scrambled to her feet, punch-drunk but clearly ready to kick some more ogre backside. She caught Vaughn's next haymaker punch on her shield again, but the force of the blow sent her staggering back. The gong of fist on metal resonated out.

By this point, bloody froth had surrounded the ogre's mouth, and it was being spritzed all over the place by his roaring, creating some rather interesting pointillism in some of his latest works that would probably have been praised as groundbreaking progress.

At last the archer came into sight, tall and lithe with the distinctive pointed ears and gender ambiguity that only came from being an elf. While the warrior woman wore the kind of armor that could generously be called leather lingerie, they were instead garbed in something resembling actual leather armor. Boiled slabs of it that were thick enough to turn a blade or arrow. Very sensible, were it not for the rather artful way in which it was draped across their body, intermingled with green silk. You could take an elf out of their commune, but you couldn't take the commune out of the elf, and while Vaughn had struggled against his nature for his entire life to grasp the fundamentals of aesthetics, this elf, like every elf, was born with the kind of killer fashion sense that made them unnaturally stylish and driven by their inherent nature to dress in a manner that accentuated their appearance, even when it somewhat interfered with the functions of their armor.

Vaughn hammered blow after blow into the woman's shield, sending her staggering with each mighty blow. He roared in victory each time she stumbled back, and snarled in rage every time she returned, an emotional yo-yo that just would not stop flicking back and forth.

Even with the ongoing arrow volleys, Vaughn did not seem to be slowing. In a body that big, there was a lot of blood, and they'd need to spill considerably more before the message finally got through to his walnut brain that he was dead.

Hefting his easel, Vaughn charged for the elf. He was making no progress getting through the warrior's defenses, but this other target looked markedly softer. I would like to have said that it was due to the longstanding enmity between the elves and the ogres, but in all honesty, everyone has longstanding enmity with the elves, because they've been around forever, which provides a lot of opportunities to piss people off, and everyone has longstanding enmity with the ogres because of the way that they like to massacre and eat other sapient creatures, often just for the fun of it.

The elf looked unnerved, or as unnerved as it was possible to look while also remaining model perfect in every way. They cast a glance to their side, and the third and final member of their party stepped up.

This one was a human, like the woman, but unlike the woman, his long hair was pulled back into a ponytail to keep it out of the way, and his armor covered more skin than it left bare. Of the three of them, his was the only set of armor that couldn't have doubled as a sieve in a pinch. It also looked to have been considerably more worn, leather blackened with age, metalwork stained with the soot of a looted city or two. He carried in his hands the kind of sword that ends up with a truly ridiculous name, Bloodthirster or Stormbringer or something equally redundant. It was black and covered in runes in languages that even I couldn't remember, and it glowed faintly like it was haunted by the ghosts of a cadre of rather ineffective fireflies who had opted for blue instead of the traditional yellow. All of which added up to the impression that of the three of them, he was the one most likely to gut you just for the fun of it. A glance up at his face did nothing to disabuse me of that notion. There were scars there, not just one or two like a hero might have to show that they'd been through the wringer, but a whole host of them, like the owner of the face was trying to map out some sort of underground rail system and only had a mirror and knife handy. And there in the midst of that face was the kind of glower I usually reserved for people talking in the library. He growled, "Is it bad?"

The elf shrugged one shoulder gracefully, backing away slowly from the oncoming ogre. Rolling his eyes, the swordsman tried again, calling out to the woman. "Is it evil?"

She seemed to weigh the question in her mind for a moment, glancing around at all the severed ears pinned to canvases before giving a firm nod.

That nod signed Vaughn's death sentence, as it turned out. The scowling swordsman took one step, swung, and then sheathed his sword in more or less the same motion.

Vaughn carried on charging at the elf for a moment before he noticed that he'd left his legs behind him. "Oh."

His broadly muscled torso landed with a thump on the mossy flagstones, and he managed to groan out, "Everyone's . . . a critic." Before he expired. I cannot say that I was sad to see him go, but neither was I particularly delighted at the new company we had just made.

Adventurers were their own whole category of problem that I had not been prepared to deal with. They may not have been possessed of the intellect required to perform the High Art of magic, but they were familiar enough with it, from their encounters in the wilds, that if one of them were to put on a new hat and suddenly start behaving differently than the rest of the group were liable to yank said hat off and toss it in the fire faster than you could say, "Please don't incinerate me."

It had crossed my mind that there might have been the odd adventurer out here in the wilderness, but you must note that at no point did I consider them to be a valid solution to my problems. If anything they would only exacerbate them.

An ogre might have killed Ig for the fun of it, a panther for some food, but an adventurer was the only one that I know who would kill him simply so that they could brag that they had killed slightly more kobolds than somebody else. In normal circumstances, in which I myself was out in the Badlands having my ears torn off, I would have been utterly delighted at their arrival, but since I was currently a kobold, or at least riding on one, the situation was very different.

The swordsman strode past the bisected corpse of the dead ogre to check on the blonde woman. "That was a bad hit, you okay?"

"I am well." She groaned, as though embarrassed to have been beaten about with an easel. "Simply foolish for being taken unawares."

"Happens to the best of us." He clapped his hands together. "Alright, let's get to looting!"

He turned with the closest thing to a smile on his stubbly face that we'd so far seen to meet the elf's placid stare. The elf still had an arrow nocked and was nodding at something deeper into the room. Something suspicious. Whatever it was, it was right behind Ig.

Tensing up once more, Ig tried to turn around, only to remember he was trying to lie low. Whatever nightmarish creature they were still hunting was right behind us, but so long as we did not move, it would be dealt with faster than you could say "guild-approved bounty."

All three adventurers began to spread out and stalk our way. Each one readying their respective weapons.

I must admit that I was so taken in by Ig's version of events that it was only as they closed in around us with their weapons raised that it finally occurred to me that the monster that they were hunting was us.

Ig sprang up out of the heap as my realization spread to him, yelping all the way, "No hurty! No hurty!"

All three adventurers leapt back in dismay. The elf managed to make that look cool, landing with a little twist that brought their bow back to bear. "It can talk!?"

My hope had been that the realization that kobolds were capable of thought and speech might have encouraged these lowlifes to reconsider their career choices, but mostly it just made them seem like they were going to torture Ig for a bit before killing him, just in case he knew why he was capable of speech. And given that I did not currently have a large pouch of money to offer them, and whosoever murdered me likely did, I didn't like my odds of laying out the truth for them and expecting them to help. More likely it would result in my immortal-hat remains being turned over to whoever had killed me to start with so that they could finish the job more thoroughly.

The truth would not do, so I seized control of Ig and told them a beautiful lie off the cuff. "I am not a kobold."

All three adventurers were frozen by this second outburst. Then the swordsman carrying Doombringer or Wrathswinger asked out of the side of his mouth to the elf, "Why can it talk?"

The elf seemed to weigh this question for a moment before nodding. A decision had been reached with all of their ancient wisdom. "We should kill it."

Ig cast his gaze around the narrowed eyes of the adventurers, hoping that any one of them might have offered succor and kindness in our moment of desperation—of which we seemed to be having a great many of late—and finally he locked on to the moderately more sympathetic face of the buxom young woman with the shield and no openly expressed desire to see us dead.

"We can't kill it . . ."

Ig breathed out a sigh of relief.

"A talking kobold is probably worth something. We could sell it to a circus."

I opened Ig's mouth to object, but the scowling warrior beat me to it. "You know a lot of circuses touring the Badlands, Rhine?"

She shrugged her shoulders, setting off an array of extremely distracting movements a little lower that neither Ig nor I were capable of explaining our fascination with. "Better just kill it then. We do not want it running loose, telling everybody and their mother that we're out here."

And there went that vote of support. Out the window with all my other hopes and dreams. "If I might interject . . ."

The elf talked right over me. "Why is it wearing that thing on its head?"

"Mind-controlling parasite?" The grim, dark blade of Bloodsever or Throngslicer was drawn out all too swiftly and pointed not at Ig, but at me. The hat.

Bending down to peer closer at me and once again forcing Ig into an embarrassed flush as this once more prompted other motions, the one they'd called Rhine examined me. "Aww, it is wearing a little hat."

Ig had no experience with women because his species treated sexual dimorphism as an afterthought. I had no experience with them because I was a wizard, devoted to the high calling of academia, which typically ate up the majority of the time that most people spent dating, and whatever social muscles I had in that respect had long ago atrophied. Yet seeing a beautiful young warrior woman ready to murder me for the crime of existing did draw a small twinge of regret from me that I hadn't ever been the fool learning to play the lute.

Regardless, neither of us had any experience whatsoever as to what to do when some gorgeous buxom blonde began cooing over us, so for a moment we were both paralyzed.

And that moment was all that it took. The swordsman holding the Black Blade of Doomy Doom or the Soulsickle asked of her, "But is it evil?"

It seemed that the elf had all of eternity to live, but no patience to wait the half second until that question could be answered. He fired an arrow straight at Ig's stupid little head, which would normally have been fine, as it was the one part of his body I judged to have the least useful organ in it, but it was also going to go right through me.

Taking all of the Quintessence that I'd managed to siphon from Ig during our travels, I threw out one desperate act of low magic, and stopped the arrow dead in the air.

It drained me more than I could say. My ability to control Ig directly was gone, at least until I managed to siphon another few micro-thaums from him. I also suspect that I had to jettison some of my childhood memories as bits of my awareness fell away, but it was a choice between my mother's face and a whole dead language of runes that might have one day proven useful, so it was hardly a decision at all.

As such, it was all Ig's natural charm at work when all three adventurers gawked at him as he said, "Me is wizard. And me is good! Not bad. Good." He gave the looming warrior a pointed look. "So no stabby."

Now, I had a sneaking suspicion then and there that the lie might have been somewhat more believable if I had been the one to deliver it. The grammar of a kobold left a little something to be desired, and his inability to form complete sentences might have suggested to the suspicious, murderous adventurers that perhaps he was not actually one of the most highly educated people on the planet.

Luckily for Ig and me, these people wouldn't know intelligence if it crept up behind them in a dark alley and slit their throats.

Rhine cooed over us once more. "Oh, it thinks it is people!"

The other two looked less convinced. The elf in particular seemed skeptical. There was an upward slant to elf eyebrows at the best of times, and one of this particular elf's brows was practically vertical by this point. "A kobold wizard?"

And they were correct to be dubious, because the very idea of it was laughable. A kobold could no more be a wizard than a dwarf could reach a high shelf;

it was a physiological impossibility. Yet it was the lie to which we were now committed, so I turned all of my thoughts towards feeding Ig the next line to keep us from being exsanguinated.

"Me . . . not kobold." Ig drew himself up to his full height, resisting his natural urge to curl up into as small a ball as possible in the hopes that delivering the next lie with enough authority might see him survive. "Me am wizard. Me be Absalom Scryne."

The announcement of my name should have been sufficient to silence even the most low of lowlife adventurers, but all that Ig's grand announcement drew from these was guffawing.

"What?!" cackled the swordsman. "You're meant to be Scryne?"

The elf's other eyebrow ascended. "Absalom Scryne, Archmage of Arpanpholigon, is a kobold. Dubious."

The young lady in leather was at least a little more receptive, "It's very nice to meet you, Mr. Scryne." She held out her hand to shake one of Ig's and he looked at it, perplexed.

This set off another bout of cackling from the bearer of the dark blade Gloomtickler or whatever. A bout so severe I had some concerns that he might lose consciousness.

"I am quite certain that Absalom Scryne is a human gentleman of considerable age." The elf scoffed. "And more pressingly, regardless of his appearance, he would not be seen dead here in the Badlands. He is more of an ivory tower academic. Field work is not his forte."

"Ah, you has heard of me." Ig tried to wedge his way back into the conversation. "Me is not usually kobold. Me is usually man. But I still has hat!"

The three of them did pause in their hilarity to look at me. Me, the hat in question, that is.

"That is definitely a wizard's hat," opined Rhine.

The swordsman nodded. "And that was definitely magic, the bit with the arrow."

"But why would Absalom Scryne be out here?" The elf's eyes narrowed. "Or a kobold?"

That was unfortunately a question that I did not myself have an answer to. Not even a good excuse. There was no feasible reason for me to be out here.

"A curse."

All of the laughter stopped as the swordsman said that. All three adventurers fell into stern silence. Ig nodded sagely, even though he knew as much about curses as he did hygiene.

"How better to be rid of any city dweller than to curse them into the form of the most pathetic of monsters?" The swordsman's demeanor had changed now, all levity leaving him as soon as the subject of curses came up. One had to assume that he had some personal experience with the matter. "He'd have to flee just to survive, or the first wannabe adventurer to cross his path would chop him up and trade his tail for bounty."

"That would explain his distance from civilization, but not his continuation in this form. An archmage could break a curse like this as easily as you or I make water." Damn his calculating elf brain. He was entirely correct. I'd have shrugged off such a curse without so much as a flex of my mind if I were myself.

"Magic no work," Ig opined. "Little body not hold croissants."

The three adventurers stared at him for a painfully long moment. Rhine mouthed the word, "croissants?" to herself.

Quintessence. Good lord.

To his credit, Ig did his best to sound it out. "Quin-tess-unce."

The elf looked genuinely surprised at the mention of one of the mechanics of magic. If they had been kicking around the world for long enough, it was likely they had come across some degree of learning, if only by accident.

Rhine glanced at the elf, taking in their expression. "That mean something?"

"Only to a wizard." They shrugged one shoulder. Too cool to shrug both.

To my surprise and delight, it seemed that we were not about to be murdered. The swordsman brought that evil-looking black blade up over his head, flipped it in his hand, and then slid it back into the sheath on his back. The elf let their hand drift away from the quiver of arrows hanging at their hip. Ig looked up to Rhine with as endearing a grin as he could muster and was met with the sight of her falchion descending upon us.

CHAPTER EIGHT

CONCERNING THE INHERENT INSANITY OF ADVENTURERS

Ig managed to squeeze out a squeal as the blade came down on us. My own dwindling reserve of Quintessence was too depleted to have any effect upon the world directly, and I lacked the mouth to cast anything even if there were time to do so. It seemed that both the kobold and I would be divided neatly down the centerline, and after the day that we'd had thus far, it felt like something of a relief. At least dead, neither of us would have had any further worries, unless you wanted to get into some sort of religious debate.

Once more Ig's life flashed before his eyes. Mud, worms, kobolds sleeping in a heap. And by the time that it had passed, we should have been well and truly dead. Except we weren't.

The nightmare sword, Spookidoomicus or whatever it was called, had been drawn from its sheath and thrust between us and the descending blade, catching the falchion and stopping it in its tracks.

Ig did not piss himself, which was a pleasant surprise, or possibly an indicator that he was dehydrated.

"He has done nothing to warrant death," the swordsman growled.

Rhine grinned wickedly. "I'm putting him out of his misery."

"Not on my watch."

And then they were off, blades spinning and clattering against each other, punches and kicks flying. If you'd made some study of the art of war then it was probably very impressive, but to my eyes, all that they were doing was creating a slightly mobile hazard. Ig dropped to all fours and scuttled away as they went at it, stopping only when the elf's elegant yet sturdy boots came into view.

The elf looked bored.

Elves usually look bored; it is part of that façade of superiority that they project. They've been around the block a few hundred times and nothing surprises them anymore. I imagine that if I had been entirely devoid of all drive and curiosity about the universe after my short century upon the face of the world, I might have managed a similar expression on my own face, before my face became the front-facing part of a hat.

Rhine performed some sort of acrobatic flip over the swordsman's head, and he had to flip his sword around behind his back without looking to block the coinciding thrust of her falchion.

This elf's expression of boredom went beyond the usual too-cool-to-exist schtick that elves liked to project and made it all the way into surly teenager territory. Ig looked up at him. "They fights a lot?"

They deigned to glance down, then nod.

Ig couldn't quite comprehend this. "But they friends?"

The "friends" had their blades locked together now, twisting and turning so the repeated slams of the warrior woman's shield were met with the flat of his blade each time. In reply, the swordsman's foot shot out and hooked her ankle.

"The best of friends." The elf sighed. "Yet she wishes for more."

Even as she fell, Rhine hooked ahold of one of the ogre's eerie paintings with her sword tip and swung it at the swordsman. The canvas bounced off his elbow, showering him in dislodged ears, and bought her the time to roll back to her feet before he could deliver a killing blow.

"Me not understand."

He gave Ig a look that implied that the list of things that the kobold did understand could probably be written on a grain of rice. "Rhinolyta hails from a tribe of famed warrior women that live in the deep jungles of the south, questing out from their lady-only paradise solely to complete deliveries for their busy mail-order service. They swear an oath that they shall lie with no man unless he can defeat them in battle. I believe this was intended to improve their breeding stock."

From this I was abruptly able to parse that the screaming and slashing going on in front of us was a form of foreplay, and I became immediately embarrassed to have been watching. Ig did not understand any part of what had just been explained to him, but that was hardly surprising.

With a little mental prod, Ig asked, "What hims story?"

"Ildrit?" the elf asked, causing the man's head to snap around, and Rhine to land a solid blow to his chest with her shield. "Some say that he was a prince in his own lands before he succumbed to bloodthirst. Others that he was a warlord, raining terror upon the cities of the plains."

Ig scratched under his chin. "Don't look very princey."

"That was long ago. He has turned over a new leaf since then, devoting himself to using his skills with the sword to do good." He was currently using his skills with the sword to stop the endless flurry of slashes from Rhine. Kicking off her shield when she pushed in with it to keep her at a sufficient distance for his longer blade to still be advantageous.

Without my guidance, it seemed that Ig was quite the curious little fellow. "Why change?"

The elf glanced from Ig to the swordsman beating back Rhine's latest offensive with a swooping, almost dance-like motion of his sword. Knocking her defenses out wide with each swoop and spiral. Finally they replied. "That is his tale to tell."

Ig settled down on his haunches to have a good scratch, finally remembering that there was someone next to him when the elf let out a polite cough. "What we be calling you?"

"In the language of my people, I am known as Angharadfflamddwyneuroswydd."

With my extensive knowledge of ancient languages, it was simple enough to translate the name into its component parts. This elf had just described themselves as something like the best loved flame bearing golden enemy. My knowledge of elvish did not extend to any desire to speak in the hideous tongue, however. Reading it was enough of a headache without introducing attempts to pronounce such words.

Ig pointed to the duelists. "And they calls you?"

Another long, tired sigh. "Wyn."

"Okay, Wyn. Nice meet you." Ig did not offer to shake their hand, and the elf seemed relieved that they would not need to touch his grubby little paw.

The attempts that I had made to improve upon Ig's general cleanliness had been somewhat undone by our passage through the forest and the paint pile. He was certainly eye-catching now, but without a thick crusting of filth, the things that caught your eye were not things that you necessarily wanted to see.

Under my direction, Ig set out to hunt for something like clothes in the debris of the house, taking care to keep his distance from the ongoing brawl. Wyn called after us, "For the record, I do not believe your tale of transfiguration."

Ig held up his hands. "Explain how else kobold wizard?"

Ogres were built to a markedly larger scale than humans, and humans in turn were markedly larger than kobolds, so all of the clothes that Ig was able to uncover buried amidst the heaps of miscellanea were quite a bit too large for him, with the exception of those tattered and bloody scraps that had at some point served as wrapping for the ogre's meals, which I refused to wear on principle.

I had no superstitious objection to wearing the clothes of a dead person, I just disliked the idea of parts of that dead person still being crusted onto them.

Finally, when it seemed that all was lost, we came upon what had once been some sort of bathroom to the rear of the cottage, where there had been a window, and beyond it, a water barrel to catch the rain. Within that room was a verdigris-coated bathtub that would never see use again, and more importantly for us, a bathrobe.

Much of it was covered in stains from what I could only hope were artist's pigments, and there were some fairly distinctive mold spots down by the trailing hem, but the important thing was that it was a *robe*.

Wandering around naked was all well and good when you were entirely alone, but now that we were in company, and mixed company at that, something more was required. Were there trousers or a shirt here, perhaps I might have convinced Ig to put them on, but ultimately they would have done little to make me feel as though I were garbed. From as early as I could remember, there was only one sort of clothing worth wearing, and that was a robe—a wizard's robe, to be precise.

This towel cloth thing was not that. It lacked the many hidden pockets, the soft lining, even the embroidered astrological patterns that one might have expected from a robe—though I could not deny that some of the bright spatters staining it could have been attempting to form little constellations. Regardless, it took only a moment's internal arguing with Ig before he wrapped it around himself and secured it with a length of string that I suspected the ogre had meant to use as dental floss. As we had already established, oral hygiene was not high on his list of priorities, so it remained coiled and untouched.

Enrobed, we returned to watch the final few blows of the battle unfolding in the ruins of the studio. There were few paintings still standing, and the ears that had been set loose from them littered the floor and made Ig all the more hesitant to pick his way across in case of an unfortunate squish underfoot.

Both Rhine and Ildrit were flushed and panting by this point, although she was the only one still smiling. Neither had drawn blood but there had certainly been a few blows traded, judging by the purplish swelling around the pale man's eye socket. There was a hint of a curve on his high cheekbone too, where the edge of the shield had caught him.

"Peoples is crazy," Ig said, to himself as much as to me, but I could not help but concur. There had to be easier ways to romance someone than beating their face in with a shield.

Finally it seemed that the battle had come to its end. With a heavy, hammering blow, Rhine slapped the great dark sword that probably had a name like Soulcleaver or Heartripper from Ildrit's grasp with her falchion, driving forward with her shield to knock him off his feet. He went down, toppling over backwards, and Ig and I both felt quite certain that was the end of the matter, but it seemed that he just wouldn't stay beaten. As he went down, his legs entangled with Rhine's and they both ended up falling over together in a mess of bare skin and leather and . . .

Ig flapped his hands at his face, accidentally drawing the elf's attention. He cleared his throat and awkwardly explained. "Toasty warm."

Legs locked together, the two combatants twisted and rolled over one another, weapons torn from their grasps, every blow countered, every grapple twisted into a different grapple going the other way. And just when it seemed they were going to go on writhing on the floor all day, they rolled the last of the distance to put the black blade Midnight's Bane, or whatever it was called, back into Ildrit's reach. It leapt into his grasp as though called by magic, laid flat along the side of his arm so that as he rolled on top of Rhine and pressed his arm across her throat, she could feel the sharp edge.

For a moment, there was some heavy eye contact and panting, then Rhine flung her arms and legs apart and cried, "You have won! Do as you desire with me!"

What Ildrit desired was apparently to get up off her as quickly as possible and put some distance between them.

She sat up, pouting. "You have defeated me in battle."

"Not really," Ildrit said, trying to adjust his armor back into its normal position without looking like he was adjusting anything else.

"You did!" She flipped onto all fours and crawled across the ear-littered floor in what she probably hoped was a seductive manner. "It was well fought, and you are a formidable foe. Now take me manfully!"

He had his hands up, as if demonstrating to the room how much he was not touching her. "I thought you said I could do as I desire?"

"You can, anything." She lowered her voice, aiming for a sultry whisper. She instead got something throaty and uncomfortable, even to Ig's untrained ears. "Even the weird stuff."

His upheld hands moved to his face and Ildrit groaned. "Rhine . . . you don't even know what the normal stuff is."

She lunged forward, hands catching on his belt. "But I'll do it anyway! And the weird stuff! And any of the other things in between that you'd really need to be in a committed relationship to even bring up in conversation."

That brought a puzzled silence over the room until Ildrit wet his lips and asked, "Have you been talking to the seamstresses again?"

She pouted in a manner that had nothing to do with attempted seduction. "They say I need girl time."

"And you do, you absolutely do. Next time we're in town, you should absolutely spend time with your girly friends." He carefully unhooked her grip from his belt without letting her touch anything beneath it. "Just don't take relationship advice from folks who only want to live through you vicariously."

Ig had been watching all of this with what I can only describe as prurient interest, but now he had tripped on his path to understanding. "What vicariously mean?"

You can't do the fun thing yourself, but you can watch someone else do it.

"We gonna watch them do the fun thing?!" He had not quite shouted it, but it was certainly close. Ig and I became aware that we were now the subject of several pointed stares. He looked at his feet, and the tattered fringes of our new robe.

He shuffled his feet, then headed for the door. "Me go stand outside until you done."

After an afterthought he paused in his flight and added, "With fingers in ears."

But then Ildrit was by Ig's side, scooping him up in a one-armed hug and half running, half carrying him out. "Let's all get some fresh air and calm down."

"There is only one thing that can calm the burning in my heart," Rhine called after him, still doing her best at a seductive tone, but there was no mistaking that it was also her voice stripped of artifice that we heard immediately after the door slammed shut behind us saying, "Oh bugger."

Ildrit let out the breath he had been holding in the whole time, groaning as the cool air touched his bruised cheek. "That woman is going to be the death of me."

Ig completely overcame all of my attempts to silence him and practically yelled at the man, "Why you no fun-thing her!?"

The man was completely mortified, as was I, and probably Rhinolyta too if she could hear through the rickety door half as well as we could.

He was unnaturally pale, with white hair and eyes so blue they might very well have been white too, and as such when he blushed and blustered only the faintest glow of red came to his cheeks. "I am . . . That is to say . . . she is . . . It's weird. Alright? The whole thing about beating her up to win a date? It's really weird. It makes me uncomfortable. I don't want to be a part of it."

Ig still couldn't seem to get his head around the idea that anyone might reject such a beautiful woman, regardless of the circumstances. "But you beats her ups anyways?"

He continued to look horrified to be having the whole conversation, as though we had joined him in the bathroom and were now discussing optimal technique. "To defend myself, not so that I can . . . take advantage."

Ig . . . gods help me . . . Ig nudged Ildrit in the ribs with his elbow. "Me thinks she is wanting you to take idge."

Advantage.

"Dantage."

Advantage.

"Vantage."

Close enough.

Desperately casting around for a change of subject, Ildrit immediately started onto safer ground. "So you've been cursed into a kobold? How did that come about?"

Ig started to answer before I managed to reassert some degree of control over him. He might have managed a few haphazard lies up until now, but I knew that he lacked the moral fortitude and intellectual flexibility to maintain a deception in the long term. I would have to be the keeper of our secrets, so I should have been the one inventing them. "Me not remember. One day I normal. Next day, poof, out here."

"Well I'm certain that we can offer you our assistance in getting out of your current predicament."

Ig was startled as his hat abruptly jumped for joy, very briefly leaving the dubious comfort of his scalp. I forced my own voice out through his mouth when I landed, before he could screw this up for us. "That would be much appreciated."

"I do not wish to speak of it, but I too labor under a curse . . ."

I would bet good money it is the evil sword.

He rambled on, ". . . I travel even now through these blighted lands so that I might discover some way to bring about the curse's end and reclaim my life from the cruel twist of fate."

It took me a moment to understand what he was saying. But when the penny dropped, it fell like a lead weight into the hollow where Ig's brain should have been. "Wizard? Out here?"

Ildrit chuckled. "Is it so hard to believe? You are out here, after all. And is it difficult to imagine that some wizards might choose to live out here? Beyond the confines of the rules and regulations of the university that prevent certain paths from being walked . . ."

This was rapidly spiraling out of my control again. Any wizard worth his salt would realize fairly swiftly that Ig was not in fact a transmutated human wizard, but a kobold in a hat that did not fit him. After which my little deception would be deciphered, and we could only hope that I was not entirely obliterated in the rain of fireballs that would follow. My only hope would be to get this wizard separate from the adventurers and explain my true situation to him, flinging myself upon his mercy.

That did not bode well. When it came to mercy, wizards are notoriously lacking.

Ig's eyes narrowed with my unpleasant suspicions. "Not druid, is he?"

"Ah no." Ildrit rubbed at the back of his neck awkwardly, trying to work out one of the kinks that had been beaten into it. "I believe that he is possibly . . . a necromancer."

He tensed, as though expecting some sort of uproar, but I had no issues with the gentleman's academic area of expertise.

"Well that okay then."

Some wizards animated furniture to make it perform menial tasks, and nobody got out the pitchforks and torches for them, even though they were functionally doing exactly the same as a necromancer in a graveyard. Though admittedly, the brush sweeping up behind you as you walked was considerably less likely to be your beloved granddad if there wasn't a necromancer involved.

Like most aspects of life beyond the study of magic, death wasn't something I considered all that much. I vaguely recalled those students who were on the necromancy track back at the university. They tended to wear quite heavy makeup and dye their hair black, but compared to some of the really annoying cliques, I don't think they were anything to write home about. Some of them looked a bit thin, with the usual jokes about them perhaps being a skeleton that had been raised from the grave themselves, but I didn't partake in such fun-making. Theirs was as valid a field of study as any, and I felt no need to persecute them just because the names of the bands that they liked to listen to were unpronounceable and sounded like screaming. I could understand the desire for some good solid screaming after a day at the university.

"We got a map to lead us to his tower from a mysterious stranger in the last inn. When they heard we were looking for a curse breaker, they said that there was nobody in this world who knew curses better than him."

It was entirely possible that this was all the prelude to a trap, that this mysterious wizard was in fact the one handing out maps to his own property with the intention of massacring all the foolish adventurers that came marching out with demands. Foolish adventurers that it was reasonable for him to believe would be weakened by the fact that they were cursed. It sounded more and more like a trap the longer that I thought about it.

However, if it was a trap that resulted in the death of everyone other than me, it had the possibility to be advantageous. There was not a wizard in the world that could look at the finery that was my new pointed and wide-brimmed form and not feel some degree of compulsion to at least try me on, and then I'd be in control of someone with a decent brain, a decent reserve of Quintessence, and quite possibly an entire undead army with which I could rain havoc and vengeance upon my killers. In essence, traveling along with these adventurers would protect me from harm, and then once harm befell them, there would be a new, ready-made solution waiting for me.

"Me am . . ." I forced Ig back from control of his mouth, brandishing his brainstem like a bullwhip. "I am only sorry that I am not at the height of my powers, or I would have been delighted to remove your curse myself in exchange for the kindness and aid you have offered me."

Taken aback by my sudden loquaciousness, Ildrit stared at me for a time, then seemed to shrug it off. This seemed to be something of a survival mechanism for him. Moving past anything he didn't want to think about before he could strain something.

"Anyway, with that ogre job handled, we should be on our way promptly. Not sure why there was such a high payment attached to 'deal with the ogre menace' when he was mostly just taking ears. I mean yeah, you can't wear hats afterwards, but who really wears hats anymore?" He glanced at Ig then coughed. "Present company excluded, of course."

Ig nodded curtly at him, and I blessed my lucky stars that only the most minimal of attention had been directed towards me, where I sat perched atop his head.

CHAPTER NINE

ELEMENTARY EDUCATION

That first night in the company of adventurers was nothing like I had assumed it would be. There was no rough-housing or cussing. The few jokes being tossed around couldn't have been called bawdy by any stretch of the imagination. They even had a campfire set up outside of the ogre's cottage, which made the whole experience a drastic step up from our previous night sleeping in the forest.

While we could have spent our evening under the cover of the building's roof, that would have required enduring the smells of a deceased ogre, not to mention ears in various states of decay. After my experience of Ig's burrow, it was the aromatic equivalent of a mild itch by comparison, but I wasn't going to argue with my saviors about sleeping arrangements. Unlike Ig.

While Rhinolyta was not looking and I was not in control, Ig continually shuffled his way along the log to be closer to the woman, and in turn she kept shuffling her way along the log when he wasn't looking to be farther from Ig's smell. She was too polite to mention it, or to repulse him with some good old-fashioned violence, but my only consolation at this point was that soon they'd all be dead in this necromancer's trap and I wouldn't have to worry about acquiring a reputation as a shape-changing lecher.

Worse even than his attempts to cuddle up to her were the smiles. A kobold's face is not made for smiling. Grimacing, certainly, but smiling was not something that they were equipped for. Given the state of perpetual misery and near starvation that they existed in, I wasn't surprised that they weren't built for cheer, but Ig was surely trying with all his might to contort his horrid little mouth up at the corners.

"So . . ." She tried to break the awkward silence. "How long have you been a kobold?"

Ig began counting on his fingers before I leapt in to answer, "Three days since awareness returned to me. Three days of being hunted by every living thing in creation."

She shot Angharadfflamddwyneuroswydd a desperate look and they visibly wilted at the prospect of being dragged into our incredibly boring conversation.

"And why is it that sometimes you speak like you're a wizard, and sometimes like a moron?"

I tried to pretend that there was no venom in that question, but I knew that of the three of them, the elf remained the most suspicious of me and this was yet another attempt to make me incriminate myself.

"Me talk smart!" Ig began before I wrested control back. "When I am able to concentrate. Without deliberate effort the kobold brain reverts to form."

There was a hint of a grin on their perfectly smooth face. "So really, you are part kobold at this point."

They were attempting to antagonize me in the hope that I would slip up, but when you enter a battle of wits with a wizard, you are bringing a knife to a cosmic death-beam fight. "Only the least important part. The body. My mind remains perfect."

Ildrit cut in before any more prodding could occur. "We're going to help Mr. Scryne out of his predicament because it is the right thing to do. Okay?"

The elf's eyes rolled with such vigor that I feared they would escape into the undergrowth, but they fell silent. Rhinolyta, for her part, had just been making conversation anyway. Something she returned to immediately. "So what's it like being a wizard?"

"To wield the power of the cosmos is a solitary life. To master the High Art of the Arcane requires a degree of mental discipline that few in this world are capable of, and mastery of the magical world leaves us changed by the experience of our learning. We can see the beauty in all things, and peer deep into the atomic heart of creation, flexing and pulsing just beyond the periphery of mortal vision."

Was what I wanted to say, but instead Ig blurted out, "Me can make fish scared and pluck plums with brain bullets."

Ildrit tried to muffle a laugh, but Rhine looked suitably impressed. "Wow."

"But there was angry cat, so my no get plums," Ig continued as I shrank in on myself, mortified to be associated with this imbecile.

For a moment there was silence, but for Ig softly repeating the word "plum" to himself, then Ildrit very deliberately yawned. "Welp, time to hit the sack. Who has first watch?"

By all rights it should have been the elf, since their kind didn't strictly need to sleep as such, but I wasn't going to be so impolite as to point such a thing out. Instead Ig declared, "Me take it."

Why on earth did you offer to take a watch?

"You want creepy elf watch you sleeping?"

It was a valid point that I wish that he had voiced internally rather than to the group at large. Wyn's near-lipless mouth pursed in annoyance then they flounced off to their bedroll without another word.

Ildrit looked like he was choking on his own tongue as he tried not to laugh, and Rhine's eyes followed him longingly all the way to his bedroll. Which even Ig noticed was very deliberately positioned on the opposite side of the fire to hers. She sighed. "You know, when I dressed as a boy to run away and be an adventurer, I thought that everything would be so romantic. I'd meet the right guy, he'd beat me in mortal combat, and then we could settle down and raise a horde together, but life just doesn't work out how you want it to."

Due to the differential in height when he was sitting beside her, Ig was eye-level with her chest. This resulted in a rather pointed question regarding logistics. "In only girls kingdom . . . you dressed as boy?"

She laughed. "Of course. If I'd dressed as a girl and they caught me trying to sneak out, I'd have been taken home. If they found a boy, they would have exiled him."

There was a degree of logic to that which couldn't be denied, but the logistical question still remained. "How you manage to hide your . . ."

She glanced down at what Ig was staring at and laughed again, taking hold of the thick golden braid of hair that had been hanging down onto her chest. "I just put it in a bun and covered it with a scarf."

Thankfully this was enough to redirect Ig's already rather confused attention. "Hair lunch?!"

"What?!" she asked.

What?! I asked.

"Weh?" Ig replied to the both of us.

"Shut up," came the answer to all our questions from over on Ildrit's bedroll. "Some of us are trying to sleep."

Rhinolyta took this opportunity to extract herself from our conversation, such as it was, and slip into something more comfortable. Given that an iron maiden would have been more comfortable than this conversation, I had to imagine that her bedroll on a pile of gravel was probably several orders of comfort higher.

And so our watch began. The moments stretched out into minutes as Ig's hyperactive imagination made every sound into a rampaging monster just sneaking up on us. Worse yet, he kept glancing to the bushes to check for panthers with such regularity that I genuinely felt like I was becoming dizzy following that same darting pattern of his eyes.

Yet through all of his anxiety, I noticed that there was one other place that his eyes kept diverting to. The gently snoring lump under a heap of blankets that was Rhine. It was perhaps best to nip this burgeoning crush in the bud. If she was going to die soon, I would not like for Ig to get too attached.

You know that it would never work out between the two of you.

Ig let out a sigh so heavy it straightened out his tail for the briefest of moments. "Because she pretty and me . . . me?"

Because you're a kobold and she's a human, I'm not even certain that there could be any sort of... interlocking. I was trying very hard not to think about what any attempts at interlocking involving Ig might look like. *You are entirely different species.*

Another long sigh. "But she so pretty."

I cannot deny that she is aesthetically pleasing, however that does not mean that there is any possibility of the two of you...

"You not know that," Ig snapped at me. He actually snapped at me. For the first time in his entire life, he showed the slightest smidgeon of a backbone, and I was so taken aback that I let it happen.

They say that love is blind, but I have noticed that the reason behind its blindness is often blind avarice. For instance, it is considerably more common for a very wealthy hideous man to find himself a bride than a pauper with a face like a beaten potato. And of course there are a great many creaking widows with remarkably young and attractive men lavishing attention upon them. Regardless, Ig was both broke and had a face that could charitably be described as atrocious, so I didn't like his odds.

Still, it would do no good to tell him that he had absolutely no redeeming qualities whatsoever and would spend the rest of his existence without love or affection because he was so awful. It might impinge upon his self-esteem somewhat, and I needed him confident to proceed. So I elected to take a different tack.

Ig, dear sweet Ig, to romance her, you must first best her in mortal combat. Do you think that you can best her in mortal combat?

He paused in his mounting squirrely wrath to check details. "What mortal mean?"

That losing will result in your death.

He shivered at the mention of his inevitable demise.

"And combat means..."

Without lungs, I lacked the apparatus for sighing. *Fighting, Ig.*

He contemplated this new information solemnly then finally came to the same conclusion that I had reached hours beforehand. "My cannot do that."

No, Ig, you cannot.

It was a strange sensation to be in Ig's mind, and for him to have thoughts of his own. They sort of tickled when they brushed up against me. "Buut... you could teaches me the magic and I could win."

If this pathetic crush on a different species was what it took to inspire Ig to action, then I was willing to entertain it. Most likely he would be dying fairly soon anyway, but having him capable of performing the most basic acts of magic might convince this necromancer with his trap that I was a party worth parleying with rather than slaughtering alongside these fools.

Because you have been such a diligent student thus far . . .
"Me cans be diligent," he protested.
You literally do not know the meaning of the word.
"You can teaches me that too," he replied with a certain smugness, as though he had found a loophole in his own idiocy.
Perhaps I can, Ig . . .
The elf cut us off curtly. "Wizard! Would you kindly speak to yourself silently? Some of us are attempting to sleep."
"Sorry," Ig whimpered back.
They aren't even trying to sleep. Elves don't sleep. This is all just a power play. To assert dominance.
Ig, bless him, attempted to whisper back to me, contorting his face as though he could speak into his hat. "Why do?"
I cannot say for certain, but I suspect it has something to do with them being a stuck-up, pompous ass who thinks they're better than everyone else.
Ig nodded solemnly at this new wisdom, then went back to nervously twitching around, looking for any hint of danger. Between the fire and the people who murdered monsters for a living, I was feeling as secure as I had since becoming a hat, so I allowed myself a little while to compose my thoughts, and lesson plan, in peace.
The next step of your training, now that you have acquired Quintessence and learned, to some degree, how to release it again, will be to teach you some spells.
Both of Ig's ears, blessedly saved from artistic predation, pricked up at the mention of spells. Everyone who is not a wizard gets very excited at the prospect of spells. They're the things that magic is made of in the mind of a layperson. Would that it were so simple as learning the magic words and saying them, all the people of the world might be mages.
To cast a spell requires three separate things operating in perfect harmony. The first you have already acquired: Quintessence, the raw building block of magic, transmutable into every other element.
Ig's head bobbed along excitedly, but he managed to prevent himself from squeaking anything out and antagonizing our elvish companion.
The third, which we shall address last, is the language of the Arcane Archons: Archaic. It is the most ancient of languages, and some say the very sounds that the gods spoke the world into existence with. It is a dense and complex language, where the slightest change in intonation and pronunciation can produce an entirely different effect from the one which you intended. If you speak a magic into existence that is beyond your stores of Quintessence, then the remainder required to cast the spell will be torn from your body, rendering you a corpse. As such, it is most important that you never attempt to cast a spell that requires more Quintessence than you know that you hold, and for preference to never come close to that limit.

The mention of death had yet again put the fear into Ig, and he sat quivering for a time with his eyes still darting around, as though words of mispronounced Archaic were going to creep up on him in the night and drain him of life.

I would have preferred to skip past that particular warning given the emotional toll that it had taken on my most worthless apprentice, but unfortunately he really did need to understand the risks involved so that he did not attempt anything so foolish as experimentation. He had little to no control over his Quintessence as it was, and if he started blurting out Archaic, he was liable to drain himself to a husk quicker than you can say *CREPITUS*.

As such, we are first going to make a study of the other part of spellcraft before we begin learning to actually cast our spells. And that, my dear Ig, is the study of the elements. The fundamental building blocks from which the universe and all magic is made.

He perked up immediately at the mention of the elements, practically bouncing up and down on the spot. "My knows this! Me knows the ments. Fire and Water and Earth and Air. Me knows already, me is ready!"

Oh, dear, sweet Ig. No. Those are not the elements. There are not four simple forces of which all things are constructed, no matter how the peasants and buffoons of the world might wish it to be so. No, there are not four elements, there are one hundred and eighteen, with research mages hard at work constantly attempting to discover new ones.

Ig blinked. "One hundred."

And eighteen.

Ashamed of himself, as he often was when confronted with his overwhelming inadequacies, Ig looked down at his grubby little feet where they stuck out from under the hem of his robe. "My cannot count that high."

Fear not, my dear apprentice, for you shall, at best, learn three or four that will serve you the best in navigating our current circumstances. Combined with the Quintessence that you are cultivating, and a small vocabulary of words in Archaic, those three or four will provide you with an ample array of solutions to most of the problems that we are likely to encounter.

"I cans count four."

Without looking at your fingers.

"You no say I need to do that."

And so let us begin your education with the fundamental building block from which your own body is composed. Carbon . . .

CHAPTER TEN

CONCERNING THE OGRE MENACE

The night had passed us by with great haste. No sooner had Ig gotten to grips with Carbon and Potassium than we were disturbed from our reverie by the gentle touch of Ildrit upon Ig's shoulder. I will admit to some mild amusement that Ig leapt up into the air at that touch with sufficient height that, had we earlier employed the same method of propulsion, he may have managed to snare a plum the prior day.

Then, with a degree of kindness that I must admit that I would never have been able to muster myself, the swordsman silently guided Ig to his own bedroll and let him lie down on it. Ig was unfamiliar with the concept of blankets, pushing them aside as he walked repeatedly in an ever-tightening circle before finally sinking down, curled into as small a ball as he could muster, and tucking the tip of his tail into his mouth out of habit. For a long moment, the bearer of the dark blade stood over us, staring down at the ridiculous creature that he had welcomed into the ranks of his party, before he crouched down and laid the blanket over Ig himself.

It had been something of a stressful day for Ig, all things considered, and he had exerted himself to a degree that he never had call to in his normal life, so immediately after that blanket landed on him with all of its woolen warmth and comforting weight, he was unconscious.

The plan had been for us to rise again when the elf's watch began, and resume our studies, with the intent that they were never put into a position of power over us and our helpless sleeping form. Sadly, sleep disagreed with our assessment of the situation and decided that it should continue uninterrupted.

You may think that, given I remained as perpetually conscious as an elf, I might have been capable of serving as some sort of timekeeper, aware of what was going on around us, but as it turned out, with the complete lack of sensory information at my disposal, I found myself somewhat adrift. It was not so awful as the vacuum of nothingness that I experienced when my hat form was removed from the head of a host, but it was similar enough that I lost my grounding in reality.

My vast mind turned to matters beyond the ken of mortal kobolds, I began attempting to decipher the mystery of my own assassination, and the manner in which my consciousness had transubstantiated into an item of clothing. Such things were not entirely unheard of in the history of magic, but typically only occurred with some degree of intention established prior to death. Intention, planning, ritual, and a magic item designed to contain the sapience as it fled the mortal coil. Such rites were typically undertaken by the kind of mustache-twirling maniacs who meant to extend their lives through magic eternally, either by the inhabitation of a golem, or some similar construct. Sometimes it was intended to be a temporary situation before some other practitioner of the High Art could transfer them into a fresh and often unwilling body. None of these were options that I would have chosen for myself, and even if in a moment of madness, realizing that I was dying, I sincerely doubt that I would have selected my current form. My hat had not even been enchanted prior to my mind being cast into it. It had just been a rather nice hat that I'd hung on to for many many years out of a desire to not go hat shopping again when it would take valuable time away from my work.

In the midst of trying to work out what particular set of circumstances might have convinced me that becoming a hat was my most viable option, I was stirred awake by a gentle kick to Ig's midsection.

Predictably, he bolted upright at the first sign of trouble, only to be immediately silenced in his attempted scream by soft hands clamping his snout shut. Rhine. She was cradling him in her arms, and he went from the blissful release of sleep to terror, then back to an entirely different kind of bliss in rapid succession.

Do try to focus, Ig.

The other two adventurers were awake, armed, and on their feet, dawn was prickling through the eastern trees, and there were sounds of movement beyond the little clearing in which Vaughn had made his home. The black blade Murderificus, or whatever it was called, was already in Ildrit's hands, the elf had an arrow nocked back, they were all ready for a fight.

All except Ig, of course, who was instead squirming around and trying to scream now that he'd recognized that there was trouble afoot.

Be quiet, you little buffoon, you'll bring them down on us.

"There are ogres coming," Rhine said breathily into Ig's ear. "Dozens of them from the sounds of it. Do you have a magic that will hide us from their sight?"

We had not made it that far last night, and even if I did give Ig the correct word of magic to use in conjunction with his absent knowledge of the element of Helium, he would almost invariably say it wrong and send the whole group of us blasting up into the stratosphere. He managed to shake his head despite her grip on him.

She let out a rather imaginative cuss in her own language, dropped Ig, then looked to Ildrit for his wisdom. Judging by his rather pained expression, his wisdom was that we were all about to die. Leaving only the elf to save us all with some sudden twist of genius. A glance at their placid expression, even in the face of an oncoming horde of ravaging ogres, would have been quite soothing were it not for the way that their knuckles had turned white as they tightened their grip on their bow.

Ig made a suggestion. "Run away?"

The adventurers conferred among themselves with only a glance before all three nodded. Grabbing what they could of their campsite and cramming it into backpacks, they picked the direction as far from the sound of approaching ogres as possible and they bolted. Leaving Ig trailing behind them as he was somewhat lacking in the stride department.

But what dear Ig lacked in physical fitness, he counterbalanced with an overabundance of absolute terror. He ran as though death itself were on his heels, because, let us be honest, it was. And while the elf may have been indefatigable, the same could not be said for the other two. After only a mile of cross-country running, Ig caught up to Ildrit, who I had to assume was being weighed down by the massive slab of black metal strapped to his back, seething with the weight of all the souls it had reaved. Not far ahead of him, Ig caught up to Rhinolyta, who was younger, in better condition, and weighed down with both a sword and a shield of burnished bronze.

Yet despite this mad flight, there could be no denying that the sound of the ogres was not abating. Quite the opposite, in fact. It was as though they had merely been marching before and had now caught the sound of quarry fleeing and taken off after it. There were whoops and roars from among their ranks, and while they had not caught sight of us, and we had not caught sight of them, they must have been able to hear our flight. Speed had taken precedence over stealth, and now we would pay the price for that oversight.

It did not matter that these adventurers were in the prime of their life, or that Ig's flight or fight response was lacking option two. The stamina of the hulking slabs of meat that made up an ogre would be beyond what any of us could have mustered on our best day.

Ig had managed to make good distance with remarkably little slapstick thus far, but while glancing back he tripped over a leaf-covered log and went soaring. He hit the ground hard, and for an awful moment, I fell off.

There was only darkness and confusion. Residual terror still clinging to me from Ig's mind. I couldn't see what was happening. I couldn't do anything to stop it. I was lost and powerless and then I was back on Ig's head and I couldn't help but wonder if I'd been better off in the boundless void of nothingness, because frankly the sudden influx of sobs and adrenaline were quite unpleasant.

"How me magic this?!" he yelped as he got me secured on his scalp.

We cannot, you are not prepared.

"Me am not got time for more prepared!" The kobold had found a surprising amount of courage to talk back to me in such a manner. I suppose that the certainty of death would instill that in certain people. "Now or no more Ig."

It seemed that his assessment was not entirely devoid of merit. There was no happy ending to this tale for either of us if the ogres caught up to us. He would become their dinner, and I their napkin. Not to mention all the unsavory things that would happen to the adventurers if they were caught. Kobolds were a prey of necessity in times of hunger; humans and elves were a delicacy, seasoned with vengeance.

In fact, it was possible that if we were to part ways with our adventuring party at this point, then our chances of survival might increase markedly. They were certainly making a great deal more noise than Ig smashing through the undergrowth. All that he would really need to do was find somewhere quiet to lay low until the ogres had passed, then we could set off on our way for Arpanpholigon again.

When it came down to it, it was a matter of simple mathematics: either four people could die horrible gruesome deaths and become an ogre's stew, or only three needed to. In terms of ethics, abandoning the adventurers to their untimely fate was essentially correct. Not to mention that they had come out here specifically to murder ogres. You might even call this a sort of poetic justice, or divine punishment.

Ig, I believe that I have an idea that might save us.

"Forget us," Ig blurted out in between gasps for air. "How I save pretty lady?"

And so it was that I was taught a lesson in humility and heroics by a kobold of all things. A kobold quite willing to sacrifice his own life because a girl with nice hair had spoken to him politely.

You have a solid knowledge of the element of Potassium by now, and from it comes the Golden Flames of Galgalagrin the Great, one of the most potent destructive spells that one can wield with the relatively minimal supply of Quintessence at your disposal. A bolt of blazing flame that water cannot quench, that erupts into explosions the moment that it draws blood. It is a truly fearsome weapon, and you have just about scraped together enough Quintessence to cast it once. Give or take a microthaum or two.

"Potassium," Ig wondered aloud. "That the not-Carbon one."

Yes, Ig, that is the one of the two that you know that is not the other one that you know.

"I knows it!"

We were all doomed. This moron had somehow shamed me into performing heroics and he was going to mispronounce something and immediately implode, taking me with him.

When the time is right, I will speak the word of Archaic into your mind, you will repeat it, exactly as I say while focusing on your understanding of Potassium, and pushing the Quintessence stored inside you up and out through your mouth to infuse the word with power. You shall also point at the particular ogre that you wish to see exploded, so as to provide some sense of general direction to the spell, as I do not trust that you can concentrate sufficiently to guide the arcane missile without that crutch. Are we clear?

"That so many words."

We were doomed. Utterly doomed.

Up ahead of us, the elf had come to a halt atop a vast stump overlooking a drop-off into a gully. They were waiting for the other adventurers to catch up and catch their breath so that a decision could be made. And I knew just the decision it was to be. Would they make their last stand here, or risk being caught while attempting a crossing so that they might gain the advantage of terrain?

While Ig's brain left much to be desired, his ears were pretty effective at their assigned task, and by my guess there would not be time enough to slide down the muddy slope and scramble up the other side. Not with Ig slowing them down anyway.

As Rhine and Ildrit pulled up short in sight of the gully, they both ran headlong into the same problem. Well, at least I could eliminate that problem for them. Ig was intent upon making his own last stand, and it would be for the best if everyone else was out of his blast radius before he attempted it. He opened his mouth to make this heroic declaration, but it was somewhat undercut by Ildrit snarling, "Leave the stupid runt to die," then storming off down the slope. The elf did not even blink before turning their back on us, but at least sweet Rhine had some kindness left in her soul. She gave Ig an apologetic look before abandoning him to his death.

All thoughts of heroism departed from Ig's mind, overtaken by a terrible intermingling of his rising anger and my own disgust at how he'd been treated. He was trying to make a heroic sacrifice of his own life to save theirs and this was how they repaid his kindness?! The utter bastards.

With a ferocity that I did know he had in his tiny form, Ig flung himself, bouncing and rolling, down the gully after them.

On each thump against the ferny slope, he let out a squeak like a kicked rat, but when he finally arrived at the bottom of the gully, and the pathetic little trickle of muddy water trapped there, the sound was definitely more akin to a balloon being deflated. With quaking arms, he pushed himself back up.

Then, as abruptly as he had hit rock bottom, Ig was soaring. Twisting his head around, expecting to see an ogre and possibly some sort of barbecue, he was delighted to realize that he had been hoisted from the bottom of the gully by none other than Ildrit himself. Who seemed to be propelling himself back up the other slope powered by panted mumbling. "I didn't leave him. I just said it. Saying things doesn't matter when you do the opposite. Look, he's fine."

"Me fine," Ig opined, dangling from his fist, battering off the ferns and protruding roots as we ascended.

"He's fine. No harm, no foul. Right?"

Ig nodded, though he was now more than a little punch-drunk, but Ildrit rambled on.

"This was the right thing to do. I did the right thing."

Ig could barely get his feet beneath him before they were slipping away again, but the heavier human was able to get some traction on the muddy slope. He had boots on his side. I made a mental note to get Ig some boots, should the opportunity ever arise.

Then, abruptly, all thoughts of boots, or indeed any sort of future, were knocked from my mind with the arrival of the ogres.

Now as a rule, ogre fashion is fairly relaxed. They will wear such clothing as they have managed to piece together for themselves from the remains of their victims, supplemented with the odd item that they've managed to trade or torture from subjugated peoples. People who more often than not also constitute their living larder. But this little group of raiders were entirely more put together than one might have expected. They weren't exactly in uniform as such, but there were distinctive elements that all of them bore in their garments that nonetheless presented a unified theme. Matching caps on a few of them, perched atop heads far too large to be encompassed by their rims. Long coats as one might have expected from a soldier's dress uniform, gone rapidly to tatters. Some shoulder pads still intact upon those jackets with what had once been some sort of filigree before it had spent time in the company of ogres and immediately begun showing signs of verdigris.

At a glance, the overall appearance was of a small troop that had been lost for many years behind enemy lines, except of course for the fact that to an ogre, absolutely every living thing was both an enemy and food, so presumably they were always behind enemy lines.

The closest of them, distinctive from his kin from the one protruding tusk of a tooth, pointed at us and roared. Ig screamed back in response before I could attempt to assert any sort of control over him.

He then proceeded to attempt to climb Ildrit, as he in turn attempted to climb the hillside. It was futile. The more that the two of them panicked, the less progress they actually made. None of which was helped by the encouraging shouts from Rhine atop the slope, or the dry commentary on the approach of the ogres from the accursed elf. "They are heading down the other slope now. They are drawing their weapons. I should hurry if I were you; they don't seem to be having as much trouble with that slight incline."

Ig was in histrionics by this point, as likely to die from hyperventilation as anything else, and the only thing that I could say in his favor was that at least now he'd stopped wriggling so much, allowing Ildrit to focus on the climb.

On the climb, and yelling up to the elf, "Shoot them!"

As though they had only been waiting for the command, Wyn swung the bow from their back and began a volley of such precision and speed that I would have called it magic were I not better educated in such matters. What we saw was not magic, it was practice. Hundreds upon hundreds of years of repetition, wearing away the rough edges of technique like rain smoothing down a mountain until only the perfect form at the heart of it remained.

From behind us, the roars of fury became roars of pained fury. All around us, arrows buzzed by. Ig would have likely flailed his way into the path of one if he were not clinging so firmly to Ildrit.

The arrows bought us time enough to clear the last few feet of the gully and scramble back upright, but even still, Ig could not be detached from Ildrit. So as he turned atop the hillside to face the oncoming ogres, he did so wearing a kobold breastplate to shield him from harm.

Ig, you worthless ignoramus, let the nice warrior go so that he can fight.

"No!"

Ildrit reached up and drew Slaughterasmus, or whatever it was called, the black blade practically vibrating with excitement at all the death that it was about to unleash. My only hope was that unlike me, it did not contain some sapience. Having to sit on a kobold's head was horror enough without having to be pushed through an ogre's innards.

You are going to get us all killed!

"No!"

There was no strategy at play in the ogres' charge over the crest; they came on as swiftly as they could, peppered all over with arrows, and all the more furious for it. Rhine sprang forward to meet them, roaring defiance in the face of the oncoming monstrous horde. Wyn unleashed arrows point-blank into eyeballs and gaping maws alike. The only one to remain entirely immobile was Ildrit, who had his sword in position, and just waited for them to come.

Ig, will you just listen to me?!

Apparently, he would not.

On the plus side, there could not have been a better spot on all the battlefield to witness the horrors that were about to unfold. Tusko the ogre came right at him, ignoring the other two, hefting a club that had started life as a whole sapling.

The ex-tree started to come down on us and then . . . Ildrit's wrists did something. They spun, or they twisted, it was so quick I doubt I'd have seen it were it not for our awful proximity. And then the hand holding the club was off, and the club was bouncing back down the hill to trip the next ogre and Ildrit was finally in motion. He stepped into the reach of the ogre's arms as it goggled at the sight of its new stump, then brought the blade Murderificon around in one smooth and fluid cut, severing Tusko's head from their body.

He brushed past the still-standing corpse and met the blow of another ogre's rusty cleaver with the very tip of his sword, prodding it aside so that it didn't pass through him. We had watched him fighting with Rhine earlier. Seen the way that he struggled with just one human opponent. He shouldn't have been able to breeze through an ogre like that, not unless . . .

He was holding back.

Instinct fueled his movement now, hard-won muscle memory that he couldn't have trusted in a fight that he didn't want to end in death. He hadn't been fighting Rhine back in the studio, he had been fighting himself.

One after another the ogres broke away from their clashes with Rhine and Wyn at the sight of one of their kin falling to Ildrit's grim blade Slaughturnicus. At a glance, Rhine seemed to be mostly succeeding only in fending off the blows of the ogres, while Wyn had scrambled their way up a tree to rain arrows down from above. Against humans or elves, such a rain would have been lethal, but there was a great deal of thick skin and muscle between the world and anything vital in an ogre, and it didn't look as though the elf's arrows were making it through.

Not without help anyway.

The flat of Ildrit's blade smacked into one ogre's face on the backswing, slamming an arrow already protruding out of its eye socket all the way into the brain. The slaughter that had so impressed upon me that I never wanted to be on this gentleman's bad side was starting to slow now. Skilled and trained or not, you can only swing a giant lump of metal around for so long before your arms start to get tired.

Rich, oily-thick purplish ogre blood was splattered all over us by this point. Both Ig and Ildrit were drenched in it, the dirt underfoot was muddied with it, even the gully that had caused all of our problems was now getting a steady flow running down to its lowest point.

Yet despite this veritable flood, more of the ogres kept lumbering in. I could not say the exact moment that the battle began to turn, but it must have been somewhere between Tusko's timely decapitation and the elf's tree getting chopped down.

As it fell, the branches raked over Rhine, knocking her from her feet, and allowing the ogres who had been held at bay by her swiping sword to close in over her.

"They don't deserve this." Ildrit panted in pain, more to himself than to Ig. "I might, but Wyn, Rhine, they deserve to make it."

Instead of slaughtering his way through the ogres as though they were not there, Ildrit was sweating hard enough to leave lines through the blood, and barely managing to dodge and parry their attacks. He was staggered by every blow now. Panting and increasingly desperate.

Carrying the extra weight of Ig was probably slowing him down also, but I couldn't continue suggesting to the kobold that he let go. Not when this had become a killing ground and he was so tiny and defenseless.

Except he wasn't. Was he?

Ig! Cast your magic.

"Me not know words!"

Just throw the Quintessence out, like before.

"But I no . . ."

DO IT, IG!

And who said that yelling was not a useful teaching aid?

All the Quintessence that he had managed to gather since the last time he had unleashed it flooded out of him now. Double what he'd managed the last time around, or possibly even more. I had been so distracted with other developments that I had not been keeping an eye on his gradually expanding reservoir.

For the longest moment it seemed that his magic had come to naught, dissipating into the world it had first been pulled from with no effect. Ildrit took a heavy blow across his back as one of the fancy spinning parries that he liked to do completely failed to make contact with the club descending upon him. It knocked the wind from his lungs, and the kobold from his chest.

Ig and I went tumbling and rolling, end over end to the lip of the gully, and then, only then, at the very edge of destruction and doom, did we hear it. The rumbling.

At first the battle raged on as it had before, Rhine managing to raise her shield against the bludgeoning blows of the gathered ogres. Wyn was springing and leaping around to avoid being torn asunder by a species that I seemed to recall treated theirs as something of a delicacy, not unlike veal.

Then slowly the clubbing and thumping and slashing and roaring stopped, and all turned their heads to the coming sound.

This was the Badlands, and as fearsome as a horde of ogres might have been, there were considerably more dangerous things out there. A cockatrice or wyvern would have made quick work of all of us. A turtle-bear or a dire louse would likely have been sufficient in itself. Anything might have been approaching through the trees, drawn by the sound of slaughter, and given that whatever it was had decided to charge towards the noises of large armed forces colliding, it suggested that it was not afraid of what some ogres with sticks and knives could do to it.

Behind an ogre's eyes, there is not a great deal going on. They are wicked, not out of some conniving, glowing-eyes evil, but because of the most banal reasons.

They were hungry and people were available as a foodstuff. They wanted something that somebody else had, and they were strong enough to take it. They are essentially every dumb toddler of the human race, granted superhuman strength and dumped into a society of likeminded bastards. Yet despite this intellectual absence, these particular ogres seemed to be piecing things together.

Something big and scary was coming.

Most of their best fighters were already in a half dozen pieces each.

Whatever was coming might not have been on the squishy human's side, but it definitely wasn't on theirs.

Without discussion, the ogres beat a retreat.

If it hadn't been for the sturdy blow to Ildrit's back that had knocked us off, it would have been a bloody rout, with him chasing them down and stabbing them in the back, but as luck would have it, he was still wheezing for breath, trying to get back onto his feet to face whatever horror was coming next.

Staggering over to where she lay, he retrieved Rhine from beneath the fallen tree, and Wyn popped into view immediately beside him once all the heavy lifting was done, declaring, "Something approaches."

Ig surprised me by calling out, "That my bad."

CHAPTER ELEVEN

INTO THE DEEP DARK WOODS

The three adventurers looked upon him in abject terror. "Your bad, how?"

"Wells, you sees . . ." Ig began. But then it was too late. From amidst the trees it came, lumbering and bounding, as broad across as a barrel-chested warhorse, but with the lop ears of its domesticated kin. It was a soft orange-brown that put gingerbread in mind, and it was by far the largest rabbit that I had ever seen in my life. Ig's jaw fell open. The others spun to look upon it. It would have been twice the weight of Ig quite easily, not to mention the size of the terrifying incisor teeth protruding from beneath its quivering nose. A rabbit, yes, but such a rabbit as has never before been seen. A monster of a rabbit, a dire rabbit!

Wyn fired a single arrow into the titanic bunny and it promptly dropped dead. "It would seem that we shall eat well this night."

Rhine, scarcely aware of what was going on around her after the concussive force of a falling tree striking her in the head, let out something like a sob. Then a slow, trailing, "Nooooooooo," as she slumped to her knees.

"To be fair to Wyn, if we didn't eat it, something else certainly would. We're really just sparing it an awful fate."

"It was so cute." She groaned.

Ig jealously huffed, "Was not cute. Was monster."

The adventurers looked from kobold to bunny and back once more. "A monster?"

"Look how big is!?" Ig exclaimed. "Is . . . dire bunny."

Still grotesque from the battle, Ildrit staggered across to the fallen beast and gave it closer consideration. "It doesn't look very dire."

"Beastie get big, you call dire." Ig squeaked in annoyance.

"Well, yes and no. You can't just go declaring every animal that's bigger than normal a whole different species, can you?"

"Consider the cow," Wyn opined. Despite all of the fighting, there was not a single hair out of place on their head. If I had not witnessed the elf leaping and shooting and all of the rest, I would have said they hadn't been involved in a backwoods brawl at all. "A cow ranges in size from shorter than myself, all the way up to the height of those low branches, yet we do not call the tallest of cows a dire cow, do we?"

No, we call them Aurochs, because they are the megafauna predecessors to cows that interbred with some of them before their extinction, producing the gigantic bloodlines that farmers still try to preserve to this day.

"Nah, you won't get anybody offering a quest to slay a dire cow. Would you?"

This is all going to be about money. They can't get paid to kill animals without dire before the name, or some such nonsense. Mark my words.

"That is an irregularly large rabbit, no denying that," Ildrit pressed on. "But dire?"

Wyn had joined the man in prodding at the corpse, although at least they were doing so with a skinning knife in hand, to some greater purpose. "It lacks the bony plates usually associated with dire beasts."

"Fine! Bunny!" Ig threw up his hands. "Me makes bunny. Scare ogres. Saves you alls."

There were some significant glances in the aftermath of that declaration, and for a moment I wondered if Ig had perhaps overplayed our hand a little. Yes, we were responsible for the arrival of what would most likely be our meals for the next three days, but to claim that we had saved them all was a great exaggeration. If anyone was the hero of the day, surely it was Ildrit, who had carved a bloody swathe through the ogres. Although admittedly, that didn't seem to make any of the living ones reluctant to attack in the same way that an approaching gigabunny did.

I opened Ig's mouth to try to take it back, but Ildrit raised a hand to stop me. "In a moment of . . . weakness there, I almost left you behind. And I'm sorry for that. My first instinct isn't always to do the right thing, and doing the right thing . . . well, sometimes I need a second to think about it."

In all of the chaos that had followed, Ig and I had both more or less forgotten about our plans for a last stand, and our subsequent betrayal, but now, after what we had just survived, it was surely water under the bridge.

Ig nodded. "No worry."

"It just goes to show that assisting this little kobold wizard was the right thing to do though, doesn't it?" He was speaking to the other two now. "We helped him, he saved us."

Rhine snuck a smile to Ig that he would likely treasure for the rest of his life, but the biggest change came over Wyn. They threw their hands up in the air with a groan. "If the curse says that helping that creature is the right thing to do, then who am I to argue?"

Ig cleared his throat politely. Or as politely as a kobold can clear its throat, which is a sound rather like someone trying to dislodge a stuck boot from a swamp. "Curse?"

The elf's eyes darted sideways to brush over Ildrit for only an instant before they corrected themselves. "The universe. Cosmic forces. Whatever you wish to call the forces of fate. Forgive me for misspeaking; common is not my first language."

Not their first language, but they've been speaking it longer than all of us put together. This is all about that curse Ildrit is trying to break. Mark my words.

"How I mark words?" Ig asked the group as a whole. If I could have slapped a palm to my head I would have, but I lacked both hands and a head at present.

The adventurers were kind enough to overlook his gibberish and press on with the messy business of bunny butchery. Ig, with no experience in such matters, sidled off to where Rhine had turned her back on proceedings. Unsure of his approach, he started with what was typically the safest way for him to start any conversation. "Sorry."

Rhine had laid hands upon all of their packs and was working to repack them now that there was time. She kept her attention firmly on that and ignored the sights and smells unfolding behind her back. "The fault is not with you, but with my own soft heart. In my own lands, we live in harmony with nature; we kill only what we must. I forget sometimes that the world of men is so very different. It is a weakness, and I shall purge it."

Well, Ig, this is your chance to say something profound and poetic enough to win her heart. Give it your best shot.

"Me am not used to kill stuff. Home was . . . safe. Scary sometimes, but not . . . not safe."

To my immense surprise, I found myself quite touched by his statement too. My mind hearkened back to the gentle and quiet years of study and solitude that had shaped me into the genius of the High Art that I had become.

"You are truly wiser than your stature would imply, my friend."

Ig's snout curled and contorted into a hideous rictus that startled her before she and I realized as one that Ig was attempting to smile at her. Ig's hideous smile cracked a little as he mumbled mostly to himself, "Friend?"

She patted him on the back, which was unfortunately where he was the soggiest with ogre fluids. "Friends."

A tap on the shoulder sent Ig rocketing up to plum-catching heights once more, but when he came down, the elf was standing there. They really needed to attach a bell to that elf so you could hear them moving around. They were entirely too quiet when left to their own devices.

"I too wish to extend my friendship to you, wizard. Without your intervention, we most assuredly would have been overrun. It would have been nice if you could have intervened somewhat sooner, of course . . ."

"Me am still learning how make magic," Ig began, before I jumped in to add, "In my new kobold form."

There was the faintest line between Wyn's brows then, practically as expressive a contortion as Ig's attempt to smile on an elf's face. It was as though there was some puzzle that they were working through that they couldn't quite solve yet, and I had just handed them another piece of that puzzle that didn't fit with any of the rest.

"Regardless, you have earned my trust." They held out a hand. It was slick with the blood of rabbit and ogre alike, with a sodden leaf stuck to the smallest finger, yet without hesitation Ig reached out and shook it, amidst some truly awful squishing sounds.

"Lots friends." Ig smiled.

Ildrit cut us all off. "The rabbit's done and the bags are packed. We should get moving before the ogres come back."

Rhinolyta piped up at that, "I thought our quest was to tackle the ogre menace."

When we all turned, it was to discover that Ildrit had already started off into the woods, and we all had to jog, or in Ig's case, outright run, to catch up to him. He called back over his shoulder once we were in earshot. "When the ogre menace is one ogre stealing ears, it's worth the gold. When there is a whole army of them, not so much."

Wyn fell into a graceful lope beside the swordsman, brows doing all the expressing for them as always. "What makes you think that there is an army to face, and not that simple warband?"

"Because they were wearing a uniform, which you only need if you've got an army. And because they had a leader calling the shots."

"I didn't see any evidence of leadership." Rhine hadn't even broken a sweat despite carrying all three packs, which she now dispensed to their correct owners with a degree of violent throwing.

"Because you don't speak ogrish."

That drew us all up short. I hadn't even realized that the ogres were speaking. Ig piped up on my behalf. "Me speak some ogrish."

"Oh you learned some Ogrish Battle-Cant up in your ivory tower, did you?"

That promptly shut both Ig and me up immediately. I was not even aware that ogres had a secondary language, let alone one communicated entirely in screaming. Still, Ig was now a wizard, and had some portion of a wizard's pride, so the last word had to be ours regardless of how good that particular word happened to be. "Was marble, mostly."

"An army of ogres, has such a thing ever occurred?" Wyn ignored us, and he was entirely correct to do so.

Ildrit's expression had been getting darker and darker the deeper that we went into the woods. "It can't be done. You can have an ogre mercenary in your army. You can even have a few of them if you spread them out, but you put more than two ogres together for any length of time and they'll end up killing each other."

"So how army?" Ig asked between pants for breath. His little legs were struggling to keep up with the longer stride of the taller people around him. The whole party was still keeping up an extremely brisk pace. A pace that had only grown more brisk as we all realized that the ogres who had gone running off likely meant to come back with reinforcements, and we very much did not want to be around for that to happen.

"That is very much the question of the day, friend wizard." He managed a little smirk to Ig as he said the word friend, as though he were sharing a little treat with a child who wasn't meant to get any. "Who or what could unite any number of ogres when chaos is the fundament of their nature?"

The whole group fell into silence to consider this question. Silent, that is, except for all the gasping and panting coming from Ig, who it was becoming increasingly apparent was going to be slowing them down regardless of the terrain. Yet Ig, despite his obvious exhaustion, made no complaint, nor did he slow his pace. I could feel the bandy little muscles inside of his legs twanging and aching with each step, but still he asked for no quarter. I'd have been impressed with him were it not for the simple fact that I suspected he was too stupid to understand that he could ask them to slow down without any risk of them leaving him behind.

The forest that we had delved into was becoming progressively less welcoming as we proceeded, the trees looking less luscious and more cadaverous with every step until I began to wonder if we had been hiking so long we'd ended up in the dead of winter. Whatever was impeding the healthy growth of the trees did not seem to be impeding any of the thickets that blocked our way, nor the thorny vines that reached up to not only strangle the trees, but to dangle down off their branches in their attempts to scratch out eyes and tangle in hair. Ig's short stature was something of a blessing, as the others were ducking and weaving to avoid being hooked almost constantly.

Were we in a child's fairy tale, I might have thought that there was some great evil dwelling in this land, but as an educated adult I knew that evil did not politely limit itself to only the dingy areas of the map. It lurked in golden palaces and the wild woods in equal measure. In civilization, it simply wore a veneer of respectability that allowed it to proceed unchallenged.

Loathsome though ogres might be, there was a refreshing honesty about their desire to brutalize and dominate all around them.

Thick cobwebs soon hung in dense swathes across the branches overhead, but of the spiders that had squirted them from their hindquarters I could see no sign. Bones protruded here and there amidst the tangled roots of this deadwood. Even the bark of the trees seemed contorted into monstrous forms, faces peering out from amidst the twisted wood.

Wait a minute.

Ig slowed his pace, and by my direction, approached the nearest tree with its terrifying countenance. Entirely against his will, he leaned in closer to the leering, demonic face staring out at him with dark pits of eyes that seemed to follow his approach, and there I saw it. The telltale mark . . . "They carved."

The other adventurers had still been keeping up a steady pace, but the general malignance of their surroundings had unnerved them. They were all huddled together, as though proximity might save them from being snatched up if evil trees did suddenly grab for them. They weren't quite cringing, but they definitely did look uncomfortable in a way that I had not observed before. Perhaps not fearful but intensely wary.

But at Ig's statement, the three of them stopped dead and Ildrit gawked at him. "What?!"

"Somebody carved trees!" Ig exclaimed in excitement, before dashing over to a bone protruding from amidst the dark and tangled roots of another tree and yanking it right out. There was a short metal post on the other end of it, to keep it standing upright when pushed into the soil, and a quick lick confirmed to Ig that it was not in fact a bone—which kobolds would have considered imminently gnawable—but rather some sort of ceramic creation. "Bones fakeses too!"

As the other two went through various stages of confusion, Wyn reached up to pluck a handful of cobweb down. "Wool."

Ig pointed at them. As though a point had been made.

My mind was of course racing, trying to decipher why somebody would blight a perfectly good stretch of forest, fill it up with false faces and bones and attempt to frighten passersby. More specifically I was trying to work out who on earth would be out here in the middle of nowhere trying to spook the place up.

"Why would anyone do this?" Rhinolyta wondered aloud.

Her pondering was interrupted by a cough. The adventurers, predictably, drew their weapons and spun around to face the teenager peeking out from behind one of the trees. "That's us, sorry."

This time, Ig did not jump. If he had, he likely would have ended up tangled in the carded wool strung from tree to tree, so it was for the best that he remained firmly on the ground. Admittedly, his foot was stuck under a root, but there had been barely even a flinch. I was almost proud of him. Almost.

Realizing that they were being confronted by a small human rather than a rampaging monster, the adventurers gradually eased their weapons down. Ildrit looked furious enough to decapitate the girl regardless, so it fell to Rhine to make conversation. "Um. Could you tell us why you've done this?"

"Monsters," the girl replied. She was a plain-looking thing, in the typical peasant garb, distinguished from others by the density of freckles across her face, which rendered her nigh-on piebald. She even had a little cloth bonnet holding down her hair. The very picture of normalcy.

Finally Ildrit seemed to move past his initial surprise and stepped forward, ready to do some heroics. "What monsters have captured you and made you redecorate a forest to their grim design? Do not fear, we'll set you free."

In normal circumstances that probably would have been quite a cheering thing to hear for a human child out here in the middle of nowhere, but the girl did not look cheered so much as amused. "No, you dope. We do it to scare 'em off."

Ildrit mouthed the word "dope" to himself, and Rhine stepped back up before he could properly respond. "Scare them off from what, exactly?"

"Home, obviously." Eyes were rolled, and it occurred to me that the suicidal overconfidence and bad attitude of most adventurers wouldn't have looked entirely out of place in the average teenager.

Perhaps a solution might have been found where teens were armed and cast into dungeons, removing the requirement for adult oversight during a trying time in their development. Some would die, of course, but that was a small price to pay not to have to deal with teenagers.

One year of teaching new intake students to the university had been more than enough for me.

"And where is home?" Wyn asked drily.

The girl pointed vaguely in the direction that we were headed. "I can take you, if you want. But don't, like . . . tell people I brought you. It's meant to be secret."

Ildrit opened his mouth to snap at her, but Rhine raised her voice so he couldn't be heard. "I promise that we won't tell anyone about your secret village in the Badlands."

The girl snorted as she turned her back on us. "Badlands."

There was some very brief conferring amidst the adventurers as the teen began plodding off, the stack of firewood loaded onto her back now fully visible. Ig overheard only parts of the conversation, like Ildrit growling, ". . . clearly evil and needs to be destroyed." Or Wyn saying, ". . . provide us with guidance, direction, and a defensible position should . . ."

The only one staying relatively quiet was Rhine, and that was because she was focused on paying attention to where the girl was going. Ig probably should have weighed in too, but at present he had no opinion because I had not informed him of what it should be.

A village would indeed have been a nice change of pace after several days out here in the wilds, but I could not allay my suspicions about the matter. What could have driven a people to live so far out here in a place of obvious danger?

While I had not been intimately familiar with the Badlands before my murder, I did know that each time any venture into them was undertaken, it generated a great deal of excitement and furor. A grand expansion of civilization into the wild parts of the world, untamed natural resources available for collection by hand, gold by the bucketload, just waiting to be mined. Farming land if you had the courage to clear it. There had been a half dozen attempts over the years to push out into the Badlands and tame them, and every one had ended in bloody disaster. The idea that there could be a village of humans out here, surviving using a mummer's farce to distract the native monstrosities, seemed extremely unlikely. Which in turn suggested that this was some sort of trap.

Had I my full repertoire of magic to hand, I might have cast a spell to remove any disguise from this teenager. To reveal whatever monstrous form she truly possessed. Or failing that, I could have at least woven a temporary enchantment that would have helped us to decipher her deceptions. As it was, I had Ig, who believed literally anything that you told him. An aspect of his personality that had come in quite useful when I was hoodwinking him into doing what I needed from him, but which now was creating the potential for trouble.

The woods became more and more grim and horrifying as we proceeded. The tangled cobwebs gave way in places to trees with dense thickets of dangling thorns wedged up into their branches, constantly dripping with blood. The teen brushed her finger over one as she passed, then popped it into her mouth. "Syrup."

Ig's stomach grumbled, and it was all that I could do to keep him from launching himself at the drizzling ichor and getting caught like a fish on a line by the thorns beneath.

There will be food in the village.

This seemed to content him for now, though he still looked at each pool of blood, and the misshapen ants supping at them like vampires, with envious eyes. Whether he longed for syrup or bug, I could not have told you.

"So you all just . . . live out here?" Rhine was doing her best to make polite conversation with a teenage girl, which is somewhat akin to drawing teeth at the best of times, even when there are no secrets being kept.

The girl shrugged, and Ig soon found himself being shuffled into place beside her, presumably on the assumption that just because he was short, he might pass for someone closer to her age and open up the conversation a little more. He of course interrupted the delicate waltz of Rhine's interrogation by blurting out the first thing on his mind. "Why you be livings out here in scary place?"

The girl was unwaveringly polite, to her credit, and while she had managed to hold off on the obvious question of her own up until now, Ig's bluntness seemed to give her the permission to ask what she wanted to ask. "I'm sorry, are you a goblin or something?"

Ig had never met a goblin in his life, which was probably for the best, as they are something of the opposite of kobolds in many ways. Small, certainly, ugly, most definitely, but possessed of a kind of intelligence that is more commonly associated with used horse salesmen or other, more subtle con artists. A goblin encountering a group of kobolds would likely have either become their god by lunchtime, or convinced them all to roast themselves for that same lunch. And they would have done so, gladly, now that there was someone with three brain cells to rub together calling the shots.

He drew himself up to his full height, which wasn't much, and said with as much dignity as he could muster, which was even less, "Me am a wizard."

You have not experienced dubiousness such as can be found pouring forth from a teenager. "A wizard?"

He pointed, pointedly, at his hat.

She raised a rather unkempt brow. "A goblin wizard?"

Wyn intervened before Ig could get himself into any more trouble. "Our companion labors under a curse that has changed his shape."

I personally would have thought this would be a source of considerable interest for a rural child, even one accustomed to life in the Badlands, but it seemed that even transmogrification was old hat to a teenager. She rolled her eyes and muttered, "What must that be like."

Giving up entirely on conversation, the adventurers and Ig trudged after the girl in equally sullen silence.

The forest did not become more pleasant as we went. The barren trees grew into ever more monstrous shapes, which I now had to grudgingly admire the artistry in. It must have taken forever to cultivate them into those particularly threatening shapes. The skull dangling with a branch growing through an eye socket was particularly well executed, though if it had been real decomposing remains, I suspect that the jaw would have fallen off entirely rather than being trapped in an eternal scream of terror.

While we continued to plod in a more or less straight line, I began to see that fear alone was not the only snare that these villagers had laid. There were sudden pitfalls down into heaps of false bones poorly hidden by ferns and the like, not to mention some particularly juicy swamps that they'd cultivated with their red syrup that were just begging to eat some unfortunate traveler's boot. Given sufficient anxiety, I imagine that many an intruder would have sworn blind that something in the morass had attempted to eat them whole and scampered off, one-booted as a result.

Despite knowing that there was artifice behind the bad vibes penetrating these woods, it did little to soothe Ig's fluttering heart. With every step he became more and more afraid, as though there were something that was actually a danger out here, rather than some clever peasants playacting at it. Some degree of this I could attribute to the excellent mummery that they had accomplished, but the majority had to be blamed entirely on the ignorance of Ig. It took an impressive degree of stupidity to know that something was a lie, to have evidence that it was a lie, and to act as though you believe it all the same.

Just as we were approaching a point in the forest so deep and dark that even I was beginning to wonder how we might go on, our guide ducked into a thicket as dense as Ig. That startled us somewhat, but not so much that we did not immediately plunge in after her rather than being left out here in the increasingly terrifying deep dark woods. For Ig, the passage was entirely comfortable, though I myself was almost slapped off his head several times by low-slung bushiness. The other adventurers most likely had a far less enjoyable time of it. They were doubled over, banging into one another and complaining more or less the entire way through the pseudo-maze that was hidden inside of this shrubbery.

When we broke free of the tangled plants, it was as though we were emerging into an entirely new world. An arcadian utopia. There were fields stretching out around the village, basking in sunshine and bursting with crops. There were hedgerows with flowers growing along them, and winding paths picking their way through the streams and fields that had likewise been lined with all of nature's beauty. Fruit hung ripe and thick from the branches of the trees on every corner. Ig was salivating.

"This is home, I guess," announced our incredibly disinterested guide.

CHAPTER TWELVE

THE COMPLETELY UNREMARKABLE AND NORMAL HUMAN VILLAGE

Rhine's eyes were shining in the sunlight. "What is the name of this wondrous jewel hidden in plain sight?"

"Uh . . . not much point giving a secret village a name. Since it's . . . secret."

I will admit that there have been times in my life when I have been somewhat contemptuous towards the intellect of others. Not only Ig, who was entirely deserving of such treatment, but also my peers in academia who proved themselves to be less capable than me. Which is to say, all of them, as I am the greatest wizard of my age. However, no matter how refined my sneering tones may have become, I do not believe that I've ever struck upon a note so condescending as this teenager managed when speaking to Rhinolyta.

At what age does it become acceptable to hit a child? I understand that the smallest ones are meant to be exempt from violence, but sometime between the ages of ten and twenty there must be some degree of allowance bleeding in. This one was somewhere between fourteen and eighteen; surely a short, sharp lightning strike would have been a useful disciplinary tool to help reform her behavior. A mild fireball or two, applied gently?

Finally we came into sight of not one, not two, but three adult human beings. Three of them, with slightly unpleasant expressions on their face when they saw the adventurers that told me immediately that they were a sensible lot. I was almost overwhelmed with relief. The broadest of the specimens stepped up with a rosy-cheeked smile. "Oh my goodness, ain't often we've got visitors here. Welcome!"

The other two, both considerably more slender and sallow faced, dragged the teenager away behind the blocking mass of their companion to begin lambasting her in whispers. I could just imagine how that conversation was going.

"Why the hecks did you bring those psychotic murderers here?"

"Because I'm a bored teenager or whatever."

"Well, we're just going to have to murder them in their sleep now, aren't we."

"Whatever, I'm bored with sleep murder. Let's murder their faces off, and reveal ourselves to be horrible monsters masquerading as humans. Teenage monsters."

"Whatever."

Alright, perhaps that wasn't exactly how the conversation was actually panning out, but of course I had no way of knowing how the conversation was actually panning out because of the rotund farmer's wife currently gushing over my companions. "So handsome, and so strong to carry that big sword around with you. You must be a prince somewhere, am I right?"

Ildrit looked intensely uncomfortable, so in came Rhine to his rescue. "I am actually considered a princess among my people."

Until now, all of the observations had been undertaken from a distance, but when Rhine spoke up, it apparently invited a hug. This woman was a hugger. She did her best to crush Rhine, then held her out at arm's length to study her with the kind of attention to certain details that would have gotten Ig slapped. "Well, of course you are, sweetheart, just look at you. So beautiful with that lovely pair of . . . pigtails. Golden hair so shiny. Even though you've been out in the woods, you look like you could have just stepped out a portrait. So pretty."

She turned to Wyn, who endured her hug with stoic silence, as though they were a mannequin rather than an extremely disgruntled elf. "And you there, I reckon you've got to be an elf, am I right? Never seen nobody so handsome . . . pretty . . . elfin before in my life, I swear!"

It was a pretty impressive save, all things considered, but Wyn managed to contain a sneer only barely.

Finally she turned to the last little member of their group, ready to overflow with more nice distracting compliments when she set her eyes upon Ig.

His little snout turned up as he attempted to smile again. I really would have to insist that he stop doing that. Not because it was hideous and scaring folks off—that part was rather funny—but because it was not appropriate for a wizard to smile. We gave stern looks and booming laughs exclusively.

The cheerful farmer's wife froze in place at the sight of Ig, desperately searching for something nice to say about a creature that by its very nature had nothing nice about it. He was filthy once more, with an aroma to reflect that, his attempts at a robe had been entirely drenched in ogre blood and mud, and his personality did not in any way make up for the massive gap where an appearance would normally be. Her mouth flopped open and shut a few times like a grounded fish, then finally she managed to mumble out, "Nice hat."

Ig was delighted and immediately started preening and adjusting the angle I sat at on his head. I, of course, was not quite so susceptible to flattery, being the more advanced mind that I am, though it was nice to hear that even though

Ig was to all intents and purposes the kind of nightmare that a fashionista might only glimpse in the darkest recess of their psyche, the inherent stylishness of the hat that I had become did some good work to counterbalance the kobold-ness of him.

The argument that had been played out in hushed tones behind her back was now at an end, and we were confronted once more with a united front of sullen villagers. "Girl says you've a wizard with you?"

This insightful commentary came from the dour gentleman.

"Me is wizard," Ig answered before I could stop him.

There are a great many times when it is advantageous, as a wizard, for others to not know that you are a wizard. For instance, when some slack-jawed yokels think that there's a spell making their milk sour, or that you might resolve their troubles with rats in the chicken coop with a swift application of chain-lightning. This felt to me like one of those times, when I would have flat-out denied wizardry as my vocation, hidden my hat behind my back, and insisted to all and sundry that I was in fact a cartographer. It didn't often work, as I am so incredibly famous for my prowess with magic, but it was necessary to make the attempt, lest I get dragged into problem-solving every minor issue that every person in earshot has.

The peasants looked down at Ig with a degree of dubiousness that it would have taken literal decades to cultivate in a lab. If you had a whole team of dedicated research wizards, devoted entirely to isolating and identifying doubt, using the most cutting-edge techniques, they still could not have achieved so singular a concentration. All of which is to say, they were not sure if what may have been a sentient tumor of some sort could actually be a wizard.

Rhine piped up on his behalf, "He's been turned into a kobold. But he is still a wizard in all the ways that matter."

The smile that she flashed Ig hit him in the chest like a sixteen-megaton explosion. I could actually feel all of the aches and pains of the day fading away as he basked in it.

It was advantageous that a kobold was not physically capable of blushing.

Regardless of the rollercoaster of thoroughly misdirected emotion that Ig was on, her word was good enough to convince the farmers of his veracity. "Chief will want to talk with you then."

On the downside, the "chief," whoever they might be, was most likely in charge of doling out quests and demands in this region, and accustomed to a whole village of inbred hicks leaping to obey their every word. On the positive side, at least they hadn't called upon the whole set of adventurers to come along, which showed that they had some discernment as to who and what actually mattered in the world.

I was guided on through a fairly standard-looking village towards the largest and most impressive building on the dirt road, which is to say, it had two stories, compared to the one that the rest had accomplished, and looked to have tiles on its roof instead of thatch. There were also no chickens in an attached coop, or randomly defecating animals in the vicinity, which put it a cut above everywhere else that we'd seen so far. The dour farmers led Ig inside while their noxious daughter was halted at the door by a stern look from the mother, and presumably the adventurers were similarly detained, because I saw neither hide nor hair of them from that point on.

An entrance hall with scrolls pinned to the wall gave way to a small office, dominated on one side by a massive hearth that was radiating heat and licking flames despite the seasonable weather. I could see why a moment later: behind the desk was as skeletal an old woman as I had ever encountered in my life. Skin like badly sun-scarred leather, wrinkles so complex that they may have comprised a map of an underground train system in some distant city. There were still wisps of ginger hair strung over the top of her withered head, which was somehow worse than if they'd been white.

With milky eyes, she peered at Ig. "This is a wizard?"

"Me am! Me am Ig . . ."

I intervened before he could make any more of a fool of us. "—salom Scryne, master of the High Art."

She blinked at Ig like a constipated owl, waiting for him to continue talking, but I had a stranglehold on the little brat now, and if he thought he was getting another word out the whole time that we were in here being threatened with questing, he had another thing coming.

"Then you know a thing or two about curses . . ." she began, and inwardly it took all of my efforts not to groan. Of course there was a curse, why else would anyone be living out here instead of someplace with tillable soil and the absence of hot and cold running monsters.

"Me . . . I have encountered a few in my time. As you can see, I labor under one myself at this moment."

Despite looking like a decrepit corpse in the latter stages of decay, there was a sharp mind still ticking over behind the old woman's rather unfortunate face. "So you're no good at breaking them then. Otherwise I wouldn't be talking to a . . . whatever you are."

It was a well-placed dig at my ego, and in truth it was the sort of psychological ploy that likely would have been very successful with me in life, when I had relished proving the superiority of my amazing intellect at every opportunity. Unfortunately for the old woman, I had just spent the past several days being debased and terrified, so the reflexive action of my ego had been somewhat tamped down by the reality of living as a kobold. "It's a matter of leverage. You can't lift a flagstone when you're standing on it."

She nodded at that, as though any part of the nonsensical statement made sense. I couldn't break the curse on me because there was no curse on me. I couldn't break the curse on our swordsman friend because I could just barely get Ig to fail at doing magic. Actually succeeding was so far beyond him at this point that I suspected the whole process of kobold education was doomed from the outset. So if she presented me with a curse needing broken, the odds of me successfully doing so were somewhere in the vicinity of none. None percent chance.

"Let me ask you a hypothetical question then."

This is, of course, the cursed person's equivalent of "my friend has this embarrassing medical condition; how should he treat it?"

"Let's say that a man came through your village, a handsome man, charming really. A man who could play music and tell tales and everyone loved him from the moment they set eyes on him."

So far it was sounding less like a curse, and more like the story of the mysteriously pregnant virgin, but I let her carry on.

"Let's say that man who everybody loved changed when the sun went down and the moon went up; let's say he grew fur all over his body, and jaws like a wolf, and he went around biting everyone, not enough to kill them or hurt them, but enough to break the skin. Men and women, children and little old ladies. Then let's say all of them started getting a little hairy too. Maybe all of them turned into something like that man had, and ran around, and ate some sheep."

Lycanthropy. Somewhere between a curse, a disease, and a strange hobby, whereby the afflicted individual would transform under duress or the light of the moon into a ravening beast of varying proportions. The wolf form was of course the most commonly known, but turtles and geese were quite frequently recorded in historical documents too. Although the rampages of wereturtles tended to end as soon as a cabbage patch was discovered, and the rampages of weregeese went entirely unreported because there were never any survivors.

At least it explained why they would have relocated out here. Wolves were never terribly popular in farming communities, and the kind of wolves that then refused to make eye contact with you the next day because they felt awkward about chewing on your shoes in the night were probably less popular still.

"Let's say that the next day that same man, let's call him Stjepan the Bard, let's say that he offered to remove the curse from everyone in the village in exchange for a portion of gold, and in their stubbornness and self-righteousness, the people of the village turned him down instead of being extorted. Let's say that they realized before long that they'd made a mistake, but weren't able to find this bard. Do you think that is a curse you might know how to break?"

Ig opened his mouth and I snapped it shut again.

No. We do not know. We cannot help. Even this Stjepan person could not have helped unless he had suicidal tendencies, as there is no cure for lycanthropy other than the destruction of the source by silver blade, in this case the itinerant disease spreader. Most likely he would have sold them a snake oil cure and fled before the next full moon.

"Snakes has oil?" Ig mumbled to himself before I once more leapt down to seize control of his blathering mouth.

"With regret, madam. I am afraid that there is no spell that can undo the state of lycanthropy. You shall need to seek out your bard and encourage him to depart this mortal coil."

She seemed to shrink in on herself a little as I told her this before looking up with desperation in her eyes. "Have you ever heard of such a man?"

"I'm afraid this is the first and only case of a ransom-were that I've ever heard of."

At that moment, I had to release my grasp on Ig. As it turned out, completely controlling his body by weight of will alone was not particularly difficult, presumably because a contest between our two wills was akin to a clash between a hammer and an egg, but maintaining control of him for extended periods was more difficult. Not just because of his consciousness wriggling around in the background, but also because I kept on having to remember to do those things that his own brain could undertake automatically, such as keeping his heart beating. Explaining why, the moment I released my control of him, he began frantically gasping for air.

The old woman was too lost in her own thoughts to even notice his histrionics.

She mumbled a little to herself, then dismissed Ig with a wave. "Stay the night. Get some food in you. We'll see you off when you're ready."

"Sorry me no helping."

She didn't seem to register that either. Already ancient, she looked like I had just dropped an additional century upon her shoulders. At my silent urging, Ig slunk out, almost colliding with Wyn, on the other side of the door, who had been in the process of slinking in. "Oh."

With a degree of foresight, their hand was already out and moving to pinch Ig's mouth shut before he could let out a yelp and give the game away. Clearly, the adventurers wanted to know what was being discussed behind closed doors. Dragging Ig by the lips, Wyn proceeded back through the town hall until a quiet broom closet could be secured.

They had to drop into a crouch to be level with Ig and prevent their whispers carrying too far. This put Wyn in the unenviable position of being face-to-face with a kobold. Admittedly a kobold with excellent fashion sense, but a kobold nonetheless. "What have you learned, my friend?"

"They is wearing wolfs." Ig tried to explain, despite knowing nothing himself. "They is wanting me magic away, but I no can."

Wyn nodded sympathetically. "Because you're a kobold masquerading as a wizard?"

"Because I is kobold with wizard in hat."

Shut up!

But it was too late. Wyn was already leaning back from Ig, stroking their chin. "A wizard in your hat, eh? And how exactly did that come to pass?"

"Me founds hat on tree and wizard says hello and tells me he need ride me home, and I says yes because we is good friends."

Will you close your mouth, you insufferable imbecile, every word that you speak brings us closer to ruin!

". . . And wizard is yelling now me is telling you, but I is thinking we friends too now. Right?"

The idiot, he was putting himself entirely in the power of the elf. All it would take was for the adventurer to reach out and snatch me from atop the kobold's head and it would all be over. He had ruined us both with his blind, trusting nature. I mean, we wouldn't have been here at all unless he had that blind and trusting nature.

Gently, oh so gently, they laid a hand upon Ig's shoulder. "Of course, you need not fear any harm from me, small friend."

We had a good run, all things considered. A solid few days, that was practically a lifetime in kobold years. The fact that we would now be parted was a sweet sorrow, sorrowful because all of the plans that I had been making would fall apart, yet sweet because I would no longer have to endure his ceaseless utter incompetence.

Yet the snatch did not come. Nor did the loud declarations, or the violence. Instead Wyn's brows drew down and they added, "I suspect that my companions may not understand the nature of your being. Perhaps it would be in your best interests to keep this information between us for now."

Blackmail, that was the elf's game. Hold the truth over Ig like the dangling pendulum of doom and threaten to let it drop when they required the services of a wizard. I might have known that so long-lived a creature would be cunning instead of reactive. All of my arcane knowledge would now be at their beck and call. We would become a slave to the whims of this elf.

Ig said, "That is smarts."

"Your situation is most uncommon, and my companions are not so well versed in the ways of magic. I do not believe that Rhinolyta would have any ill will over your deception, but it would instill confusion, and may result in her attempting to liberate you from the wizard's yoke. Something that I assume you do not desire . . ."

"Me is Ig and hat is Absalom Scryne, and we is best friends . . ."

That was a statement of such magnitude that even the unflappable elf was given pause, but it lasted but a moment before they moved into action once more. There was a small window in the broom closet, a glimmer of light. It was towards that light that Wyn hoisted Ig up. "Then I shall endeavor to see you and your dear friend are not parted. Let us make haste."

We made our way out through that window with only the bare minimum of Ig falling directly onto his face, and then returned with as much stealth as we could muster to the other adventurers, who had settled at an outdoor dining table in the village square.

The whole place was decorated with garlands of flowers, as though those who dwelled here were trying to counterbalance the ugliness that they had created beyond the thicket fence protecting them. As though their new nature could be hidden under a façade of nicety.

Ildrit leaned across the as-yet empty table to ask Wyn, "What do you know?"

"The villagers are werewolves."

The news was taken in with stony silence, but you could tell from Ildrit's expression that certain things were beginning to make sense. Such as the small children who had been playing on the other side of the green having paused to scratch behind their ears with their feet. And the howling noises they kept on making every time their ball was thrown up into the air. The permeating aroma of wet dog may also have been relevant.

Trying her best to put on a happy smiling face for those watching, Rhinolyta asked through a rictus grin, "Are they planning on eating us?"

That was a grotesque and offensive stereotype about werewolves and she should have been ashamed of herself, but also, I wished I'd thought of that. We had been invited to feast with them that eve. What if we were the feast in question?

"Me no want be eat," Ig opined with all the gravitas he was capable of mustering. The others ignored him, thankfully.

Wyn seemed to be weighing the question. "They moved out here, and concealed their location so that they would be safe. Allowing a group of adventurers to discover them and then depart to spread word of their presence would somewhat destroy that safety. It may be in their best interests to eat us."

Ildrit was much better at subterfuge than the other two, leaning back as if stretching, and scoping out the whole village green in the same motion. "So if we try to sneak out before dinnertime . . ."

"It would also be in their best interests to prevent that from happening. As of this moment, they assume we do not know the danger that we are in, and they will continue their masquerade until they are forced to unveil themselves. We will be protected by our ignorance until then."

A middle-aged farmer with a straw hat and dungarees loped past us on all fours with a hoe in his mouth. I was beginning to wonder just how oblivious they thought we were. Although on reflection, if you'd asked me if an adventurer could count to three before today, I'd have guessed not, so perhaps their assumption was correct.

Rhine attempted the stretch-and-look-around move that Ildrit had pulled a moment before but got it mixed up somehow, and ended up with her arm around his shoulders instead. He looked irritated, but was obviously intent on not causing any sort of scene in case we were set upon by ravening werewolves. Ig seethed with jealousy at the sight of Rhine's muscled arm holding Ildrit snug against her side.

I really don't think your chances with her were all that good anyway; she is a shining golden goddess walking the earth and you're a kobold.

His little ears perked up, tickling under my rim. "She what?"

Pretty, Ig. She is pretty. And you are not.

His ears flopped down again.

Exceptionally unattractive in every way, really.

Thankfully Ildrit piped up at that moment before I butchered the poor creature's ego any further. "If they think we're just going to sit there and let them chew on our bones, they've another thing coming."

The other adventurers glanced his way nervously. I could understand that glancing. It was a fairly ominous statement. Ig, meanwhile, remained blissfully unaware of the slaughter that the swordsman meant to begin. "What plan?"

Memories of the battle with the ogres came back to me now. The hot wet blood spattering across Ig's back. The groans, not just of pain, but of muscle and bone prying slowly apart where the cursed black sword had done its awful work. There were so many children scattered around us playing, frolicking really. Fighting them would be like massacring a village full of innocents and a pack of happy puppies simultaneously. We needed a better option.

Thankfully one of the adventurers in our company had more going on behind the eyes than the faint plinking noise of a single brain cell bouncing back and forth from one side of the skull to the other. Wyn sighed, "I'd propose that we do nothing. Wait for an opportunity to present itself."

"What is it with you elves and doing nothing, anyway?" Rhine grumbled. "Oh here comes another dark lord going to conquer the world, guess we'll just kick back and let the humans handle it. Again."

"Given time, most problems resolve themselves to our satisfaction."

"You mean other people fix things for you if you leave them to it," Rhine snarked back.

Wyn was not troubled by this in the least. "A policy of non-interference would have kept us from this situation to begin with."

"Can we not have this argument again for the nine hundredth time," Ildrit finally interceded. "Some of us aren't immortal."

"What's your idea then?" Rhine asked him, eyes shining bright, full of expectation that he'd have some heroic solution.

"Cook up some chocolate pudding for their dessert?"

To the others, this had doubtless sounded like an admission of defeat in the face of an impossible situation, but I was not the others, and the selection of chocolate, a substance known to be toxic to canines, had not been accidental. There was an intelligence in this swordsman that went beyond mere cunning. Intelligence, mixed with a bitterness I couldn't yet comprehend.

Unbeknownst to me, Ig had been thinking. It had been such an unusual sensation from him that I hadn't recognized it until it was too late and the words were already out of his mouth. "What if me says me can fix them?"

What.

"What?" Ildrit echoed.

"They be wanting to not be wolveses no mores." Ig was clearly struggling with the unfamiliar task of composing whole sentences. "What if me says me can fix 'em."

Wyn raised an eyebrow. "Then I'd imagine that they'd tear you apart the very moment your lie was exposed."

"Nots if they be sleepies." Ig tried for a grin and overshot into grimace once again.

"Drug them?" Ildrit asked.

"Me is making potions!" Ig declared, springing to his full height in excitement. His full height wasn't much, but it was sufficient to draw attention from all the gathered werewolves.

In short order, Ig was guided to the herb garden of the village to look for what he needed, and the other adventurers were in the process of getting a fire started under a rather large soup cauldron on the green, with little assistance from the bemused villagers.

The other adventurers in this case excluding Ildrit, who had somehow laid himself out on one of the benches and fallen asleep. How exactly he was capable of sleeping in a situation like this was entirely beyond me. Death hung over us all, and he went for a nap. The prospect was inconceivable to me, let alone Ig, who was so highly strung that you could craft some sort of airborne harp from him.

At last it seemed we were alone, and Ig felt safe to speak. "So how is we making sleepy potions?"

Oh, you finally decided to actually ask my opinion on your plan. What luck that you consulted with me prior to announcing it to everyone so I could inform you of all the myriad reasons that it absolutely will not work.

I hoped that my searing contempt was sufficiently conveyed through my tone, but honestly it was hard to measure tone when you were merely thinking very hard into another person's head. Not that Ig was particularly capable of parsing sarcasm, tone, or indeed much of anything from the words and actions of others.

"It work! So work," he proudly declared. "Me makes potion and then we sneaks when they snoozing."

And you are of course aware that the condition of lycanthropy renders its victims immune to all manners of sedation.

There was a long pause as Ig dug through my imparted knowledge in search of the word sedation, then he attempted to cover for his idiocy with bravado, as idiots often do. "Me knew that. Me didn't know you knew."

What Ig knew could quite readily have been transcribed into a hefty tome about the size of a single square of toilet paper.

And I'm certain that you also knew that while I am intensely competent in the fields of magic, alchemy is in fact an entirely distinct discipline with which I've had little to no experience.

There was a certain kind of courage in sticking to your position, even when you knew that it was atop quicksand. The kind of courage usually only found in those people written about in legends of heroic last stands. And in the great many millions of people who were never written about because they died before doing anything of note. Presumably the monuments erected in their honor were also placed atop said quicksand.

"Me knew that too."

Oh, my apologies, I did not realize that I was nestled upon the head of one of the preeminent alchemists of the kobold world. When I found you living in that hole in the mud, I had no idea you were merely on a sabbatical from your much vaunted alchemical practice.

"Me am making the potion for 'straction, then you be doing the zappy magic."

There was a sort of base animal cunning to be found in kobolds. The fact that I currently occupied the brain that he was trying to use to lie to me about his deception obviously rendered the act of lying somewhat pointless, but there was a swiftness in his jump to the new plan that I might have called sharp wit in another person. Sadly, his newfound ability to leap to new conclusions was going to end about as well as his ability to crawl to them at agonizingly slow speeds.

Werewolves are equally resistant to magically introduced torpor.

Ig turned to desperate flattery in his hour of need. Though calling it an hour of need when his need had been pretty much constant from the moment that I met him is perhaps downplaying the neediness of the average kobold. "Ah, but you is bestest wizard in world."

Perhaps, had I been a young and foolish wizard, desperate for approval, then such a comment might have spurred me into spurious action. Sadly for Ig, I had a lifetime of experience with sycophants begging for my assistance to draw upon.

Whether the best or the worst, I cannot alter fundamental laws of the universe. One of which is that the arcane disease known as lycanthropy renders its victims immune to magical intervention. It is why I couldn't help them even if I wanted to.

Had I my own body, Quintessence reserves and resources at my disposal, I may very well have been able to craft some arcane solution to the situation . . . a combination tracking spell and purging curse to seek out the vector of infection and . . . But I am not, and we are not. We have but a speck of Quintessence at our disposal despite your ongoing efforts, nor a competent caster to make use of it even if we did.

I do not have the time to research means by which we might make magic affect those afflicted with lycanthropy, and you have neither the time nor the ability to learn multiple new elements and words of Archaic before nightfall. I may be the greatest wizard to ever live, but I am but a single man.

"Hat," Ig corrected me. Had I teeth, I would have grit them.

I am but a single hat. And you, my friend, are buggered.

Despite being damned, I could not help but note that Ig was still going through the motions of collecting herbs from the garden, almost as if he had the faintest idea of what he was doing, other than possibly preparing some seasoning for himself so that wolves gnawing on his corpse later would have a broader flavor palate to enjoy.

You did hear me, there is no way that you will be able to drug these creatures. Perhaps the knowledge hadn't quite sunk in yet. Or he was so slow-witted that his body was still continuing the last action it had been told to carry out because the signal to stop hadn't yet reached it.

But no, he was aware that all he did was in vain. You could hear it in the misery of his croaky little whisper. "Me know."

Yet still I see you tinkering with the plants here as though . . . wait, don't touch that one.

Ig's hand stopped an inch from the frostwort's leaf.

Touch that and your fingers will go entirely numb.

There was that itching sensation below my brim once more. The unfamiliar sensation of Ig forming a thought. "Me thought you says you no know potions?"

I said that I knew little, not nothing. I'm sure everyone has read some herbals in their spare time, concocted a few little brews to stave off sleep or cure minor ailments.

"So me cans cures them!" Ig declared, as though he had outwitted me. As though a battle of wits between me and him could possibly end in anything other than a smoking pair of shoes where he had once stood. As though in a battle of wits, he was not bringing a rusty spoon to a knife fight.

The village elder, resting her elbows on the garden wall, let out a sigh. "It is such a relief to hear you say that."

Ig jumped into the air, yelping, "Old lady!"

Thankfully she was either remarkably hard of hearing, or simply too polite to acknowledge that comment. "I must admit that when you told me that helping was beyond your power, I was doubtful. Was it the plight of our children that convinced you to help?"

Ig's heart was hammering in his chest. "Me didn't knows you is there."

She was smiling beatifically at him. "Or perhaps you spent some time talking with the people of our village and came to realize that all they want is a peaceful life?"

Ig's poor brain was backpedaling as fast as possible. Trying to work out how much he had given away about our current situation with his rambling, one-sided conversation. "How long was you there?"

She reached out her hand, and tentatively, Ig crept closer to take it, as there didn't seem to be any other polite response. "I came as soon as word of your change of heart reached me."

He tried to tug his paw back after the initial squeeze but found that despite her hands having skin like a well-roasted chicken upon their back, they still held an uncommon strength. One borne of either her lycanthropic curse or a lifetime of hard labor in the fields. I could not say which. "Me think me can fix. But no promise. Magic be tricky hard."

She clasped his paw all the tighter, tears brimming in her cataract-smudged eyes. "Oh, I completely understand now, you didn't want to give us false hope but planned to do your magic secretly. Claiming none of the glory for your heroism."

What possible purpose would be served by such a thing? To deprive yourself of any possible reward for your actions? To convince others that their good fortune was simply that, and not the work of some higher power? To hide your puissance from a world that stomps readily upon those who appear weak? Even if you were of the more vacuous and naïve sort who wanted to help all they met, surely telling those that you'd helped that you were helping would have served as the best sort of advertisement to others who needed you. There was literally no benefit to such an act.

Ig did seem to understand, however. An occasion so bizarre I felt it should have been marked on the calendar. "Me no want you sad if no work."

Ah. To cover for the potential for incompetence. That had never occurred to me as a reason. Presumably because I have always been so supremely competent in all that I sought to achieve. It must have been some trick that the less capable bandied about so that when they failed, others could not assign them blame. That made more sense.

"We have every faith in you," the old woman said, before letting Ig's hand slip from hers.

I think I would have been more comfortable with threats, to be honest. If she had come out snarling about how she was going to tear out my gizzard and devour it if I failed in this task, then at least that would have been something tangible to work with, but having the now overwhelming danger of letting down a nice little old lady . . . that was not something I was emotionally equipped to face. And the awful truth was that whatever I said to Ig to convince him that this plan was never going to work, we were committed now. There was no way out.

This is why we do not offer to help people. Just so you know for the future, supposing that we survive until the future.

Ig was whispering under his breath to me, hoping that the old woman now watching us with a smile so wide I feared her face might rupture would not hear him. "You can do the tracky zappy on bad man who bits them."

Given enough time, Quintessence, and resources, I might be able to compose a spell that would help, yes. But we have none of those things.

"You is clevers," Ig said as though trying to convince himself as much as me. "You is working out."

Then he reached down without looking and grabbed a handful of frostwort, turning his whole hand numb.

CHAPTER THIRTEEN

WHO IS AFRAID OF THE BIG BAD FARMERS?

In heroic tales, the amazing wizard who claimed that he had no time to solve a problem would nonetheless have created an arcane quick fix long before night fell, so it should come as absolutely no surprise that here in reality, when I said I needed more time, resources, and power than we had at our disposal—by the end of the three hours of Ig puttering around with the cauldron of what was now probably the most disappointing tea in all of the world—I had absolutely nothing. I mean, not even the first inkling of a clue as to how I could save us. I'd have needed a month in my library back in the university to have found a way around werewolves' resistance to magic in general, not to mention their specific immunity to soporific effects, then I'd have had to combine multiple elements into a single spell, then I'd have had to really dig into the etymology of the Archaic words I meant to use to ensure that there could be no ambiguity whatsoever. Plus, Ig would have needed about a year of cycling in and out Quintessence to increase his reserves to a usable level for something so complex, which would also have been about the length of time it would have taken to actually teach him the spell. And that was all assuming I'd been working on the idea that he'd come up with rather than the one that I'd arrived at in the brief moment when confronted with the problem. That would have been markedly easier but would still have required at least a few weeks. In the library I had no access to. While Ig cycled Quintessence and learned the specific words I needed him to learn, alongside the nature of the specific elements we would be invoking.

All of which is to say. We remained, as we had begun, entirely buggered.

Another factor on the side of heroes in the tales is luck.

Luck would have come in extremely handy in the absence of any practical solutions. I would have delighted in even the slightest glimmer of luck. And in this case, good luck would have been that the random day on which I had awoken in the forest atop Ig's head was not just a few days before the full moon. You would have thought that even if there was no luck, and merely random chance, with there being only one day out of each month when everyone in this village was guaranteeably going to turn into ravening wolves, there would have been decent enough odds that we could have sidestepped it.

But it seemed that either fate was against us, or the one in thirty odds we had been working with were simply too potent to overcome. As the sun began to set on the tree line, the moon was already entirely visible. Round as only a perfectly spherical lunar body could be. Full and ripe with possibilities. In this case, the distinct possibility that I was going to be in someone's stomach by the end of the night.

The villagers, who had now all gathered around the village green, were looking a little less friendly by this point. The majority of them definitely looked in need of a good shave and a haircut, and there was no small portion of the population that appeared to have already been replaced with rather large and unfriendly-looking dogs. Wolves, one might say. If one were so inclined.

The adventurers were huddled close around Ig, and Ig was stirring his cauldron as though he hoped that if he went fast enough, the little spiral in the middle might suck him down and he wouldn't have to be present for the impending slaughter.

The leader of the village was beginning to look . . . the word *anxious* wasn't really appropriate. She had cast aside the stick that she used to walk, and was now pacing relentlessly back and forth. There was something about her stride that I didn't much care for. Perhaps the suspicion that at some point underneath her skirt, the joints of her knees had reversed direction. "You must hurry," she growled to Ig.

"Me going fast as me can."

Wyn leaned down to whisper, "You really do need to stop delaying. They will never be more ready than now to sup your poison soup."

"Me going fast as me can!"

Ig was stalling, of course. Hoping that if he bought enough time then my brilliance would shine through and save us all from the impending doom. He had even, to my immense amusement, been cycling his Quintessence all day. There were a half dozen tiny bunnies scattered throughout the village who would most likely end up a wolf's snack before the night was through. And he had once again doubled up the amount of Quintessence that he had stored. Not that it would help all that much since he seemed to be clinically incapable of focusing on anything for the required amount of time to actually cast a spell, and all of his attempts thus far had missed the mark by a hare.

Alright, they were rabbits, not hares, but you get the point.

I had briefly considered whether another attempt at wild magic might have been in order. If Ig could have gathered sufficient Quintessence and released it to create a veritable horde of small fluffy creatures, that instinct might drive the wolves to pursue rather than coming after us. Unfortunately, this would likely have worked if we had been confronted by perhaps a handful of werewolves, but we were now well beyond the point of Ig being able to count them all upon his fingers, toes, tail, and any other appendages brought into the mathematical system. Dozens upon dozens of farmers were ready for their cure, and all we had to offer them was a tepid green broth, served up by a kobold who still hadn't regained full feeling in one of his grasping little paws.

It was less than ideal.

The bunting that had been strung up around the green to make the place look cheerful was seeming increasingly sinister as the night drew in and the wind picked up, fluttering as it was like the wings of a thousand tiny bats. The fact that every hair on the back of Ig's neck was standing to attention as his hind brain screamed at him about being surrounded by predators obviously wasn't affecting my perception of the situation at all.

Casting a glance to our companions—Ildrit, with his arms stiff to stop himself reaching for his sword, Rhine as close to scared as she'd ever allow herself to look, and Wyn, who looked very much like this was an average day for them, and that they were somewhat bored by the prospect of being chewed to pieces—I tried to psychically convey to them all that at any moment, the screaming was going to start and they should all take off running. They all looked down at Ig with momentary confusion as he tried to convey with his expression what I was trying to tell them by thinking extremely hard at them.

They were all doomed.

We had delayed as long as it was possible to delay. The wolves were at our door, so to speak. Less figuratively, the gathered mass of farmers at various stages of transformation into wolves were coming closer and closer with each passing moment. Most of them also tumbling down the evolutionary ladder onto all fours as they approached, until the most human-looking one was the village elder, and even she had a pretty serious snout protruding.

"The . . .cure . . ." she whined out, and Ig, poor Ig, reached down into the pot with the nice long spoon, scooped up an abundantly herby spoonful and held it out towards her mouth.

Her ever-sharpening teeth clacked shut around the spoon, biting the head clean off, then she cocked her head back to let the potion flow down her throat as the very last of humanity left her and she stretched up and out from her withered frame into a seven-foot-tall, white-furred wolf woman. You will note that I said wolf woman, not wolf man. And that is because with the loss of opposable thumbs, she had also lost all dignity and all six fuzzy teats were now swaying in the wind at Ig's face height.

Needless to say, the herby concoction did absolutely nothing to deal with her transformation into a werewolf, except perhaps to give her slightly better breath.

It would be nice to be enveloped in a miasma of mint as Ig's skull was crushed between her jaws.

Around about three seconds after she realized that the potion we had given her was going to do nothing, the adventurers, who had been hoping for her to immediately pass out on consumption of the grassy-smelling fluid, realized that it was going to do nothing. They looked at Ig with dismay, and all that he could do was shrug. Hands splayed, goofy little apologetic smile on his face, as though he hadn't just condemned us all to end the evening as wolf droppings.

"Wizard, what have you done?" Ildrit asked, finally drawing his doom sword Blackstabber, or whatever it was called, after a long day of desperately longing for it.

Wyn answered for Ig. "Absolutely nothing."

All of which Ig could have coped with—being a disappointment to them was more or less par for the course—but then he turned his gaze to Rhinolyta. Her big, beautiful blue eyes shining with unshed tears in the moonlight, the stricken look of utter betrayal upon her face.

Oh, damnation.

"Help now?"

The wolves began to circle around as their leader licked her lips, waiting for the magical transformation to occur, and finally, after a considerable delay, regurgitating the head of the spoon.

Congelo. Repeat it back, enunciate it clearly, do not touch your Quintessence. Congelo.

Our deception had quite firmly been uncovered by this point, and the white wolf now dropped to all fours before us, growling, rendering our view blessedly free of nipples.

"Con-jello."

If I could have screamed, I think that it is safe to say that I would have. *Wrong! Congelo. Congelo!*

The adventurers had all drawn together now and were backing away from the stalking wolves. The moon shone bright and full in the sky above, reflecting back to us in dozens of eyes out there in the ever-deepening shadows.

"Congelo!"

Yes! Again! Congelo!

The wolves began to shepherd us backwards, blocking off our path towards the exit, and at their head was the white wolf, snarling with barely contained rage. I could not say for certain whether a werewolf retained any part of the intelligence and personality of the person that they were by daylight after their transformation. It was another subject that I supposed I must study when I returned to my beloved library in Arpanpholigon, but for now, I had to make assumptions, and it seemed to me at least that the white wolf remembered that we'd lied to her.

"Congelo!"

He had it. Somehow, despite his mouth being the wrong shape and his brain being the size of a walnut, he had successfully pronounced a single word of Archaic flawlessly. Now we just had to hope that he could do it again when it actually counted.

Now focus upon Carbon.

A hand, Wyn's hand, seized Ig by the back of the collar and jerked him back out of reach of a wolf's snapping jaws. It made sense that they'd pick on him first; he was the smallest and weakest of the pack. Not to mention the fact that kobolds walked through life with the genetic equivalent of a "kick me" sign on their backs.

There was a momentary pause as pants-pissing terror washed through Ig, then he returned to the task at hand as competently as I had expected. "Which one be Carbon?"

The one that isn't Potassium. For the love of the gods, Ig, surely given two options you can . . . right. Focus. Carbon. Carbon.

It really was for the best that I didn't have a mouth or eyes in my current form, as I would be screaming and sobbing in frustration. All of my boundless wisdom, bound in the form of the most useless creature on the planet with no way out. Surely this was some sort of divine punishment for my hubris, though for the life of me I could not recall a single moment of hubris in my life.

"Carbon," Ig yelped. "Carbon."

The wolves' circle tightened in. Ildrit's sword rose, ready to sweep through them. Even softhearted Rhine had her blade at the ready. Wyn did not draw an arrow, nor nock their bow. Their hands were full of kobold, and while it would have seemed entirely in character for the elf to fling me to the wolves in a very literal way after our latest cock-up, they resisted the urge.

Carbon Congelo.

"Carbon. Congelo," Ig yelped out. Word perfect. How I hoped that he was actually focusing on his knowledge of Carbon, and not devoting his entire mind to remembering the word.

Again.

"Carbon. Congelo."

A wolf lunged in, only to be batted away by Rhine's shield, falling back into the less hasty members of its pack in a spattering of yelps and snarls. Ig's eyes had widened to the point that I had concerns they might plop out of their sockets. I was having to constantly dip down and exert control over his body to prevent bowel leakage.

Again!

"Carbon! Congelo!"

Here goes nothing. Focus upon the white wolf, and the white wolf alone. Push your Quintessence out through your mouth as you speak the Archaic word Congelo, and concentrate with all of your might upon your understanding of Carbon.

"Do which?"

All of them at once! Now! Do it!

With an awful groan that made me double check whether some pee had finally escaped him, Ig cast his first true spell.

"*Congelo!*"

And because it was Ig, it was a complete and utter failure.

If he had been competent, then the Quintessence, shaped by his thoughts of Carbon, would have escaped from his body and flowed into the magical word that he had spoken; it would have followed the line of focus that he had formed with his target and it would have turned the white wolf to stone.

Given the rather paltry amount of Quintessence at his disposal, she would only have remained stone for perhaps a few minutes, but once the rest of the pack had realized what we'd done to their leader, they would have drawn back in terror, for fear that they too would become statuary. It would have provided us with the opportunity to take flight and escape the village.

But of course, Ig was Ig.

His ability to focus on anything at the best of times was . . . limited. When placed in a situation where he was surrounded by dozens of snarling wolves, with hundreds of extremely sharp teeth, his attention and focus was divided in a hundred different directions. As such, when the Quintessence, shaped by Carbon and cast out through the magical word, was released, instead of focusing in on a single target where it could have its potent effect, it instead blasted out in every single direction at once.

A puff of soot.

Now don't get me wrong, it was a very impressive cloud of soot, puffing out every which way, painting the faces of all the wolves black and making a very impressive *poot* sound. But it did not have the desired effect of paralyzing all our foes in terror at our mastery of magic.

What it did do was blind them all.

The wolves began to howl, but no sooner had their sorrowful wailing begun than they became a blur of motion passing us by. I had assumed that this was all of them charging in to devour Ig after he'd puffed them, but a swift reassessment revealed that in fact, we were in motion towards the exit in Wyn's arms, the two human warriors at their heels.

The wolves milled around behind us, blinded and deprived of their sense of smell by the sudden influx of soot. Some had dropped their heads to the ground and were pawing at their own faces. A few had even taken a frantic dive into the pond on the green to be free of the black dust, startling the ducks still afloat on its surface and making such a raucous ruckus that it completely covered the sound of Wyn's soft footfalls.

We were going to survive. Somehow, despite all of Ig's best efforts, we were going to survive.

"That was a rather impressive trick, my felted friend," Wyn whispered to me, atop Ig's head. "Though next time, I would prefer to know precisely which trick is being planned ahead of time."

"Immune to potion." As Ig was dangling like a burlap sack in their arms, it was no trouble to briefly seize control over his speaking organs without fear of him tripping over his own feet. "Had to improvise."

The yowling behind us was now becoming a more coordinated howl as the initial effects of the soot began to dissipate. What would have lasted minutes if focused upon a single target lasted only seconds when it was so divided and misshapen. A quick check revealed that Ig was almost entirely devoid of Quintessence now, and it would take him a long time to recoup what he had spent. There would be no second wind in terms of a magical fix for this impending problem.

Over a short distance, four legs are actually something of a disadvantage. On a long-term trek, obviously the wolves could quite readily outpace us, but in a sprint, they had twice as many legs to get into order and moving in synchronicity. Wyn, despite the current kobold-shaped burden, remained at the head of the pack of adventurers, though what they had in natural superiority the other two seemed to be trying to make up in blind panic.

We were nearly to the exit. The gap in the bushes opened up ahead of us. To one side of the path, a teenage werewolf who was presumably meant to be on guard had hoisted herself up onto her rear legs, leaning against a hay bale, and was trying to file her claws. Ildrit freed one hand from his sword to flip her the bird.

She didn't even look up.

The exit hung open before us like the waiting arms of our mothers, we were almost out, almost safe, when the telltale growl sounded behind us. Quite firmly being made from in pouncing distance.

We froze in place.

The growling continued.

Wyn slowly, oh so slowly, so as not to invoke any sort of wolfy wrath, turned around to face the pack gathered behind us. The white wolf, now only white on the back side, was at the head of them and looking absolutely furious. I mean, she probably looked furious at the best of times, what with her being a snarling werewolf, but I suspected that this was an extra level of angry.

There may have been only a dozen wolves gathered there on the path out of town, but it may as well have been seven hundred for all our odds of surviving.

Well, Ig, I will not pretend that it has been nice knowing you. As you are an absolute cretin. But I am still sorry that it ends like this.

An unfamiliar sensation passed through Ig once more. The other half of the fight or flight survival instinct that kobolds never seemed to be able to access. Anger.

He raised the chewed-off handle of the spoon that he'd still been clinging to all of this time like it was a magic wand, perhaps hoping to scare them off with the threat of a spell, and all of a sudden, every single one of the wolves froze. Their eyes locked upon his makeshift wand.

Perhaps they truly did fear this kobold's arcane might after the soot blast. Perhaps we would be able to bluff our way out of this.

Ig waved the stick as though he were about to cast a spell, and every one of the wolves' heads swayed and bobbed to follow it.

For the first time in his life, Ig had power. And like most people the first time that they have power, it went immediately to his head. He was not physically capable of cackling, with the noise instead coming out like a series of odd squeaks, but internally he might as well have been standing atop a heap of skulls on a mountaintop with lightning flashing behind him. The Dark Lord Ig, in all his majesty.

Then, because he was Ig, he made too dramatic a flick while performing a wide sweeping motion, and the stick went flying from his hands.

As one, the wolves all surged forward and I prepared myself as well as I could to die, but it was not us that they were bearing down upon with all their ferocity. It was the stick.

Ig had thrown a stick for them.

There were certain things in this universe that I would never have considered given all the time that there was from now until the stars dying. One of them would have been pursuing a career as a druid. Or having my soul trapped in a hat. Another would have been throwing a stick for some werewolves. But despite my incredulity, it worked.

Wyn caught on to what had happened considerably faster than me, sprinting off with Ig still clenched tightly to their chest through the maze of thicket. The other two adventurers may not have had a thought in their head at that moment, but what they did have was muscle memory on their side, an instinct that told them that when the elf ran, they should run too.

Brambles whipped past Ig's face, close enough that he could feel the sharpness against his snout, though not a one made contact. Wyn moved through the forest like a fish through water, and it seemed that their awareness of their body and the world around them had been extended to the kobold pinned to their chest too.

While I have spoken much of the bravery of Ig thus far, I believe that it is only fair to provide some context to the previous sequence of events. The context in this case being that he was in fact screaming the entire time all of it was happening. It started off high-pitched, and then only scaled up from there into a frequency that only the werewolves and elf were liable to hear. Even kobold ears could not grasp the heights to which his terrified wailing rose, and I like to imagine that this was some sort of evolutionary response to being constantly surrounded by other kobolds in various stages of mental breakdown at any given moment.

CHAPTER FOURTEEN

THE LARGE CRAB APPLE

As we broke out into the ghost-house version of a forest beyond the village perimeter, a hand clamped shut around Ig's snout, silencing him at last, and for one long, awful moment, Wyn lingered, awaiting the arrival of his companions from the maze.

Typically, I would measure the passage of time in heartbeats when I could not spare the attention to it, but that was somewhat impossible as Ig's heart didn't so much beat as vibrate so fast that I had concerns it would phase out of the mortal planes of existence. But even without a sure measure, it seemed to me that the humans took an exceptionally long time to emerge from the maze.

When they did burst out, whatever hardness of breath Wyn might have previously been experiencing was long gone, and they looked entirely bored with the situation once more. I felt for a brief moment as though I had glimpsed behind the curtain to see how the trick was done, then we were off again, heading alongside the tangled thicket of thorns in a curve around the opposite side of the village, presumably working off the assumption that the wolves would come shooting straight out. Or perhaps working off some knowledge of the area that I was simply lacking. Perhaps both.

Regardless, we silently trekked on through the night for hours on end until finally arriving at the outermost edge of the spookified forest. And it was a harsh edge, I must admit, because one moment we were beneath the cover of the trees that had extended as far back across the Badlands as we had traveled, and the next we were out on barren soil, looking up at the stars and full moon shining above.

"What in the nine hecks?" Ildrit began, before Wyn's upheld hand silenced him. It was the same hand that had been silencing Ig all this way, and also the main means by which he had been secured to the elf. Ig fell directly into the dirt the moment he was released, gasping for air as though he hadn't been breathing through his nose the entire time. Perhaps he didn't realize he had nostrils, or what their purpose was. That would explain his propensity for mouth breathing.

As far as the eye could see, the forest ahead of us had been cleared, not just trimmed back, but sheared down to ground level, with only stumps remaining.

Had they been blackened, I might have assumed that a dragon had swept over, but there were still boot-tracks in the earth and drag marks from where the felled logs had been dragged off.

It was for the best that Wyn was no longer holding Ig, as their hands had tightened into fists, and now shook. Rhine gawked at the destruction, mouth hanging as open as Ig's. "What could have done this?"

Wyn spat out the word, "Civilization," and left it at that.

Ig clambered back to his feet, staring around in absolute confusion as the other three moved off once more. "Where trees gone?"

I believe that they have been cut down, my friend.

"You can do that?"

Someone did.

In truth, even I was somewhat flabbergasted by the scale of the destruction. This had been one of the oldest forests in the world, older than mountains and oceans, and now it was an empty slope, and I could not for the life of me fathom why.

Dire termites would not have left such tidy remains, nor consumed so much. There was no sign of fire. There was no possibility that anyone from Arpanpholigon would have hiked all the way out here into monster-infested badlands to harvest trees that could have been grown in their own backyard. There was no logic to it whatsoever.

Under the cover of darkness we moved, not along the comforting tree line and all of its cover, but out into the open expanse, where Wyn would sometimes drop to one knee and lay a hand upon a knotted stump where it still showed signs of axe-work. "They were all felled near the same time, within the last year. Rot has not even begun."

Rhine pointed off into the center of the dark expanse, where even the stars above seemed to be dimming. "Smoke."

"So are we ever going to talk about how the wizard completely screwed us?" Ildrit began, the anger that had been powering him all this distance finally simmering to the surface now that we'd paused for a moment.

Ig shrugged. "Improvised."

"You were meant to put them all to sleep," the swordsman growled.

Another shrug of the shoulders. It appeared that Ig was too stupid to realize that he was currently in as much mortal peril as he had been in the presence of the accursed wolf-farmers. "Didn't work."

"And you don't think that us being relentlessly pursued by savage wolf men is a problem?" He didn't just look angry; he had passed beyond the warmth of anger into the cold shadow at the far end of the ravine: murderous rage.

"They lose dogbodies." Ig pointed at the slowly lightening sky. The subtle hints of purple and pink spreading out from the distant horizon. "We lose them."

I was not entirely clear upon when he had inherited the natural arrogance of a true wizard, but now that it had arrived, I was more than a little impressed. Even I would likely have faltered in the face of Ildrit's wrath, but little Ig, he was just treating this like a vaguely contemptable conversation. Perhaps there was hope for my young apprentice yet. At least . . . I assumed that he was young. For all I knew, kobolds might have been venerated elders at three.

Despite Ig's ignorance, I couldn't help but note the way that Rhinolyta placed herself between Ildrit and the kobold as we proceeded towards whatever fresh nightmare was at the center of the vast expanse of truly blighted land. Though given her specific relationship with violence, and Ildrit, it was entirely possible that she considered preserving Ig's life to be her best chance at knocking boots this evening rather than feeling any moral or personal compunctions about his bloody demise.

Note to self, find out what that magic sword actually is so you can counter it when it gets turned on you.

Wyn led us on, every bit the woodland ranger with the complex hand gestures and the bird calls. They needn't have bothered really since we were all in plain sight of one another in the deforested expanse, but nobody had the heart to tell them to stop. All the dead trees had clearly hurt their feelings.

I cannot say with any specificity what the relationship between elves and forests is, or why they feel such kinship with what are, to me, planks that just haven't realized it yet. But there was definitely some connection between elves and the woods of the world. Those of them that do roam beyond their hidden villages in the depths of the forests tend to be rangers, attuned to the ways of the woods and intent upon their preservation in the face of expansion at the hands of us lesser races. The fact that we need to chop down trees so we can build houses and make fires never really factored into the bloody vengeance that elves have historically rained down on us for our awful sin of converting vertical logs into horizontal ones.

Perhaps it is because they both have the same rather laid-back approach to gender? Perhaps when your lifetime spans centuries, it is a comfort to see a familiar twig? Perhaps there is even some spiritual connection between the elf with its slow-moving iridescent blood and the vital sap of the tree?

Regardless, when we came upon whoever had committed this grievous act of logging, I would not have liked to have been in their boots when Wyn finally caught up to them. That much I can say.

As though to add insult to injury, the smoke that we found rising from across the horizon turned out to be a fairly substantial charcoal-making operation. It was not enough to simply hack down all of the trees; they were being burned using the corpses of their kin, into blackened husks of their former selves. Or at least, that is how I'd imagine an elf would feel about it. Not that Wyn was giving much away with their expression.

Whoever attended to these burners by day was entirely absent in these early hours of the morning. It had been my understanding that peasants were of a generally industrious persuasion, rising before dawn to tend to such things, but in this case, we were apparently earlier still.

The only positive thing that I could say about the rows upon rows of fairly substantial charcoal kilns heaped up out of the clay-rich mud was that someone had laid a gravel road stretching out from them towards whatever civilization might be afoot out here. Following every city-boy instinct in my body, I urged Ig onwards. Only to find our progress stymied when he was hoisted from his feet by the scruff of his neck by Rhine.

It was the most physical contact Ig was liable to get with her, or indeed any woman, so I let him enjoy it while he could.

She twisted him around so she could ask him to his face. "Where do you think you're going?"

"Follow road." He pointed to what I had rather generously called a road. It was road-like. Road-esque. A section of mud with cartwheel marks dug in and stone fragments scattered across it. It was hardly the royal highway but it at least pointed us in the right direction.

She rolled her eyes as Ig slowly rotated by his collar. "We're in the Badlands, home only to monsters and those brave enough to fight them. What do you suppose we will find at the end of that road?"

"Soft bed? Good food? Help?" I could almost feel a feather down mattress beneath me as I spoke. It had been many years since I'd stayed in an inn rather than the spartan luxury of my own chambers, but I could remember the fine treatment I'd received there very well indeed. I was remembering it so well that Ig had begun to salivate, leading to Rhine finally dropping him, lest her bracers began to rust.

Wyn opined, "By my estimations, we are far more likely to find monsters."

To my immense surprise, it seemed Ildrit was in agreement with Ig. "Monsters don't build roads. They don't make charcoal. This isn't monster's work."

Wyn examined the funeral pyre for an entire forest with a look of disdain. "There is more than one kind of monster in this world."

Ildrit groaned. "I'm not getting into this again."

Apparently, we had stumbled upon an old argument, judging from the way that Wyn actually raised their voice ever so slightly. "You know that my words are true, so you will not deny them."

Ildrit rolled his eyes and started walking away down the rickety trail. "Are there bad humans in the world, yes. Are we all ravening murderers, no."

"No?" Wyn spoke softly enough that it took Ig a moment to realize anything had been said.

Ildrit spun on his heel and pointed right past both Ig and Wyn to our rear-guard action. "Look at Rhine. She's never murdered anyone in her whole life."

There was an eyebrow raised on Wyn's face. An accusatory eyebrow. "Less than one day hence, I saw her cut the head from an ogre."

Rhine opened her mouth to speak, but Ildrit scoffed. "That isn't murder."

"Because *they* are monsters . . ."

"We are adventurers, Wyn. We can't stop and puzzle through moral quandaries every single time we meet something trying to kill us." Ildrit was practically shouting by this point. "Besides, I'd say we've got a pretty good system going to tell us when we're doing the right thing."

Throughout all of this, we had been toddling along in the direction that I wanted to go, so I felt no real compulsion to interrupt their arguments. But that last bit had perked up my attention once more. Something to do with the curse on the swordsman. Something to do with moral quandaries. I hadn't quite deciphered it yet, but I was getting closer with each hint.

Wyn jerked a thumb at Ig. "What of the wizard?"

What?

Ig startled. "Weh?"

Ildrit's eyes narrowed. "What about the wizard?"

Wyn stepped up beside Ig and gestured up and down the length of him. "At a glance, he was but a kobold, a thing that you would have slain without a second thought. But on learning he was *human* beneath the surface, he was granted a leave of execution."

"Why do you keep saying human like it is a dirty word?" Rhine snapped at Wyn, to their continuing disregard.

Wyn was now between Ildrit and Ig, their face hidden from my sight. Anxiety was mounting in both Ig's fluttering heart and my industrious mind. Wyn had not yet used their knowledge of our unique situation to their advantage, and I feared that at last it was going to be used like a bludgeon. "It was not enough that the kobold could speak and think and mean us no harm. What if you were to learn now that our wizarding companion who has twice saved our lives was a kobold in truth? What then?"

Rhine shouted over the mounting argument. "But he isn't."

"Me is." Ig bit his tongue. "A bit."

"Don't be silly, you're as human as me." She patted Ig on the head, then wiped the greasiness off onto her trousers. "What you look like it is just . . . a trick."

Ig squirmed uncomfortably beneath her pat and words. But he had the good sense to keep his mouth in the closed position without further intervention from me.

The road was being eaten up beneath our feet as they bickered back and forth, and the sun was rising ever so slowly, bathing the dirt slopes in colors at last. Shame that all that was being painted was dirt really. A few rocks thrown in for good measure, just to break up the monotony. A few stumps in various stages of being dug up for extra charcoal material. A whole load of nothing, in short.

I wondered if this argument had been provoked for my benefit, so that I might hear the reasoning behind Wyn's suggestion that our true state of being remained hidden from the other adventurers. Thus far, it had been relatively successful in convincing me not to trust them. I, of course, required no convincing. I had hopes that something was sinking in for Ig.

Though of course, for things to sink, some depth would have been required.

The argument came to an abrupt end with a single gesture from Wyn. Not the rude gesture that I would have expected, but one of his ranger codes that were entirely unneeded.

We all dropped back into a crouch, shuffling off the road despite the absolute absence of any cover to hide in. The adventurers drew their respective weapons; Ig readied himself to sprint. And then, as the sun finally peaked over the horizon, the approaching enemy came into sight.

It was a troll.

Trolls are huge, murderous creatures with a faint aroma of mushrooms who dwell almost exclusively underground due to their unfortunate propensity to immediately turn to stone when exposed to sunlight.

The actual mechanism by which they undertake such a transformation was the subject of a paper I published early into my magical career. They consume high volumes of various minerals throughout their lives in lieu of protein and undergo a process of rapid calcification when suffering burns, presumably as a defensive mechanism. This provided some sort of evolutionary advantage for the troll, as it prevented them from being burned to death: one of the few things liable to get through their thick hides and actually do them harm. As such, the more reactive a troll was, the more likely they were to survive, and across successive generations, the sensitivity increased exponentially until finally reaching the point where contact with direct sunlight was sufficient to trigger the reaction. At which point they adapted once more, electing a subterranean life rather than one where they spent all of their time cowering under cover until nightfall.

I closed out my treatise with the suggestion that the next phase of troll evolution would likely be a sensitivity to moonlight, then torchlight, then starlight, culminating in their inability to be exposed to any light source whatsoever and losing their ability to see, like many troglodytic species.

This particular troll was ahead of the game in this regard.

While it was tramping along the road with a hefty wagon of barrels just waiting for charcoal, it was not aware of us camped out on the roadside, because to prevent its inevitable transformation in sunlight, it had been covered in what appeared to be a complex interlocking series of parasols. The soles of its feet were more or less the only thing visible, and judging from the crunching sounds as it walked, they had already become stone boots. Beyond that, it was completely concealed from sight. Were it not for the telltale troll stench, I likely would not have been able to identify the beast at all, at a glance.

"What in the nine hecks?" Ildrit whispered in confusion.

Blinded though it was, encased in an amorphous layer of bubbly wired cloth, still the troll's preternaturally sharp senses were not entirely dulled. Its head, or at least, the section of umbrellas that I assumed were attached to its head, swiveled around towards the sound.

We held our breath, well aware that despite its incapacitating allergy to daylight, this monstrous cretin could still do us substantial harm before succumbing to the sun. In truth, even if we were successful in removing its protections, it would result in us being struck by a landslide rather than a troll, with rather similar results.

For a long, arduous moment it waited, listening, and then it set off along the road once more. A road that I increasingly suspected was lined not with gravel, but with broken-off chips from the creature's feet.

Once it was out of earshot, Ildrit dared speak again. "First, organized ogres, now a domesticated troll. What is going on out here?"

"One must assume that a dark lord has risen and is assembling a force to be reckoned with. Perhaps a dark wizard of some sort." That was another rather pointed question from Wyn.

Ildrit's teeth clattered together as he tried to speak and grit them at the same time. Like he was a snappy dog. "The wizard we are out here to see is not dark lord material. I can assure you."

"Then some other has arrived." Wyn shrugged. "Some dark wizard, or a dragon with an industrial mindset. A mortal warlord with might enough to sway the militant-minded monsters . . ."

"Whatever evil may be out here, we shall put an end to it!" Rhine chimed in, drawing some slightly nervous looks from the more experienced adventurers.

Situations such as a dark lord rising typically required fewer adventurers and more heroes to resolve.

The primary distinction between these two categories is that the former expects to return home from their quests and to be paid for their trouble. The nervous look between the other two may very well have been the long-awaited moment of recognition that their traveling companion was hero material, and that they may want to retreat to a safe distance beyond the inevitable blast radius.

Ildrit decided to risk answering her. "Or . . . we could scout things out, head back to the city, and report what is happening to the proper authorities, who'll be able to deal with it properly?"

"And give whichever bold hero they assign the task to all the glory?"

Glory is another one of those wonderful abstract ideals that heroes like to chase after, like truth, justice, and so on. As far as I've been able to work out, glory basically translates to bragging rights, except nobody dares calls you a braggart. And for a while, you might get your dinner and drinks bought for you until someone else does something impressive and your glory dims and dims until there is nothing left.

It's a trap. Like so many other things in life. Because the problems, they never stop. There is always another dark lord, or evil wizard, or dragon to be slain, and it is always worse than the last one, and when your old glory fades in the face of the new darkness and you strap on the old armor that doesn't fit very well anymore and stride out to face evil in its prime, your odds get worse. Every comeback you make is another chance to die in a not-very-glorious way and be completely forgotten about. But if you don't make the comeback, well then, you're forgotten all the same.

The only way to win these games is to not play them, which is why in all of my life, there has not been a single occasion on which I have considered committing an act of heroism. I was the greatest wizard that had ever lived, and that meant I would focus exclusively on magic, and the rest of creation could just go about its business and leave me the hecks alone.

There, some wisdom for you.

Ig came to the rescue, to everyone's immense surprise. "Me need fix magic first."

Rhine turned to him, empathy overtaking her lust for glory, and the rather manic expression on her face fading back to its usual pleasant shape. "Of course, friend wizard. We would be delighted to have you at our side when we face this evil. We shall complete your side quest, return you to your natural form, and then you can really give them what for." There was such optimism in her face that I decided I couldn't bear to burst her bubble so I just let Ig nod along.

We started trudging along the road once more, but Ildrit leaned in close as he passed and whispered, "Nice save."

Ig snickered. "Thank."

You have kicked the problem farther down the road, not resolved it. Try not to be too insufferably smug.

We plodded on along what I insisted upon calling a road towards what I insisted on imagining would be civilization. It wasn't so obscene to imagine that someone with a little moral flexibility might have enslaved a troll to do their drudge work. If I'd had any drudge work that didn't require a level of competence higher than a grad student, I'd have considered it myself.

The ogres spotted us before we spotted them, which was, I suppose, the purpose of the guard towers and all of the cleared forest. Some flags were waved atop the towers, with the begrudging stiffness of a creature that had never waved a flag in its life, nor had any inclination to do so. And the message was thus carried along the line of towers and to the distant horizon where our road, and indeed a great many that we were now beginning to intersect, met.

There was not a single ogre up in those towers that would not have preferred to get out of the tower, climb down the wooden post that their little tree house was attached to, and ram their little flag through our entire alimentary canal, which suggested one of two things. That they had been nailed inside those little wooden boxes, or that they were absolutely petrified of whatever was in charge. I could not think of any other way to make an ogre obedient than the threat of imminent agonizing death, nor do I think that any ogre would have liked to have been thought of as obedient without the threat. It would probably be quite offensive to them culturally, to not be threatened with gruesome agony in exchange for getting things done. Ogre chore wheels must have involved at least one person being racked on the wheel at any given moment.

Regardless, the ogres did not give pursuit, a flag did not abruptly sprout from Ig's mouth, and we continued on our way with a new sense of urgency. On the periphery of the kobold's admittedly rather myopic vision, I could make out movement as we continued to accelerate. Anywhere else, I imagine we would have been run down by cavalry, but horses and similar creatures tend not to like having an ogre riding on them, in much the same way that I'd imagine a fly doesn't like having a spider riding on it, so it was a footrace. And why were we racing instead of standing our ground and fighting them off in a heroic manner, you might ask?

Well, as I explained to Ig as he panted out a similar question, borne of exhaustion rather than any desire to fight: *Because they're trying to catch us before we get to the city. Which implies that if we get to the city, they can't catch us afterwards.*

And now that we were close enough, there could be no denying that there was a city up ahead. Not a city in the way that Arpanpholigon was a city, built up over centuries into a vast architectural masterpiece, but definitely a vast collection of buildings where people most likely lived. To a certain interpretation of the word "people." Given the rather militant nature of ogres, it should also come as no surprise that they went in heavily when it came to the city-walls aspect of a city. They were big and tall and sturdy looking, despite having been constructed exclusively from fresh-cut un-aged wood and whatever spikey affectations the ogres could manage to attach. There were a few buildings made of similar material poking up over the other side of them, but I struggled to imagine what sort of insane creature would deliberately live in a tower like that. With one household stacked atop one another, all the way up to the cloud line. Or smog line, as the case may be.

What wood they hadn't used up building their rickety skyline was clearly alight somewhere in the city, judging from the voluminous clouds of smoke clogging up the sky, and the sounds of industry were nigh on overwhelming from within. Hammers and shouting and the like.

We were in a full-on sprint by this point, all four of us impaired by lungs desperately gasping as the ogre patrols closed in. The ogres, for their part, had not even broken a sweat. Actually, I'm not sure ogres do sweat, now that I think about it. Perhaps they are more like a mollusk, with a constant coating of viscous slime. Regardless, they certainly weren't breathless and heaving like Rhinolyta.

Sorry, my brain stalled for a moment there.

We stood before the very gates of the ogre city, the vast edifice of the gates graven into a rather predictable gaping skull-maw. If it had been done in stone, it probably would have been rather imposing, but with the fresh sap scent still in the air, it felt rather like a rebellious carpenter's child trying to make a statement about the unfairness of curfews and not allowing your teens to date forty-year-old bards. We were almost through, we were almost to . . . well, perhaps safety wasn't the correct word for diving right into a den of monsters, but certainly we were almost where the ogres didn't want us to be, which was surely to our advantage in some way.

But just before we passed under the threshold, we crashed in a tragic three-adventurer pileup that resulted in Ig's face and Ildrit's hindquarters making close acquaintances with one another. It was only once he had been extracted that I could see clearly what had caused the delay.

Standing there, waiting for us, beyond the city gates, was an ogre.

Now, an ogre in itself would hardly have been notable in this situation, and while this one was markedly bigger than the others that we had encountered, I doubt we would have given that too much of consideration either. Having seen Ildrit swinging his sword around, I'd have said most ogres would have ended up about a head shorter by the time we stopped to chat regardless. The thing that made us stop dead in the face of this ogre was that he was not smiling.

An ogre's smile is a terrible thing to behold. Their dentistry is on par with kobolds' personal hygiene, and their diet consists mostly of whatever can't run away fast enough, but it is still a constant of the ogre that cannot be ignored. They may be utterly malevolent in every way, but there is still a jolly air to them, as though they're having a blast as they flay all the skin off your body. They might be lining up everyone in your village to be cut in half vertically using a rusty spoon, but you're guaranteed service with a smile.

Even when the ogres earlier were being slaughtered, it was with a very sportsmanlike attitude, as though they'd been dealt a bad hand and fully expected to win again next time. They had died as they'd have killed, with joy in their heart.

They would kill you, your whole family, everyone that you knew and loved, they'd do it all out of pure, unabated spite, and they'd do it all while having the best time of their lives, because that was what ogres were. Evil idiots.

They did bad things because it was fun to do bad things. When they cut off your toes one by one and force-fed them to you, it was all just a joke that you weren't getting. There was always that tiniest glimmer of cold comfort that even though you were currently having the very worst experience of your life, at least they were having a nice time.

This ogre was not having a nice time. He wasn't smiling. Not even a gloating smirk. It was unsettling enough to make the adventurers entirely forget about their impending death by all of the very-much-smiling ogres pounding along the various roads to intersect with us.

In addition to not smiling, the ogre was also wearing a suit. It is a testament to how unusual a sight an unsmiling ogre is that the suit took so long for me to notice. I'd have said that it was poorly tailored and ill-fitting, but that wouldn't really have been correct. It was perfectly tailored, to the body of an ogre, which inherently looks misshapen and bizarre to the human eye. Perhaps to an ogre, the vast wedge of muscle protruding up to connect the back of the head to the shoulders, where other species would have had a neck, was a singularly attractive attribute. The fact that he still managed to wear a perfectly tied bowtie around that assemblage of flesh, bone, and cloth was quite remarkable too.

"You is welcomated to New Orc City," he announced, politely, gesturing for us to step inside. Still not smiling.

The other ogres, still smiling broadly, were almost upon us, close enough that I could see the steam rising off their backs. Ildrit, Rhinolyta, Wyn, they were all paralyzed in indecision, but Ig had one advantage over them all. He didn't have enough room in his head to hold two thoughts at once. All he had was terror. So when he flung himself forward and caught the three of them by the backs of the knees, they all went tumbling down in a heap on the other side of the gate.

Immediately, the ogres outside started loudly cursing.

"No fair!"

One pulled off his little helmet and threw it at the dirt so hard that it bounced. "So close!"

"Boo!" said one of the heavier ones to the rear of the pack. "Stupid rules."

That statement brought a sudden silence over the whole gathering. The grinning buffoonery that was at the core of all ogres' being seemed to pale in the face of the unsmiling one's blank expression.

Softly, and surprisingly politely, he inquired, "You isn't liking me rules?"

Immediately, all of the friends of the ogre who had misspoken leapt to his defense. "Love the rules, boss."

"Good rules!" one announced while trying to retrieve his helmet from a roadside ditch where it had rolled. "Very fair."

"No fights in the city." The ogre who had booed finally had a chance to speak in his own defense. "Good rules!"

It seemed that the unsmiling ogre still wasn't entirely convinced. He ran a hand along his sleeve, dislodging some imaginary lint. "If you isn't liking the rules, you could be interlocuting to jail. Do you wants to be interlocuting to jail?"

"No!" came the immediate, terrified cry from all assembled ogres.

It did make me wonder what in the nine hecks an ogre jail might be like, given that their usual punishment for any slight greater than eye contact tended to be a brutal fight to the death.

The ogre in the suit raised a hand to cup around his ear. "Me can't hear you?"

"No, boss," they replied again, in a rather more singsong tone, as if they'd done this before a great many times.

"What was that?" The boss ogre's eyes narrowed behind a pair of half-moon spectacles that I couldn't believe I hadn't spotted until that moment.

"No boss, sir," they all sung back.

"That's right." He jerked his thumb. "You want to kill 'em, you catch them quicker next time."

Well, that is certain to make leaving New Orc City an absolute delight when the time comes. Perhaps I'll have you throw me into one of the ogre's latrines before you depart. Cut out the middleman.

Turning back to us and providing a firm nod, the ogre resumed. "As I was expectorating before me was so rudely interpulated, you are welcome to New Orc City."

The adventurers glanced at one another and then around at the streets, where ogres were going about their ogring. Ildrit was the first to gather the courage to point out the obvious. "I'm not seeing any orcs around here."

Contradicting an ogre was not typically a good way to extend one's life expectancy, but there was so much contradictory here that I imagine the man could not resist letting his curiosity run wild. I was fully anticipating the response to that question being an unseasoned knuckle sandwich with a side of stomping, but instead, the suited ogre tilted his head ever so slightly. As if he'd been ready for the question.

"There was an orc village situated here."

Feeling encouraged by the non-trampled state of their de facto leader, it seemed the other adventurers were growing more courageous. Rhine scratched her head. "Why not call it Orc City, then?"

"Because we just built it." The ogre knocked on the side of a rather greenish-looking panel of wood on what I hoped was not a load-bearing wall, given the way it wobbled under the impact. "It new."

"But why not call it Ogre City, if your kind built it?" Wyn was getting in on the inquisition too, it seemed.

The ogre drew himself back up to his full height and adjusted his bowtie with fingers thick enough that you couldn't even call them sausage-like, because everyone's appetite has a limit. "Because we is a civilized society, we did democracy on what it should be called. The peoples decidederated they liked the name Orc City so much, they called it that twice." He held up two of those gargantuan fingers for us, and pointed to them in case we could not count. "Once before, and once now."

Wyn's eyes had been drifting around from the moment it became clear that they weren't about to be attacked, taking in every detail with a sort of clinical efficiency. To the others, I imagined that the elf looked as tepid as ever, but having spent some time in their company, and that of others of their race, I was not so sure of their even temperament. All of this wood had once been trees, and the wholesale felling of the forest was clearly the responsibility of our current host. "And where are the orcs now?"

"Moved out." The ogre shrugged. "Couldn't afford the rent."

I shuddered atop Ig's flaky scalp. The ogres had become something even more frightening than giant murder babies. *Gentrifiers.*

Ildrit had now gathered his courage once more, and with all of the subtlety of a chainsaw to the shins, he outright asked the question that I imagined was on the tip of all our figurative tongues. "I can't help but notice that we aren't currently being slaughtered by the hordes of ogres living here . . . I'm not complaining but . . . why?"

The ogre still did not smile, but it did manage to look a little smug. "We is a civilized peoples. Which means we has laws. Which means, no murder in New Orc City." He cast his glance around, and then pointed. "Look, look, watch this. Murder situationary. But watch . . ."

There were two ogres heading along the same street at the same time, heading in opposite directions to one another. The street was broad enough to comfortably run a carriage along, but that meant that it was only barely going to be wide enough for the two to pass each other by, and neither one of them seemed inclined to give an inch of ground. On each of their faces was the grim certainty that the other would move out of the way, because of course they would. Each of these ogres was convinced that he was the bigger and tougher of the pair, practically guaranteeing that the matter would need to be resolved. Animals may roll over and show their stomach after losing a dominance battle, but ogres roll in one another's entrails after winning a dominance battle.

The two of them collided, shoulder to broad muscled shoulder, with a thump heard down the street, not unlike a small meteor colliding with a planetary body. Then, just when blades should have been drawn, both parties seemed to remember themselves and start reciting, as though from a script, starting with the more scarred, one-eyed ogre. "Me walking here!"

"Me walking here!" the other replied.

One-eye bellowed back, "Me walking!"

"ME WALKING!" At a deafening volume, they roared in one another's faces, and at any second there was going to be blood, but then somehow, miraculously, it did not come to pass. They were by each other and carrying on along their merry way. Turning to shout back over their shoulders. "Me was walking there!"

"Me was too!"

One-eye pointed to a side street. "Me walking over here now!"

With surprising enthusiasm, his one-time enemy cheered him on. "Keep walking!"

For the longest moment, the adventurers were silent, gawking open-mouthed at the whole display. Then, finally, Wyn managed to open and shut their mouth enough times to form the word, "Remarkable."

Rhine leaned over to Ildrit in confusion, as if they were watching a play together and had come upon an improbable twist in the tale. "Nobody died?"

The ogre nodded firmly. "Civilized."

There was no dangerous edge to Wyn's voice. There never was. "And I take it you're the one responsible for civilizing them?"

"Me do what me can."

How austere! He isn't even claiming credit for this impossible task.

Ig was unfamiliar with the term. "Oz tear?"

The ogre dipped an imaginary hat at the kobold. "Why, thanking you kindly, me good man."

With no better idea of how to respond, Ig dipped me in turn.

The ogre raised a hand, and almost immediately a more traditionally attired ogre lunged forwards out of the shadowy alley between two of the leaning highrises with a vague air of panic lingering around him. "Grubbly Dave, please be showing me honorary guests around the city. Me have some meetings this afternoon, but would like to . . ." He glanced across to find that the ogre had extracted a notebook from under his loincloth and was attempting to write everything being said down. Something that probably would have been more effective if the quill he'd plucked from behind his ear had any ink in it, and was not, in fact, just a feather. "Is you listening, Dave?"

Grubbly Dave bolted upright. "Yes, boss, sir."

"Bringulate them to the Mayoralty once you done." The suit ogre sighed.

"The what, boss, sir?"

If I had not performed the particular action myself so many times, I likely would not have recognized the bridge of the nose pinch being used to fend off an impending stupidity-induced headache that the ogre in the suit was now engaged in. He had to lift his little glasses up to slip his gigantic fingers underneath, and ogre noses, while bulbous in other ways, don't tend to have much in the way of a bridge. Even when broken repeatedly. "Me house."

Dave bobbed like a nervous duckling in a crocodile-infested pond. "Yes, boss, sir."

"Very goodly," he said in a tone that strongly suggested that nothing good had ever or would ever occur from that moment until the heat death of the universe. "Me look forward to speaking with you after youse have seen the wonders of ogre civilization."

And with that, he set off briskly. And we were left alone with Grubbly Dave, who was staring after his master with the same expression of amazement as the rest of us.

Ildrit risked asking this other ogre a question. "Who was that?"

"King Ron." The hulking ogre flinched. "Sorry, Mayor Ron."

"Ron," Ildrit repeated back.

"Yeah."

Rhine deflated ever so slightly. "I expected something more, for some reason."

"Sour Ron, we calls him."

Wyn nodded. "Because he has no joy in him."

"Yeah." Grubbly Dave nodded along. "Good at king stuff though. Look at this place."

"It is quite something," Rhine carefully replied.

We moved off, trailing after Dave for a lack of any better direction to head. Still securely under the protective aegis of the laws of civilization, backed up by the violent might of enough ogres all operating in consensus that I kept catching myself checking for mind-controlling enchantments.

Surely all of this couldn't have just been the work of an ogre?

"So this bit is . . ." He flicked back through his notebook to where there were some illegible blobs, presumably made with an actual pen rather than something pulled raw from the rear end of some unfortunate goose. "Downtown. Over there's uptown. Where Ron lives with all the other ones what has gone civilized. Down that way's the Old Town, where you can sample traditional orc queasy. Then there's the Arse N' All, what the fires are lit under. And the Financial District."

Ildrit mouthed his way through the word arsenal, as Rhine's beautiful brows scrunched together in a most adorable way. "Financial district?"

"Yeah," Dave agreed.

"What's that?" Rhine pried.

"Dunno, Sour Ron hasn't found the right book to read that bit yet." That seemed to jog Dave's memory of what he was meant to be doing, at least. "You lot got any books? We's meant to tax them all from you and give 'em to the boss."

"Take them?" Ildrit stiffened at the prospect of being robbed, even though I'm fairly confident that the only time the man was happy to see a book was hanging on a nail in an outhouse.

"No. Tax," Grubbly Dave explained with relish. "That's the kind of taking other people's stuff that isn't yours without asking that's legal."

While my companions may not have been aware of it, adventurers actually pay considerably more tax on their income than everyone else. One would have thought that being violent folks of no fixed address would have helped them to avoid the tender ministrations of customs and revenues officers the world around, but in fact, it turned out that when you have a whole subset of people perpetually flush with freshly found tomb gold who had no idea of the actual value of things outside of their weird little adventuring world, you could more or less charge them whatever you pleased for your goods and services. Inns, armorers, and houses of ill repute all offer substantial discounts for brave adventurers, but mysteriously, they all underwent drastic price increases mere moments before the adventurers arrived, resulting in them still paying at least double what the regulars had to fork over even with the discount. Quite tragic really. And of course, once a bunch of adventurers have swept through the town, you barely have enough time to get your trousers back on before the tax collectors arrive with wide grins and even wider sacks.

As to the matter of taxing wizards, it has always been a subject of lighthearted frivolity between institutions of arcane learning and their local governments. It isn't possible to put a price on education, say the wizards. Then explain your tuition fees, say the government. Then, once everyone has agreed that there is perhaps some price that could be attached to education, it all becomes rather granular, trying to determine which particular pieces of knowledge being shared are worth what, with the educators having to perform their jobs busily, explaining to the taxation officials all the details of what they teach, so that its value can be evaluated. After which, of course, with the value of that education now set in stone, they would request precisely that amount from the taxation officials, generally considerably more than the tax bill would have come to, and the whole thing would be called off.

That, or the wizards cut out the middle steps and jump straight to turning any tax collectors into newts. It does not take long before the economics of caring for a vast collection of newts and training new tax officials becomes more expensive than simply writing off any imaginary debt attached to any given wizard.

Wyn's eyes narrowed slightly as we came into a new region of the city and the sooty expanse of the Arsenal came into sight. All the charcoal being made out in the forest was being shipped here, into the vast furnaces operating everywhere the eye turned. "I'm afraid that we have little in the way of reading materials."

"What?" Dave had to raise his voice to be heard over the thundering hammers of the smiths, though I suspect it was the verbose response that was causing more trouble than the volume it had been spoken at.

Up until now in our adventures together, I had been acting as a go-between for Ig, explaining things from the real world in terms that the profoundly stupid could understand. Well, now finally it was his turn to shine, doing the opposite. "No books."

"None?" Dave squinted at Rhine, as though she might have had a small library stuffed down her breastplate.

Alright, it was admittedly possible, but it would have had to be a very tight selection of abridged volumes at best. Rhinolyta shrugged her shoulders. "I don't know how to read."

"What about you, Big Man?"

It took Ig a moment to grasp that he was being spoken to. A moment longer to recognize that a joke was being made and to blart out a laugh.

Then finally, after that goose-like response, he managed to reply, "Me don't even have paper."

Grubbly Dave's vast shoulders couldn't really slump, as such, being underpinned by such a dense and complex layer of muscles, but he did seem to droop ever so slightly. "Boss likes new books."

"Your boss seems like a real interesting guy." Ildrit sauntered up to the ogre and was about to throw an arm around the man's shoulders before realizing the myriad reasons that wouldn't work, other than the fact he'd need a stepladder. But to his credit he still maintained that jovial attitude. "What can you tell us about him?"

"Sour Ron is the best boss we ever had," he replied out of some sort of flinching instinct for self-preservation that reminded me entirely too much of Ig. "He has showed us the wonders of civilization and we is all grateful."

That second part sounded like it had been learned by rote too.

"For a thing to provoke wonder, it must be beautiful, and there is no beauty in this place," Wyn replied.

With her background living in some hidden kingdom of ladies only, it sometimes seemed like Rhine wasn't quite as street-smart or . . . dungeon-smart as the other two adventurers, but in this case, she was flinching just as much as Ildrit as Wyn called this ogre's home ugly.

I don't even believe that the place was particularly ugly—for something to be ugly, it would have required some effort being made to give it an appearance. The entire city had been built exclusively around the principles of functionality. Once a roof held out rain, no more work was done. Once a floor held someone's weight, no more work was done. Even the vast city walls, in the hands of a more aesthetically inclined leader, might have been decorated with blood or skulls or tribal symbols, while here they were blank.

"He made it so we's all work together for the greater good." There was a turn of phrase that could make anyone who'd ever read a history book flinch. "And we isn't murdering each other and stuff no more neither. Because that is Wrong."

He definitely enunciated a capital letter at the beginning of the word Wrong. The way that a child first encountering the concept of morality would. I wasn't actually certain that giving ogres morals was a bad idea, in the abstract, but I had my suspicions that they were going to have morals in a particularly ogrish way. Which was to say, someone would be burning at the stake for using the wrong spoon at dinner fairly soon.

I'd have to go over etiquette with Ig if we were invited for a meal.

"And did he happen to mention why he is doing all of this?" Ildrit pried.

"You littles has everything. We's stuck outside, looking for scraps. Ron says, we want a share, we got to deserve a share, got to act like you littles. Got to be civilized"—he said the word with the same hint of venom that Wyn inflected it with—"if we want what you's got."

"So he intends for ogres to assimilate into human culture?" Wyn's disgust oozed out of their every pore.

Dave laughed. Ogres have very good laughs, starting low in the stomach and rumbling up from there. Usually you only get to hear it briefly before something sharp intersects with you, but this time we got to bear witness to the entirety of it.

"Nah, mate, he wants us to be ogres, but like, posh. With fancy words." He pointed at one of the signs dangling from the side of one of the manufactories. A swinging piece of weather-bent plank that someone had drawn a crude representation of a hammer on in what I could only hope was not blood. "Sent boys to learn human stuff, so they can do it ogre style."

"The artist . . ." Rhine trailed off when she realized the trouble she was about to step in. Killing ogres outside of New Orc might still have been legal for ogres, but it was a fair bet the rules were going to be different for us. Luckily for us, Grubbly Dave was as astute a listener as he was handsome.

"Wrote them letters, telling littles not to stab 'em on account of 'em being super smart and good ogres what will learn and not squish 'em for giggles."

As far as apprenticeship planning went, it wasn't the worst I'd ever heard. Send an ogre off with a letter like that and it might very well come home with a trade. I could imagine many a carpenter's yard would be happy to have a massively strong apprentice to do the heavy lifting, even without the apprenticeship fee. And your average peasant would likely be as flabbergasted to be presented with a letter as any given ogre.

"And has there been a great uptake of this program among ogre kind?" Wyn was not sneering. Elves are too austere for sneering. "A vast number of you volunteering to improve yourselves?"

Dave paused in his ambling to tackle the puzzle of that sentence. "What volunteering mean?"

Wyn gave a thin-lipped smile at having their suspicions confirmed.

Rhine and Dave went back and forth for the remainder of our tour, with her trying to explain volunteering, free will, choice, and a variety of other complex subjects of that sort in a sufficiently monosyllabic way that the ogre might grasp the concepts. By the end of that, she was frustrated, he was more confused than ever, and it was well past noon.

A whole morning spent in the company of ogres, with not a drop of blood spilled. It was nothing short of a miracle.

CHAPTER FIFTEEN

AN OFFER YOU CANNOT REFUSE

With the tour concluded, we arrived at the Mayoralty uptown just as the dinner bell was ringing. Trying not to assume that we were going to be the main course, we made our way inside, parting with dear Dave at the door, as he clearly did not meet the dress code.

Inside there were other ogres dressed in costumes. The butler ogre in particular took several looks over to parse, but in comparison to the maids' uniforms, his unnecessary monocle and drawn-on hair were only mildly traumatic.

It was the only building in the entirety of New Orc that looked finished in any way. There were some unfortunately thick-fingered weaver's first attempts at rugs strewn across the floors in a slapdash manner, there were what I at first mistook for giant versions of children's finger-painting pictures of random objects from the world nailed to the walls, and the furniture looked as though serious attempts had been made at various items without any real understanding of their purpose.

The ottoman in particular looked as though it may have started barking at any moment.

We were placed in seats around a dining table that had clearly been crafted for considerably more voluminous posteriors, doubly so for poor Ig, and then, finally, given a moment's peace.

Rhine was the first to break the silence. "This is so weird."

Wyn may not have used the same word, but they conceded their agreement. "A truly bizarre turn."

"Easy fix at least." Ildrit had been lost in his own thoughts throughout the entire tour, so it was nice to know that he was still in there somewhere. "Ogres are hierarchical. They follow whoever is strongest. We take the head off the snake and escape in the chaos."

That brought the pre-dining conversation to a stilted halt again abruptly. With a quick glance around to make sure none of the servants had come back, Rhine whispered, "Kill Ron?"

Ildrit shrugged, reaching for a clunky goblet that was sadly empty of wine. Though on reflection, I wasn't sure I'd like to taste an ogre's idea of a good vintage. "Seems like the right thing to do."

"But . . . why?"

That question seemed to stymie both Ildrit and Wyn for a moment. "Because he's an ogre? With a giant army of ogres? It's just a matter of time before they attack somewhere."

"But is it though? This all seems like the opposite. It's like they're trying to stop being monsters . . . Surely that's a good thing? Surely this is what we want? No more monsters."

"If that is what's happening—and it isn't—no more monsters would put us out of business."

Rhine rolled her eyes. "Don't be silly. You don't really care more about making gold than about protecting people. If you did, you wouldn't be an adventurer."

That seemed to surprise Ildrit into silence long enough for someone else to get a word in edgewise. Sadly the first one to do so was Ig. "Me think we should be friends."

Personally, I could not have disagreed more. The ogres were one minor mishap away from a complete societal collapse, that would likely spill over into gruesome destruction for everyone in the surrounding area, and I wanted away from it as quickly as possible. Unfortunately, I could no longer say so without contradicting Ig, or . . . myself . . . Life was easier when I only had my own brain and mouth to contend with.

Regardless, I couldn't throw in with Ildrit's assassination plot, as it seemed the most likely course to set off said societal collapse, with the full weight of the collapsing society aimed to land directly on top of us. So I supposed that Ig and Rhine's pro-ogre policy was the one I'd have to support at present.

I had until now fully expected Wyn to fall in line with the kobold and the maiden, what with the whole debate as to the nature of what made a monster with Ildrit earlier, but it seemed that I did not quite have the elf's measure yet. "Ogres do not have friends; they have victims in waiting."

Ildrit nodded his agreement. "This is going to turn to fighting sooner or later, and I'd rather hit first while we have the chance to make it count."

Ig and I unanimously agreed that given the choice between sooner or later, we'd prefer later, actually, and he had just opened up his little yapper to say so when the door to the room swung open and Sour Ron and his entourage marched in.

There was Ron himself, still resplendently dull in his suit, a white mound that resolved itself into an ogre in a chef's uniform, and a third, even larger ogre in a chef's uniform, carrying a cleaver as big as Ildrit's terribly impressive evil dark sword. The first chef had a tureen of soup clasped between his hands, and an expression of eye-bulging agony as it seemed that in his civilization education, they had foregone the section about oven gloves.

With a sigh of relief, the chef dropped the hulking metal can onto the table, grumbling off back towards the kitchen. "Me hates that part."

Ignoring the other ogres entirely, Ron had taken a seat at the head of the table and now clapped his hands together. "How is you findulating New Orc City, friends?"

Were he capable of a smile, I suspect that would have come across as almost jovial, but without it, everything he said came with the sense that he'd rather be dead than talking to us. Or that he'd rather we were all dead, which would at least be more in keeping with the usual ogrish behavior.

"Truly remarkable," Wyn replied smoothly.

Rhine seemed a little more capable of genuine praise, though the possibility she was merely using the conversation as a pretext to continue the argument from earlier could not be denied. "It is amazing how much you've been able to achieve. To take ogres from being savage monsters and turn them into citizens, with their own homes and jobs. To make it so they're no longer a danger to the world. It is more than remarkable. It's amazing."

Ildrit placed his palms down on the table. "Only if it sticks. If they go right back to . . ." He glanced at Rhine, and internally corrected the next word before it came out. ". . . murderhumping everything the second they're out of his sight, what difference does a delay make?"

"My boys go where I tell them." I think it would have been less unsettling if Ron were to sound angry; instead he mostly came across as bored. "New Orc Militia isn't out . . . murderhumping?"

Being so short, Ig was well situated to see exactly what was happening on the tabletop, and very little much higher than that. His nose actually rested on the table an inch from where the ogre chef was laying out bowls. As such, he was looking right across at Ildrit's hands on the table as the knuckles began to turn white. Ildrit was obviously trying to match the ogre's calm demeanor, but neither I nor Ig expected him to have much success. "Well, that isn't entirely correct, now is it. Because we've already seen them out there doing just that."

"You is referating to the squad I sent to check on me artist laureate," Ron conceded. "Half them boys died, half got magicked. Ran all the way back home."

It felt rather like we had been prancing along through a field of wildflowers only to realize our foot wasn't coming down on soft moss, but a bear trap.

Sour Ron pointed to each of the adventurers in turn. "You isn't a wizard, elf isn't a wizard, girl isn't a wizard. Leaves one."

Ig had been trying to follow this ogre's mental calculus. "Me?"

Ron settled back in his seat looking self-satisfied, if not content. "Kobold is a wizard."

"He mean me?" Ig still hadn't caught up.

Yes, Ig. There aren't any other kobolds here.

Ig's jaw dropped. "How he know me am wizard?"

Sour Ron brushed an imaginary piece of lint from his sleeve. "Process of elimination."

"And the hat," Rhine added.

Ildrit also had to admit, "The hat is a big giveaway."

"Maybe me just like hats!" Ig cried, his terror already mounting.

"When I sent ogres to Arpanpholigon to study magic, they says lesser races don't have the brains for it. Lesser races. They says ogres are too dumb for it." Ron was leaning forwards now, his eyes locked on Ig, and Ig beginning to squirm at being the center of attention. "Kobolds is dumber than ogres. Kobolds is dumber than rocks."

Ig snatched on that train of thought with both hands, and hoped that his arms wouldn't be torn from the sockets. "Can't be a wizard then."

For all the attention Ron was giving Ig, it was almost impressive how thoroughly he seemed capable of ignoring everything he said. "But this one, he a wizard. Means he knows wizard secrets. Means . . . he can teach them."

I tried to snatch control of his mouth from Ig before he could jam his foot in there, but I was too late. "Sorry, not taking apprentices right now, going through own personal stuff."

Ildrit trying to be polite was a rare sort of entertainment. There were few people in the world, ogres included, who could make every little politeness seem so begrudging. "However it may appear to you, rest assured, our companion is no kobold."

"Or wizard," Ig chirped again, desperately hoping anyone might buy it.

"He labors under a curse," Wyn added. "One that has changed his appearance."

Ron peered at Ig, considering what had been said, then arrived at his own conclusion. "Me see kobold wizard, can teach me how to magic."

Wyn's eyes narrowed. "And what precisely would you need magic for?"

Sour Ron's entire name was predicated upon how utterly devoid of joy he was. His inability to find delight in the little things, or indeed the big things. So when I say that he was overtaken with an even more grim and dour attitude now, you must understand that it was a truly fearful sight. "Long as littles have something we don't, they's going to thinkify they's better than us. They ain't. And we's going to show 'em that. We's got a city and books and magic. Same as 'em. They needs to take us serious."

"You are giant, rampaging murder monsters, and you're concerned that people aren't taking you seriously?" Ildrit scoffed. "I can assure you, everyone takes the ogre menace extremely seriously."

"They treats us like we is animals. Like what we says don't matter." Ron settled back in his seat and steepled his fingers. "Me making it matter. Me making them listen. Ogres is going to be civilized, sovereign nation. The Badlands be our homeland. New Orc be our capital."

Wyn came close to hissing. "You will be inviting every people that ogres have ever harmed to wage war upon you if you declare yourselves so. And there is no nation that has not felt the pang of predation by your kin."

The thick ogre fingers, previously steepled, now interlocked, the huge, powerful hands squeezing one another until the knuckles within popped. "We is going to do diplomacy to them."

"That's why half this city is a forge," Rhine realized aloud. "He's arming for the war he knows he's about to create."

"We don't want fight nobody," Ron reassured her. "Civilized people talk. If they don't want to talk instead of fight, they ain't civilized."

"Justifying whatever violence you choose to inflict upon them." Wyn's usually placid face had become truly emotionless now, as it did when they were fighting.

"They'll learn not to hit. Just like the ogres did." Ron shrugged, proving the quality of the tailoring on that suit when it didn't immediately burst at every seam. "Just takes a few lessons."

"Which is why he needs wizards, of course. Arpanpholigon is the nearest city, a city renowned for its magic. The one craft he hasn't stolen from its creators. He's getting ready to go to war with them as soon as they find out the ogres are out here, but he lacks the vital weapon required to match their strength." Ildrit's eyes looked a little glazed over by the enormity of it all. "By the seven hecks, this isn't a city, it's the staging ground for an invasion."

"Actuality, is a city," Ron corrected. "In the name. New Orc City."

The weight of our mutual realization had brought the whole conversation to a grinding halt. Except for Ildrit, of course. There was a man all too used to damning revelations. For us, this was a huge event; for him, it was just another day ending in y. "So what do you want from us?"

Ron uncrunched his knuckles and settled back down. "All me wants is to talk. Like we is all civilized peoples."

"We're talking," Ildrit snapped. "What else do you want?"

Without missing a beat, Ron pointed to Ig. "The wizard."

Now, I must admit, up until this point I had suspected that this was the direction things were going to go, and I had not piped up or intervened in any way because I retained a degree of ambivalence about the entire situation.

On the one hand, this ogre was clearly a terrible tyrant, intent upon waging genocidal war on any who would not kowtow to his regime. On the other hand, if he were to wear me, I would be guaranteed my vengeance against whosoever slew me and consigned my soul to hat-based purgatory.

Sneaking into the city of Arpanpholigon as a kobold, trying to track down my killer, trying to bring them to some semblance of justice, these were all going to be arduous tasks, even if I did somehow manage to train Ig to use magic. Rolling in atop an invading army that would already have a vested interest in killing most of the wealthy and powerful of the city would have made matters considerably easier.

There was something of an ethical quandary about teaching a megalomaniac how to use magic just so that I could use him as a cat's-paw in a conflict with some shadowy opponent, but given I was a murder victim, I immediately had some sort of moral high ground to begin from.

I could do considerably worse than to acquire Ron as an ally, or even a new host. I would not be certain that I could mentally dominate him the way that I could Ig, but I was quite accustomed to manipulating others with markedly more skill than was required to squeeze obedience from a kobold. And ultimately, was it really so terrible if I allowed all the citizens of Arpanpholigon to die? They had let me die. Surely it would have been fair play, if anything. Not a one of them had leapt in the way of the crossbow bolt or knocked the poisoned chalice from my hands, and at least some of them must have had some opportunity to.

Ildrit's immediate response prevented me from answering for myself. "No."

"No? Just no?" Ron's sour expression became darker. The bulbous humps below his forehead that probably constituted a brow, minus the hair, were drawn down, casting shadows over his face. "That's not very civilized. Civilized folks be all about compromisation."

"You can't have him," Rhine piped up, filling Ig's little heart with joy. "He's a person, not a trinket to be traded."

"Looks trinket sized." Ron sneered.

Ildrit pressed on. "You cannot have the wizard; we are on a quest to rid him of his curse."

Ron sought clarification. "The curse that made him a kobold?"

Wyn nodded. "The very same."

Once again, it seemed an opportune moment for a sinister smile, and Ron just couldn't muster it. "No."

Rhine gawked at him. "Excuse me?"

"Wizard belongs to me now. Taxing him." Ron only had eyes for Ig—throughout all of this conversation, his gaze had not turned away, even as the adventurers prickled with anger at his dismissal of them. "You all be free to go. Or stay. Opera house opens tonight. Should be a very good show."

Ig finally found the gumption to pipe up. "And what if me no want teach magic?"

Ron cracked his knuckles. "We persuade you."

Ig seemed to weigh this option for a moment. "What if me no want be persuaded?"

Ron settled back in his chair, emanating smugness from every pore. "Then you teach ogres magic."

Ig seemed to consider this too as I frantically tried to make myself heard.

There are worse things than teaching the tragically stupid to do magic, Ig. Trust me. I think that we should give this offer serious consideration.

But Ig did not give it serious consideration. He answered immediately, speaking not to Ron, but Ildrit. "Me change my vote, chop ogre's head off."

"Finally!" The warrior sprang to his feet, yanking the black blade Massacrox or whatever it was called from its sheath. "Come taste the blade of democratically decided death!"

Which was about the moment that the ogre chef we had all more or less forgotten about grabbed Ig from behind and hoisted him from his chair. Typically, this would not have been a huge issue—the kobold was extremely accustomed to being manhandled by this point in his life—but unfortunately, in the process of the scuffle, I was knocked off his head.

While I was atop nothing there was only silence and darkness. The borders of my universe snapped tight against the outer brim of my form. Time lost all meaning as I tumbled through the air. It could have been for the breadth of a breath, or it could have been ten thousand years, and I would have perceived it in precisely the same way.

Then, abruptly, awareness came back. I was fat and full and heavy. To move a single part of this new body would have been arduous, and I would have sloshed with the movement, the steaming hot fluid within me shifting around.

Oh dear gods, I'm the soup tureen.

What can be said of the senses of a soup tureen? It had no eyes, no ears, only mass and weight. I could feel both of those shifting as the table was knocked about. I could almost hear, with the vibrations of battle cries in my internal lake of soup, but more specific awareness eluded me at first.

Given that my new perch was possessed of no mind of its own, I couldn't achieve much in the way of complex thought while atop it, but I could swivel, trying to point the front of my hat self in the direction of the various players in the cacophony of violence occurring just outside my ability to perceive.

There was definitely fighting going on. Shouting too. And I suspected more ogres had come into the room than had been present previously. Though telling ogre from adventurer was something of a struggle in my current predicament.

That was, at least, until I realized that the soup within me tremored not only with the shaking of the air and the table, but also with terror. When I faced an ogre, the soup knew its apex predator was there, and it began to quiver and bubble within me.

Whatever else I may be accused of in the years to come, no matter how my legend may have been sullied by the words of others, know this: when I was in the presence of frightened soup, I gave it recourse for revenge. Raising my brim like a puckered lip, I took aim at the nearest ogre and then spat.

A stream of scalding soup fired forth from the tureen I had become.

In the vibrations that returned, I could feel the screams of the soup's ogre nemesis learning to fear and respect liquid lunch options the hard way.

We spun, this way and that, me and the tureen below. Firing blast after blast of vegetable broth into the eyes of our oppressors. No longer would soup fear the spoon. No longer would soup fear the mouth. Now let the eaters be the ones who were afraid. Now let the ogres cower at the might and majesty of our projected wrath!

I was snatched back off the top of the soup tureen, still dripping no small quantity of its contents from my rim, and wedged back down on the more familiar shape of Ig's head.

"Me got you!"

I had never expected relief to be the emotion I felt when I was forced to touch Ig's waxy scalp, but here we were. You lived and learned.

What did I miss?

As Ig babbled more or less to himself, I used his eyes to take in the scene. The seats had been more or less matchsticked. Six dead ogres, most of them soup-blinded before the lethal blows had been delivered, but no sign of Sour Ron among their number.

". . .and then they was shouting and me . . ."

Ig. Where is the ogre leader?"

"He runned aways when you souped his suit."

In an instant, Ig was snatched from his feet once more, and it was as much luck as anything else that kept me intact atop his head as Ildrit pulled him into a bear hug. "That was a spectacular showing, friend."

"Weh?"

He thinks you were responsible for the soup artillery.

"Oh."

Do not disabuse him of this notion, please. When he likes us, he is less likely to murder us.

"Agh." The last noise was not one of confusion, but of crackling ribs as Ildrit's expression of affection became a little too intense for kobold physiology to hold up to. Realizing his mistake, Ildrit dropped Ig, right into the waiting arms of Rhine.

She smiled down at him; he tried to smile up at her. It would almost have been sweet if he weren't a horrid little gremlin of a creature. "Well done!"

"No problemso," he replied. Ig trying to play it cool was somewhat akin to a hypnotic serpent. You wanted to look away, but it kept drawing you back in. As though he had traveled so far from charisma that he had reached it again from the other side. Mesmerizing.

The tureen that I had been was knocked to the floor as Wyn flipped the table onto its side, and I felt a brief pang of paternal sorrow for the soup within. Then both the elf and Ildrit set their shoulders to the substantial piece of furniture and shoved it across to barricade the door and stop the onslaught of more ogres.

"I do not suppose that you have some arcane means of escape about you as well, wizard?" Wyn was the only one who didn't seem overly impressed with the soup shooting. Perhaps because he'd seen the same trick done a few centuries back.

"Me got nothing," Ig replied before I could formulate any sort of witticism.

"Then it seems we have made the gravest of all possible mistakes, striking at the ogre king and failing to secure the killing blow." Wyn didn't sound particularly upset, mostly just like they were accepting the inevitable.

The table rocked as the ogres on the other side pounded against the door.

Rhine stood back from it and tried to assess the situation. Needless to say, it was not looking pretty. "We've got to get out of town; every ogre in New Orc is going to be after us."

"How? We're bang slap in the middle of their city." Wyn hadn't sounded too upset, but Ildrit more than made up for it. "How are we getting out of this alive?"

There are instincts deeply rooted in the kobold mind, the very reason that the species has survived when it thinks at a speed comparable to trees, and in this situation Ig's instincts told him to run, and then run, and then run some more.

He burst through the door into the kitchen in a blind panic, briefly comprehended the absence of any additional ogres, and then bolted on through the next open door that he could find. This led him into a cupboard, where his instincts stalled for a moment. It was a small, dark hole. Ideal for kobolds. Perfect place to hide. But the manic energy that had already been driving him fired him back out of the cupboard like a cannon, scattering pots as he went and skidding across the room with a foot stuck in one particularly ill-fitting saucepan. There was a door into the kitchen that we would need to barricade posthaste before the ogres remembered it. I saw it whip by briefly during one of Ig's pirouettes.

Then he was at the stove, and the front door of that was also hanging open. Instincts that would have been for self-preservation in your average kobold's life were now actively working against us.

Ig, no!

But he was too terrified to even hear as he went barreling on towards the opening into warm darkness. Some little lizard part of his brain was screaming to him that this was safety. The larger part of his brain, which is to say, me, was screaming at him to stop before he broiled himself.

Ig! Fire! Fire bad!

He was already in mid-leap when my words penetrated the thickness of his skull. He let out a little yip, flung his hands forward, and pushed with all of the Quintessence that he had in his body while chittering and gibbering in terror.

I suspect it was the gibber-chittering that caused the problem. It may have been inane nonsense sounds in our tongue, but in the Archaic language of the Arcane Archons—a vast and complex language made up of thousands upon thousands of individual syllable and letter combinations with entirely different effects depending upon tone and enunciation—there may have been some brief moments when there was a degree of crossover.

As to the element that he was invoking at the time by focusing all of his attentions on it, I believe it was fair to say that for the first time since I had met him, Ig was entirely focused upon the fire in front of him. And while fire is not an element if you have an understanding of elements that goes beyond elementary school education, it can be closely associated with several, in particular Sulfur.

The Quintessence flooded from his body, shaped by his words and thoughts into a massive, reeking cloud of rotten-egg-smelling fumes, which in turn flooded across the room and into the vast cast-iron oven that our dinner had been in the process of being prepared in.

At this point, there was an elemental reaction.

Everything turned white.

The boom left Ig's ears dead and ringing, stripped him of what little body hair he had on the forward-facing side, and flung him back across the room to land in the dining chamber.

For a moment, as he lay there with the adventurers staring down at him and mouthing words of panic, I truly thought that he was dead, even the most rudimentary functions of his pathetic mind turned off by his proximity to the explosion. Then Rhine reached down to cup his scalded cheek and his heart thumped back into action again. "Ow."

She said something, presumably something sweet and heartwarming that Ig couldn't hear. Ildrit also mouthed his way through some presumably clever quip about roasted kobolds. Wyn, as the only sensible one in the group, had traversed to the smoldering chaos of the kitchen and peered inside before calling back and gesturing for the others to follow.

Ig was scooped up by the collar and dangled at Ildrit's hip as they charged off, giving him a wonderful view of the slightly scalded dining room as the ogres burst through the barricade en masse. His little feet began to cycle as though he could run away in midair.

Where there had been a kitchen, there was now soot. Where there had been an oven, there was now a hole and some shrapnel. Ildrit dropped Ig to the floor and stared down at him in amazement, as I in turn stared out in awe at the destruction that his clumsy mumbling had wrought.

The rear half of the Mayoralty was now unsupported by ground-floor walls, and the upper floors were already beginning to tilt inevitably downwards towards total collapse. The building behind the Mayoralty had also suffered a similar fate.

Presumably. It was possible that the lower level of that building had simply vanished of its own accord, dumping the second floor onto the ground, but judging by the flames licking up that now grounded floor, I'd make some assumptions as to Ig's guilt.

The buildings to either side of that one didn't look much better either. It was almost as though building everything out of wood and placing it all incredibly close to everything else was bad city planning. Of course, Ron had looked at human designs and optimized them using his superior ogre intelligence. After all, you only had to worry about fires if people made mistakes, and nobody would dare to make a mistake when he was in charge.

He was so smart he had actually managed to ascend to a new plateau of stupidity.

Ig's hearing was starting to come back now, mostly as a very high-pitched ringing in his ears as the adventurers leapt from the burning building before it collapsed and he followed, tumbling end over end to land spine first on the fence separating the Mayoralty from the next house over. If anything, it would improve his posture, assuming that he could still walk.

Ildrit kindly assisted by hoisting him up by the scruff of his neck once more, so we didn't have to worry overmuch about spinal damage just yet. Ig was in a great deal of pain, of course, but right now I couldn't really concern myself with it. Being in a great deal of pain meant that he was still alive, and that was the important thing at the moment.

Faint snippets of conversation were making it through the shrill trilling in Ig's ears now. Wyn's perpetual calm. "... whole city is going to burn down ..."

Ildrit's gruff complaining. "... imbecilic ogres ..."

"... get out of here alive ..." Rhinolyta, Ig's beloved.

There was a catastrophic smashing sound from behind us as the Mayoralty toppled, the flames already licking up to consume its higher floors now spreading to the building next door as it impacted against it, setting the whole thing rocking on its apparently absent foundations. They had built their houses out of sticks and now they were all going to come tumbling down.

One by one the ogre's houses toppled into the next, a vast, burning domino effect sweeping through their alleged uptown. Each time one of them collapsed, a pyroclastic cloud was thrown up, embers raining down on all of the other wooden houses around it. The fire spread so swiftly that if I had not known better, I would have said it was magic.

"Oh, you thought they were mad before." Ildrit laughed to himself as another boom of a collapsing building swept over New Orc City. The high-pitched whine in Ig's ears had finally abated, replaced only by the high-pitched whines that he himself was making each time he was jolted by a sudden change of direction as the adventurers sprinted.

Rounding a corner, we were confronted with a barricade of bodies. A mass of ogres, blocking our way. Fury was upon their faces, and many of them held improvised weapons from the trades that they had been forced into. For every baker with a rolling pin, there was a butcher with a cleaver and a candlestick maker with a heavy lump of pewter, partially shaped into its final form. We were grossly outnumbered.

Yet they did not charge. Rather, they stood their ground, paralyzed. They were trapped more surely than us, because while every instinct in their monstrous bodies was telling them to crush and kill, there was a higher directive that had been handed down to them. One of civilization. It had been forced on them as surely as their trades but with such threats of violence that they could not overcome it.

And so it was that, using my incredible intellect and the voice of Ig, I saved us all once more, by calling out with the specific combination of ogrish words that would see us through.

"I'm walking here!"

The ogres were taken aback, shocked and confused, presumably because Ig was not in fact walking, but being dangled ahead of Ildrit like a lantern. They were unmoved.

Pouring more of Ig's breath into a bellow, I decried to the ogres, "I said, I'm walking here!"

There was a ripple in the crowd, and seeing their opportunity, Wyn plunged in.

The ogres closed in tight behind them, hiding them from sight, but with a glance to one another for moral support, the other two adventurers plunged in behind the elf, all three beginning to bellow as they went, "I'm walking here!"

From up ahead, we could hear Wyn's progress. "I'm walking here!"

"I am trying to walk here," Rhine called out from our left flank.

The ogres closed back in around us, their massive porcine bodies pressing hard against our progress, but Ildrit set one shoulder to the task and drove on, parting the sweat-slick flesh and leather to make progress. In the distance now, muffled by the press of bodies, more buildings caught flame and collapsed, but still no organized response seemed to have been made. No order had gone out for our capture. We were outpacing the ogres' ability to think.

Of all the experiences I had endured since landing up in Ig's frail frame, I must admit that being pushed face-first into a load of sweaty ogres ranked near to the top of the list when it came to unpleasantness, but all the same, there could be no denying the success of our exodus thus far. Sure, Ig was smeared in foul, milky ogre sweat, but we had made such good progress that I could swear I saw light beginning to peek through the gaps in the forest of overly muscled bodies.

"Me walking here!" Ig bellowed once more, entirely on his own. And the solid wall of flesh before us parted, just enough for him to be wedged in and used to pry a path for Ildrit.

There was one unexpected benefit to our impromptu sweat bath. Quintessence flows through all living things, which is why druids are able to gather it so easily in their natural foci despite having all the mental discipline one would expect from people that go to the toilet in the woods, and ogres, despite their other less admirable qualities, are most assuredly living things. All of the Quintessence that Ig had poured out into the world in his little kitchen fire was now flowing back into him.

Nature abhors a vacuum. The more Quintessence that a wizard uses, the more rapidly it is drawn back into them, and the more that is drawn into them, the more their capacity to retain expands. In such close proximity to so many living things, Quintessence was positively rushing into Ig, restoring all that he had so clumsily spent.

Admittedly, this was rather like being excited about how quickly one was able to fill a thimble with water, but I was attempting to cling to the positives at present. If only so I would not have to think about the fact that an ogre nipple had just rubbed over my eyeball.

By the time that we emerged back into breathable air, Wyn and Rhine were already out, gasping and looking immensely traumatized by the whole experience. It was certainly not one that any of us were liable to forget in a hurry, at least without the heavy application of liquor.

The sky had gone dark. Smoke billowing up from the already-consumed uptown forming a vast black cloud over us and blotting out the sun. Embers carried up into that cloud by the rising heat raining down to set new buildings ablaze. Wyn had been entirely correct in their half-heard assumption: the whole city was going to burn.

Wyn cast a glance up at the rain of fire. "We should endeavor to be somewhere else as swiftly as possible."

"Agreed." Ildrit snapped a nod and dropped Ig to walk for himself once more.

His legs were a touch wobbly after the fence's cruel back-crack-attack, but he was able to stand, so I was considering that to be a win.

He wobbled and hobbled for a moment as the other three ran on, trailing behind at a time when being alone really wasn't going to be all that advantageous to us.

Perhaps you might go a little faster.

Ig, not usually inclined to ill will towards me even when I was driving him towards his doom, snapped back. "Me trying!"

It is just that Sour Ron and his little posse will be in pursuit of us, and most likely rather unhappy about the whole city-wide incineration situation.

There was a little simmering spark of anger in Ig's belly that I had hitherto been unaware of. "Me knows!"

Yet even as he became more and more irritated with me, I could not help but needle him on, as our adventurer bodyguards got farther and farther away. *Just a little turn of speed until we're out of . . .*

"Me is going as fast as me can!" Ig squealed, while simultaneously increasing his speed.

As you say. I'm sure you've definitely never gone faster.

He chirped, "Me is hurt!"

And I imagine that the ogres will give you a lovely backrub for setting their kingdom ablaze.

At this point one could definitely argue that I was bullying the poor kobold, but if it hadn't been for his repeated rash actions, I could have been comfortably nestled atop an ogre warlord instead of a kobold, commanding a legion to march on Arpanpholigon and exact my revenge. Besides, when he was riled, he moved faster. "That was accident!"

Once again, I'd strongly recommend that you pretend it was deliberate. Better you are thought of as puissant than clumsy by your allies.

So long as Ildrit thought that his repeated attempts to save Ig were resulting in their ongoing survival, he would continue saving Ig. If it were proven otherwise, I was not so certain. The whole matter of curses and moral guidance threw all of his actions into doubt, and I'd prefer that he maintained pragmatic reasons for not decapitating Ig alongside the ethical ones.

For instance, right now, he thought Ig had just annihilated half a city so that we could make our escape, which was presumably why he halted in his flight to glance back and realize that Ig, with his markedly shorter stride, was trailing behind. Also most likely why he had drawn his sword and come charging back towards Ig.

He made one final leap, just as Ig was catching up to him, and there was a clatter of steel from behind our collective head. The black blade Sliceyermush, or whatever it was called, had intersected with Ron's own staff of office. A large metal cudgel that even with ogrish strength I was amazed anyone could lift.

"I must be requesticating your returnify to my office, Mr. Wizard," Ron growled out, muscles straining against Ildrit's surprisingly strong parry.

"Me no want go with you thanks bye," Ig squeaked, bursting into another sprint.

At Ron's back, there were a few more besuited ogres, carrying weaponry that could not have been mistaken for anything else. Yet they kept on casting glances towards Ron instead of advancing. Even as he was doing his darndest to crush the life out of someone in front of them, they were scared of breaking his rules about violence in the city.

But they would work it out eventually. Even if an ogre's mind usually moved at a speed typically reserved for tectonic plates, they would work it out, and they would attack Ildrit, and with his weapon pinned between him and Sour Ron, there would be nothing he could do but die.

To me, that was an acceptable loss. He was already something of a dangerous wildcard, and the distance that he might buy us in death was probably going to be immensely valuable to us if Ig would just keep running. Why had he stopped running?

It was quite impossible for a kobold to grit their teeth, as no two teeth on the upper and lower jaws quite lined up, but Ig did his best. "Me no leave him."

He left you.

Had he been possessed of a chin, Ig would have stuck it out. "He came back."

You can learn from his mistakes.

"Me is a wizard." Ig tried to square shoulders that were never meant to be squared. "Me can do this."

I'm fairly confident that you cannot.

"Me is thinking of not Carbon," Ig announced, raising his hands.

Potassium?

"Me is thinking Potassium and me is going to do Goldy Fires of Goggy the Good."

Goggy . . . The Golden Flames of Galgalagrin the Great? Oh no.

"Me is." Ig's announcement broached no argument. And the fact that he was not running away meant that I didn't really have much in the way of a better option. "Gives me the word."

For a moment I dithered over whether or not I should in fact supply him with the word in Archaic that would have his desired effect.

The word in Archaic that you are seeking is "Fragor," but you absolutely will not succeed.

"Me is thinking of Potassium. Me is going to say that word. Me has Squintysuns."

Quintessence, you buffoon, good grief, are you getting more ridiculously stupid by the minute?! At best you're going to explode yourself. At worst you're going to . . .

He did not take the moment that I might have hoped to consider my words. Instead, he pointed with the index fingers of both hands at Sour Ron, who had forced Ildrit to his knees by this time. "***Fragor!***"

His second spell was precisely as successful as the first.

Hope is an odd thing. It can creep up on us in the most surprising of places, when we finally thought that it had lost our scent forever. His focus was entirely on Ron, no distractions to dissipate the spell. When I heard Ig perfectly pronouncing the word of Archaic while his mind was entirely full of the secondhand understanding of Potassium that I had bestowed upon him and I felt all of the

Quintessence flood out of his body, I had one genuine moment of hope. One moment where I could deceive myself into thinking that this useless little rat in a bathrobe could successfully perform a spell.

If I had a heart, it would have beat faster. If I had eyes, they would have widened. If I had a stomach, it would have flipped. But I was a hat, and had none of those things, so could only experience what felt like a slight tightening of my embroidery before I perceived the exact manner in which everything had gone horribly wrong.

Betwixt Ig's pointed fingers, a golden light coalesced, what should have been a bolt of golden flame ready to leap out and strike down our foe—and there was something there, something glowing and golden, but it did not burn, and it had an odd curvature to it.

Nonetheless, it was launched at the head of the ogre, who jerked up suddenly in surprise at its approach, opening his mouth to roar fury and vengeance at Ig for daring to use magic against him.

Then the banana shot right to the back of Sour Ron's throat, and he gagged.

It seemed that unexpected oral penetration was exactly the distraction that Ildrit needed to turn the tide, surging up, knocking the ogre's weapon aside, and delivering a powerful boot to his midsection.

Which in turn made Ron's jaws snap shut, trapping the banana inside even as he was trying to eject it.

Sour Ron was already turning a little blue as Ildrit made his escape, sprinting off as the rest of the ogres present finally seemed to realize that they were capable of movement. He swept Ig up under his arm as he passed, panting and gasping all the way, but still managing to squeeze out a little, "Nice one."

To my continuing dismay, Ig's endless litany of failures was once more being considered cleverness. I must admit, nobody would ever have expected to be bananaed, nor prepared any countermeasures against intrusive fruit, but that did not mean that a fireball to the face would not have been more effective in this case.

In the distance, Ron was receiving a round of slaps on the back trying to dislodge the banana, but from his watering eyes came forth a baleful stare. Pure unadulterated hatred.

It was my sincere hope that we never crossed paths again.

Regardless, from that point on we encountered little resistance from the ogres of New Orc on our way out of the city, probably because the majority of them were dealing with the massive city-wide fires and toppling buildings, and the remainder were desperately trying to remove a banana from a very angry wannabe gentleman.

CHAPTER SIXTEEN

NECROPOLIS NOW

There was very little in the way of adventurer banter for the rest of the day. Which was something of a shame because I could have done with a distraction. As it stood, I was left alone in Ig's head, feeling the warm glow of satisfaction that he had derived from "saving" his companions. When, in effect, he had completely failed to cast two different spells in catastrophically awful ways. Back in the kitchen, he had achieved what I'm going to politely refer to as a passing of gas, and on the streets of New Orc, he had managed to deliver an early dessert. Neither of these were acts of magic worthy of note. Neither were the spells that he should have cast, and when put into the context of his complete flubbing of the petrification spell, it was rapidly becoming a pattern.

I should not have been teaching a kobold magic.

Not for the moral reasons relating to arming simians, babies, and the otherwise mentally deficient, but because he was succeeding. Utter failure would have been preferable to the travesty that he was inflicting upon the High Art. The conjuration of fruits through magic is of course a possibility, but it should be an apple that grants eternal life, or a pomegranate that traps you for ten thousand years in the underworld. Not a banana.

Never a banana.

Despite the relative quiet, we seemed to be moving with some purpose again, rapidly clearing the stripped areas of the woods and delving back into cover soon after. We very well might have expected to have been intercepted by some of the ogre patrols, but it seemed that the sight of their homes ablaze distracted them somewhat, and those that we did catch sight of were in a full-on sprint back to New Orc. Presumably intending on putting out the fires with the sweat from their brows, given that I didn't see a single bucket anywhere in town.

I pondered for a moment, at the sight of all those ogres, whether they would choose to call it New Orc City for a third time, if they bothered to rebuild, or if this might have been the turning point when they shucked off the oppression of Sour Ron and made a go of it themselves.

Admittedly, them making a go of it themselves would involve roaming warbands slaughtering innocents wherever they found them, but at least they wouldn't be pretending to be civilized while they did it.

Night fell earlier than I would have expected, but still we trudged onwards, with Ig having been deposited back onto his own two feet once it was apparent that there was not going to be any pursuit. I suspect that Ig would rather have been carried everywhere, like the world's ugliest baby, but life was unkind, particularly to the world's ugliest babies.

Deep into the woods, I expected us to make camp, and judging from the way that Ig's stomach was attempting to digest itself, he expected some dinner, having missed out on the weaponized soup earlier.

"Maybe we be stopping soon?" Ig asked.

But Rhine was paying no attention at all. Her eyes were turned to the darkest shadows of the woods, where Ig could see nothing at all. So too were the eyes of Wyn and Ildrit now that Ig glanced over to them. All three were staring off into the distance with their mouths hanging ever so slightly open.

It had been a long day, I supposed. No reason to jump to any conclusions. Ig made another attempt. "We stop soon for sleeps, weh?"

Once more he was entirely ignored. While I personally felt that anyone in the world was well within their rights to completely ignore a kobold, and in particular this useless, wretched excuse for a waste of skin, it was out of character for the trio of adventurers, and as such, it concerned me.

Something is not right.

Ig nodded, as though I could see him, instead of seeing the world rocking up and down through his eyes. "They is magicked."

Oh, do us all a favor and close that vapid flap you call a mouth. You would not know mental domination if it slapped you in the face.

I was surprised at just how much of my vitriol towards the obnoxious little runt had just slipped out after me spending so much of my time and effort in the past few days desperately suppressing it, but I supposed that it was time for some sort of reckoning for this kobold.

He did not make it easy, of course. His jaw wobbled with upset and he sounded like he had tears in his eyes when he blubbed out, "Why is you being mean?"

Trying to keep my own voice sounding calm in his mind was something of a struggle, in truth. When really I just wanted to start screaming and never stop. *You just annihilated an entire city by accident because I have been trying to teach you magic; I believe that I am entitled to be a little upset.*

Ig waved one of his little paws. "They was bad."

Bad. Evil. Wicked.

"Yes!" Ig agreed. "Bad."

These are all words that I have heard applied to kobold-kind too. Do you believe that you are bad?

He was gobsmacked by this turn of events; his little muzzle literally fell open. "No! Me is good."

Yet there is no shortage of people in this world who would have seen you in your hole in the ground, surrounded by your kin, and set you aflame for the crime of being a kobold. What right have you to judge the goodness of an ogre?

Asking a kobold to present a cogent moral explanation for their actions was probably some form of cruel and unusual torture for the poor creatures, but to Ig's credit, he did at least make an attempt. "They is stabby."

As well they should be, after millennia of being shunned and sidelined. It is not the place of a wizard to judge all the world and divide it into the righteous and the wicked. Leave that to the priests.

His mouth flapped open and shut a few more times as he tried to gather his thoughts. All two of them. "But they was bad! They was trying to make me slave."

And what of the next city? When a single person crosses you in Arpanpholigon, will you scorch it down to its foundations too?!

"No!" Ig wailed in horror. "Because they is goods."

Just as the ogres believed themselves to be.

He dropped down onto his haunches and put his hands on his head, just below my rim, as though he feared his brain might explode out of his skull otherwise. "My is getting more confused."

Because things are not so simple, and the path of destruction and domination has no end. The moment that you set yourself above all others and make choices for them is the moment you cease to be a wizard, and begin to play at being a god.

"Maybe should be kobold god." Ig pouted, liplessly. "Lots of food and nices."

And from whom would you take the "food and nices" to give to your flock? Everything has its price, Ig. And the price you paid this day was in creating a legion of enemies. They will remember what you have done, and their children, and their children's children, and all shall loathe kobolds above all else, for it was a kobold that destroyed their homes, killed their families, brought all their hopes to ruin.

There was a screaming edge to his voice now. "My didn't do all that?!"

It may not have been your intent, but it is most assuredly what you did. So might I suggest that until we are more confident in your ability to use magic effectively, you stop trying it out at every opportunity? It has been frankly miraculous that you haven't destroyed us both so far.

"My was just trying to . . ." Ig's attempt at an explanation trailed off. I lived in his head, I knew exactly what he was thinking at any given moment, that was why I spent so much of my time in silence and boredom.

There is no trying in magic, there is success and there is death and nothing in between. Luck alone has preserved you thus far, and I'd wager you've drunk from that cup well past the point of emptying it.

For a moment, Ig tottered on the precipice of rebellion. Of telling me, his master, to shove all of my hard-won knowledge directly up my hat-hole and to find someone else to ride around on top of. I could almost hear every word of his tantrum simmering beneath the surface of his mind, just trying to break through, but in the end, Ig was a kobold, and confrontation was not a part of their nature. "My is sorry."

I do not need for you to be sorry, Ig. I need for you to be better.

That sounded like something a kindly teacher might say. I was absolutely killing this apprentice-master relationship thing.

"My will," Ig said, tears still pooled in his eyes.

I know, dear sweet kobold, I know.

He let out a heavy sigh, then gestured after the rest of our party, who had continued lumbering off into the dark woods without our intervention. "But they is magicked though?"

Oh, most assuredly. There is some enchantment calling to them from the depths of the woods. At first I had hoped that it was perhaps some forgotten elf encampment and we might be drawn in to have a pleasant stay, but judging by the tang of necromancy in the air, I suspect it is something more sinister.

Ig mouthed the word tang to himself. Then asked, "What necromancy smells like?"

Dust, predominantly. With a hint of hot metal as the radiation tears through the cell membranes of your nose.

Ig's eyes bulged out in terror at so many long words. "Weh!?"

Rest assured that I know it when I smell it, and I smell it now, dear Ig. We enter the domain of a dark sorcerer, a warlock, a weaver of shadow magics that animate the bodies of the dead and put them to work.

"My is thinking maybe we go other way now?" This was possibly the first time that Ig had said something intelligent in his entire life, and I felt like I had borne witness to something truly amazing. Had I eyes, I might very well have had to wipe them. Had I hands, I might have snatched up a quill and made an entry into my diary: Witnessed baby kobold's first thought today.

I could not let my emotions carry me off, however. *That would be preferable, yes.*

"How stop magicked friends though?" He had more or less caught up to them. Wyn was striding ahead as always, and Ildrit's bulk allowed him to pass through the thicketed areas without slowing, though he was now scratched up more than a little bit from the various thorns and whatnot that had once blocked his way. Leaving poor Rhinolyta as the closest in range of Ig's scrabbling little claws.

Most likely they are being guided by some hypnotic light in the distance that your kobold eyes are too feeble to make out. Try covering their eyes.

Stepping in front of Rhine, Ig was immediately trampled. And while in other circumstances I'm sure that he'd have paid good money for a leather-clad warrior woman to trample him, these were not those other circumstances, and his primary reaction was in the form of pained yipping.

He rose with newfound resolve, scampering and capering ahead of Rhine by a good distance, turning on his heel, and then sprinting right for her.

The one advantage that I could see to armor such as that which Rhine wore, other than the obvious aesthetics of the style, was that there was no shortage of little leather straps crisscrossing over her perfectly sculpted musculature. The perfect handholds for enterprising little climbers like Ig, who leapt to hook onto a foothold near her knee, and then ascended from there.

Once again, were circumstances different, I imagine that Ig would have been having the time of his life scrambling up the front of Rhinolyta, but with me scowling down from above his brow, his hands did not even pause for a moment as he made his ascent, until finally, with a yip of victory, he slapped his hands down over her eyes.

All at once, she was stilled in her motion, the hypnotic hold of the necromancer broken. Then she began to cause a commotion. "Why are my eyes covered?!"

Ig yelped out, "Bad light brain melt."

Shaking with barely contained rage now that her mind was her own again, Rhine begged the all-important question. "Why is your hand upon my breast?!"

"That my foot. You is tall," Ig yelped in terror, flexing his little feet for a better grip as she rocked back in revulsion.

"If that's your foot, why is it squeezing?!"

Normally it would have been appropriate to make a joke about Ig never washing that foot again, but honestly, it was a running battle to get the kobold to wash anything, and I had no intention of providing him with any semantic ammunition for our next bout.

"You is slippy and tall!" Ig yelped again.

Almost screaming now, Rhine grabbed hold of Ig around his middle and tried to pry him off. "Why are you on my face, wizard?!"

"Ah! You was hypotenused."

Oh come on, there is no possible way that you knew that word and not . . .

Yet somehow, Rhinolyta understood. "I was what? Mind magic?"

"Yes!" Ig squeaked in relief. "You was being led into the woodses."

"Then I thank you for your swift intervention." Rhine gritted her teeth. "Now get off."

"Be closing your eyes first."

Honestly, even I, with my limited upper-body strength in life, would likely have launched the kobold into a tree by now. Her self-control was remarkable. "I assure you, they are firmly shut."

"Okies. Then I is getting down . . ." Ig looked down and considered his potential hand holds and exactly what would happen to him if his hands held them. "Coulds you put me down?"

Very carefully, Rhine plucked Ig from her face and set him on the mulch. "It is taking all my good manners not to."

"We must be saving the others," Ig announced, as though this was not abundantly obvious.

Beneath their lids, Rhine's effervescently beautiful blue eyes shifted, almost as though they were being rolled. "And how do you propose I do that when I'm blind?"

"Me steer you?"

She reached a hand down for Ig's grubby paw. "Then lead on!"

Tripping and stumbling over every uneven surface, the pair of them made their way towards the swiftly disappearing back of Ildrit first. And then Ig left Rhine to deal with him while chasing on after Wyn.

This proved to be somewhat more difficult than little Ig had anticipated, given their respective strides and the amount of time he had spent on Rhine alone. The same dim vision that protected him from whatever guiding light was drawing the others like moths to candles also made it impossible for him to make out the elf ahead, and we had no option but to charge blindly on into the dark, in what he could only hope was the same direction that we had been heading all along.

It was, in my opinion, a very good thing that Ig was entirely focused upon his task, because if the entirety of his peanut brain had not been occupied with chasing down the elf then he might have run the risk of noticing things.

The things in question were predominantly my own creeping sense of dread as we drew closer to the baleful light, the skeletal hands protruding from amidst the roots, and the general decrepitude of the forest gradually giving way to decay. It was much like the deep dark woods that we had encountered previously, which had been rigged up to be unsettling to passersby, but this time there was a degree more authenticity. For instance, the bony hands poking out of the roots were grasping spasmodically for Ig's ankles as he tiptoed by, the stench of decay was seeping out of the blackening husks of trees, and there was an ambient green tint to the light filtering through to us that spoke of radioactive death. Typically I would have cast some protection spell on myself, invoking the element of lead to prevent ambient damage to my body just in case, but not only would Ig be incapable of such a complex spell; being far more likely to encase himself in metal and suffocate, there was also the sterilization to consider.

If exposure to radiation prevented Ig from ever having little baby Iglings, then I would consider a little mutation to be a small price to pay.

Still he strode on as the trees began to decline into the blighted earth around us. The closer that we got, the less lively the forest appeared, and we had not heard a peep from a bird in an hour at least, now that I thought about it. Not even the macabre *crawing* of crows that would have set the mood beautifully. The night was silent and the darkness drowning deep.

Then Ig laid eyes upon the first tombstone.

It must have been an ancient thing, crumbling away to practically nothing, but still distinctive enough in its shape that it could not be mistaken for anything else.

Of course Ig had never seen a tombstone before, so it had no impact on his usually terror-filled little heart at all, and I meant to keep it that way for as long as possible. If there was a dark wizard out here, then my current vulnerable state would make me a particularly appealing target, and given their already shown propensity for mind magics in addition to necromancy, there was a real danger that I might be recognized for what I am and stripped from my hat home like an oyster being shucked from the shell. All the delicious knowledge I had spent a lifetime accruing could be sucked out of me by the right dark wizard and used to do unfathomable damage. As such, I needed Ig to have his wits about him. Inasmuch as he had wits at all.

The gravestones grew ever denser as we proceeded, statuary lurching up out of the green-tinted mist at odd moments. Vast sepulchers and monuments to the long departed blocked our path, and Ig had to weave his way between them to keep heading towards where we could only hope Wyn would be found. Then came the other statuary.

Hills had begun to build up around us as we went, lined with worn-down humps that had once been grave markers, but amidst them stood tall pillars of stone, newly hewn to my discerning eye. To be generous, I would have described them as obelisks, but in reality, they looked rather distinctly like a certain part of the male anatomy that I had never expected to see thrust up from the earth in such a manner. They were surprisingly detailed, exceptionally large, and, I had to assume, the result of some very puerile humor on the part of their craftsman.

Ig stared at them as we passed them by, and I willed him not to ask any questions that I didn't want to answer.

Down in the valley between the two great slopes of graveyard, I saw at last the guiding light that had drawn the others in. It was an obelisk, grander in scale but otherwise much like the others. Atop its tip shone a great green gem, illuminating the entire area. Seeping into Ig's mind like a spoon into custard.

He was entranced the very moment he caught sight of the glowing green, but since it was the direction that we were headed anyway, I left him entranced. It would have run the risk of him enquiring as to the helmeted top of the obelisk if he were conscious and aware, and besides, I had no real desire to seize control of his little kobold body and force his eyes shut unless I had no other option. So in blissful silence we proceeded onward.

Wyn stood in the great obelisk's shadow, head tilted back so their vision of the bright green light would not be interrupted. From within their eyes it would be reflecting back, consuming all that they had been. At least until something interrupted the light.

Which brought me back to Ig.

It is said that when a carpenter has only a hammer in his toolbox, every problem that he encounters begins to look like a nail. Within my metaphorical toolbox, the only tool that I had was an enchanted kobold, and thus every problem looked insurmountable.

Ig continued his little waddle, and slowly the words being beamed into the hollow bean rattle he called a skull became clearer and clearer to me. A musical, lisping voice. *Come to me.*

While Ig and Wyn remained blissfully unaware of his presence, a figure emerged from the deeper shadows, clad in dark robes with gold filigreed skull designs upon the shoulder pads. Everything from the hood atop his head to the considerably too many rings upon his fingers—also embossed with skulls—screamed necromancer.

Yet there were no lurking legions of the dead at his heels ready to feast upon the flesh of Wyn and Ig, nor was there any horrid dark cloud of doom swirling around him as he readied himself to strip their souls from their body. Rather, he gazed upon them in confusion for a moment, then turned to peek up at the radiant green gem atop the obelisk, before finally muttering to himself, "Oh bugger, I thought I turned that off."

There was a brief moment of showy casting with a great deal of arm waving, swooping sleeves, and distant screams of the damned, and then his nightlight blinked out.

"So sorry about that, gentlemen. Gentlewomen. Gentlewhatevers." He flung back his hood with equal amounts of drama as had been established with the swishy sleeve spells. "And welcome one and all to the Necropolis!"

Wyn and Ig both stared at him blankly. Though, to my amusement, Ig, who was more accustomed to arriving in situations with no rational explanation that he could grasp, was a lot quicker to adapt to his new situation. "Weh?"

"My darling boy . . . girl . . . thing . . . this is the Necropolis!" He paused again for effect, to little or no effect. "The greatest undead-themed dungeon in all of the Badlands. Home to some of the most fearsome constructs of bone and decaying flesh that humanity has ever laid eyes upon. Adventurers travel from distant lands to come and explore our many levels, seeking treasure and excitement and . . ."

While it may not have been apparent to Wyn, and definitely was not apparent to Ig, most dungeons are not, in fact, operated like theme parks. The typical process for dungeon construction is that a monster, dark lord, or otherwise socially undesirable creature comes into possession of a great deal of wealth and needs somewhere to put it. Initially they may hit upon the classic solution of burying it in the ground, but soon after that, they are typically struck by fear of theft. So they go back and dig deeper and bury it all over again. Then, when they've had more time to think, they go back, dig it up, set a lot of traps on top of it, then bury it again. And so on and so forth over a period of decades with new traps being added, then monsters, and by this point there has been so much coming and going between the surface and the treasure that there are now several flights of stairs, sometimes an elevator, and an entire hierarchy of various monsters initially employed to guard the treasure, but now fighting to defend the home that their family had occupied for generations.

The idea that someone could have taken the end result of that and constructed a dungeon in its final form, so that people could enjoy delving into it and killing monsters and finding treasure, was frankly mind-boggling, but I suppose that it would make sense to a necromancer. Eventually every adventurer's luck ran out, and then you'd have a whole new attraction for the next adventurer to fight, and at the end of the day, after the adventurers had been through, you could just pop in the back door and raise all the skeletons that they'd knocked down to fight again the next day. As far as business plans went, it was actually relatively solid. Nefarious and bizarre, obviously, but smart.

And the orchestrator of this conniving plan was now before us, simpering insufferably. "I don't suppose either of you are gentlemen in truth? It has been such a long time since someone made a social call."

From across the breadth of the graveyard, a bellow was heard as Rhine and Ildrit finally arrived to rescue us from the mounting confusion.

"Bonetaker!"

It was a good shout. A solid battle cry that jerked everyone's head around. Though in the case of the necromancer, only for long enough for him to sashay forward and peer out. "Is that Ildrit Blackblade, the Curved Swordsman? As I live and breathe!"

Cursed, surely?

They continued their charge through the graves, though I could not help but notice that the pre-combat banter seemed a little bit more lighthearted than I was accustomed to from this lot.

"Bonetaker, you vile reprobate! What are you trying to pull, ensnaring us with that glowing dong-star?"

"Terribly sorry about that, little bit of a misfire," Bonetaker demurred. "Thought I'd turned it off after the last ogre came through."

That managed to stop Ildrit in his tracks for a moment. "Good gods, Bonetaker, ogres?!"

"What can I say?" The necromancer shrugged. "The pickings are slim out here."

The charge had now slowed to something of an amble as Ildrit tried to measure something in the air with his hands. "But the logistics . . ."

"With a little bit of magic you can make anything work, darling." There was some unmistakable smirking going on now, and I could already tell that we stood upon the very edge of tittering. Probably from Ig, if he ever worked out what the Bonetaker was actually talking about.

Rhine's head snapped back and forth between the swordsman and the necromancer in confusion. "You know this blackguard?"

Bonetaker drawled, "Know him, darling? I've . . ."

Before the nature of their prior meetings were revealed, Ildrit shouted over the top of the necromancer's sly comments. "He is the wizard that we have traveled all this way to see."

What.

"This guy?" Rhine gawked.

Wyn had begun to slowly back away from the necromancer throughout all of this, clearly not appreciating the appreciative looks that the scrawny man was giving them. "We have traveled the Badlands in search of this evil . . ."

"Madam, I am no more evil than you." Bonetaker genuinely looked offended this time, instead of the faux-offended he'd mustered up until now while he'd been smirking his smarmy face off. "I happen to have a talent for the reanimation of the departed, but I'm sick and tired of the stereotype that this makes me a grave robber or a wicked witch. I'll have you know that . . ."

"His name is Bonetaker!" Rhine shouted over the top of him. "Of course he's a grave-robbing necromancer."

Ildrit rubbed the back of his neck, trying to defuse the situation without actually saying anything. "Well, to be fair, that isn't actually why he's called that."

"Why would he be called Bonetaker if not for the thievery of bones?" Rhine's sculpted brows drew down and that adorable little line between them appeared once more. Poets could have written epics about that little crease between Rhinolyta's eyebrows when she was perplexed, but luckily for us, Ig was no poet.

"Well . . ." Wyn began trying to formulate an answer that wasn't too crass.

"Uh," was all that Ildrit could contribute to the cause.

"Well what?" Rhine demanded.

Throughout these proceedings, the shit-eating grin upon Bonetaker's face had grown wider and wider, and now he was looking so excited it was a wonder that he had not taken off.

"The statuary is a hint," Wyn suggested.

She cast around, looking for some hint from the stone pillars raised all around her. "The obelisks?"

Ildrit tried to guide her to the obvious conclusion with the minimum amount of actually having to say anything out loud. "They don't . . . remind you of anything?"

There was an extremely long pause as Rhine cast her eyes about the various erected monuments. "I suppose they look a bit like mushrooms if you squint?"

"Mushrooms . . ." Wyn replied flatly. "Not . . . anything else?"

"Satyr pillars, I suppose? Like they use to support their temples."

Anticipation boiling over into frustration, the Bonetaker squealed, "Seriously?!"

She examined them a little more closely, running her hand up the length of the grand obelisk that had summoned us all here in a manner that would have left Ig a gibbering mess if he too were not completely oblivious. "Well, merfolk pillar designs are more elegant and less squat."

By this point, it seemed that amazement had given way to slow realization that growing up surrounded exclusively by women and having her rather odd rule about only making love to a gentleman who could best her on the field of battle—when she was a particularly able fighter—had left a particular gap in Rhine's knowledge of anatomy. Ildrit spoke ever so softly, as though concerned that he might frighten away a baby deer. "You can't think of anything else that they might look like?"

She weighed the question for a moment, clearly not understanding what all of the fuss was about, before finally returning her reply. "No?"

Almost at once, the Bonetaker swooped down on her, wrapping his arms around her and cooing. "Oh, you poor, deprived darling! You have so much to learn about the joys of life." He gave her a sly smile when she looked uncomfortable about his proximity. "For instance, when it comes to satyr pillars, you should know that your friend there has an absolutely fabulous . . ."

"Bonetaker!" Ildrit screamed. "How long has it been?"

He kept an arm draped around Rhine's shoulders—prompting immense jealousy from Ig—but spun to face Ildrit all the same. "Since your letter or since we last . . ."

Ildrit's voice actually broke this time as he shouted over the end of that sentence. "Saw each other, how long since we last saw each other, five years?"

The Bonetaker leaned in close to Rhine and stage-whispered, "And I haven't aged a day."

Necromancy will do that for you. You look absolutely pristinely preserved, right up until the moment that you don't, then it is all decaying flesh and exposed bones.

"You know, typically you'd wait for someone else to compliment you." Ildrit could not help but laugh.

"And run the risk of it going unsaid? I don't think so, darling." He unhooked himself from Rhine and sashayed over to catch Ildrit by his stubbly chin. "Meanwhile, you've aged like a cabbage in the sun."

Wyn was not smiling, but somewhere behind their placid expression, there was a hint of bemusement as they announced, "Your friend is quite charming."

"Oh, you." Bonetaker batted his eyelids at Wyn. "You'd know all about charm, you gorgeous creature, you."

It was at that moment that an unfortunate and extremely unlikely event took place. After having spent the past several minutes staring at them, Ig had finally managed to put together what the others had previously been speaking about in regard to the pillars. With a gasp, he announced, "They looks like . . ."

Ildrit cut Ig off just in the nick of time. "Wizard! Why don't you introduce yourself to our gracious host."

That was sufficient to shut him the heck up, if only because he'd been having a low-energy anxiety attack about what he'd say to the wizard we were out here to meet when we finally met him for the past day and a half. In between more pressing panics.

Right, Ig, just like we practiced.

In one continuous stream of sound, Ig unleashed, "Me-is-Absalom-Scryne, Wizard-of-Big-Good-Magic-ness. Me-has-been-cursed-with-kobold."

That last part is truer than you know. I tried not to groan.

"A wizard, eh? Have you got a big-good-magic staff hidden somewhere about your person?" Bonetaker giggled. "Ildrit, darling, why have you trained your pet rat-lizard to tell such preposterous lies?"

"Is not lies," Ig squeaked in indignation. "Me is wizard!"

"Darling, your little hat is absolutely adorable, but you must know that clothes maketh not the man." He cackled. "Why, otherwise I'd be some sort of fabulous gothic peacock."

"He really is a wizard." Rhine stood up for Ig. "We've seen him do magic."

"But darling, he's a kobold. They aren't big in the thinking department. Or . . . any department, tragically."

Ig crossed his twiggy little arms across his chest. "Me is big in the magic department."

"Oh ho! Sounds like we have ourselves a challenger." Green light shone out from the hook-nosed necromancer's eyes as he touched the Quintessence within. "What shall the contest be? I'm very good at making things disappear."

This gentleman is getting on my last nerve. Here we have a classic example of what a well-executed version of the Golden Flames of Galgalagrin the Great could be used for. Insufferable necromancers.

Wyn stepped up to try and defuse the situation, clearly aware that when you put any two wizards in close proximity to one another, they're liable to fight. We are somewhat like betta fish in that regard. That and the trailing robes and sleeves. "There is no need for that. He cannot perform all of his usual magic because of the curse. But he remains the only reason we made it here unharmed."

Bonetaker arched a wry brow. "Can't do magic, but he's a wizard. Methinks I smells a liar among us."

"Stop winding him up, Bonetaker," Ildrit finally intervened. "I trust his word as well as I'd trust yours."

"Then I'd say you are entirely too free and easy with your trust, because I'm deplorable." He glanced across to Rhine to reassure her. "For reasons completely unrelated to necromancy, darling. Deplorable reasons."

Throughout all of this conversation, Ig had been blissfully silent, and I had ignored him utterly, but as it turned out, that was an error in judgment on my part. I should really have borne in mind that my primary role within this group was babysitting the imbecile I was riding around on.

With his knowledge of Potassium fixed firmly in his brain, Ig cried out, *"Fragor!"*

The banana launched from his pointed finger, soared through the air, and slapped Bonetaker across the cheek, drawing a rather unseemly-sounding gasp from the man. After the moment it took him to compose himself and examine the piece of fruit that had now gotten stuck in the folds of his insidious black robes, he took a steadying breath. "Well, I stand corrected."

Ig nodded firmly. Proud of himself.

Idiot.

If he had actually cast the spell that he had intended to, then this would have been a situation worthy of some pride and praise, but instead he had just made the same ridiculous mistake all over again. Consistency in your failures is not admirable.

And in truth, it was something of a small tragedy that Ig's ill-thought-out assassination attempt had failed, because despite the immediate uproar that it was liable to have caused with the other adventurers, at least it would have been better than what was going to happen now, when the necromancer outed us as a non-cursed, non-transfigured, perfectly normal kobold and an enchanted hat. At best, I'd be claimed by this flamboyant buffoon and dyed black. At worst, they'd part me and Ig through murderous means and I'd never be worn again, instead cast into eternal nothingness, just waiting for my soul to be reconnected with a living body. After all of this time, it seemed we were about to reach the crisis point of our relationship with the adventurers, and with each other.

"Well, given that you've all had a long day on the road, with little time for beauty sleep and pampering, might I invite you to spend the night at the Boneyard Bordello and Spa, free of charge to friends of Ildrit, of course. You can have a wash, relax, have a little cocktail, use some of the scented oils and tinctures, try some of the treatments, take a bath, get a little makeover, scrape off some of that road dust, sleep in a bed after you've showered . . ."

Wyn surprised us all by agreeing so swiftly. "The message has been received; we smell."

"Oh, darling, it isn't a matter of your muskiness. I love a little musk." He seemed to be practically salivating each time he said the word musk. "It is just that I don't want to have to throw out all the bedsheets after you go."

"I'm sorry, did you say bordello?" Rhine interrupted.

"Oh yes, adventurers tend to be very particular about their needs after they've been off exploring a dungeon all day. They want an inn, a bed, and . . .

company." The Bonetaker sighed, as though it were a genuine imposition on his morals.

Ig's excitement rose in time with my own trepidation. "So there is other peoples here?"

"Well, my diminutive darling, that would very much depend upon how you define people. If you are prejudiced, like certain people around here"—he cast a bitter glare at Ildrit—"then you would say that personhood is a 'til death do you part' sort of deal, while more enlightened people might consider . . ."

"Nobody is going to have sex with your zombies, Bonetaker!"

"I keep them very clean! And with the perfumes and correctly positioned and timed heating, they're extremely lifelike." The necromancer was petulant.

Ig did not know what sex was. Not really. He knew that in the close company of Rhinolyta, he started to get some odd tingling sensations in places that were usually hidden well away and to make decisions based upon increasing his proximity to her, but the actual act itself entirely eluded him. The mechanics of it, the specifics, all of the things that as a wiser older man, I probably should have been able to enlighten him about. Sadly, while I understood the process in academic terms, I had never had much in the way of hands-on experience, due to my focus upon my studies.

Yet we shared a natural revulsion at the prospect of an undead bordello. I supposed that there was a certain eyeliner-wearing subsection of the world who would be taken with the idea of a vampire lover, but even they would most likely balk at the prospect of making love to undead who were actively decaying.

I hope.

Throughout Ig's moment of inward contemplation where we mutually agreed that he should not make use of the services here without debate, Ildrit and the Bonetaker had continued bickering. Culminating in the conversation having reached an unexpected point by the time that we returned to paying attention. The Bonetaker shouted, ". . . you are a bigot! You are homophobic against the undead. People like you disgust me. You are a small-minded bigot and you should be ashamed of yourself."

"Maybe I am!" Ildrit yelled back. "I'm still not having sex with a zombie."

"Fine!" In an instant, the Bonetaker's tone switched from argumentative to flirtatious. "We'll just have to find you someone living and willing!"

Ildrit burst out laughing. "It is good to see you again, old friend."

"Less with the old, if you please." Bonetaker preened. "I'm still as lithe as a teenage boy."

Is . . . is that something people want?

Ig was briefly stunned into silence by the horrific flashback to my own teenage years that I had endured: the communal showers, the dorm rooms, the . . . smells. No. Nobody would want to be like teenage boys.

There had been some more conversation while we were trapped in my own personal heckscape, but it seemed that we were all taking this necromancer's word thanks to his prior association with Ildrit, and actually planned on spending the night in the somewhat ramshackle inn that he'd constructed beside the entrance to his dungeon. The others traipsed inside, still chattering away, but I, like Ig, found myself drawn to the dungeon itself.

I assume in Ig's case it was because of his predilection for dark holes in the ground where he might hide, but for me there was an unfortunate draw to such places. Ancient secrets long lost to the sight of man. Monsters against which to test my arcane might without any need to hold back for fear of collateral damage. There was much about a dungeon that might draw in a wizard. Many of my peers had gone down the adventurous path, tiring of the true calling of academia and succumbing to the urge for worldly possessions and exploration. It had never once appealed to me, but after this last little jaunt through the wild places of the world, I had to admit that there was something to this adventuring nonsense. The appeal of it, that had entirely escaped me on paper, had now arisen once I was faced with the reality of it.

Perhaps, once my vengeance was done, I would find some way to grow a new body for myself to inhabit using the apparatus in the College of Arpanpholigon. And with that new lease on life and my soul returned to the mortal coil, I might *do* more. There was no denying that my studies had made me the greatest of all wizards, but now that I was no longer nestled comfortably in the heart of my tower, there was a vague sense of unease about returning. As though it were a gilded cage in which I had been trapped through all the decades of my life.

Maybe that feeling was simply a holdover, bad memories of my assassination associated with the place, but it was equally possible that despite the truly wretched company I was currently being forced to keep, there was something of value to be learned out here. Something that had not been bound in tomes or inscribed in scrolls, some understanding of the world that had thus far eluded me. Perhaps I'd take a sabbatical, travel a little, pick up some books from far off places for the library back home.

Creeping ever closer, at last Ig's feeble eyes took in the entrance to the dungeon fully. The cave mouth carved into the likeness of a gaping skull, the overgrowth of ivy, the sign strung up above it that read "Out of Order."

Surely not . . .

"Come along inside, my little snack-sized friend," Bonetaker whispered into Ig's ear, his breath tickling over the kobold's neck. "There's so much more to see."

CHAPTER SEVENTEEN

CURSES!

The evening actually ended up relatively pleasant despite the somewhat shaky beginnings. Bonetaker, despite his rather salacious demeanor, was an excellent host, plying us all with drink and spinning tales that always bordered just on the right side of obscene.

At some point, I suspect that Rhinolyta's innocence may have been fractured somewhat, and she began to understand at least a portion of the anatomical unlikelihoods that he was describing, but any blushing that she might have begun to do was just as likely caused by the frankly copious amounts of wine that the Bonetaker was pouring. There was a green wine in particular that had the faintest taste of pine to it that absolutely intrigued me. My own wine consumption had always been relatively light, as it muddles the mind and I perpetually needed mine in the finest working order, so I will admit that the varieties I recall consuming over the years have been fairly limited, but this too seemed like an area of study that I might want to expand upon after acquiring a body of my own.

Unfortunately for Ig, having lived his entire life in a muddy hole in the ground, he was not entirely accustomed to wine, or alcohol of any sort. After the first intriguing sip, the shiver running down his spine all the way to the tip of his tail, and the resultant spread of warmth throughout his bony little torso, Ig could not be restrained from guzzling wine at a frankly terrifying rate. Admittedly, to those around him it probably looked like he was just slightly more intent on getting to the bottom of the one glass he'd been poured than them, but to someone who could feel his brain cells popping and his liver shrieking in terror at the new horrors being unleashed upon it, it felt like a lot.

Approximately one hour into the proceedings, just as the conversation was beginning to get interesting, Ig traversed from vertical to horizontal, in more or less a single movement. He sloped down off the bench to slither to a halt beneath the table, and as his hollow head passed over the rim of the bench, it hooked under my rim, tilting me down to cover his face. He began snoring gently just a moment after.

There was uproarious laughter from around the table at his departure, and then the conversation went on as if nothing had happened at all.

Although Ig was no longer conscious and aware of his surroundings, I remained connected to his senses, and as such, had the benefit of listening in on the conversation unfolding overhead without the downside of having to police Ig's responses. If I could just keep him blind drunk from now on, things would likely be much easier. I'd have to arrange for him to be carried, but frankly he weighed about as much as a wet dishcloth, so it was unlikely to create much of an issue for the adventurers.

As the wine went on flowing, we got little more out of Wyn, who I suspected was very carefully pacing themselves so that they didn't let too much of their real personality slip out from behind the mask of dulled disinterest. Rhine, on the other hand, was almost as unfamiliar with liquor as Ig, but had a constitution that proved a fairly worthy match for the fresh bottles that kept on appearing as though they'd been conjured.

She devolved into stories about her upbringing in the world without men, and Bonetaker almost immediately became fascinated with the prospect of a single-gender civilization. Though it seemed as though the feminine aspect was of less appeal.

The vast majority of her time and efforts as a child had been spent in training incessantly to be the very best, running marathons, riding horses, running marathons on horseback, shooting things with arrows, shooting things with arrows from on horseback, and practicing time and time again with every weapon that they could conceive of to hone her into the ultimate weapon for the defense of her homeland.

Ildrit was quite taken by these tales, having come from something of a martial background himself, but it rapidly bored Bonetaker and he began interjecting his own commentary into the descriptions, usually referencing something sordid. This was a man who had never met a euphemism that he did not like. He suffered a serious allergy to single-entendres, doubling up all of them as he went and sometimes even achieving a third secret entendre that nobody could have foreseen coming.

It would most likely have made him a hilarious delight at a dinner party. Once.

After an hour or so, the "charm" was wearing thin. It was as though someone had taught Ig a joke, and he had told it once and got a laugh, so now it was the only thing he would say. Different iterations of the same joke. Over and over again.

It made me truly wonder how it was possible that Ildrit had befriended this one-trick pony of a wizard. Certainly he was a skilled necromancer, and that enchanting gem trick had been quite impressive, but generally speaking, one did not become a necromancer because one had a wide variety of options outside of the shambling corpses field. You hyper-specialized in the one thing you were good at if you only ever became good at one thing. Otherwise you'd have become a wizard. He had duplicated this crippling overspecialization in terms of his conversational gambits too. Every other word was an eyebrow-wriggle reference to genitalia, and the line between salacious and boring did not take long to cross. I wondered, briefly, if he had perhaps been inflicted with some sort of head wound to the part of the brain responsible for talking like a normal human being, not overwhelmed by the prospect of coitus.

Either recognizing that she'd overstayed her welcome by rambling, succumbing to what was the fourth bottle of wine by my count, or ultimately tiring of the Bonetaker's incessant dicking about, Rhine announced, "Bed now. Alone. Again."

Wyn, being a gentleman . . . gentlewoman . . . gentle-elf, offered to escort her to the designated chambers and ensure that it was bereft of any of the undead harlots that we'd seen scattered around the place. There were few things in the world I could imagine were a worse surprise to wake up to. Other than discovering that you'd become a piece of headwear.

And then it was just the two old friends, reminiscing about good old times. It was my sincere hope that they would not recount any sort of romantic trysts, but I could not deny that I had some curiosity as to how these two had crossed paths. The brave adventuring hero and the necromancer with a fixation on the size of his lovers' . . . equipment.

"Darling, it really has been too long. I know you like to play it mysterious and all, but even you have to admit that vanishing off the map for half a decade is a little over-the-top."

"I assure you it wasn't by choice." Ildrit groaned, and the table above Ig groaned too, as though he had leaned heavily upon it. "Circumstances . . . changed for me."

The Bonetaker sniffed. "Well, darling, I never once assumed that you'd deserted an army you'd pulled together all by yourself just because of a run of bad luck."

"It wasn't . . ." Ildrit was trying very hard not to slur his words, and I had to assume that he too had consumed a quite copious amount of wine. "It wasn't luck. It was a curse."

When the Bonetaker laughed, it should have been high and cruel like the necromancers in the tales of great heroes, but it came out, tragically, as a prolonged bout of tittering. It went on, and on, with not a single word of interruption from Ildrit, until finally, wiping the tears from his eyes, the Bonetaker continued, "A curse. Oh, my sweet man, you have no idea about magic at all, do you.

"You kept stubbing your toe because of a curse? No. The ground was uneven. The elves cut us off at the bridge because of a curse? No. They just had good scouts. You decapitated your horse with a bad swing. That's why they sell more horses.

"Those are just things that happen, darling. And while I'll admit they seemed to happen to you an awful lot that last month or so, that doesn't mean that there was anything supernatural going on."

"I was cursed, Bonetaker." Ildrit's voice was uncharacteristically cold. "No sneaking around with dolls and pins. To my face. By a shaman."

For the first time, the Bonetaker seemed at least a little interested in what Ildrit had to say. "A shaman?"

"You remember we took that village, the little one, with all the sheep."

"Darling, you just described half the villages I've ever seen." Bonetaker yawned. "More specific, would you please?"

"The village with all the sheep on the hills and the big wicker sheep outside the village that they filled up with the wool. Do you remember?"

"Oh yes! I used some of the horny skulls to make new skeletons and we set that big wicker sheep on fire with the village chief inside it." Bonetaker giggled.

"That's the one," Ildrit confirmed in a matter-of-fact way that slightly glazed over the whole conquest and slaughter thing. "Anyway, I cut my way through their militia, and we were putting torch to the wicker roofs."

"As you do," the Bonetaker conceded.

"As you do." Ildrit continued, irritated at the asides and interruptions. "And then out of one of the burning huts there comes this old woman. And I mean, really old. Like, there were mountains younger than her. She looked like she was made of dried-up chicken skin."

Another faked yawn. "Hideous old woman, got it."

"Well, she took hold of my face, just before I stabbed her. And she said to me . . ." He dropped his voice into a throaty whisper. "You will get what you deserve."

I couldn't see the Bonetaker at that moment, due to being perpendicular, and beneath the table, but in my mind's eye I could picture his lank black hair, his sallow face, his hooded eyes, rolling. "Darling, that isn't a curse. That's barely even a comment. That's just something old people say sometimes to fill the quiet."

"It was a curse," Ildrit insisted. "I felt it. Like . . . tingles all over me. Right up my back."

"That also isn't a curse," the Bonetaker tittered. "That's a breeze."

Ildrit pressed on again as though he had not been interrupted. "And ever since she said that, and I stabbed her, I've been getting what I deserve."

"Well, I think there's an argument to be made that we all put a certain amount of effort in, and the rewards that we receive are commensurate with . . ." The Bonetaker began to wax philosophical, but I did not get the sense that Ildrit was being any less than literal. At least this curse explained a few things about why the elf trusted him.

"When I do bad things . . . bad things happen to me." Ildrit sounded truly heartbroken at being unable to commit acts of evil. "I can't even be rude to people anymore. Not even . . . when they're badly dressed."

There was a crack in the Bonetaker's façade, and his voice. "Oh, darling, oh no. My sweet baby boy."

"Murdering people is right out. Every time I've killed someone since then when they haven't been evil, it has come right back at me. Broke my arm slipping on some wet grass the first time. Sat on an Ortharion Torture Bug the next. Lost almost a whole cheek before I could get an antivenom."

Even I winced at that one. We used OTB venom to clean ancient artifacts sometimes, when the millennia had layered on too much in the way of organic matter. It wasn't fast, but it was very effective.

It was difficult to tell from the usually sarcastic-sounding necromancer, but I think that he was being genuinely sympathetic when he replied. "You don't look too lopsided."

"It grew back, eventually, but I was riding side-saddle squint for months."

"But all that still doesn't mean a curse." The Bonetaker was clearly trying to dismiss the possibility of a curse by now because the alternative was to deal with it. Something that I personally also would have preferred to avoid if possible. "It could all have just been bad luck."

"But it wasn't, Boney. It wasn't. I worked it out, see? I worked out that if I did bad things, bad things would happen to me, so if I did good things, it should work the other way, right?" There was a manic edge to his voice now. "I helped an old woman across a road. Turned out she was the mother of the owner of the inn I was camped out at. When the guards came around looking for me because of the wanted posters, the innkeeper said he'd never seen me."

Even the incredulous necromancer couldn't entirely dismiss that. He seemed to doubt his own words. "Just luck again, surely?"

"Well that's what I thought. So I tried again. Did something else 'good' and do you know what happened?"

"Money fell down from the sky to land in your lap?" The Bonetaker attempted to scoff, but given the way that things had been going thus far, it would not have surprised me at all.

"No, sadly. But when I stopped a mugging because they were making too much noise and I had a hangover, it turned out their victim was the king in disguise, and he gave me a full pardon."

There was a long period of silence, then the Bonetaker said, "Oh, you must be joking."

"Do I look as though I am jesting with you, old friend?"

Giving up entirely upon skepticism, the Bonetaker leaned forward over the table to hear more. "So what happened next?"

"Well, for a while, I just sort of . . . stagnated. I didn't know how to be good, it was foreign to me. I didn't like it."

"Understandable, darling. Hearing about you helping old ladies cross the road is like hearing a fish discuss the finer points of cycling."

For me, it was quite the opposite. We'd had a rough few stops and starts when Ig first met Ildrit, but he had quite firmly formed the moral core of the adventurers; now it turned out that the core was rotten, and had half a worm sticking out of it.

"Anyway, I realized I could do small good things all day and get some of the same results as one big dramatic good thing, and then I started trying to work out what sort of work might be out there for someone who is only good at killing, cast aside by society, a little rough around the edges. Being good might have protected me from consequences, but I couldn't eat good luck. I had to do something."

The Bonetaker followed through his logic quite easily. "And what better job for an old warlord than an adventurer?"

That drew a little chuckle from Ildrit. "It's basically the same job, just with more remembering people's names."

"Well, you have to, if they're going to survive meeting you." The Bonetaker giggled back.

"And of course being an adventurer meant there was plenty of opportunity to get out there and do good. I know they have a bad reputation, especially among people in our line of work, but adventurers are alright people mostly."

"Like the sweetling who won't stop making eyes at you?" the Bonetaker teased.

"Rhinolyta? She's fine." He was clearly embarrassed about the whole thing. "Does her job well, can hold a shield line."

"And what about the elf? How did that happen? Last I heard they still considered you a war crime."

"You travel far enough, you eventually meet people who haven't heard of you."

The Bonetaker seemed to be lost in memory. "Weren't you officially banned from every standing forest in the world?"

"And then those people who haven't heard of you introduce you back to the people who have heard of you, and from there it is all smooth sailing."

"But an elf, really? Protectors of the natural world?" Bonetaker jibed. "Slayers of everything a little bit fun and naughty?"

"Wyn's a good one. Once they understood the curse, they started trusting me. Once they understood I could only do good things, and doing bad things bring down doom, they started using it as a yardstick to measure everything. I ended up as their compass."

"So now you've come running along to me, begging to get the compass broken. So you can stab your elf in the back?"

That seemed to put Ildrit on the back foot, as there was a distinct and definite pause as he tried to put his next words together. I strained Ig's little ears to be sure and hear the answer, as it would determine whether or not I needed to murder the adventurer in his sleep. "I don't . . . I have no enmity towards either one of them, but I'm not . . . this isn't me. I'm not some goody-goody out to save the world. And the sooner I can get back to myself, the happier everyone is going to be."

The Bonetaker tittered. "Except all the folks you'll go back to murdering."

"Well, yeah, except them, obviously." There was a glugging sound overhead as the ex-villain poured himself another glass of wine.

"And the elf and sweetheart sword swinger you've befriended."

Ildrit's voice became cold once more. A hint of the man he used to be shining through. "It feels like you've a point you're trying to amble towards."

"Well, darling." There was a cruelty to the Bonetaker's amusement now. An edge to his jibes that I hadn't noticed before. "I think you're underestimating just how unhappy they're going to be when you switch teams on them."

Ildrit swirled the wine around in his glass, probably staring down into it instead of having to endure any more eye contact with the necromancer. "Why would I do a thing like that?"

"Because they're goody-goodies. And you . . . you, my darling, are a very naughty boy." The Bonetaker sounded utterly delighted about that.

"I'm not . . . I don't know what I'm going to do once the curse is broken, but I do know I want it gone. So I don't have to spend every minute worrying about doing the right thing. So I don't have to worry about the universe reaching down to spank me every time that I put a foot wrong. I want to be free again. That doesn't mean I'll go right back to doing what I did before, or that I'll keep doing what I'm doing now. It just means I can choose. I should be allowed to choose for myself. Shouldn't I?"

Bonetaker went back to tittering. "Darling, I thought you were doing fantastic as a tin-pot dictator, so I'm really the wrong one to ask your big philosophical questions to."

"So, can you do it?"

"Do what?"

"Can you break the curse?"

"Well, curses, curse-breaking . . . it's a whole other thing. They usually have some condition attached that you need to fulfill if you want to break them, and if you try to brute force them, you end up getting the twanging back in your face. And while I've always been a big fan of things twanging in my . . ."

Ildrit cut the man off before any more penile humor was waggled around. "Can you break the damned curse or not?!"

"I can take a look for you in the morning when we're both sober enough to see straight." He giggled. "But I don't think the chances are good."

There was a thump as Ildrit set down his glass. "You're my last hope, Boney. My last chance to be myself again, without this muzzle and chains."

"Of course I'll do everything I can, darling." Bonetaker was clearly uncomfortable being party to a serious conversation, even one so brief as this. "Though I must admit, the image of you in chains is . . . appealing."

Ildrit chuckled. "You get rid of this curse, then we can talk."

They went back to drinking then, in companionable silence. Bonetaker lost in some fantasy or another, Ildrit sinking into his own thoughts. Then, abruptly, it was interrupted by another jibe. "I just don't understand why you want it broken, given what a lovely time you're having playing at being a hero. Why, surely it would be a truly evil thing for me to let you off your magical leash?"

He let out a heavy sigh. "It's about survival, Boney."

"How's that?"

"I've been getting paid back for all the bad I've done recently and all the good, but before I got cursed . . . there was a lot of bad. I've still got that balance hanging over me like a headsman's axe. I'm tired of waiting for it to come down. I'm tired of waiting to get what I deserve, spending all my life wondering when it is going to catch up to me."

I will admit that this was an aspect of his curse that I had not yet had time to consider. If it truly was enacting some sort of karma upon him, then surely simple redemption would not be sufficient. My initial horror at learning both the nature of his curse and his desire to be free of it now seemed somewhat limited by my own perspective. Of course I wanted him to be forced to continue being good, because it greatly benefited me for him to serve as Ig's protector, but he was essentially strolling around with a karmic bomb strapped to his back, ready to go off without warning.

"And what about your wizard?" the Bonetaker asked, far too casually for my liking.

That startled me back out of my reverie.

"My what? Oh, the kobold? He's my backup plan. Supposedly he's some sort of big shot wizard back in the world. I figure that if I get him back home and he can fix himself up, he'll owe me; might take a swing at my curse himself."

"Well, that's a relief." The Bonetaker tittered. "I thought you were going to ask me to break the curse that made him into a horrid little gremlin man."

"I think that's just his personality."

Rude.

Clearly deciding that he wanted salacious gossip instead of serious conversation, the necromancer switched subject. "So you must tell me why you and that lovely young lady haven't . . ."

"She's young and innocent and I'm . . . me. There is no way that the curse would let me get away with messing around with her."

Bonetaker let out a little sorrowful sigh that was painfully rehearsed. "And here I thought you'd been pining after me all this time."

"Oh yes, I swore myself to celibacy until I could be reunited with your scrawny backside again." Ildrit's flat tone belied the sarcastic jab.

"Darling, this is the scrawny backside that launched a thousand ships. Wars have been fought over scrawny backsides like this. Artists have tried to recreate it in their masterpieces . . ."

Ildrit broke down laughing all over again.

CHAPTER EIGHTEEN

THE HIGHEST FORM OF FLATTERY

At some point, the two chattering old friends gave up on wine and went off to their respective rooms, leaving me and Ig lying on the hard flagstones to wait out the remainder of the night. I had been looking forward to introducing Ig to the joys of a mattress and reveling in his comfort vicariously, but it was not to be.

The only benefit of our abandonment was that when dawn came creeping around and the massive hangover struck the kobold in the head like a hammer, we had some privacy to talk.

"Me is dying," he moaned the moment he awoke.

You are not dying, Ig.

"My heads is going to pop."

It is just the wine. This is why you should not indulge in it so deeply.

"Me is dying, and you is making jokes."

I assure you, my friend, that if you drink some water and give it some time, this discomfort will pass.

"Discomfort, he says." Ig groaned, still lying immobile on the ground. "Me is dying and my heads is going to explode, and he says discomfort."

Get up, Ig.

"Can't. Dying."

I will admit that there was some degree of cruelty involved in what I did next, but we had scant precious time to pursue his education when he was under constant observation, and I was not about to let this opportunity pass. I raised my voice.

GET UP, IG.

The words reverberated back and forth within his tiny skull, with each bounce setting off a fresh gong of pain. He shot from supine to sitting in a single movement, and it was only pure luck that he was just short enough to hit me off the bottom of the table and not his own head. That impact might actually have finished the poor little bugger off.

"Me is up." He opened his eyes, very very slowly, already aware of the detrimental effect that light would have on him. Luckily for us both, the candles of the previous night had burned down, and no sunlight was streaming in through any windows. "Why is me up?"

Because today we resume your education, my friend.

"I thoughts you was angry at me banananananaing." It seemed that banana was a very easy word for Ig to say, and very difficult for him to finish saying.

I must apologize for my frustration; it was unbecoming of a good teacher. I fear only for you, my dear apprentice. While the magic you have been achieving has been incredible, it has also been outside of your complete control, and while none of the bananas you have thus far unleashed have presented a danger to you, when we move on to other elements and words of power, you run the risk of you producing something truly harmful rather than merely useless.

"Me is not useless." Ig attempted to pout. Not easy without lips. "Me can do magic!"

Ig, my dear boy, you can do something. But to call yourself a wizard, you must have control over the effects that you create, you must be able to predict them, to shape them into a grand strategy. A single spell, born of desperation and achieving nothing that you meant it to is not . . . Once more, I must apologize. You are quite right. You can do magic. Now we merely seek to refine your skills to produce the results that you are seeking.

This seemed to placate the little imbecile and we headed out.

None of the others were anywhere to be seen in the dim morning light as Ig padded around the inn, and that was just as well, as I had no real desire to concoct an excuse to sneak away from them once more. They had been trusting, thus far, of the small monster in their midst, accepting the lies that we had told them, with the exception of the elf, of course. Yet even though Wyn knew more than the others, I could not say how they would feel about my teaching a kobold the arcane arts. When asked to teach an ogre, all of us had rebelled against the idea. We could all see the horror of putting such power in the hands of such a beast, yet here I was doing exactly the same, using the justification that the monster I was empowering was so pathetic that even with the cosmic power of the arcane at his disposal, he could do no harm.

I knew that it was a falsehood. I knew that I was lying to myself if I believed it for a moment. Even with no thoughts behind his eyes, he was a danger. Bananas and rabbits were all well and good, but they would not be the limits of what he could achieve in his folly, and all it would take was the wrong element, misplaced focus, or a slip of the tongue and he might unleash a true terror upon the world.

The necromancer invoked Plutonium. Ignorant as the kobold was, he was not blind. Eventually he would notice, he might even ask as to the element, and then he would have an understanding of it. A faulty understanding, inevitably, but in many ways that would be worse. I would be at a crossroads, with the choice of letting him carry on with his flawed grasp and risk all that he might cause or teaching him the true nature of the element. Providing him with an element of utter destruction that he would invariably invoke in a moment of panic.

An accident when invoking Plutonium would not be a banana.

So he needed to learn. He needed to ensure that the results he created were deliberate. There was no other option. I needed to make him a wizard before he could become a disaster.

Outside of the inn, the dim light of dawn was barely penetrating the fog that lay heavy over the valley. It would provide us with cover for our experimentation, even as it obscured the path that Ig needed to walk.

Luckily for him, my memory provided us with our course, winding us through the standing stones and graves until we came upon the entrance to the dungeon.

Ig shivered at the sight of it, having at least absorbed some portion of the danger of dungeons from his fellow travelers. "Is you sure about . . ."

Have you ever known me to be unsure?

As he passed beneath the jagged toothed entrance to the tunnel system, I could feel Ig shiver and shudder as fear washed over him. If anything, this should have been a pleasant experience for him—he was used to living underground. I was the one who should have been frightened, as my natural habitat was a tower high above the earth. With that said, it was somewhat understandable that he'd be a little nervy, what with us entering a complex series of rooms, divided by traps and filled with various monstrosities.

A kinder teacher might have thought to ease his fear, to assuage his quivering, but I, sadly, was not so kind, and I had joined the dots between some data points from our previous attempts at performing magic that made maintaining a state of terror necessary.

Focus was what Ig lacked above all else. The misfiring of spells was an inevitability until he had mastered pronunciation and internalized the essence of each element, but the inability to direct his magic to where it was meant to be presented the greatest problem for us both. Even when he achieved a spell's intended effect, he could not direct it, and it was wasted, as it had been with the werewolves. Thus, I needed to find a way to bring Ig's attention to a singular point of focus.

In the first chamber, there was a scoreboard, graven into the stone in the likeness of a vast ribcage, with each gap betwixt the ribs filled with the green-glowing names of the various adventuring guilds that had made their attempts upon the Necropolis Dungeon. I was not clear upon the scoring system, as such, but many of the various names were well-known notables of the adventuring field.

And into such company now winced Ig. Who was on the verge of pissing himself.

The door to the next chamber was sealed with a stone door, carved in the likeness of a skeleton, hunched and crushed into the doorframe. I had a suspicion that I was going to tire of the décor choices long before the designer had.

Ig attempted to push the door open to no avail, before I suggested pulling, and when he could find no purchase upon any handle and stepped back, I realized that this must have been one of the puzzles that so teased the brains of adventurers. A puzzle that I was disgusted to solve as swiftly as I realized it was a puzzle at all.

Ig, pull on the bone.

"Which bone?" His eyes raked up and down the cadaverous carving. "They all bones?"

The one that is not in its normal place.

He stared witlessly at the deceased door decal. "I not be knowing normal place."

The . . . femur protruding from the pelvis.

"The what what what?" It sounded as though he was almost as frustrated as me.

I seized control and thrust his hand forward to grab onto the knob of stone in the shape of bone.

"Ah! The sticky-outy one," he announced, as he pulled down hard on the jutting lever.

Indeed.

And so we began our progress through the dungeon, surging on from the first entryway into the first chamber. Once more the décor ran to the skeletal, and once more there was nothing of real note to be seen. A few more doors exiting the chamber, a cleared space in the middle of the room where you could likely have had a decent fight if you were so inclined to, and in the middle of that space, a heap of bones. Not stone bone décor, but actual bones that had once belonged to a human. They were yellowed and notched from years of post-meat use. Raised time and time again to face whosoever came charging into the dungeon looking for a fight.

But not today, it would seem.

Today it remained a heap, and Ig was confronted with the choice of multiple doors. As he swiveled back and forth attempting to decide between the three identical courses for us to follow, I used his ears to pay very careful attention to the heap of bones, just in case it was animate after all, and merely playing dead. I mean, it was dead. But also . . . you understood perfectly what I meant.

That one.

Ig stopped his fretting and reached for the next doorknob. "You be sure?"

Not even slightly, but since they're all equally likely to lead us to our goal, this one will do.

It must have taken a long time to build up a creak like that door had. The Bonetaker must have been down here with a little misting bottle, building up the rust to just the right point in the hinges to make such a resounding racket as the door was pulled open.

Pulled open to reveal another empty room, with three piles of bones scattered around it.

Oh, come on.

Ig let out a sigh of relief at the absence of anything trying to kill him. "He did be saying it was outs of order."

This was no use at all. Ig had descended back to his usual general anxiety, somewhere about the level of a rabbit surrounded by wolves. Not nearly scared enough to be focused.

Surely there must be some monsters still in here.

"Nopes, no monsters, me go back out now," Ig loudly announced to the next empty chamber.

Ig . . .

"Darling, if you wanted to see a monster, you could have just asked." The Bonetaker's high voice reverberated out from the deep shadows, and but a moment later he sashayed into sight.

Ig's mouth opened and closed a few times, heart palpitating away as was usual when he was surprised. It was remarkable his species still existed given their propensity to self-destruct at the first sign of danger. "Me is . . . Me was just . . ."

Bonetaker dropped down into a crouch to scratch under Ig's chin. "No need for excuses, darling, not with me. I can understand better than most the desires that drive men to seek out great big monsters in dark places. I promise, I make no judgment."

Oh, that is just . . . crass.

"Me needs a monsters to practice on."

The Bonetaker glanced around conspiratorially, before leaning in closer to whisper into Ig's tufted little ear. "Well, darling, you know, I don't offer this to just anyone, but if you don't want to go monster hunting, I'm always here if you want to experiment a little."

Ig jerked back in surprise. "You want I cast Goggy's Gold Fire at you?"

"Oh! You want to practice your magic . . ." There it was again, that little hint of suspicion upon his face. We should have been the ones who were suspicious, with some necromancer popping up out of nowhere in the middle of the dungeon, but he was the one acting like we had something to hide. Which we did, obviously, but damn him for knowing that. "What an odd thing to do for an alleged wizard. I would have thought that you'd have the whole magic thing down by now."

Ig fell into our rote repeated answer to this particular question. "Kobold body not good for magics. Speak different. Not have quen-ters-unce."

You must be getting that wrong deliberately at this point.

The Bonetaker had risen back to his feet, the belt cinching his robes now just about level with Ig's eyes. "I suppose that mouth must be a wholly different shape than what either one of us are used to."

Ig craned his neck and blinked up at him innocently. Uncomprehending. Until finally the Bonetaker gave in. "Oh, very well, darling. If you must have something to zap at, let me take you to one of the living monsters of the dungeon to have your way with."

Ig bobbed along beside him as he strode off. "Thank."

We passed from one chamber to the next, with each puzzle being solved with a literal wave of Bonetaker's hand and a mild application of low magic. Deeper and deeper into the dungeon of his design we went, with Ig not pausing for even a moment to consider that this might be a trap.

To break the silence, Ig elected to attempt small talk. "How you meet Ildrit?"

I had not yet made Ig aware of what I had overheard the previous night, fearful that he might randomly blurt it out, but it seemed that he was doing his best to jam his foot directly into his mouth without any assistance from me whatsoever.

"Oh, that is quite a tale, and not entirely mine to tell, darling. It was a rough and tumble affair, eyes meeting across a battlefield and all that. He may not look it now, but old Ildrit used to have quite a presence to him, one might even call it charisma. If one were so inclined. We worked together for a while, then, somewhat unexpectedly, our ways parted."

"Why you live out here?"

"Well, darling, much as it may surprise you, I am not particularly well-liked in those areas of the world that have dubbed themselves civilized. Nor was Ildrit, if it came to that. We were two outsiders who found comfort in each other. Quite deep within each other."

Ig was blessedly immune to double entendres, given that he rarely grasped single entendres. So he pressed on, blessedly oblivious. "Why you outsides though?"

"As I said before, I cannot speak for he of the long sword, but for me it was my obvious talent for necromancy that set me apart, and made society reject me."

As it should. Disgusting habit. Most of us grow out of it by the time we're teenagers.

"So you come all way out here?"

"Well, darling, I tried doing a few different things through the years to make use of my talents. Raising armies for warlords, fighting the bad fight and all that, but no matter what happened, I knew I could never make a home for myself where there were people and prejudice, so I settled myself down in the only place in the world I was liable to be left in peace." He shrugged. "The locals have never bothered me much, and they're all outsiders too, in a sense."

He stopped before the next door and rapped on it three times before opening the door into a nondescript room with a large chest in the middle. "Here we are, my little pet, I hope you have fun. Come and find us when you're done.

Ildrit has me doing some little job for him today, then we're doing cocktails and commiserations afterwards when he realizes I can't do what he's asking me to."

Curse-breaking was arduous work. I didn't envy him. "Good luck anyway."

And so Ig turned to the now abandoned room and said, "Me no see monster."

The chest, Ig.

He looked around the room again. "Chest has monster in it?"

The chest is not a chest. Take a better look, but do not come too close.

Ig, with his dim eyesight, could not make out the telltale signs that this particular piece of cabinetry was not in fact a storage receptacle. Even the most highly trained of adventurers were sometimes taken in by such creatures. The trick, as with most things, is not in studying the thing itself, but the places where the thing meets other things. The seams that in a real chest are ever so slightly open are sealed perfectly tight. The place where it meets the ground, where usually shadow is cast, is absent, for there is no gap between bottom and floor; it is sealed down. The hinges, which should have gaps to allow movement, are snug. In these ways you can tell a mimic from a real object.

Although I will admit that in this case, I was mostly relying upon context clues, like being told there was a monster in the room before we got here.

The mimic is an ambush predator capable of disguising itself as various inanimate objects. It is possessed of only the most rudimentary of intelligence, so we need feel no guilt over what comes next.

"What do come next?" Ig asked, still mystified by the idea that something could look like something else.

Potassium.

"Weh?"

Focus upon your understanding of Potassium and let us begin.

What followed was the most pathetic magic lesson in the entirety of human history. Not since the dawn of time has a student learned so little, and a teacher tried and failed so hard. Ig's first attempt at the Golden Flames of Galgalagrin the Great had no result to speak of, though I suspected that if we were to open the door to this chamber and look outside, we might have encountered a lop-eared banana.

For a time, he gathered fresh Quintessence from the world around him as I tutored him on the fine points of concentrating on the one bloody thing that is in front of you, before he made his second attempt at the Golden Flames of Galgalagrin the Great. This time he managed to maintain his focus for all of the split second that the spell required to cast, but instead of a roiling ball of golden fire that would rend our enemies to their component molecules, there came forth a banana. It was flung at considerable speed, I must admit, yet it remained a banana.

Now, some might consider this to be another failure, but not I. This time, I had been carefully listening to the exact pronunciation of Ig's spell, and I had been carefully monitoring his understanding of Potassium throughout. Neither was entirely perfect, but it was imperfect in a consistent enough way that I still had hope. He was not blurting things out entirely incorrectly; he just needed a little directional tweak. The other reason that I did not consider this latest bout of fruit summoning to have been a failing was because as the banana soared across the room, the mimic suddenly burst into action. The chest's lid flapping back, a long, froggish tongue extending out to snatch the banana from the air, and all of the many many rows of sharklike teeth lining the top and sides of the chest's opening smashed together to render it into a creamy yellow paste.

Before, Ig may have been told that there was a monster in the room that was capable of killing him. Now he believed it.

He shook and shivered, resisting the urge to run from the room screaming as he gathered Quintessence for his next attempt and tried to listen to the improved pronunciation that I was repeating to him.

Once I believed that he was entirely ready, I paused for a moment to ask, *Did you see how long its tongue was? Anything it touches becomes stuck and is dragged into reach of the mimic's jaws. Just imagine that moment, when it seizes hold of you and yanks you off your feet.*

"My is imagining it!" Ig screamed.

Good, now take one step forward, focus upon your understanding of Potassium, and cast the spell.

Was the spell perfect this time? No, it was not. Was it actually worse? Also no.

Another banana leapt from Ig's outstretched hand to be gobbled by the mimic. Ig turned to scamper back to a safe distance at the sight of the monster's tongue, but I seized control of his ankles to keep him in place.

There is no need to be running off, Ig.

"There is many needs to be running." Ig squeaked in fear. "Like big chompy toother thing."

Stand still. If you fall, you may land in reach of it.

Careful examination of the process had revealed the root of our problem. While Ig had spoken the Archaic perfectly this time around, his understanding of Potassium was limited.

This was not because he had not been granted the wealth of information on the subject that still resided within my hat-shaped mind, but because his understanding of all things was limited. His world was smaller than most other people's and it had been built around some central pillars. Fear, of course, but also lesser pillars such as hunger. No longer was he a creature of base instinct alone, but neither was he capable of the full breadth of higher thought that a fully sentient creature that had spent all of its life sentient could achieve. All of which is to say that his division of the world into things to run away from and things to eat had filed Potassium as something to eat, and thus, each time he cast his spell, the fruit of his obsessive dreams manifested itself.

In short, he was an idiot.

He shook and shivered like a mildly inconvenienced chihuahua in a thunderstorm. "Why is you making me stand closer?"

Oh, Ig, don't you understand I mean only to help you? Fear brings the world into focus for you in a way that rational direction cannot. So long as you have something tangible to fear, we do not need to police your attention, and thus we can focus upon more important things.

"There not be any more important things than big toothy chompers."

Precisely, it holds your gaze in the ideal manner. Now take another step forward and ready to cast again. This time, we shall work upon your understanding of Potassium.

The better part of the morning was spent down in the dark of that dungeon, launching banana after banana into the maw of the mimic. By the end, Ig was swaying on the spot from exhaustion. Yet that was not the reason that our practice came to its end. Nor was it the fact that he was now standing well within the striking distance of the mimic, having edged forwards a step at a time over the course of the hours. No. The reason that we gave up for the day was that from deep within the wooden frame of the mimic there came a dread rumble, the lid flapped open, and a fountain of partially digested banana puree was launched into the air.

We had overfed it.

Allowing Ig back the control of his ankles, we fled with all haste ahead of the churning, chunky spray, slamming the door to the chamber shut behind us and hoping against hope that the Bonetaker did not go and check up on the place before we were already well away.

As if he were summoned by my thoughts, we encountered the very same lank figure in dark robes just outside of the dungeon entrance. "How was your private session with the biggest tongue in the dungeon?"

Ig blinked before mumbling a confused, "Okay?"

He pursed his lips. "I do hope that you taught that naughty beastie a very serious lesson in why it should pay me my rent on time."

Unfamiliar with the concept of rent, Ig had no real comment to pass on that. "Is left alive but is not forgetting what me did." Ig nodded firmly. "Not never."

It was remarkable how often Ig's rambling nonsense was technically true while entirely failing to accurately describe the situation.

The Bonetaker clapped his hands together, putting his flimsy wrists at risk. "Well, come along then, darling, let's get the drinks in."

The sun was still high in the sky as we emerged from the cavern into the fog. "Is early?"

"It is five o'clock somewhere, pet." The necromancer tittered.

Ig attempted to set his jaw, which likely would have been more effective if he had any jawline to speak of. He barely even had a chin—mouth basically flowed right into neck in kobold anatomy. "Me is not a pet."

"Oh, I'm well aware, darling, it's a term of endearment." The Bonetaker bent low to place a kiss on the top of Ig's hat. Which is to say, me. "I like you, pet, so I call you pet."

Uncomfortable at this turn of events, having never been liked before, Ig attempted to change the subject. "You fix curse?"

"Now how did you know about that, you naughty little creature?" He snickered, but there was a distinct edge to his voice as he asked, "Were you listening in on our conversation after you were meant to be sleeping?"

"Me couldn't work out cursed man want curse gone on own." Ig actually rolled his eyes. Eye rolling and sarcasm in one fell swoop. What an overachiever. He was learning well from his civilized companions. A little too well for my liking. "Me is so dumb."

"Haha." When he wasn't deliberately snickering for effect, the Bonetaker's laugh was actually quite fun. A little high-pitched and nasal, but otherwise charming enough. "Fair play. Fair play indeed."

The others were lounging around outside, as only adventurers can lounge. Ildrit looked a little worse for wear after his late night and was flat out atop a stone bench, resting his head upon Wyn's lap. Wyn was idly braiding the man's hair while staring out into the mist as though they could penetrate the fog by will alone. The only one not in the pile was Rhine, who was instead scowling at anyone that she could, fairly ineffectively. Whether her scowls were a result of a hangover or the casual intimacy of the other two which she was being denied, I could not say.

"Look what I found lurking in a hole," the Bonetaker called out as we approached.

Wyn glanced at us, Ildrit waved a hand vaguely in our direction; only Rhine seemed genuinely pleased at our arrival. "I was worried you'd gotten lost."

"Me is fines." Ig smiled at her so widely his face began to ache. "Was 'sploring dungeon."

That was sufficient to draw the attention of the other two fully, with Ildrit swinging up to sitting with only the one side of his hair braided back.

"On purpose?" Wyn asked at the same time that Ildrit said, "Why?"

The Bonetaker intercepted that question like a champ. "There was something of an arcane problem that needed attending to down in the deeps, and like the hero he is, your . . . brave companion volunteered."

All three of them cocked their heads to the side, trying to fit the word brave and hero into their mental picture of Ig.

The Bonetaker, however, seemed to have frozen up for a moment with a little frown on his sallow face. "You know, I'm terribly sorry for the rudeness, but I don't know your name. I don't believe that we were actually introduced."

Ig turned and stuck out his little hand, which the Bonetaker shook, as you would the proffered paw of a well-trained dog. "Me is Absalom Scryne."

The hand-shaking halted. "You are Absalom Scryne? Archmage of Arpanpholigon? Imperator of the Invisible College? Lord of the Lost Library?"

Ig was suitably impressed by my many titles but remembered to answer. "Me is."

"I thought you'd be taller." Bonetaker managed to titter despite his obvious surprise.

"Me usually is." Ig grinned.

"I had no idea that I was in such esteemed company. I wouldn't have treated you like . . ."

"Stop fussing, Boney, if he'd wanted to be primped and petted, he would have told you his name upfront," Ildrit interrupted. Though he too was now looking at Ig in an entirely different way than the barely contained contempt that he usually managed.

Wyn was unmoved, what with knowing the truth of our situation, but poor sweet Rhinolyta looked thoroughly taken aback. "Should I have been curtseying? I'm really bad at curtseying."

"Me is still same man kobold thing you knows yesterday." Ig fumbled his way on. "Nothing change."

"This changes absolutely everything. If we'd known you were the head wizard, instead of just some wizard, we would have made getting you home our first priority," Ildrit announced. "To think we've been dragging you around on our adventures. Making you sleep in the dirt . . ."

"Me didn't mind!" Ig announced, contrary to all of my recollections of the times being described. "Me like spending time with friends."

I think you could actually see the moment that Rhine's heart swelled with affection for her little kobold companion. If it were the real me, rather than this falsehood in kobold skin, I doubt I would have been quite so magnanimous, but none of these people knew the real me, so the deception would still hold without any issue.

"Well, my darlings, in recompense for the fine company you've given me in this lonely place, you must allow me to accompany you on the rest of your journey to see your wizard safely returned home."

"Really?" Ildrit's head snapped around, suspicion writ across his features. "Now that you think he's a big deal, you're all about helping him?"

I had my own suspicions already bubbling beneath the surface about the dubious help that a necromancer might offer. He might very well be planning to make a name for himself among the wicked by taking me down while I was in my vulnerable state. There certainly wouldn't be a warm welcome awaiting him in Arpanpholigon.

"My sweet man," the necromancer pressed on. "I feel just awful about not being able to help you with your little issue. Let me make it up to you. Please."

I could see Ildrit trying to decipher exactly what his old ally was up to, but he couldn't very well accuse him of impropriety when he was the one that had vouched for him so vociferously. Wyn was implacable as always. Only Rhine seemed to be happy about the arrangement, clapping her hands together. "Wonderful, we'll get to hear more of your wonderful stories about how stupid young Ildrit was."

Ildrit groaned as the Bonetaker clapped his hands together in equal delight. "Oh, my darling, I haven't even begun to tell you all the depravity your friend there used to get up to. I have tales to tell that would put hair on your chest. Well, perhaps not yours. Or the svelte elf. And Ildrit's chest is quite hairy enough, as I'm sure we're all aware, what with him going shirtless to show off his alleged muscles at every opportunity. I suppose we shall have to settle for a particularly hirsute kobold in our company."

The currently un-hirsute kobold was following all of this with his usual vacant smile, but the hat upon his head, the hat which was me, was filled with trepidation.

CHAPTER NINETEEN

IN THE REALM OF THE BLACK HOOD

Another night was spent in somewhat more subdued revelry as the Bonetaker put his house in order, with Ig being a mite more careful with his consumption of wine after his unpleasant morning. Come the dawn, Ildrit and Rhine were both hunched ever so slightly, as though straightening up might raise their poor aching heads into the maelstrom of the hangover floating just above them. Wyn and I had not a single moment in privacy to confer as I would have liked, but every attempt to separate from the pack had resulted in a degree of lewd commentary from the Bonetaker that had made even the elf blush, at least a little.

With his preparations complete, the Bonetaker emerged from his private chambers with but a single satchel slung about him, also in corresponding black leather with his boots and belt. A construct of bone and Plutonium-infused unlife would stand guard over the place until his return, and the "Out of Order" sign on the dungeon had been enchanted to draw the eye of any who came wandering by. Between the giant stone statues and the bone-golem, I'd say the place would likely do a decent job of dissuading visitors anyway, but the Bonetaker was nothing if not fastidious. He turned slowly on the spot then pointed off into the distance. "Arpanpholigon is that way. Shall we be off, my darlings?"

I must say that it was sort of nice to have someone along who actually knew where they were going, even if they did plan to use that superior knowledge to murder us all in our sleep.

Heading out in this direction, there was a lot less in the way of ominous and foreboding undead and considerably more in the way of large flashing signs that read "Dungeon This Way." It was a subtle enchantment, by comparison to the draw that the Bonetaker was clearly capable of inflicting upon passersby, but I suppose that it wouldn't do to draw in too many non-adventurers.

Before noon, we had passed beyond the reach of his advertising and pressed on towards the still-distant sound of running water. Had I a heart, that would have gotten it beating faster. A river, a big river, the big river that divided humanity and all her kingdoms from the Badlands. The Whitewaters.

Our progress would be stymied upon arrival there. While in my usual state I could simply have flown across, leaving these ingrates behind, as a hat upon an inept kobold, such things were out of reach, and we would likely have to rely upon the raft-building talents of all these outdoorsy people.

While we stopped for a lunch of dry rations, I cannot say that anyone found them particularly filling after the lovely food prepared in the Bonetaker's brothel. Though now that I thought about who was probably doing the actual cooking in the bordello, I immediately lost any remaining appetite that I might have retained when I became a hat. Ig was thankfully not privy to that particular thought of mine, having instead been instructed to spend his time working on his understanding of Potassium, and being fed a steady stream of my knowledge on the subject. It was my hope that eventually my wisdom would manage to overpower his natural ignorance, but that hope was fading as the day went on and his attempts to cause minor forest fires instead furnished the party with a great many fruit snacks.

Even Ig himself happily munched on a banana as I abandoned all hope of a different result. Perhaps I needed to move on to a less edible element. A change of direction might be just what his education needed. Though I was frankly fearful of what might be produced if I were to point him in another direction.

The Bonetaker, now outfitted with a small satchel filled with bananas, was walking alongside Rhine, having decided that she was the only one who was going to be nice enough to engage him in the endless conversation that he apparently desired, and was now making an attempt to challenge her.

"I'd bet that I can swallow the whole thing in one go," Bonetaker bragged.

"Nobody could take the full length of that down their throat without choking."

Ildrit's ears twitched, but he very carefully did not turn around.

"Just you watch, my darling. There are talents in this world that it takes years to master, but if you put in the time . . ." There was a grotesque wet gulping noise as he inserted the banana into his mouth, flattening the back end of the fruit with the palm of his hand as he shoved it in deeper and deeper while Rhine watched in awe. Yet for all his protestations of his superiority in this skill, it seemed that even the Bonetaker had his limits. At first he merely gulped and gagged, but soon it became apparent that the banana had struck upon some solid surface somewhere in the apparatus of his neck and could proceed no farther. His eyes watered and his sallow skin flushed as he tried to force it farther despite the barrier, but it was not to be. Coughing, he regurgitated the banana and it fell sadly to the forest floor.

"Hah!" Rhine cried. "I told you it couldn't be done."

Panting for breath, the Bonetaker snapped back, "I'd like to see you do better."

For reasons that he could not explain, Ig found that he would also like to see her do better. Judging by the way that Ildrit's upper body had entirely frozen, it seemed likely that he'd also like to see her do better. The sly smile now appearing on the Bonetaker's face suggested that he himself could have done better, but was now attempting to goad Rhine into trying to do better for his own amusement. The only one who was not having some visceral reaction to this whole matter was Wyn, who might very well have been having a massive visceral reaction that they had spent centuries schooling their face and body not to show.

As though caught in the pull of some potent magnet, Ildrit's head was dragged around as Rhine lifted the banana to her plump limps. Ig had never taken his eyes off her throughout the entire exchange, forcing me to watch the Bonetaker's attempt from the corner of his eye. Even Wyn tore their eyes from scouting ahead to watch the show that was surely about to unfold.

Rhine licked her lips as she peeled the skin from the banana, running a finger down the length of it, as though taking its measure, then she bobbed her head down, opening up to accept it inside her . . . and bit down, severing the tip in a single chomp.

Every man present winced.

She chewed it a little before taking another bite and glancing up at the wide eyes locked on her. "I don't waste food."

Ildrit let out a little nervous laugh before snapping his head back around and carrying on along the rabbit trail we'd been following through the underbrush.

Knowing he was beaten, the Bonetaker shrugged. "Darling, that is no way to get a husband."

For the first time, Rhine looked offended. "You think I'm too fat?"

So accustomed to living in his own filthy world of fantasy, it took the Bonetaker some time to recover from what was to him a non-sequitur and realize that she thought it had been a comment on her eating habits. "Oh, darling, no. Look how you fill out all that leather so perfectly; I wouldn't drop a penny-weight if I were you. If I had a body like that, I'd never be off my back."

She nodded her flawed understanding. "Because you would not need to get up and exercise. I assure you, I put a lot of work into maintaining my fighting form. Out here in the wilderness, I remain toned enough from all of the fighting and walking, but back in the city I have a strict regimen of . . ."

She began listing off exercises that were as foreign to me as they were to Ig. Crunches and curls and belching or something. A whole swathe of actions the body could be forced to perform if one wanted to develop bulging musculature beneath one's skin. I had never much seen the point personally. When other young wizards had spoken of getting fit, I had explained that my own somewhat podgy body was in fact a perfect fit for the tasks that were required of it. I was built to sit for long periods of time reading and stand for short periods of time providing lectures to the less well-educated, with the odd periods of lying down in between when the words began to blur together.

The food that she described eating sounded to me like the kind of thing that would make a gruel-devouring peasant turn up their nose and ask to speak to the chef. Protein was the primary point of all that she devoured. Protein and no fat whatsoever. In my experience the fat was the part that tasted good, but I supposed that this too was further evidence that we wanted different things from our bodies. So long as mine could remain upright in a chair, I was fit for purpose. She had to fight things and do backflips and . . . whatever else it was that warrior women did.

The Bonetaker's eyes had also glazed over. It seems that he had the same care for personal fitness as I. Presumably this was a trait inherent to those that plumb the depths of universal knowledge, and we weren't just both lazy bastards.

With that particular detour into debauchery completed, I was able to return to my contemplation of the next element that I might teach Ig. He'd had some success with Sulfur thus far, so that seemed like a viable contender. The fire that it created was a little more difficult to control than that of the Golden Flames, but at least he could consistently produce some sort of defensive ability, or possibly just more rotten egg smells. Of course, it did run the risk of conjuring demons if he put too much Quintessence into a spell, but what was a little heckish invasion between friends?

Admittedly, it would take either magic or a magical weapon to dispense with any fiends, but I had little doubt in Ildrit's ability in that regard, and there was a fair chance that any chaotic denizens of the nether planes would be just as likely to attack anyone trying to kill us, so it still felt like a net win.

Though that was of course assuming that Ildrit's black blade was actually magical.

Ig scampered up beside him. "Swords is magic?"

The warrior looked down at Ig in surprise. "Uh, yes. My sword is . . . how did you know that?"

"Looks magic."

Bonetaker chuckled from behind us. "Yes, Ildrit my lovely, why don't you tell them what incredible enchantment the Widowtaker has upon it."

Finally the black blade had a name, and it was just as ludicrously evil sounding as I had expected. Both Wyn and Rhine looked taken aback by the name of the thing, presumably because it was so ludicrously evil sounding. Ildrit scratched the back of his neck, failing to meet their gaze.

"It, uh . . ." He trailed off into a mumble.

Ig cocked his head to the side. "It what?"

"Well, it, uh . . . it rends through the armor of my foes about as well as any sword . . . and uh, any injury it deals to . . ." more mumbling, ". . . on the other."

"Any wound it deals to who?" Rhine enquired, with her eyes narrowed.

His shoulders slumped. "Married people."

"You'll need to say the whole thing, without any mumbles." Wyn sighed.

"Any wound it deals to one married person, it deals to the other."

It was hard to make out much more over the sound of the Bonetaker's wild cackling, but through that cacophony I could hear Rhine's cry of dismay. "What?! Why?!"

The cursed swordsman's pallid skin was now showing a rosy red upon his countenance, creeping up from his cheeks to envelop his entire head. "I didn't ask for it to . . . I found it in . . . listen . . ."

For Wyn's part there was only confusion. "What possible purpose could such an enhancement serve?"

"Look, I don't know!" Ildrit was now drifting ever closer to the color of a tomato. "Clearly somebody somewhere in history had some issues with commitment, or marriage or . . . something."

"Darling, don't be so silly." Bonetaker giggled. "There was clearly a cuckolding warrior who needed to defend himself from the obvious repercussions and thought that stabbing the one he was already *stabbing* was the easy solution."

"What is this cuck holding?" Rhine asked sharply, before Ig had the opportunity to blurt out the very same question.

"Oh, my sweet girl, you see, sometimes when two people love each other very much, or one of them gets knocked up, or their families want to inherit what the other family have, they get married, and sometimes one or more of the married people decide that they'd like to get a little bit of strange . . ."

Ildrit silenced the Bonetaker with a glare before he could elaborate further. Given the heat rising off his head by this point, it was surprising that flames had not shot forth from his eyes.

"Regardless of the circumstances of its creation, it is mine now, and I use it simply because it is a superior weapon. I've never had any call for its . . . special traits."

That seemed sufficient to placate the others for now, though I could still hear Bonetaker heaving with laughter behind us. It seemed that the whole debacle was over until Rhine asked in a whisper loud enough to raise the dead, "Strange what?"

We made camp that night on the banks of the Whitewaters, and I had never been so happy to see a large body of water in my life. On this side of the river, the Badlands had the same yellowish clay soil and wild-growing spiky plants as it had throughout our journey, but on the far side, grass grew, and it was in fact greener than anything on this side of the river.

Technically speaking, this river was not in fact the border of the Badlands. The official border as marked on maps could be found several miles beyond it, abutting the great wall that had been raised to divide the wicked world out here from the beauty and peace of civilized lands, but the official and practical definitions differed somewhat. With such an impassable natural barrier, the vast majority of the monsters and chaos that occurred out here stopped dead. Our travel across the far side of the river should have been moderately safe by comparison. Not entirely safe, because there would always be some unpleasant creatures lumbering around, just waiting to pick off anyone fool enough to leave behind the safety of walls, but safer than anywhere I had experienced since becoming a hat. That was worthy of celebration in my books.

Almost there, Ig. Just another day's travel and we shall walk among mankind once more.

Ig shifted uncomfortably on the fallen log that had been dragged over beside the fire. "Me is not sure mankind will be liking me walking there."

Do not fear, my little companion, in the company of these fine adventurers, I'm sure we will be quite able to traverse the distance unhindered.

"Fine? Me thoughts you said they was scums."

I mean, they're adventurers . . . but as far as adventurers go, I'd argue that these are some of the better sort.

Ig nodded contentedly. "Me is liking them too."

Especially Rhine?

"Who are you speaking to, pet?" Bonetaker called out from the tree line behind us. He had wandered off in search of the minor privacy required for his pre-dinner ablutions. Twice in the direction that Ildrit had gone, before being rebuffed, and once after Wyn, who had made themselves scarce rather than be observed. I had rather thought that we might have had more time alone before his hunt for prurient curiosities came to an end.

"Me is just talking to me," Ig blurted before I could intervene.

"Talking to yourself, darling. That is never a good sign." He tittered, coming to sit beside us with what I considered to be an unnecessary amount of sweeping robes and drama. "Could be dementia setting in. How old were you before your little transformation?"

Ig opened his mouth, but I clamped it shut again just as quick. He may have thought that this was just impolite conversation, but I could sense a snare hidden somewhere in there. *One hundred and six. The prime of my life.*

"Me was prime numbers."

Bonetaker's plucked eyebrow rose. "Beg your pardon, pet?"

Ig tried again. "Hundred six."

"Oh. I suppose that isn't so old, for a wizard. So the dementia must be the result of your transformation." He went on tittering, and I hoped that someone else would show up soon so I could get Ig out of this conversation politely. "How did that happen exactly?"

Careful, Ig.

"Me not remember." He started, "Remember was wizard then woke up as hat."

IG!

The Bonetaker turned to look at me curiously. Not at Ig, but at me. "Hat?"

"Kobold," Ig yelped quickly. "I means I was kobold. With my hat."

"So let me get this right, pet. You were transformed into a kobold, with no memory of how such a thing was done through the doubtless many layers of enchantment intended to protect you from such things, and despite every other part of you having been transformed, you kept your hat."

"Is good hat," Ig proclaimed, loyally.

"How curious." He reached out towards me and Ig jerked away. "Might I examine this object of arcane power that has somehow resisted so potent a curse?"

"No. Is my hat," Ig yapped with a degree of hostility I had not been aware that he was capable of. "Get own."

Ildrit stepped out into the fire's light, still fussing with his belt. "What's all the arguing about?"

At once, the Bonetaker went back to his usual simpering self. "Oh, darling, I just wanted to try on your little friend's hat, but he's quite resistant to sharing."

Ildrit shrugged as he hunkered down to feed the fire. "Suppose if I was turned into a creature and only had one keepsake from being human, I'd be pretty attached to it too."

"I'd give it back!" The Bonetaker pouted.

"Boney, you look awful in hats, you know that. Like a crested bird or something."

The pout remained. "I thought that the width might balance out the noble elegance of my face."

"No take. Mine," Ig grumbled.

"Well, there's your answer." Ildrit plopped down onto the packed earth with a groan. "What's for dinner?"

"Bananananana?" Ig offered.

"If I ever see another banana again in my life, I may vomit," Ildrit replied without even glancing around.

Wyn staggered into sight holding one end of a deer. Or rather one end of about three quarters of a deer, because the front half was missing and Rhine, at her end, was covered in blood. "Venison tonight!"

"Dear gods, woman," Bonetaker exclaimed. "Did you kill it with your teeth?"

"Shouldn't bother a lady in the powder room" was the only answer he got.

The adventurers set about diligently preparing the meal while Bonetaker and I sat as idle and useless as you might have expected, though I suppose you could call his running commentary of suggestions and recipes helping, if you were exceedingly generous.

Finally, by the time that the moon had risen, the delicious smells of roasting meat were wafting out through the woods and we were all set to tuck into what had to be the most appealing-looking meal that Ig had ever encountered in his life. Small as he was, I had no fear of him gorging himself to the point of interfering in the others getting a good meal, but I did have some concerns he might rupture himself if left to his own devices.

Ildrit jammed a knife into the poor dead beast to watch the rivulets of juices dripping down into the fire and throwing up black smoke, and declared the meat, "Medium rare."

Which was the very moment that an arrow slammed into the poor dead deer's rump. From this close it was quite easy to see, even if its abrupt appearance was rather alarming. It was fletched with what looked like crow feathers.

Just as abruptly as the arrow had appeared, all of the adventurers had frozen in place. Quite the opposite of the usual explosion into action that they normally performed in times of crisis. They seemed almost as paralyzed as the werewolves would have been if Ig could cast a spell worth a damn.

From out in the dark woods there came a call. "Prithee be still, knaves! Your money or your life!"

It sounded as though someone was reciting it from a cue card that had in turn been cribbed from some old book on how to be a bandit. The more modern bandit tends to have a more "beat people to death first, ask questions later" approach.

"We haven't got any money," Ildrit called back.

The voice from the dark paused for a moment, then came back to us, presumably after consulting their notes. "Jewels?"

"None," Rhine declared.

"Silk?" There was a pang of desperation in the voice.

"Do you wish for us to give you a full catalog of everything of value we carry, for it would be a very short list." Wyn sighed, turning back to dishing out the now punctured venison. "One might even say, no list at all."

"Oh, come on, you must have something," pleaded the bandit.

Ildrit gestured around at the log, backpacks, and absolutely nothing else that we had scattered around us. "You are looking at the sum of our worldly possessions."

"We could shoot you, you know." The bandit seemed to be extremely unsure of this idea. One got the impression that they'd never expected to get this far to begin with.

Wyn shook their head. "Then you'd have nothing, and a pile of dead bodies to deal with."

There was more distant deliberation before the bandit called back, "Can we have some of that venison at least?"

"Catch your own!" Rhine snapped.

"Please?" That plaintive cry was so pathetic it made Ig seem like a beacon of courage.

"Oh, go on, let them," the Bonetaker said, ever the voice of charity when it came to increasing the number of eligible men around his campfire. "They must be starving trying to make a living through banditry out here, the silly buggers."

"What is your vote, wizard?" Ildrit turned to Ig, who shrugged.

"We gots enough meats?"

Wyn was forced to concede that we likely would not be able to consume an entire deer in a single sitting, no matter how ravenous we may have been. They conceded this through the slightest tilt of the chin.

"We have some ale left," came the cry from the dark once more.

Ildrit and Rhine's eyes may have just caught the campfire light at the same moment, but I couldn't help but feel that the light shining there was coming from within.

"Come on then," Ildrit called out.

As Rhine simultaneously declared, "We cannot leave these poor people in need."

And out of the woods they came, the most pathetic dregs of humanity I have ever laid eyes on, so skinny that even Ig could have enclosed the whole of one's arm in the span of his spidery hand. They were dressed much as you'd expect of bandits with rusted weapons, scrappy leather armor and bandanas tied around their faces, but while desperation may have driven many to banditry, it seemed that banditry had driven this lot to desperation.

"Thank you so much," a short one said, gratefully accepting some venison and setting upon it with gusto.

"Haven't had anything but mushrooms in days, and half the time they make you crap to death." A tall one shook his head in despair.

The roundest of the trio declared, "Poor old Johnny."

From the depths of the darkness emerged their leader at last, the one who had been speaking to us from the start, and I was startled to see that rather than being a teenaged boy out here making his first attempt at breaking away from his parents' mastery, she was in her twenties at least. "He died how he lived: shitty."

Tall sighed. "Nobody deserves to die like that."

"Somebody had to try them to make sure they were okay." Short shrugged.

Round added, "They were bright red with white spots; I don't think you get bright red mushrooms with white spots that are okay to eat."

Their leader came into the firelight with her hands already held out for food, which Ildrit begrudgingly dispensed. She had a black hood pulled up over her face to hide her identity more fully than just the mask, but it was so dark anyway that it seemed somewhat pointless. She snapped, "Oh, you're the mushroom expert now?"

Round replied, all too fast, "Johnny was the mushroom expert."

"Not a very good one." Tall sighed again.

"Don't speak ill of the dead," the Black Hood cut them off.

The adventurers just sat there staring as I considered that they were for the first time on the receiving end of the same degree of pointless banter I'd been enduring since meeting them.

"Darling, love the hood, the mask, the drama, delightful," the Bonetaker piped up. "You wouldn't happen to have old Johnny's bones with you, would you? I could do with somebody to carry my bag."

The Black Hood had turned towards him as he spoke, but having heard his words, she now seemed to be pretending that she couldn't hear him at all.

Ildrit dispensed meat to the rest of us, though not in the way that Bonetaker might have liked, then turned to the bandits savaging what they'd been given. "So what brings you all out into the Badlands?"

"Well, we're bandits. See . . ." began the round one, before the tall one elbowed him and corrected, "Freedom fighters."

"Yeah, we're freedom fighters, see . . ." the round one resumed, with somewhat less enthusiasm.

The Black Hood drew up to her full height. "We rob the rich and give to the poor. Bring the world back into balance."

Ildrit offered around some dry tack and they snatched it hungrily from his hand. "That doesn't explain what you're doing out here."

"Well, as it turns out, we couldn't really find anyone rich where we stayed," said the short one. "So we had to look a bit further afield."

The short one added, "And all the rich people had private guards. Stabbed us if we tried to rob them."

"Poor old Johnny." Round sighed. "They stabbed him so much."

"So we decided that we needed to go somewhere without poor people, so we weren't accidentally preying on the people we're trying to help, and without guards, so we could live on to fight the good fight. So we came here," the Black Hood concluded.

Wyn's eyebrow was ever so slightly raised. "How well is that working out for you?"

"Well, there's nobody here at all," cried the shortest of the quartet of idiots.

"Except you lot," the tall one added. "And you're as poor as us."

"Well, nobody is as poor as us." The round one rested his chins upon his hand. "We probably shouldn't have given everything we ever stole to the poor, really. Maybe just kept a percentage so we wouldn't starve . . ."

"That sounds like taxation." The Black Hood's hand drifted down to the axe on her hip. "You know I don't hold with that."

"I ain't saying tax nobody, I'm just saying we're poor too," Round whined. "So when we rob the rich, shouldn't we give some to us?"

"But then we wouldn't be poor anymore," Tall shouted back at him.

"Perhaps there is some middle ground?" Rhine, ever the peacemaker, tried to help. She should not have gotten involved, as all four now rounded on her, and the Black Hood shouted, "Whose side of the class war are you on, exactly?"

"Uh . . . warriors? Though we've got another warrior, a ranger, and a wizard or two. So a good mix of classes really."

The Black Hood's eyes stuck on me. "That's a kobold."

"Temporarily," Ildrit amended.

"You do know it's a kobold, right?" Round seemed to be genuinely confused. "It hasn't tricked you into thinking it is something else using magic."

"Oh, my sweet, plump-cheeked boy, everyone knows kobolds can't do magic." The Bonetaker unexpectedly came to my defense. "That's a wizard that got turned into a kobold. Apparently."

"Me is a wizard," Ig agreed.

The Black Hood's eyes narrowed in the deep shadows beneath her black hood. "It sounds like a kobold."

"It looks like a kobold," the short one confirmed.

"You want us to just kill it, to be on the safe side?" offered the Black Hood.

"No!" the adventurers all cried out together. Well that was a rather nice little surprise.

"Alright." The bandits turned their attention back to the food. "Your funeral."

Ildrit finally managed to seize the wheel of the conversation. "Did you mention beer?"

"Yeah! Still got a few bottles in my pack from the last inn we knocked over before heading out past the wall." Round grinned. "One second."

He began rummaging, and the adventurers turned their disapproving gaze on the Black Hood once more. "Robbing innkeepers?"

"They're petty bourgeoisie." She refused to be shamed. "They profit off the labor of their fellow man!"

None of the adventurers were particularly prepared for this foray into economics and political theory, so they were forced to let the conversation pass them by. Ig, unfortunately, was too ignorant to realize just how ignorant he was. "Isn't you do that too?"

"What?" The Black Hood looked supremely offended.

"You is taking what other peoples made." Ig's brows had drawn down as he tried to reason his way through the situation.

"That's different. We're redistributing the wealth!"

"By taking it from peoples?" He was counting on his fingers, even though there was nothing to count.

Thankfully there was no opportunity for this to advance to a full-on debate as at about that moment, the gentleman looking for beer in his bag exploded apart into ludicrous little gibbets of meat.

CHAPTER TWENTY

JUSTICE AND VENGEANCE

It took even me some time to parse what had just happened, because of how abruptly it had occurred. It would only be after careful consideration and examination of the scene of the crime that I would realize the murder had been committed using what appeared to be a ballista bolt.

"Weh?" was all that Ig managed to say before the screaming started.

More of the same bolts began to rain down on us from out in the tree line, and with every one of us turned in towards the fire, eyeing the bandits with suspicion, every one of us had lost our night vision and not a one of us had been keeping watch for any other aggressors.

The difference between the professionals and amateurs became immediately apparent. As the Black Hood shot to her feet and both Tall and Short started wailing in horror, our own little group of adventurers sprang into action. Rhine leapt behind the log we had been using as a seat before another massive bolt could obliterate her. Wyn sprinted off towards the river to seek cover and an exit strategy. Ildrit was the most practiced of them all. He rose to his feet with an odd sliding motion, kicking dirt into the campfire and smothering it even as he righted himself and drew Widowtaker.

I had just managed to get Ig into motion when the Black Hood's black hood was separated from her neck and torso, sailing off into the dead of night. For a moment the body remained standing, spurting a ridiculous fountain of red all over us, but that was just until the wailing Short crashed into it and the two of them went down in a tangle.

It was just as well that they did. Because while that first flurry of massive bolts had been most impressive, what came next was the true horror of the evening. From out of the woods came another whistling of shots, not vast sapling-thick things like we'd suffered before, but an organized volley of perfectly normal arrows.

Familiarity with history books does a rather horrible thing to your brain: it gives you the ability to notice patterns. Things like "invading landlocked countries in midwinter is a bad idea" and "gosh, an awful lot of these legendary heroes that were allegedly unstoppable in battle seem to have died when they were made into pincushions by an organized block of archers."

Ildrit's shoulder took Ig in the gut, and we both passed briefly over where Rhine lay breathless and heaving behind her log before landing heavily in the leaf litter. It knocked all the air out of Ig's body, which was probably for the best. If he couldn't talk, there was a minimal amount of trouble that he could cause. The impact didn't seem to have done Ildrit any inconvenience whatsoever. "To the river."

Rhine rolled to her feet, already following after him. "You just want us to run?"

Behind us, the entire campsite had become a tiny forest of arrows. Where the bodies of the bandits had fallen were hillocks. Where our shucked-off gear had been pinned to the ground, I could not rightly say.

The Bonetaker, who had quite sensibly invoked Nitrogen to become intangible for a moment, returned to his solid state with an abrupt, effete cry. "That is just rude!"

Ildrit called back to him but did not stop running. The whistle of the next volley was already in the air. "Fall back to the river!"

"I shan't be falling anywhere, darling, who do these ingrates think they're dealing with?!" With a green pulse of Plutonium invoked, the dead bodies of the bandits arose then split apart, shedding their flesh to expose glowing bones alone. As the arrows came down, those bones swirled up above the Bonetaker to intercept them, then he was out of sight as we rounded a copse of jagged shrubs.

"We can'ts be leaving him!" Ig cried out.

"Old Boney has had much worse," Ildrit tried to reassure him. "Just you worry about getting us over that river."

"Weh?!" Ig yelped.

There were a great many things that Ig did throughout the day—scratching himself, examining his claws after scratching himself, glancing around to make sure nobody saw him scratching himself—but one of the things that he did not do was think. He did not plan ahead, he did not contrive solutions to problems, his brain was essentially up for grabs to do with as I pleased for the vast majority of the time, and while it was far from optimal working conditions for an intellect such as mine, it did work, at least a little. So while he had not given any consideration to the ways in which the Whitewaters might be forded, I had conceived of several potential solutions.

Invoking Gadolinum to freeze the river solid had been my first thought, and had I my own supplies of Quintessence and my own body, that would have been how the trick was done, but there was entirely too much risk involved in having Ig invoke a completely unknown element at such short notice. It would be bad if our pursuers caught up to us, worse still if they caught up to us and found that we had already freeze-dried ourselves.

Carbon and Potassium were all that Ig knew. Using Carbon would make us sink like rocks, and Potassium exploded on contact with water. In essence, no actual magic that Ig might be capable of casting would help in the slightest. So it was time to think outside of the box.

Alright, Ig, here is the plan.

"Plan." He bounced under Ildrit's arm. "Good."

You are going to use low magic to pull down one of the trees, creating a bridge across the river.

"Me no can do that," Ig whined.

I am certain that you can, Ig. We need only master your ability to focus upon a single thing at a time.

He sounded as though he were sobbing as he bounced along. "Me no can do that!"

Ig, my dear, sweet apprentice. Not only can you do that, but you are also going to do that. Because the alternative is to be peppered with arrows by our unseen assailants. Do I make myself clear?

"Me can banan them?" Ig offered.

That will not be sufficient in this case.

We arrived at the riverbank all too swiftly, and from the roar ahead of us it was quite easy to guess where this particular flow got its name from. On this side of the river, if memory served, there was little to write home about. Sickly yellow dirt, a few scrappy patches of half-dead grasses, no trees. It was that last part that concerned me. If it were a matter as simple as cutting down a tree then I feel that my more martially inclined companions might have been just as capable of crafting our makeshift bridge, but there was nothing convenient so close, and asking them to go back towards the archers to perform a little light lumberjacking felt a tad rude.

Yet by the moonlight I could already see our salvation. A solid oak, probably older than I, stood atop the far bank, its roots doubtless home to many water voles and the like, but its height more than sufficient to cross the gap.

Focus on it, Ig.

"Too big!" he squeaked.

Nothing is too big for magic to master it; all it takes is will, Quintessence, and focus. So focus, Ig. Focus as though your wretched little hide depends upon it. Because it does.

There was no telltale whistle of arrows at our heels. Instead came the heavy tramping of boots. Ig's ears could pick them up, well attuned to listening for larger creatures liable to make him a meal. His focus, his damnable focus, was split between the trees and the creatures closing in on us.

Not helping was the sudden appearance of Wyn from the shadows. "There is no better place to make our crossing. We must swim and hope for the best."

Wyn would probably be able to swim across if they were lucky and their lithe body was not broken upon the rocks. Perhaps even Rhine might make it too, but Ildrit was weighed down by his piecemeal armor and Ig had the upper body strength commonly associated with the terminally ill.

"Me is going to make bridge," Ig announced, despite being aware that the odds of him actually succeeding in the exceptionally simple task that I could have achieved at the age of five were so low as to be essentially zero.

From in the dark behind us, the stomping advance halted and we all braced ourselves for the next flurry of arrows. Yet piercing death from above did not descend upon us, even though the fear of it kept Ig well and truly incapable of just focusing upon the damned tree.

Ildrit rose from his haunches, where he had been trying to hide, and strolled out to meet our pursuers with his sword drawn. Very brave, but ultimately the stupidest thing that he could possibly have done. "I don't know who you are, but I should warn you . . ."

"You know us, human," Sour Ron called back from the shadows. "And your warnings are for nothing. You have incinerationed our city. You murdered innocent ogres for no reason. You is not giving us any warnings then."

Despite Ig's mediocre eyes, the bulk of Sour Ron and his bodyguards soon came into view. The moonlight glinted off the tears running down his leathery face. "You burninated them all. All our houses. All my books. All the civilization I was trying to make."

"Now, to be fair, you were attempting to enslave us at the time."

"We was." Ron nodded his head, which should have been difficult given that ogres' heads more or less merge perfectly into their bodies thanks to the girth of their necks. "I was trying to make things better. I was trying to make it so ogres could be educationated. So they could be respectable. I thoughts no matter what I is doing, it was worth it. No matter what uncivilized things I needed to do to make us civilized, they would all be worthwhile when there was no more looking down on us ogres."

"Well, it sounds like you've learned the error of your ways . . ." Ildrit trailed off as the ogres hefted their weapons.

"I has learned, yes." Ron strode forward out of the dark, and the rest of his body lit up as the moonlight reflected off it. Off the full suit of pristinely smithed armor that covered him. Off the massive cleaver blade he held so casually in a single meaty paw. "I has learned that trying to make ogres like you little people, it makes us weak. Trying to make ogres not ogres, made it so trash like you's could hurt us. I has learned my lesson."

Wyn had been quietly skulking around to one side, trying to find a clear shot through the ogre's armor with those incredible elf eyes of theirs. Rhine, sweet heroic girl that she was, had readied her shield and positioned herself between Ig and the horde.

In the distance, we could all hear the high-pitched scream of the Bonetaker on the wind. Even with all of his power, the necromancer had not been able to stand against the ogres' overwhelming mass and strength. Whether that was the killing blow, or they were torturing the poor man, as ogres were wont to, I could not say for certain.

"I has learned what you was saying all along. Ogres is monsters. Ogres is meant to hurt, and to kill and to laugh." With a truly sickly wet sound, the ogre's lips curved upwards. Sour Ron was attempting a smile. "All this time, I was trying to be more like you. When I was already perfect. I was already an ogre."

"Well, I'm glad that you've . . ." Ildrit began, then had to jerk to the side as Ron lunged forward, blade swinging.

"I is an ogre!" Ron screamed as he brought the blade about again, slamming it into Widowtaker with all of his considerable strength. Ildrit had solid footing, he had a lifetime of experience tanking through the kind of blows that would have turned me into a fine paste spread across the landscape, but he was only human. He slid back from the ogre's awful blow, almost colliding with Rhine before he managed to dig in his heels and stop.

Wyn loosed an arrow, but it deflected uselessly off the headpiece of Ron's armor. Naked and deranged, an ogre was already dangerous enough, but encased in steel, I had no clue how we'd get through to him. In answer to this failed assassination, Ron howled, "Get 'em, boys!"

And then the battle truly began.

Could it truly be called a battle when it was three people against dozens of monsters, each one of them strong and vicious enough to wipe out a whole village by themselves?

Ig, we need to get out of here. You need to bring the tree down.

"Me can't!" he squealed in terror. "Me can't thinks!"

The Quintessence that he had spent the whole day gathering now swirled around him, invisible to the naked eye and perceptible only to the magically attuned. All the power that he was meant to be forcing out to grab hold of the tree was instead spilling everywhere, as though his incontinence in dangerous situations had somehow spread to his magic working too.

Focus, Ig!

He grabbed control of his Quintessence once more, searching about desperately for it as his power poured out of him.

For my part, I kept my attention on the ogre king and Ildrit. The two had met now, blade to blade, at the very center of the battlefield. Sparks rained each time that their weapons collided, but Ildrit had learned from the first awful blow that he'd suffered not to match the ogre's strength head on. Every parry he made was with the black blade angled to drive the force behind Ron's attacks aside and create openings.

If he had been in his prime, perhaps he could have exploited each of those openings, but he was slowing as age and exhaustion caught up to him, while the ogre only seemed to get stronger with every swing.

Ig was so close to having his power gathered and his concentration locked on the tree, but that was the moment that Ron chose to shout out to him. "You'll pay the price for what you've done, wizard."

Ig's panic spiked; his concentration split. Both tree and ogre were jerked on ever so briefly, but neither with sufficient force to particularly help. Ron's blade swept a little farther forward than it should have as the ogre overbalanced and almost took Ildrit's face off. The tree wobbled then sprang back upright, flicking a very unfortunate squirrel off into the distance.

Why can't you focus even when it will literally save your life?!

"Scary!" Ig screeched.

The other ogres had moved in to engage Ildrit too, only to find Rhine had charged during their indecision. Wyn had begun peppering them with arrows too, though he'd only managed to down a couple of ogres, with the rest now resembling extremely overweight porcupines. They were just too dense of muscle mass for the arrows to pierce anything vital, so while Wyn would have been an utter fool not to keep on firing, the majority of their shots served only to enrage.

Ig sucked in more and more Quintessence with every frantic breath. No matter his obvious shortcomings in every other area of the art of magic, something about the frenetic pace of the kobold metabolism seemed to draw the raw stuff of magic in far faster than a human of his level of training could manage. The fact he couldn't reliably do anything with it wasn't particularly helpful, but at least he was almost back up to full stock after his misfire.

Everyone is relying on you now, Ig. You must bring down the tree or we shall all die. Do you understand me?

"Me understand, but me can't!"

Indeed, I couldn't even get the stupid little rodent to turn around and face in the right direction. He was hyperventilating even more than usual, the power inside of him building up and up as he went on frantically drawing in more and more Quintessence. He was so distracted by his own terror that he didn't even realize his reserves were full and overflowing.

Ig.

"Me tired! Okay?! Me tried and me couldn't and me isn't a wizard, me is just a kobold and we is all going to die and is all my fault!"

Ig, you must stop. You must calm yourself.

Ig's screaming was now loud enough to have drawn the attention of everyone, even over the clashing of steel. "How me calm when ogres going to make me tail a belt?!"

"I be going to make you into gloves!" bellowed Ron in answer, his old sour countenance returning as he was hard pressed by Ildrit.

"We believe in you, Ig." Wyn's voice was as soft and steady as ever, but their words hit Ig with the impact of a sledgehammer. Here was this ancient creature, wise beyond human capacity, and they were placing their faith in Ig.

I suppose everyone makes mistakes.

But Ig, he took that encouragement and his terror and all the raw power that had built up inside of him, and he believed in himself, for the very first time. Turning to face the ogre king, he raised his hands and focused on Potassium.

The power surged through him, enough to set every bristling hair on his weird little body on end, his eyes blazed bright with the raw Quintessence he was channeling, and just when I thought he was about to burst, he cried out, "*Fragor!*"

This was it. The moment that all of our hard work paid off. The moment that he truly became a wizard, casting his first real spell. The Quintessence rushed out of his body, shaped by the word, by the knowledge, by his certainty that this time there would be no mistakes, only the Golden Flames of Galgalagrin the Great!

For a moment nothing happened, and then it began to rain bananas.

Ron slapped a hand over his mouth at the first sight of them, giving Ildrit the briefest of advantages over the immense strength that the ogre could bring to bear. Wyn groaned softly behind us. The ogres that had until this moment been charging us stepped upon the fallen bananas and slipped, skidding and stumbling to land in a great heap. It may not have been the desired effect, and it may have left Ig so bereft of Quintessence that his heart was now hammering so hard in his chest, I was surprised a rib hadn't yet broken, but it was doing something.

Wyn took his shot, nailing Ron right in the left eye. Freeing Ildrit from the melee to sprint back towards us, and the river beyond.

He cried out, "Run for it!" as he passed us by.

For a moment I wondered what exactly he meant to do, given that there was still a raging river directly behind Ig, but as the kobold turned to watch him pass, the new reality asserted itself. There was a raging river there, but it was now thoroughly clogged with fruit. Ildrit bounded across, stepping from banana heap to banana heap where he could and wading through where he couldn't. I'd have said he was making good time, but honestly, if I had Sour Ron and his army on my heels, I probably would have been sprinting like a maniac too.

Ig, run!

The poor kobold was completely frazzled after his singular act of magic. His brain, never the most finely honed machine to begin with, was now operating at perhaps 5 percent of its usual capacity. He blinked dully as Wyn seized him by the scruff of the neck and carried him off towards the river.

Once or twice, he was dunked into the water, and the chill of it probably helped to clear his head more than any amount of internal screaming that I could muster. I caught brief glimpses of Wyn struggling against the pull of the Whitewaters, Ildrit on the farthest shore. Ig twisted around relentlessly in the elf's grip, though I was damned if I knew why.

It was only as we were flung clear onto the farthest bank and Wyn fell to their knees beside us that Ig's frantic attempts to get back into the danger made the faintest bit of sense.

The bananas were already being washed away, but Rhine had not yet crossed.

She was mounting a fighting retreat from the ogres, holding her footing better than them, but still not able to break and run without the danger of their superior reach bringing an axe down in her back. Ildrit was hovering on the river's edge, ready to go running back in and save her, despite the bananas now being so thinly dispersed across the surface that he'd almost certainly plunge right through. Not Rhine though; she could swim, she was strong and fast, and she could make it over.

I yelled out through Ig's stupid gaping mouth. "Get the tree down for her."

Ildrit snapped into action, sprinting to the tree with water still running from Widowtaker's blade. He slashed at it with a frantic energy, as though he could cut down Rhine's pursuers.

Ig tried to draw in more power, to launch some new spell that might get her to safety. Something, anything.

Wyn, meanwhile, was doing nothing. Their bowstring was soaked; any shot they fired would only serve to destroy the weapon. All that they could do was watch, so that was all that they did.

The tree came crashing down, exactly where I had planned for it to land, perfectly bridging the river. Nimble as she was, Rhine would have no trouble making it across—we were all going to make it. Ig screamed, "Run, Rhine!"

Her head turned at the sound of his voice, confusion and fear fighting for control of her beauty. She managed a step towards us, then an arrow took her through the knee. In through the pit, out through her shin. She screamed as she fell. Then the ogres were upon her, raining blow after blow down with their shiny, mass-produced axes. Blood splashed over their mindless grinning faces, and none of them smiled wider than Sour Ron. "I'm coming for you, wizard! You're next!"

I do not know what possessed Ig in that moment, but it certainly wasn't me seizing control of him and setting him bounding over the top of the log on all fours with about enough Quintessence inside him to fill a buttercup. He was letting out a constant screech as he went, so high-pitched it would have set my teeth on edge, had I teeth.

He would have died, just like Rhine, if it hadn't been for Wyn's swift intervention. They kicked the log out of place, dislodging it from where it rested across the two banks and sending Ig spinning downriver. Ig was already so blinded by rage that he didn't notice until he'd pounced off the far end of the log and landed back on the bank he'd started on.

"They kill her!" he wailed at me, or anyone close enough to hear. "They kill her!"

I know, Ig. I'm sorry.

"Why me be wizard if can't save?" He sobbed. "Why me do anything?!"

It was Wyn once more who came to Ig's rescue, remaining focused upon the reality in which we lived, instead of the realm of fantasy in which a kobold might have stood a chance against even a single ogre. They scooped up the kobold in their arms as he flailed and sobbed, then took off running towards the distant walls of civilization.

Ildrit still had not moved from where he stood on the banks of the river. His gaze still had not turned from where Rhinolyta had fallen. Sour Ron had his archers and ballista-men lining up on the far bank, taking their time and taking their aim. It was only Wyn yanking on the back of his collar that saved Ildrit from dying that night too.

The two of them ran, Ig dangling from Wyn's arms, Ildrit stumbling and choking as he tried to keep the tears from blinding him. Looking up at his savior, Ig saw tears on the cheeks of the elf too. I had not known that elves could cry, I'd always assumed that they'd consider it too uncouth. There was no snot and sobbing, but the tears flowed silver over their sharp cheekbones in the moonlight. Pattering down on Ig, who by contrast was almost exclusively snot and sobbing.

My opinion on the matter: adventurers die. That is the nature of their job; the vocation that they have chosen is well compensated for specifically because of the risks involved. If it were safe, everyone would do it. Instead only those on the outermost fringes of civilization go out into the wild places of the world and fight—the disgraced warlords, the exiled princesses, the pervert necromancers and even the strange silent elves like Wyn, who hold their secrets so close to their chests that none can guess at their motives for flinging themselves into the jaws of death.

Was it just that Rhine had died while Ig, the most hapless and worthless creature to ever live, survived? That Ildrit, with all the sins staining him, had walked away without a scratch? No. No, it was not just. If there were justice in the world, Rhine would still walk among us. Her beauty untarnished, her face not contorted into the awful rictus of pain and terror that I saw in the moment before she died. The image that will haunt me for the rest of my days.

Adventurers die. But she . . . she deserved better.

CHAPTER TWENTY-ONE

THE WISDOM OF KOBOLDS

To say that our entire party felt bereft come dawn would have been a vast understatement. We had proceeded far enough now that we could no longer hear the distant whistle of arrows still being launched off in our general direction, and presumably, Ron and his little minions had backtracked so that they might find enough wood to bridge the Whitewaters. It bought us a little time, but none of us seemed particularly excited about the prospect of surviving a little bit longer at this moment.

Power had flooded back into Ig as soon as his nervous system had stopped screaming, and his reserves were refilled before I could even check them, still gradually expanding with each new refill, and thankfully not damaged by the overfill that he'd accidentally committed to. It was easier, I found, to focus on practical matters, as Wyn was doing now.

They had planned out our route through to the great wall that divided the Badlands from the good, with the intention for us to travel with great haste in that direction and rely on that particular fortification to protect us from Ron's pursuit. It was a solid plan, and I had no complaints about it. But it did rely upon us moving forward considerably faster than we currently were.

Surprisingly enough, Ig was not the cause of the delays this time around. He had the shortest legs, certainly, but even though he was in emotional turmoil, he had those handy kobold instincts to fall back on, instincts that made him want to run away very fast when he knew that he was being pursued by a bunch of murderous ogres.

Ildrit was the problem.

It was strange to think that this man who had allegedly had whole kingdoms on their knees before was completely losing his ability to function just because a single woman had died. I couldn't even imagine how many women he'd killed himself without losing a wink of sleep, yet here he was, a complete mess.

For most of the morning's forced march, he made no sound at all except the odd little crackling from the back of his throat as he tried to contain a sob. He moved at about half the pace of Wyn, despite the elf scouting out ahead of us and doubling back to confirm our continuing safety. It wasn't that Ildrit was walking slowly as such, so much as the fact that he just kept stopping dead, replaying the awful sights of the last night in his mind.

I'm a hat, not a psychic, so I could not say with certainty that was what was going on beneath his silvery hair, but I recognized the haunted expression well enough. Had I a face, I might very well have been bearing a similar one.

We stopped only briefly to rest our feet and eat some hard tack at about midday. Wyn had not spoken a word to either one of us all day, but finally, seeing the state of Ildrit, they intervened. "It was not your fault."

Ildrit snapped back so fast it was as though he'd been reciting the whole argument in his head all morning. "She was only there to protect my flank. If it wasn't for me . . ."

Wyn cut him off before he could descend into more wallowing in self-pity. "They would have shot her with an arrow, or caught her and tortured her, or bludgeoned her unconscious with their bare hands. They are ogres. It is their nature."

That unavoidable truth did nothing to stop Ildrit's self-loathing. "She should never have been there."

"She chose to fight by your side, would you dishonor her memory by claiming that she did not deserve that choice?" Wyn tried an appeal to the martial code of Ildrit, whatever it might have been.

"I killed her." Ildrit's face sank down into his hands. "The minute I invited her along. I killed her."

Wyn swatted that aside too. "She was already set upon adventuring long before your paths crossed. There is no question that somehow she would eventually have encountered a problem that she could not fight her way through."

"Not adventuring. Me. If it wasn't for me. My curse . . ."

"You were not cursed with ogres. Our actions led to this conflict, not some supernatural force. And when there is conflict, there is death."

Ildrit dragged his face back up out of his own grasp and we saw all the guilt and sorrow plainly in his eyes. "She would have been fine adventuring with anyone else; nobody deals with as much crap as we do. I thought that I'd help her find her feet, train her up a bit so when the time came for her to adventure herself, she could . . . I don't know what I thought."

"You not think," Ig snapped with surprising ferocity. "Should have been you."

"You little . . ." Ildrit surged forward, snatching Ig up by the throat, lifting him up until they were eye to eye, but instead of fighting him, Ig just dangled there, glowering. "You . . . You're right. It should have been me. I'm the one who's cursed. I'm the one who did evil. I should have been the one to pay for it."

He slumped back down onto his seat on a stump, letting Ig drop.

Wyn looked to the kobold as though he might have answers, but none were forthcoming. Presumably because Ig's single brain cell was currently bouncing back and forth between the sides of his skull like a squash ball.

"You should leave me. I'm just going to bring more doom down on everyone around me. Just . . . get the wizard home, elf."

And so we all stood for a long moment, the two of them coming to terms with the fact that this was where their fellowship parted ways, and Ildrit so sunken into his own guilt and misery that he'd probably just sit there and let the ogres kill him when they caught up.

The sad truth was that there was no simple solution here. We all bore the burden of some responsibility in what had happened, from the ogres to Ig. But where this burden weighed on Ig's conscience, it was not sufficient to crush him, while Ildrit was already carrying markedly more weight.

"Me cannot fix. Me is not smart enough." Ig had his faults, but recognizing his own limitations was definitely a strength. He looked up at Wyn, stoic as always. "You cannot fix. You is not smart enough."

Wyn didn't even look offended at being called a moron by a species designed by nature to be on the bottom rung of every ladder. That was commitment to the cause of looking aloof.

Ig reached up to take hold of me by my rim. "We needs someone smart to fix."

I knew what he was asking before he had even asked it, because as Ig pointed out, I was the smartest person here, as I always have been.

There is a dreadful burden in being the smartest person in any room, the need to slow yourself down so the slower can keep up, the need not to condescend when you're simply explaining facts, the fact that you know nobody will ever be your match and you will never have a challenge. It is lonely at the top, but also infuriating, as you have to wait for the rest of the world to play catch-up to conclusions you reached ages ago.

Put me on his head.

Ig remained still, even though he was the one suggesting this absurd course of action. "You is sure?"

Do it.

Ildrit glanced askance to Wyn at Ig's monologuing, who simply waited, implacable as ever. Someday, if I should live long enough, I hope that I might learn the ways of the elves. Not their music, or their forest walking, or even their unique types of magic, but their indifference. I suspect it would be a potent deterrent to graduate students seeking my counsel.

"He is knowing secrets?" Ig tried one last time to sway me from the course he'd set me on. As if sitting there chatting to me wasn't already giving away all the secrets we'd been keeping.

I need to speak to him myself.

"Me is not smarts enough to fix you brains," Ig announced to Ildrit. "But I knows who can."

For a moment, a long, dragged-out moment, there was nothing but utter darkness. The absence of all awareness of the world around me, and then just as suddenly it all returned, and I was seeing things from much farther up.

"What the heck?" Ildrit cried, trying to snatch me off his head as I sifted through his thoughts like a showy gambler with a deck of cards.

Be still, Ildrit Elfbane.

The secret nickname that he'd earned in his old campaigns shocked him into stillness for just long enough for me to shove his arms down and out.

I could feel the weight of the curse upon him for the first time, the magic bound tightly to his soul. I could feel the lithe strength of muscles that I'd never possessed, and a sharp mind, not like Ig's or even like mine, but like some carnivorous beast, wired to kill. No wonder he'd ended up in his line of work if this was the shape of his brain—anything else would have been like draping a sheepskin over a wolf and hoping for the best.

Ig saw the world as danger, I had seen it through the academic lens of my studies, but Ildrit saw the world as a threat assessment, a constant calculation, the land dissolved into high ground and cover. The trees once more springing up around us, weapons or charge breaks.

He felt most of all as though he were missing a limb, like his arm should have been longer than it was, and it was only as his hand instinctively drifted to the baldric holding Widowtaker as he perceived me as a threat that I understood why.

It was time to talk fast.

I am Absalom Scryne, the wizard you have been accompanying home. My mind resides within this hat, and through it I command the kobold to do my bidding.

"You won't . . . control me so easily . . ." Ildrit fought the very mild limitations that I'd put on his body to stop him from snatching me off or hurting himself. There was willpower there. Potent willpower. On reflection, probably not so potent at all, more like mildly above average, but certainly significantly more than I'd been accustomed to with Ig.

He clashed with me. His mind pressing against mine, his carefully structured battle lines of thoughts being rolled out, raising walls, keeping me from the worst of his deep dark secrets. Trying to drive me off from motor control so that he could snatch the offending garment in which I dwelled from his head. I gave ground where I could and saw for the first time just how lucky I had been to have found Ig. If any creature of greater intellect had found me, then all of my memories would have been theirs for the pillaging. All that I was would have become a resource. I would have gone from a person to an artifact to be abused by whoever could lay hands upon me. A Hat of Arcane Knowledge.

Good, you have some fight left in you after all.

That brought all his struggles to an abrupt halt, and I was able to loosen my grip over his body. Images flickered through his mind. A soft smile. A squeeze of the hand. Blood spraying black in the moonlight. "Rhine . . ."

She is dead, not by your hand, but because of you.

That stopped him before he could sink into his depression funk again. When he thought it to himself, that was fine, but someone else saying it filled him with a rage I would have considered unfathomable until arriving upon this particular head. "Screw you, wizard."

You are the bearer of the curse, you are the one with the burden of the evil you have wrought upon the world, and you are, in your way, powerful. You have a strength of arms, and a talent for battle that makes you a force to be reckoned with.

He fought all the harder, gaining back mastery of his body inch by inch, snarling and straining against me. "Do you think compliments are going to stop me from stomping you flat, hat?"

It is important that you grasp that you are powerful, so that you can understand what I tell you next.

"Fine," he growled. "I grasp it."

You have been in this world for a time; you have seen the way that it works. You grasp the mechanics of reality. Not in the manner of a wizard, but in the manner of a man of experience.

"What is your point?"

Have you ever known the powerful to suffer the consequences of their actions?

His struggles stopped. All the muscles he'd set pulling against the ones I controlled eased. ". . . No."

It falls upon those around them, those that are vulnerable, those that they care about, and must sacrifice in their pursuit of power so that they do not become a liability.

"Rhine wasn't just some . . . minion. She was . . ." His voice broke, and I felt all the affection that he'd held for the girl in his chest like a tightness. All that love now turned to poison.

You cared about her. Which means that there is hope for you yet.

"Hope?" His voice broke as he forced out the word. "What hope? She's gone."

And you are not. You are still here, carrying with you the weight of all your sins. If you did not care, if you did not hurt, then you would remain powerful and that burden would fall upon everyone around you, but no part of the evil you have done could ever be balanced.

"So she died just so I'd hurt?"

Now it was my turn to be angry. I had not lusted after the girl as Ig and Ildrit had, I had not considered pressing my lips to hers or falling asleep with her in my arms. I am above such things. But that did not mean that I had felt nothing for her. She had been a sole light of kindness in the darkest time in my life, and I would not suffer to hear her disrespected. *She died fighting for what she believed in. To save her friends. To defeat evil. She was a hero. Not like us. Do not dare to belittle her sacrifice by making her death into a footnote in your own story.*

That shut him up quick enough. All the self-pity and self-loathing were easy enough to maintain when you were only thinking about yourself, but confronted with the idea that his behavior was bringing the memory of Rhinolyta into disrepute, he could not maintain his inward focus. "What do you want from me, hat? I can't keep doing this. I can't keep bringing this down on everyone around me. I should get away from other people before this happens again . . . I should be alone."

Alone, you become a monster. Other people make you human.

He cast a glance to Ig, who was now staring off into the middle distance in a state of thoughtless peace that many meditating monks spend a lifetime seeking to achieve. "Maybe I don't want to be human."

If that were true, you would be delighted to learn that the worst punishments of your curse will fall on others instead of you. You are not a monster, Ildrit. You are a man, and I can speak no worse curse upon you than that.

If you have never felt heartbreak, I do not know how to describe it to you. If you have, then you remember the moment, the exact moment that the pain inside you seems to sunder the person that you were and leave behind the person that you will be after the pain fades. Ildrit broke then, and I let him feel everything without a word.

Finally, when it seemed the worst of the ache within him had faded back to the constant of grief, he asked me, "What . . . what should I do?"

Do good. Only by doing good can you become a better man. Not like the dog with a muzzle you have been, but like every man who chooses to do what is right.

"How will I know what . . ."

You won't. But trying is what matters.

He managed a pained smile. "You're pretty smart for a hat."

Just imagine how smart I'll be when I get a brain of my own to think with again.

Ildrit's brow furrowed. "So all this time, the kobold . . ."

Has just been a kobold. He's a rather nice kobold as they go, I'm rather fond of him. But please do not let him know that. There is scarcely room for two thoughts in his head at once; if you were to put an ego in there too, I'd be squeezed right out.

He managed a little chuckle. Something I would have thought impossible just a few moments before. "Alright, wizard. I'll get you home. It's what Rhine wanted. It's . . . the right thing to do."

Much appreciated, now please return me to Ig.

He blinked. "Ig?"

"Weh?" The kobold's head turned at the sound of his name.

Despite himself, Ildrit found that he was amused. "Oh, you've got a little name of your own. Uh, hello, Ig."

Ig held out his grasping little paws. "Give. Please."

Darkness returned to me, ever so briefly, then I was back to peering out through Ig's dim and hazy eyes at the world.

Problem solved.

Ig looked up at the soft smile, so incongruous on Ildrit's face. "How fix?"

Oh, the usual moralistic nonsense and platitudes. He'll serve well enough for the rest of our journey. Even if his martial prowess is somewhat dampened by the swirling vortex of ill fortune pursuing him.

Ig mumbled to himself. "Platipudes?"

Why don't you just focus on not making any more bloody bananas when you're meant to be saving the day?

Ig announced to the group, "Me shut up now."

Good.

We were back in motion again just a few moments later.

CHAPTER TWENTY-TWO

HE WHO TAKES

Despite this land being relatively healthier-looking than the Badlands proper, it was also the most contested area of land within the whole place. Here the more powerful monsters that were not pushed to the periphery made their lairs and made their assaults upon civilization. It was for this reason that the Great Wall had been built to begin with. There wasn't much in the way of villages and farmland, even on the other side of it. While human expansion was relentless, it also typically happened at the other end, where you were less likely to expand into something vast and murderous.

Wyn slowed and redirected us time and again as they uncovered tracks. The sticky white spoor of a cockatrice, spattered across a tree. The huge bare footprints of a forest yeti. The single-file tracks of an orc war party. Hopefully survivors from the ogre takeover moving on to better things. We wended and weaved back and forth all day to avoid encountering trouble, even knowing that there was even greater trouble hot on our heels.

To stop and fight would be an unbearable delay, and we could only hope that the ogres were following our own messy trail rather than making a beeline forward.

We were hunkered down behind a fallen log, waiting for a family of gnolls to pass us by, when the hair on the back of Ig's neck rose.

This in itself was hardly surprising, given that the little creature was in a perpetual state of fear, enhanced by proximity to a posse of dog-men who'd likely make a swift snack of him, but there was something in the sensation that could not be so easily accounted for. A tingle of magic at work.

He opened his mouth to yelp out a warning, only for me to clamp his jaws shut again before he could doom us all to being dogmeat. Or in my case, a chew toy.

Wait.

Anxiety spiked in his little kobold heart, but there was nothing that we could do in that moment but hyperventilate slightly more than usual and try to sense what was afoot. There was a hint on the air of some exotic element that Ig could not place, and I could not interpret through his stunted senses. But beneath that, a pressure in the air that had not been there before. Perhaps Nitrogen or Oxygen being invoked. There were a great many potent spells that could be cast with either one, but none that I'd expect from gnolls. Their people did have the odd shaman among them who could work magic, but it was typically only a single element's worth, and only a common one. The exotic component was throwing me.

Yet as I pontificated on the finer points of magic, the spell that had been cast began to take effect: the trunk we had been hiding behind began to sprout fresh branches, blossoming with leaves. The gnolls took one look at this unnatural display and went off running with their tails between their legs, suggesting once again that they were smarter than the adventurers they usually fought, who would have taken one look at a mysteriously blossoming log and sprinted headfirst into the damned thing.

The sudden outburst of branches clipped Ig around the back of the head and sent him tumbling away from cover, while the larger adventurers accompanying him instead found themselves tangled. Trapped within the fresh grown wood where they'd been unfortunate enough to be touching it.

This smelled like the work of druids to me.

Yet it was not a druid that stepped out from behind a nearby bush, shaking his robes to try and force the seam to reassemble after it, and he, had been turned into Nitrogen so that he could cross great distances by wind-walking.

"Why hello, my beautiful darlings, how are you?" the Bonetaker simpered.

"Boney!" Ildrit cried. "I'm so glad you're alright. I told them that you'd make it out of that mess intact."

"Oh, darling, you have no idea what I had to go through to escape them. I had to take on five ogres at once." He yawned, and his jaw clicked.

There was always a degree of mincing to the way that the Bonetaker walked, but as he approached us now, it was almost as though he were tender. Or that he feared a sudden jolt of a step might rattle something loose.

"I knew you'd be alright." Despite his sorrow, Ildrit managed a smile for his old friend. "It's so good to see you."

Bonetaker counted us on his fingers and then tutted. "Oh no. The girl didn't make it. That's a shame; I was so fascinated to see what happened after temptation won out and you finally ploughed those untouched fields." He tittered. "My money was on your nether regions dropping off entirely."

"The injury is too fresh to be making jokes," Wyn snapped back with surprising vehemence.

"Oh, do be a boring little elf, darling, and shut that mouth of yours." He hissed a word of power under his breath, and the log lurched into life once more, the newly expanding leaves encompassing Wyn's head entirely and muffling any sound they might make.

Ig had been staring up at him, simmering with anger ever since his cruel comment about the fate of Rhinolyta, but now the necromancer turned his attention to the kobold himself. "It seems that the ogre king is a little bit cross with you. Sounds like you burned his city down."

"Me is nobody's slave," Ig growled. Or tried to growl. It sounded more like a ferret with a throat injury coughing.

"Oh, you silly little pet, that isn't entirely true, is it." His hand reached down to caress Ig's cheek. "You're telling me lies."

Ig drew back from his touch. "Me is . . ."

The Bonetaker cut him off with a hiss. "You are enslaved, even if you're too ignorant to recognize it. That parasite atop your skull commands you, guides you, even tries to teach you the art of magic, but it is all for its own ends."

Falling back on his classic tactics, Ig feigned ignorance. "Me not know what you talk about."

To which the necromancer merely smiled. "Ildrit knows. Otherwise, why would he have flinched when I said that?"

Behind Ig, Ildrit groaned. Then tried to salvage the situation. "Boney, you don't understand, nobody was trying to keep a secret from you, it was just difficult for them to explain."

"Difficult, because you have a magical artifact of immense value and you're letting a kobold wear it? Difficult because you planned to hand it over to the kind of people who gladly saw me banished from all civilized lands and reduced to being a lacky for monsters just because I don't subscribe to their archaic binary system of alive and dead? Or difficult because you're all so stupid that you let a hat convince you it was sapient?"

"Is you sapient?" Ig asked, in what he probably thought was a very subtle whisper.

Yes!

"Hat sapient!"

Had I hands, I would have applauded Ig's successful pronunciation of the word or slapped him for confirming all of the Bonetaker's suspicions about me.

"Well, pet, it certainly won't be once I'm finished tearing all the arcane knowledge out of it." The Bonetaker stretched out a cadaverous hand for me and Ig stumbled back out of his reach.

The necromancer did not pursue him, however, he held out that same hand in a gesture of friendship. "Come to me, my little kobold sweetheart, and I promise I won't hurt you. I'll even give you a new hat, wouldn't you like that? A hat, and some food. I'll even give you a comfy little cushion to sleep on. Wouldn't that be so much nicer than getting dragged all through the woods by a talking hat? Wouldn't you rather be free to come and go as you please?"

"Hat is friend!" Ig snapped his little incisors at the Bonetaker's fingers.

I wish that he had not done that.

Immediately the necromancer began invoking Plutonium and Ig, with no knowledge of lead, had absolutely nothing to counter it. He was dead.

A wizard's duel is not like a clash of swordsmen, a collision of raw magical talent, or even the games of strategy that those who consider themselves enlightened like to play at. Imagine that you are playing chess, but you cannot see any of your opponent's pieces. You can make moves following the rules that you know apply to the game that you are playing, and it is possible that the other wizard might be playing by the same rules. But just as likely, they're actually playing backgammon, or poker, on their side of the table, hoping that their royal flush will beat your hand—your hand, which has a bishop in it.

Now imagine this, with each wizard able to draw upon a library of over a hundred different games, and able to switch between games every move, and you come close to beginning to understand the complexity of magical combat, and why, when it comes down to it, most of us prefer not to fight one another.

When we do have to fight, most of us prefer to get off the first spell and hope that's enough to do the trick, because counter magic is a whole other realm of trouble that we haven't even begun to delve into, and our best bet at a clean win is hoping that the other wizard forgot to set up any protection spells that morning. Which was of course why the Bonetaker was flinging some Plutonium death ray at Ig in the hopes of finishing things in a single zap.

Meanwhile, Ig had prepared no defenses, did not know how to play chess, and was currently doing the intellectual equivalent of sucking on the head of a pawn.

Cast anything!

For all that he was a buffoon, there was something to be said for his rodent-like reflexes. Before the necromancer had even opened his mouth, Ig had yelped out, "**Fragor!**"

There had been scarcely a drop of Quintessence readied, and he was so surprised at the suddenness of this whole exchange that he had no time to concentrate his mind upon a single element. His focus was quite excellent for a change, as the necromancer was currently the thing he was most scared of in the surrounding area. As such, the inevitable occurred.

From his pointed finger there came a flash of light, then an exceptionally small bunny soared through the air to smack the Bonetaker in the face.

It was hardly the devastating blow that one would hope for in the first exchange of a wizard's duel, but it certainly distracted him before he could cast his own spell. The luckier of the four feet on the rabbit actually went into his mouth as he opened it to cast, and so his enunciation was . . . less than perfect.

Still, a lethal wave of green burst forth from the hand he had pointed at Ig and washed over him. Where it struck on Ig's bathrobe there was a hissing, and they were rendered clean, I myself was deprived of the various bugs and lice that had found their way to dwell within me and the thick crust of mud that had marred one side of my fabric was purged of staining.

Where it struck his bare skin was another matter entirely. Ig was enveloped in an awful hissing sound as the radiant damage seeped in, his skin was seared into tiny blisters everywhere it was facing the necromancer, and those blisters popped but a moment later with an awful spattering sound. The pain was unimaginable, and it triggered in Ig his most primal response. He turned and ran directly away from the thing that was hurting him.

A kobold sprinting at full speed isn't all that impressive, if truth be told—they aren't the quickest of creatures—but with that fresh agony still sizzling all over him, there was a relentlessness to Ig's running that served him well. He almost caught up to the wave of green light before it washed over Ildrit, Wyn, and the blossoming log.

The branches and leaves died. The brittle twigs left in the spell's wake snapped as Wyn and Ildrit hauled themselves free.

All at once, Bonetaker was no longer facing off with a tiny desperate kobold, but with a pseudo-competent party of adventurers. This adjusted the odds accordingly, and the sly smile was back on his face not a moment after Wyn trained an arrow on him.

"Darlings, this is all a misunderstanding. Just let me show you, that poor kobold has a parasitic hat latched onto its head." The Bonetaker nodded encouragingly to Ildrit as he came to stand beside poor Ig. "Just jerk it off."

Ildrit reached up and drew his sword, prompting the necromancer to lick his lips. "Why are you working for the ogres, Boney?"

"For?" Bonetaker scoffed. "Darling, I work *for* nobody, no time, not never."

Wyn cut off any further asides. "Why are you working with the ogres?"

"Well, my succulent androgyne, there are a number of important factors. Length, girth, stamina. Oh boy, you have never seen stamina like a frisky ogre, I tell you."

"Me heard you scream, when ogres . . ." Throughout all of this, Ig had been trying to piece together the various clues up until this point that the Bonetaker had been killed by the ogres that he now seemed to be allied with, and he couldn't make sense of it because he was blessedly innocent. ". . . took five guys."

"Regardless of the rewards I might be receiving for all the hard work that I'm putting in, Ronald the Sour desires only the kobold; you two darlings are perfectly safe. No reason to get yourselves in a tizzy. Why, he didn't even mention the hat at all. So I suppose that is mine by salvage rights."

Ildrit stepped in front of Ig, separating him from the necromancer. "You'll be leaving with neither."

"Oh come on, darling, I'm onto a good thing here." There was a hint of pleading to the necromancer's voice. "You get off without any trouble, I get off with a little assistance from some new friends, the only one who dies is the kobold, and kobolds are just monsters."

Wyn stunned us all into silence with the vehemence in their voice. "Ig is our friend."

"Oh, darling, that is just sad, it is like putting a little outfit on a dog and claiming it is your baby." He tittered. "It can't be your friend. It doesn't even understand the words you're saying without the hat to translate everything into moron-speak for it."

"I is not it. And Wyn is friend. Ildrit is friend. Hat is friend. Rhine is . . ." Ig briefly choked upon her name. "Only one not friend is you."

"Oh, come on, Il, you can't seriously be considering throwing away all that we've had together for some little gully goblin," he wheedled.

Ildrit set his grip on his sword, holding it level like a barrier between the necromancer and us. "I owe you nothing."

"You . . ." For the first time, some genuine emotion showed through Bonetaker's façade of pleasantry. He was enraged. "You owe me everything! You owe me your life a hundred times over! How many times was I there to pull you from the fire? How many times was I the only one who could turn the tide of battle? I gave you the best years of my life, I was the best advisor a wannabe warlord could wish for, and this is how you repay me? Abandoning me, vanishing without a trace for years, and when I finally catch up to you, I've been replaced by a rodent in a hat?!"

"Ig is not your replacement . . ." Ildrit started to explain, but Bonetaker had clearly heard enough. With a snarl, he invoked Nitrogen once more and vanished from our sight.

Immediately, Ig and the adventurers relaxed. Presumably because their understanding of magic held as much depth as most puddles. I was forced to snatch up control of Ig and rasp out, "*Do not breathe.*"

Wyn made no motion, but stilled so completely with the absence of breath that they might have been a carving. Ildrit took a moment longer to respond, slapping a hand over his mouth and pinching shut his nose.

The tingle was still in the air. The Quintessence that Bonetaker was expending, brushing against Ig's skin. The kobold cocked his head from side to side, as though intangibility and invisibility were things that could be circumvented by looking directly at them.

For one long, breathless moment, all three of them stood stock still, then, with a sudden pulse of air, Bonetaker reformed, right behind Ig. Just where I thought he'd appear. I loosed all control over Ig's body in that same moment, and the poor kobold toppled like a pile of sticks. Dragging me down out of reach of the necromancer's grasping hands.

Ildrit spun, sweeping Widowtaker with a whistle through the air, but halting just before the blade made contact with the necromancer's neck. The muscles in his forearm seemed to ripple with this display of restraint. He whispered, "Don't do this, Boney."

"Oh, darling, when I'm doing it to you, you'll know all about it." The Bonetaker blew a kiss, then exploded apart into Nitrogen once more.

Both adventurers looked askance to Ig, to see if it was safe to breathe this time around without the danger of a necromancer reforming in their lungs. The telltale tingle was gone. He had been carried off on the breeze. Ig gave a firm nod.

Wyn must have been the first to get their breath back. "Lovely friends that you have, Ildrit."

"We all make mistakes when we're young. But maybe you can't remember that far back?"

"I recall my first century with perfect clarity. Those acquaintances of bad influence that my parents disapproved of never made any attempt upon my life. Nor have they since."

"So even your friends were boring?"

Ig snorted in amusement, earning a stare from both of them.

Wyn took the high road. "It would be best if we depart with all haste; the ogres will still be pursuing us."

CHAPTER TWENTY-THREE

EVERY WALL IS A DOOR

We did not rest that night for fear of our pursuers, but neither did the creeping darkness provide us with any shield against the other denizens of the wilds. As one set of monsters drifted off to fitful sleep, the other set awoke, and if the things you could see wandering around during the day out here could make you desperately need a chamber pot, then what you couldn't see wandering around in the dark made you long for a fortified outhouse.

Ig was a little bit past tired by the time that the wall loomed up on the horizon, given that in his previous life he had been more accustomed to napping eight or nine times a day in addition to a solid twelve hours sleep by night. If he had been somewhat more aware, then he may have completely lost his mind over the sight of a man-made construction that dwarfed many of the mountains he might have encountered, had he ranged but a little farther from his mud-hole. He might have been overcome by awe at the incredible things that humanity could achieve when it put its mind to it. But instead, he saw it looming up out of the darkness with about as much awareness as a sea cucumber has of a boat passing overhead.

Ildrit and Wyn had seen it all before, so they were similarly unimpressed. In fact, I think of the three of us, I was the only one who had never actually laid eyes on the Great Wall before. Still, I felt hope stir within me for the first time. Hope of safety, hope of speedy progress towards my destination, hope even of my long-thwarted vengeance upon whoever had slain my earthly body. Everything was finally going our way.

"Nearly there," was Wyn's sole comment. Ig was too breathless to reply.

On and on we trudged, the number of trails and monster noises thinning as we got closer and closer to the vast structure itself. Once we were inside, there was no way for the ogres to follow, no matter how big their army. The Bonetaker was another matter, of course, but just as Ig couldn't go wandering through civilized lands without someone human-looking to vouch for them, neither could someone so obviously involved in the necromantic arts. Perhaps he could have disguised himself, but I doubted his flamboyance would allow for it.

We arrived at the foot of the wall just as dawn was beginning to pinken the sky. It seemed thematically appropriate for us to emerge into civilization bathed in light.

Except there was one minor matter that all of us had overlooked, ever so slightly. When mankind had collectively gotten their act together and built a massive wall to keep all the horrible things in the Badlands out, they had failed to outfit it with doors. Shocking, I know, that they had decided punching holes in their big wall for easy access might somewhat undercut the purpose of the thing. There were vast reinforced gates, of course, for those few times someone was insane enough to want to come out here, but by my estimation and vague memory of the maps I'd glanced at, they were about three days to the left.

We looked up from down in the dirt at the wall reaching to the heavens, constructed through all the arts of magic and manpower that humanity had been able to commit, and Ildrit said, "Shit."

As one, the adventurers turned to Ig for a solution.

"Time to shine, little friend," Wyn told him, stepping aside so that Ig could blast a hole in the wall. Ildrit also took a step aside, then crossed his arms to watch.

Ig had nothing.

Had his arcane training progressed at a speed faster than glacial, then perhaps he would have developed an understanding of several elements that might have come in handy here. Helium, for instance, might have made us lighter than air, and able to float up and over. Sufficient understanding of Carbon may have allowed us a stone-pass spell that would have made it possible to stroll right through the wall as though it were not there.

Unfortunately, I did not trust Ig to achieve either option with any degree of confidence. An attempt at Helium would likely have resulted in Wyn inflated like a balloon and floating off into the sky, and at best the stone-pass spell would have resulted in us becoming trapped in solid stone for the rest of our natural lives, which admittedly would not be a very long time. More likely he would cast it, then immediately turn to stone, or just fail utterly, resulting in us walking face-first into the rock with little to no effect.

In short, we were stuck.

"Me not know what do," Ig admitted, breaking one of the first rules of being a wizard—letting others know what you were capable of.

"Surely you've got some trick up your sleeve. Some climbing vines to make a ladder or . . ." Ildrit began making suggestions, only to see the expression on Ig's face.

"Me is not a druid."

Wyn cleared their throat. "No. Of course not."

"Me is wizard. Apprentice wizard," Ig clarified. "But wizard."

"So what is your wizardly solution to the impassable wall?" Ildrit pressed, eyes now drifting from Ig to the sparse forest we had just exited. The one that held hordes of monsters, just waiting for an easy meal.

Wyn stalked over to the wall and began searching for handholds, but the construction was truly exquisite, and we lacked the climbing gear like pitons that might have made an ascent possible.

"Maybe we is cutting down more trees and making ladder?"

We glanced back at the forest behind us. It would take a dozen of these trees tied end to end to reach the top of the wall, and even if one of us had a hidden talent for joinery, the length of time such a thing would take would invariably result in something coming to check on the sounds of industrious sawing.

Ildrit flopped down onto the grass, and once more made his vital contribution. "Shit."

Wyn sighed. "I must concur."

"Has the hat got any bright ideas?" Ildrit asked with the tone of an atheist turning to prayer in a time of crisis.

I'm thinking.

"Says is thinking," Ig explained.

"Great," Ildrit snarked back. "A thinking cap."

At present, the best idea I could come up with involving Ig's limited ability to do magic was to attempt to summon a heap of bananas so tall we could climb up it, but even if that were not laughable, it would leave behind a ramp for our pursuers. While I was not entirely opposed to turning over the outskirts of human civilization to a tide of ogres and hideous beasts if it was more convenient for me, the fact that the ogres would be chasing us specifically meant that it would defy the purpose of the wall I meant to put between us entirely.

Perhaps I was thinking in too complex a way. Ig was not capable of any decent feat of magic, so it was time to turn to the indecent ones, the laughable low magic that toddlers achieve by accident on occasion. He had plentiful reserves of Quintessence to draw upon now. Not as vast a pool as I personally once commanded, but more than most apprentices by a fair margin. Perhaps we simply needed to apply that directly to the problem.

Ig, I want you to focus on Wyn.

"Weh?" he asked, erudite as ever.

I want you to clear your mind, focus on Wyn, and let the Quintessence take hold of them.

"Me can't."

All you need to do is focus. Just for a little while, just long enough to lift them up on top of the wall.

"But there is sounds, and bumblebutts and smells and . . ."

And you need to forget about all of those and focus, just once in your life, Ig. Just ignore everything that your senses tell you and focus on Wyn.

Raising his hands like a conductor, Ig let the magic begin to flow.

If Wyn was surprised to suddenly find themselves floating, they made no mention of it, nor showed any sign of it in their expression. Ildrit was not so calm, unfortunately, letting out a yelp that immediately caught Ig's attention.

So he too began to float.

A bumblebee that had been flitting around passed into Ig's vision, and it too was seized by his magic and began drifting up. Then another. Then a flower twitched in the breeze and found itself plucked and drifting up into the sky.

Ig just couldn't do it. He couldn't keep his focus on any one thing for long enough. Not without the one thing being the object of his absolute terror. Fear was the only thing that could make the constant buzzing of his little brain fall silent, and though he was jumping and twitching at every sound, that was just the same general anxiety that racked him constantly. Wyn was about six feet off the ground and Ildrit four when the strain of trying to keep so many different things in focus became too much for Ig.

Everything dropped. Ildrit landed on his backside with the yelp of a bruised tailbone. Wyn landed with a cat's grace on their feet as though they had not even been moved. The bumblebees resumed their winding flights, swearing to themselves that they'd never touch nectar that had fermented for too long in the sun ever again. Only the flower remained in place, just for a moment, before that cruel mistress gravity seized hold of it too and dragged it fluttering back to earth.

"A little warning next time?" Ildrit complained, rising and rubbing at his backside.

Precisely the pose that he was in when Sour Ron, a cadre of ogres, and the Bonetaker emerged from the woods about a quarter mile to our left.

By this point in proceedings, it was unnecessary for anyone to shout, "Run." Running had become the default response to every situation, and there was some small part of me that was amused that while Ig had not been infected with too much humanity by his companions, this fundamental aspect of kobold-ness had definitely passed to them.

Yet despite the unnecessary nature of the cry, all three of them bellowed, "Run!" even as they began to run.

The logical direction for us to run would have been to the left, towards the gate, but since that was blocked off by a horde of monsters, the second-best option would likely have been to plunge back into the cover of the forest, where there was at least the possibility of us losing the ogres in the more complex terrain. Rather than pursuing either one of these options, Ildrit and Wyn took off running parallel to the wall, with Ig in hot pursuit.

There were some war cries behind us, but I didn't catch the gist of the threats being made against us because the sound of the wind whipping past Ig's little bullet head was essentially deafening. Despite his exhaustion, terror and adrenaline had once more breathed new life into Ig, and he was able to keep pace with the longer stride of elves and men through sheer blind panic.

We ran, and we ran, and with every step, Ig stumbled more. He was beyond exhaustion and into that strange valley on the far side where the world seemed almost dreamlike. Each time he fell and hit the ground and scrambled back to his feet, he should have been yelping with pain, but it seemed distant; even as his paws were scratched and his snout bumped, he felt nothing at all. This was a concerning new development.

He was going to die. He almost seemed to have accepted it now. The fear that had characterized his entire existence was beginning to fade, and the thought that dominated that little useless nugget of gray matter betwixt his ears was submission. If he were to just stop, to just lay down here on the ground, there would be some pain, yes, but also peace when the pain was done. The sweet embrace of darkness.

Cut it out.

Ig barely seemed to recognize my command. But he went on running all the same out of habit more than anything else.

All of this time, we had been fleeing. We had been afraid. We had been thinking like kobolds. I, for one, was not a kobold, and I was tired of acting like one. Seizing control of Ig's mouth, I shouted out, "Swordsman, give me a tactical solution."

Ildrit looked back with confusion and dismay writ across his features. He was as exhausted as Ig, he had just done a better job of hiding it after a lifetime where the first hint of weakness would have been exploited. "Tactics? We're in open ground. They've got every advantage. Their numbers are overwhelming. Retreat is the tactic. The only tactic."

I had been letting myself think like a kobold all of this time, and I could feel the shame of that burning within my pointy tip, but I was a wizard still, and I would not allow my error to bring our quest to an end. Returning control to Ig, and ignoring his stumble as he took over mastery of his legs once more, I turned inwards, sifting through my memories, my boundless knowledge. Something would help. Something had to.

And then I remembered.

"Break right," I called out.

Wyn was the one to give answer. "Into the woods and undergrowth that will slow us?"

"To the favorable terrain beyond it."

Ildrit and Wyn met one another's gaze, then the warrior shrugged. The ogres were gaining on us fast, we'd be in range of their arrows in moments, we were all going to die anyway, why not do what the wizard said?

He drove in ahead of us, slashing at the shrubs and thicket. Were any of the plants wed, I'm sure their partners were suffering similar injury thanks to the stupid enchantment on his sword. But it was enough to make ingress back under the cover of the woods and out of the ogre's sight. That little bit of protection would keep their arrows from our backs just a little longer. And a little longer was all that we needed to change everything.

This plan shall hinge entirely upon you, Ig.

"Then we is going to dies," the kobold mumbled, ducking a conifer branch swinging back at his face as he pursued the others.

You are going to perform the very same feat as you just achieved, levitating yourself, the elf, and the warrior, and you will only need hold it for a minute. You have already done it before, Ig. So I know that you can do it.

I believe in you.

That last part was, of course, a lie, but he needed a boost to his confidence.

Ildrit came into sight of our goal first, breaking out of the tree line and skidding to a halt at the chasm's edge. It was exactly as I had imagined it would be when I had first read of it all those decades ago. The great wall that protected civilization had not been built of hopes and dreams, but of solid stone, and that stone had to come from somewhere. All resources beyond the wall would soon be lost to mankind, abandoned to the wilds, and so they'd decided to exploit it for all that it was worth while they had the time, and here was the aftermath. A quarry, almost three miles long, deeper at the farthest point from the wall, as stone was carved from the earth and run up the vast slope below us towards the wall where it would finally come to rest.

There were dozens of these quarries stretching along the length of the wall, and this one, this was the quarry that would be our salvation.

"Great!" Ildrit bellowed into the gaping abyss of bare stone before him. "Just perfect. A pit for us to die in. Good job, wizard!"

Tantalizingly close was the far side. Too far to jump, obviously. Too far to bridge, either. If we somehow found ourselves on that far side, then the ogres would have no means of catching up to us. They would either have to make a perilous descent down the sheer quarry wall and then repeat it on the far side, or they would have to divert and work their way around the full three miles of quarry before coming back to us. By which time it was safe to say that, exhausted or not, we would have been able to put more than enough distance between us to have room to think once more.

Alright, Ig, here we go. Seize hold of all three of us with your low magic and carry us across. I know that you can manage three targets at once, I have seen you do it. Finally your inability to maintain any sort of focus shall be an advantage.

"Me isn't doing that!" Ig exclaimed. All of the fear that had faded into exhaustion had reared its ugly head once more now that he was looking down into that hole.

You shall do it, Ig. I have foreseen it.

"Me no care if you five-seen it. Me isn't doing it."

Wyn was the one who'd had the most time to come to terms with Ig and my peculiar arrangement, so they were the one to grasp that there was an argument being waged internally. "What precisely is the wizard proposing?"

"He crazy. He want me carry us over hole!" Ig's shrill cry turned into a grumbling. "Me not going over hole. Me not falling in hole."

Ildrit was quicker on the uptake than one might have presumed. "You have to do it, kobold. On the other side, we'll have a chance; here, we're doomed."

Wyn seemed to be weighing their options a little more carefully, pausing in that deliberation only long enough to turn and send an arrow flying into the first of the ogres as they appeared amidst the tree line. "It seems that we have no better option."

You can do this, Ig. I know that you can. You may have been born in unfortunate circumstances with nothing to your name, but you are more than a mere kobold now, you have been initiated into the highest order of arcane mastery, tutored by the wisest of wizard kind. You will do this, you will survive, and the tale will be told for millennia to come of your heroism.

Ig was in the midst of some sort of panting anxiety attack.

More ogres were beginning to emerge, slowing as they realized they had us cornered. There was something of the cat to an ogre, a relentless predator that immediately became playful when they realized their prey could not escape. Both cat and ogre also considered slow disemboweling to be play. Why on earth do we keep those things as pets?

Ig reached out his arms, closed his eyes, let the Quintessence within him flow, and he *lifted*.

We rose. Weightlessness washed up over us as Ig's will took over from gravity.

Perfect, now just carry us across. Do not think of anything except for the distance, do not look down, there is nothing below you that should concern you. Just go.

He kept his eyes shut, which in all honesty was probably the most sensible thing he'd ever done. There was no need to see Ildrit and Wyn being lifted up and drifting out into the open air. There was no need for him to see what was below him, or rather, what was not below him. He could feel it all through his magic; the Quintessence that carried us all was a part of him, harnessed from the world and taken inside and made a part of his being.

This was magic at its purest. No shaping it, no twisting it with meanings and words, just the power itself. And to my immense surprise, power was the one thing that Ig did not lack. He drew in Quintessence with every breath, with the frantic hunger of a creature that had always been upon the brink of starvation. Everything that made him a kobold was what made him a better wizard than any human with his intellect and training could have been.

In silence we were carried, with only the faint whistle of the wind passing around us. Carried by Ig, and his mastery of the Quintessence that, until a few days ago, he had not even known existed.

We must have been almost to the other side when Sour Ron called out. "Me is going to exsanguinate you, wizard! Me is going to exbonulate you too! You can floatify and you can flee, but me is going to get you!"

Ig's eyes shot open in terror. His focus, always so tenuous even at the best of times, was broken. For the briefest moment Ron was yanked forward off his feet as Ig's attention turned there, then in a blind panic he spun in the air, trying to catch Wyn as he lost his hold on them.

The elf had tumbled end over end down into the chasm in the brief moment that Ig had lost his grip, and when it was reestablished, the poor creature was dangling upside down.

Ildrit dropped but a moment later, falling almost all the way to the bottom before Ig managed to grab onto him again. By which point he'd lost his hold on himself too and was plummeting at terminal velocity towards the nice hard rock below.

He managed to catch Ildrit ever so briefly, cushioning his fall enough that the impact didn't shatter every bone in his body, but it must still have been a hard fall. Wyn struck down but a moment later, landing on their feet and then springing forward instantly. It seemed elves, like ogres, had some degree of felinity to them.

The spring forward was to bring them underneath Ig's tumbling ragdoll of a body. He was trying to catch himself, trying to turn the Quintessence around him back into that lovely gentle grip that he'd managed before, but all of it flowed to where his concentration was focused, and every part of Ig's mind was locked on the rapidly approaching rocks below.

Wyn leapt and caught Ig before the kobold hit the ground. It was a bone-crushing impact for both of them. I could hear the pop as the elf's shoulder was ripped from its socket, but they did not flinch, and they did not falter, rolling to absorb as much of the impact from poor Ig as they could before crashing down onto the stone below.

The stone was just as hard as Ig had imagined that it would be, when staring down at it. More solid than it had any right to be. The impact knocked the air from both elf and kobold alike. Leaving Ildrit the only one standing and breathing when all was said and done. He wheezed, "That could have gone better."

Wyn made a sound from beneath Ig that sounded somewhat like a punctured accordion, finally prompting the aching little ball of kobold to uncurl and clamber off them. Rising to his full and unimpressive height about level with Ildrit's hip, he announced, "Ow."

"Well, at least we're away from the ogres." He patted Ig on the shoulder, awkwardly.

Wyn had managed to get back up to a sitting position but had not managed to proceed beyond that. Ildrit crouched down beside the elf and they exchanged a whispered conversation. Ig probably wasn't meant to overhear it, but kobold ears are pretty well attuned. "What's the damage?"

With the usual calm tone, the elf listed off their injuries. "My shoulder is out. Both ankles are sprained, at least. My bow is broken."

Ildrit flinched at the last one. "Can you move?"

"Do I have a choice?" Wyn sighed.

Ildrit reached down as though to offer them a hand up, then set a foot on the poor elf's chest once he had a grip on their hand. "This will hurt."

Wyn pressed their eyes shut.

The wet noise of a shoulder being relocated made Ig's stomach turn a little flip, but there was no food in there for him to bring up, so we avoided that embarrassment at least.

With that done, Ildrit hunched down to help the elf to their feet before turning to Ig. "Now what?"

Ig didn't know, but he had proven himself capable of repeating things he'd heard. "Tack elution?"

Wyn mustered a chuckle. Possibly the first that I could recall hearing from them. Ildrit stared blankly at the quarry walls. "We can't climb out. Too steep. Elf is in no fit state, and they'd hit us with arrows from their side."

He glanced up the long slope towards salvation. "Can't head to the wall; they'd be able to cut us off. Rain arrows on us the whole way too."

Turning in the other direction, he nodded. "We go deeper, find a tunnel to hole up in. Even if they track us, a bottleneck will cut their advantage of numbers, and they won't be able to use their bows."

If they had been creatures of intelligence, then the ogres would have recognized that they had us trapped. They would have traveled to the entry slope of the quarry and followed it down, sweeping the area until they found us. Instead, they were ogres, so they began descending the sheer rock face to come at us as fast as possible.

The first one lost his grip pretty much immediately and plummeted down to land with a splat that would haunt my dreams. As it turned out, Ig had done a rather good job of keeping our party alive during our own descent. Gravity really did a number on that ogre.

Even from down here, we could hear the other ogres laughing at their fellow's misfortune and pouring over the rim of the quarry to descend.

"Okay, we need to go faster." Ildrit was no longer serving as a crutch to Wyn so much as carrying them outright. Ig scrambled ahead of them both, not scouting so much as just running for his life at full pelt. More thumping splats resounded behind us as we went. Thinning the horde a little, but not nearly enough.

The sun had risen enough now that the deep shadows down here at the bottom of the chasm were calming and we could see our way. There was nothing much in the way of tunnels to hide in as of yet. A few big squares cut into the solid stone, but nothing deep enough to serve Ildrit's purposes.

I kept expecting arrows to begin raining down on us, as I could clearly see the forms of ogres moving alongside us atop the ridge, but nothing so untoward occurred. Instead we carried on unhindered.

If we could have evaded all pursuit for a time, then I might have asked Ig to make another attempt at levitation, even though the last attempt had been nigh on lethal, but there was no hope of dragging his attention to only three things at once when there were so many signs of danger about.

Ildrit's plan was the better one for now: head down deeper into the quarry and take cover. We could always fall back on a blockade of rabbits or bananas if the straits became too dire. Two things that I could trust Ig to consistently achieve.

The only trouble was that as we headed towards what should surely have been the lowest point of the quarry at the farthest end, it wasn't actually getting all that much deeper. The solid stone beneath our feet had given way to gravel and shale that was all heaped up towards the middle in what it was becoming increasingly apparent was another ramp. Someone else had been digging in this damnable quarry since the wall's completion and they'd left all their mess right there to provide the ogres pursuing us with an easy means of ingress.

Spotting the very same ramp as us, the ogres that had been pursuing us on the ridge put on a turn of speed, obviously intent upon cutting us off from the escape route we had not known was there.

Every step that Wyn took upon the slope was in danger of being their last. The loose stone slipped out from under their feet. Their injured ankles, barely able to bear weight even on flat surfaces, were constantly being twisted. Though they were too composed to complain, the fact that their skin was gradually turning gray with each turn of their feet suggested a great deal of pain. If Ig would not have been more of a hindrance than a help, he would doubtless have been right alongside the elf, helping them along, but the difference in their builds rendered such things impossible.

Veering off to the far wall of the quarry from the damnable ogres, we were able to find a little more depth. Some tunnels, now plugged with shale, showed their tops along the walls, and we could only hope that we might come upon an unblocked one sooner rather than later. Particularly because the distant sound of ogres popping on the rocks behind us had now stopped, suggesting that they had made it down.

Finding the quarry had been my own personal last-ditch effort to save us. Now that that had been buggered up royally by Ig's utter inability to do anything right, I was at something of a loss.

As we headed alongside the great slope of pebbles that might have gotten us out of this hole towards the rear wall where the quarry was still at its deepest, a tunnel finally came into sight. Wide enough that you could quite easily have driven two carts side by side through it.

It was our only option. We had entirely cornered ourselves. It was nowhere near narrow enough to serve Ildrit's purposes, but the ogres were close enough behind us now that all the pebbles on the ground were bouncing with the pounding of their oncoming march. We ducked inside and ran as best we could into the deep shadows for almost a whole second before we hit a solid wall.

Just like the other square blocks that had been pulled from the quarry side farther back, so too had one been drawn from here. A perfect cube as wide as it was deep. A dead end.

"What do we do?" Wyn asked Ildrit. As though anyone had an answer to this impossible situation.

"You stays here," Ig answered.

I'm not sure that all of us hiding in this tiny crevasse is actually going to be all that helpful, Ig. They can just walk in and see us.

"Me is the one they wanting. Me is one who burn city down, banana their boss. They is wanting me." He turned back to the other two adventurers with a smile. Or as close a contortion as his kobold face could muster. "They wants wizard. Me is going to give them one."

CHAPTER TWENTY-FOUR

THE KOBOLD'S GAMBIT

As Ig emerged blinking into the sunlight, I was internally screaming at him. *What the heck do you think you are doing you overgrown rodent, you are going to get us both killed, stop it right now and go back inside before they see you.*

The ogres were arrayed around the entrance to our tunnel with their weapons drawn. They had lost perhaps a quarter of their number in pursuit of us, but that still left several hundred times more ogre than Ig could reasonably have been expected to deal with. One ogre was several hundred times more ogre than a kobold could deal with.

If you were to start running, there is a chance the archers couldn't get you without shooting their own men.

Arrayed along the slope were the archers. The heavy siege weapons seemed to have been abandoned in the pursuit, leaving behind only actual bows, which was something of a relief. At least Ig would live long enough to know what had killed him if he got shot with them.

Shouldering his way through the crowd came Sour Ron, as foul a scowl on his face as he had ever shown. All of his perpetual grumpiness was focused now upon Ig. The object of his loathing. The font of all his misfortune. His nemesis.

Ig looked at him for a moment, then turned away to examine the other ogres, with an expression that I could only describe as unconcerned.

He had gone mad. Clearly that was the only answer—he had lived his entire life in such endless boundless terror that now he was finally in a situation where blind panic was in fact the rational option, and he had plateaued into some strange level of calm.

"You is ogres. You is not soldiers. You is not civilized. Ron lied. He try make you what you not." Ig's voice didn't even crack. I couldn't have gotten through that pidgin speech without at least a nervous cough, and he was just chatting with them as though they were old friends. "You not need follow him. You not need die for him."

The threat of death drew a belly laugh from Sour Ron, one that, after a little elbowing, was picked up by all of the other ogres too.

"You think we is scared of you, little kobold?!" Ron roared with hilarity. "You is nothing."

"Me burned your city without trying. Me escaped you again and again. Me stick my banananana in your Ron! Me is not nothing." His little squeaking voice rose into a bellow. Or as close as a kobold could muster. "Me is a wizard. Me is the big boss wizard of Arpantaloon. Me is Absalom Scryne! Archmage!"

And as he spoke, the Quintessence flowed through him, out of him, surrounded him. He drifted, inch by inch, up into the air until he was level with the faces of the ogres. They could not look down on him now. They could not deny that he had magic at his beck and call. As intimidation tactics went, I'd typically have gone with turning their blood to boiling acid or something, but this wasn't bad at all for a first attempt.

Oh, bravo.

Ig pressed on, ignoring Sour Ron's mounting rage. "Me is giving you a chance to leave. I send other 'venturers away. Ron not be stopping you. You cans go be ogres again. No more boss. No more rules."

A few of the ogres in the crowd began casting one another sideways glances, but every time it seemed one might break and run for that promised freedom, their gaze went back to Sour Ron, and his misery seemed to infect them. They were more afraid of Ron than they were of Ig, and that was all there was to it.

Ron's sneer dripped contempt. "Shoot him."

Ig, look out! Look out! Run!

As one, the archers drew back on their strings, took aim on Ig, and loosed.

I would also have expected Ig's bowels to loose at the same time. It would have been fair enough. Had I the equipment still built in, his scalp would most likely have become marginally less hygienic in that moment. Yet instead, he let his anxiety leap from him like the living thing that it was. He was so very afraid of everything all the time, and now, with Quintessence at his beck and call, with the lowest magic imaginable, he finally had a way to weaponize that terror.

A hundred arrows filled the sky, arcing down towards Ig where he stood, already abandoning all attempts to concentrate in a rational manner. He could not focus on a single thing, because of the anxiety at the heart of him. But he could focus on a hundred things all at once without even trying.

The hundred arrows stopped dead in the air as he caught hold of them with his magic.

The terror only peaked for a moment before he opened his eyes again and realized that his insane plan had actually worked. The moment that the fear passed, he lost all grasp over the arrows and himself. He dropped back down to the ground, and the arrows became subject to gravity once more, dropping straight down into the mass of ogres below.

There was a great deal of roaring, screaming, and complaining in the subsequent seconds. Some ogres on the periphery of the pack took their opportunity and sprinted away. Some that had been struck down by the fire of their companions turned on them and charged up the steep, sloped side of the shale pile to attack them.

In short, chaos reigned.

And Ig . . . he smiled up at Sour Ron as though they were best friends, raised a hand, and pointed a finger.

Ron opened his mouth to roar out his next command and in the same instant, Ig yelped out, "***Fragor!***"

The banana soared through the air, following the gentle arc of its own curvature, soaring past the ogre's fat lips to slam directly to the back of his throat once more. He made a noise somewhat akin to a blocked drain, grasping at his neck, spinning around to look for assistance that it seemed quite clear was not going to be forthcoming.

Up at the top of the gravel ramp, it had become apparent to the archers that they were about to be in exactly the situation no archer ever wants to be in, which is to say, close enough for the people you have been shooting at to lay their hands on you.

They had been well schooled in Ron's many classes; they knew the correct way to beat a retreat from advancing foot soldiers if you were an archer was to shoot them in the legs as you go, and that is just what they did, unloading the next hundred arrows directly into their already enraged compatriots.

The ogres that had neither turned on their own kind or already fled were now in something of a conundrum. They had just witnessed this tiny little kobold completely mopping the floor with their entire army, apparently without breaking a sweat, and the brutish and powerful leader that they had all sworn themselves to, and completely submitted all individuality to, just because of how awesome he was, looked like he may very well die to a piece of fruit.

Understandably, this was causing something of a morale crisis.

With all of the raw magic that Ig had been throwing around, there was a massive amount of ambient Quintessence still hanging in the air. The raw stuff of life, with nowhere to go. From beneath the shale heap, vibrations began. Pebbles at first began to roll off the slope, then whole hunks of rock dislodged. A small-scale landslide that sent those pursuing the archers sliding back down into their compatriots, and the archers themselves sliding sideways, even as half of them came under attack by the ogres who'd been quick enough up the slope.

Then, just as it seemed that things could not become any more confusing, the rabbits arrived. I had fully expected to see one vast bunny bursting forth from beneath the stone, but it seemed the diffusion of Quintessence through the area had been sufficient that it could not all coalesce into one point, quite the opposite in fact. Ig had created a veritable legion of lop-eared dwarf bunnies that now came bursting out from the gravel with all the grace of an alien parasite exiting a man's chest, showering stone shrapnel and fluff everywhere.

The ogres who had held the line until now finally broke in terror as the miniscule rabbits came loping their way. As ogres, they were understandably unfamiliar with such creatures as domesticated rabbits, and between the burrowing and dangling ears being mistaken for antenna, they were convinced that they were facing some sort of giant insect swarm. Perhaps dire termites, spraying their awful acid, gnawing through flesh, bone, and wood alike.

Proving once again, that even if the whole world is full of monsters, what we can imagine is always worse.

The ogres who were not in the midst of murdering one another ran for their lives at this point. Every single one of them abandoned their brave leader, scampering off back towards the distant ramp up to the walls of civilization along the floor of the quarry.

When the rest emerged from their bloody conflict with one another and realized that everyone else had buggered off, they were quick to follow, sprinting up the gravel ramp without even noticing the preponderance of lagomorphs.

Ron had continued huffing and puffing and choking as all of this unfolded. He dropped his sword and began thumping himself in the stomach, trying desperately to dislodge the blockage in his airway.

And Ig, he walked closer and closer still, with the same silly little smile fixed on his face as he had treated the adventurers to before he came out here to sacrifice himself. Another revelation so profound that it overcame all the fear that made him a kobold.

Crouching down beside Sour Ron, he told him, "Me is not afraid of you anymore."

Then he turned his back on the ogre and walked away.

It was one heck of a way to end things, triumphant, a display of not even caring what happens to your nemesis next. Admittedly my viewpoint of his heroics was slightly tempered by the fact that I'd heard his internal monologue the whole time as he gibbered about his own certain death and absolute terror, but even so, the whole thing had been masterful.

Ig. I take back everything that I have ever said; you are truly a wizard. Capable of creating victory from nothing. I am in awe of you, sir.

Which was when the dying ogre snatched up his cleaver and decided to take Ig with him.

There was very little Quintessence inside of me, the vast majority of it being required to maintain my sapience, but everything that I had, I flung out at the ogre. It was barely even low magic. All of my attention was on the blade and so that was where all of the force I'd unleashed went. It wasn't much. Not compared to the vast quantities of Quintessence that Ig was now capable of calling upon, but it was enough to knock the sword from his hands and shoot it back into his gut, slicing all his oxygen-starved fingers as it passed.

Ron hit the ground in a heap before Ig had even turned to look back. But by then, my solitary act of bravery that had clearly surpassed everything Ig had done previously, and you should all remember that, had taken its toll.

My awareness of the world, my connection to my kobold. It was fading.

Ig . . . I need . . . I need Quin . . .

That's right, I was so heroic I sacrificed my own life to save the stupid kobold. Now who do you think is the real hero of this tale? Hmm?

A moment later, reality returned to me as he flung some spare power he had lying around up through his scalp.

Right. Thank you.

"Welcome." Ig seemed entirely too pleased with himself.

Now perhaps we should go and retrieve our . . .

Sour Ron rose to his full height once more, the remains of a banana slithering down his chin, ejected by the impromptu Heimlich maneuver I'd performed on him with the butt of his sword.

Oops.

Blood dribbled from his wounded hands; drool slicked down his chin and in his eyes. Finally, the ogre within him had been set free from all of the restrictions of civilization that he'd walled it in with. There was a beauty in that, I supposed. Like looking at a wild running river or a waterfall or something. Something vast and uncontrollable and dangerous that it was fun to look at from a safe distance but that you really did not want to get too close to.

He didn't even bother with his sword. He came at Ig with his bloody hands hooked into claws. "Die!"

And that was precisely what Ig was about to do, because I was all out of magic, he was all out of clever tricks, and when it came down to a fistfight, a kobold had several disadvantages that I did not have time to list because he was about to be massacred messily.

Ron roared.

Ig squealed.

I wondered if the next person to wear me might be slightly more capable.

And Ildrit came surging out of the shadows with Widowtaker already swinging.

It took the nearest of the ogre's arms off just below the elbow, but in his rage, nothing so simple as dismemberment could stop Ron. Frothing at the mouth, he roared over and over again, "Die! Die! Die!"

His bloody hand caught ahold of Ig by the front of his horrendously stained bathrobe, and with no other hand available to pummel him with, the ogre lifted the poor kobold up, moving instead to dash him on the rocks. A plan that would absolutely have worked if Ig had any idea how to wear clothes. As the robe went up, Ig remained in place. Naked and more than a little confused.

In the tumult, I was lifted from his head and banished into the black void of nothingness that I was becoming all too familiar with, but in what felt like a single moment I was back on Ig's head and the ogre was laid out on the floor, missing his head as well as his hand.

Ildrit was breathing heavily. Still standing ready to fight. Just waiting for the next of the ogres to come.

"They is gone."

"What?" Ildrit took a step forward towards the light, and then stopped dead at the sight of scattered corpses and fallen rocks. "What did you do?"

"Me is a wizard," Ig answered succinctly, tugging his bathrobe free of Ron's still-spasming hand and trying to get back into it.

"Did . . . did we win?" Ildrit couldn't seem to quite grasp the situation.

"Yup." Ig managed to find an armhole at last. "Big win."

"The ogres are all . . ."

"Some run away." Ig was careful not to take too much credit.

Ildrit turned to look at the kobold as though for the very first time. "Ig, was it?"

Ig smiled. "That me."

"I think that I may love you, Ig." Ildrit laughed.

"Hat helped too," Ig added, magnanimously.

"Yes, of course." Ildrit bowed to me, atop Ig's head. "My newfound respect and affection extends to the both of you."

Then let us retrieve our elfin friend, and carry on towards civilization.

"We get Wyn now?" Ig translated for me.

Ildrit clapped him on the back, almost making the poor little creature tumble over. "Yes, we'll go get Wyn now."

CHAPTER TWENTY-FIVE

THE LIVING DEAD

With his arm still slung freely about Ig's shoulders, Ildrit led us back to the rear of the cave where our companion should have been awaiting us.

You will note from that particular turn of phrase that Wyn was not in fact present. Furthermore, the rear wall of the cave, which we had until now considered to be a solid block of stone, had resolved itself into something else entirely.

"What in the nine hecks, now?" Ildrit grumbled. But quietly enough that it wouldn't carry deeper into the newly opened cavern.

Curse Ig's feeble eyes. You would have thought a creature that spent all of its time in holes in the ground would have had excellent vision in the dark, but no, he was blinder than a flatworm the moment that you turned the torches down. Yet more evidence that evolution had really only intended for the kobold species to persist for twenty minutes at most.

Along the rear wall, what was left of it, graven into the solid stone, there were runemarks. Dwarven runemarks, of the sort that they used to alert other dwarves to their secret stoneworks. For instance, if they had snuck into someone else's quarry and didn't know who the owner was, but they'd decided that it was where they wanted to mine, they might dig the entrance to the mine in an already existing cave, and then hide the entrance with a solid stone slab, movable to those who knew it was there, as guided by the runemarks. For a people deprived of magic, there could be no denying that dwarves were cunning little bastards.

More likely than not, left to their own devices, Wyn had discovered said marks and used their substantial knowledge of languages to decipher that mode of unlocking the rear exit. My only wish was that they had done so before Ig went out and was brave, as it would have saved us all considerable anxiety.

Still, the fact that there were dwarves up ahead rather than ogres did not necessarily guarantee us any sort of safety. Particularly given that we had an elf among our number.

Elves and dwarves have not, historically, seen eye to eye. And that is not just because one is lithe and tall and the other about the same height as Ig.

There were some fundamental issues that the two species disagreed on, and while many accords had been reached throughout history between the two mighty empires, one atop the surface of the world, and one down below, they kept on finding themselves drawn into conflict due to the same issues again and again.

Primarily, the elves were big fans of trees, forests, and nature, while the dwarves were big fans of exploiting the mineral rights of every inch of land on the planet, even when it meant massive slash and burn operations up on the surface to clear the way for their access.

Add onto this the fact that elves are incredibly long-lived and dwarves pass down grudges like ancestral memory, and you have what is essentially a self-perpetuating system of vengeance stretching back to the dawn of time.

So no, this new development did not necessarily mean safety was ahead, but it did mean that we'd had an option other than running face-first into a small army of ogres. Ig didn't seem to have realized this yet. Sometimes I wasn't sure that he had a sense of object permanence, or understood causality. Perhaps to him, things like a new tunnel suddenly appearing where before there had been none were perfectly normal.

I for one wasn't about to stop and explain to him that his great act of heroism and courage had been entirely unnecessary as we had a back door out. He needed the confidence, and frankly I felt that he'd earned it. I may not have particularly cared for Ig when we first met, but I must admit that after all of our time together, he had grown on me somewhat. Like a fungus. An itchy fungus.

The short passageway from the outside world was not guarded. Dwarves trusted in their craftsmanship to keep out anyone hostile. And honestly, if you were a monster that had enough intelligence to get through the door, you'd also have enough intelligence to know that making an attempt at tunnel-fighting in a dwarf's home turf, where they had designed every inch for maximum defensibility and where even the most passive of innocent bystanders was still carrying around a very sharp pickaxe, was not a good move.

From there it opened out into a large cube chamber, with tunnels extending in various directions. From the amount of dust, it appeared that this area of the dwarven mines had long since been forgotten and abandoned. It happened quite often with dwarves that the actual entrance to the mine would be supplanted by a secondary or even tertiary one constructed later when they found a more viable site. It had also been known to happen that dwarves would forget about the surface world entirely once they had their own underground farms set up, delving ever deeper and expanding ever outwards in an entirely closed system.

The dust was quite helpful, in that it showed Wyn's tracks as they journeyed in. There were the dragging footsteps of someone who'd sprained both ankles falling from a great height, heading over to a fallen hunk of masonry. There were another set of footprints, almost as small and delicate as the elf's, picking carefully across the cluttered floor. Stalking Wyn deeper and deeper into the mines.

And there atop that fallen stone there was the still-glowing outline of the elf where a death-spell had struck them. All of that Plutonium light absorbed into the body but bathing the surrounding stone and leaving it glowing sickly.

"Oh no," Ig mumbled.

Ildrit spun, blade unsheathing as the monster leapt from the dark shadows. Sparks flew from the creature's daggers where they scraped across Widowtaker's sharp edge, illuminating the strange creature for just long enough for us to recognize its features. Wyn.

In life, Wyn's face had been deprived of expression by self-control; now their face hung limp on their skull, expressionless like a hanging side of beef is expressionless. Yet all of the other motion that had made the elf alive had been returned to it by dark magic that I'm far too classy to use. The body had two daggers drawn and was doing its damnedest to mantis-slice its way through to Ildrit.

The undead are typically clumsy creatures, characterized by their slow, lumbering movements as decay sets in, but of course the elf who had been our friend was still fresh. Freshly slaughtered so that they might serve the necromancer in keeping Ildrit occupied.

Ildrit, who appeared to be currently crying. That probably wasn't a good sign.

"Why?" he begged to the still darkness of the cave. "Why would you do this?"

"Oh, don't go crying those crocodile tears, darling, it's an elf. You used to kill ten just like it before breakfast." Bonetaker's voice echoed out from one side passage, then the next. A simple distortion, a simple trick, but an effective one, nonetheless.

Ig spun around on the spot, searching for the necromancer, only to stumble over some uneven ground and land on his tail. I was starting to rethink believing in him. It had been a lot easier to assume he was useless, what with all the evidence in favor of that conclusion.

"They were my friend!" Ildrit shouted back, even as they kicked the corpse of their friend back out of reach. "They found me when I was at my worst, at my lowest, and they believed in me."

Bonetaker's sniggering echoed back and forth, all around us. "Oh, darling, were they your bestest friend before I murdered them? Did you hold hands? Whisper secrets?"

"Why are you doing this, Bonetaker?" Wyn's body darted back in, slicing in at Ildrit from both sides in a pincer, then skittering back out of reach like a startled spider the moment that he deflected the blows. "We were meant to be friends too."

"Friends? You thought we were friends?!" Bonetaker's cackle was amplified, deafening. Pounding in on Ig from every side. "People like us don't have friends, you halfwit. We use each other until we're of no more use, then we move on. Just like you did the moment that things got too hard for you, because of some nonsense curse."

Ildrit backed away, letting the dead body of Wyn lumber after him into the middle of the room, where a little of the distant sunlight was still filtering through and the green glow of Bonetaker's killing curse still lingered. "You followed me once, so at some time you must have had some respect for . . ."

"Respect?!" Bonetaker choked on their laughter. "You absolute joke of a human being, we didn't follow you because we were your good little soldiers, we followed you like hunters follow their hound. You were a very well-behaved little pup, sniffing out the places where slaughter was ripe and guiding us there, but it didn't go any further than that. Respect? Hah."

I could not say with certainty whether the Bonetaker had direct control over Wyn's reanimated body, or whether some spark of the person that they had been was trapped inside of it, guiding their movements. I would have hoped that it was the former, but the Bonetaker had never shown even a fragment of the grace with which this abomination now moved.

Daggers flashed out, deflected with a spin of Widowtaker, only to lash in again from the other side. No longer trying to best Ildrit in speed but wearing him down through relentlessness. Wyn's corpse still moved fast enough that a counter would hit only air and leave Ildrit vulnerable, so he was forced on the back foot, constantly shifting and ducking the furious flow of strikes. But despite all this, there was no exhaustion in his voice when he called out to the dark once more, only pain. "Why would you follow me if you hated me?"

"Isn't it obvious? Because I need corpses, darling. The dead are the crucial catalyst of my magic. And no matter your many *many* other shortcomings, the one thing that you did leave behind in vast, bountiful amounts was a trail of bodies."

In a move so fast Ig's eyes couldn't even follow it, Ildrit slapped both of Wyn's blades aside and hammered his head forward into the elf's face. There was no brain in there doing the thinking anymore, so the elf could not be knocked unconscious the way a living one could, but at least it was sufficient to knock them off-balance, staggering back into the shadows.

Ildrit's face was bloodied. His friend's blood running down from his forehead. It was also contorted into the kind of bestial snarl that you never expect humans to be able to express until you see it. "I meant why did you leave your cozy little dungeon and follow me now, if all you ever felt was hate."

"And lust," Bonetaker interjected, only for Ildrit to ignore him completely.

Even as Wyn darted back in to meet Ildrit's blade once more, the warrior snapped, "Why follow me?"

"Because of the bounty, darling. You were about to march yourself straight into Arpanpholigon, where there is still a posted bounty of ten thousand gold crowns for whoever delivers you. I wanted the money, honey."

Even Ig raised an eyebrow at the sheer amount of money being offered for Ildrit's capture, despite having no real grasp of either mathematics or finances. Our companion really must have been a problem in the old days.

Ildrit's jaw set and they lashed out at the dead elf. "Wyn was going to vouch for me. Tell people I wasn't like that anymore."

"Oh, whoops. Guess that's out the window." The Bonetaker tittered. "Maybe you should just surrender yourself into my hands and let me be rich and comfortable as well as clever and beautiful." His voice sounded as though it was coming from right behind Ig's ear now, and finally I realized why the elf-zombie trap had been necessary.

Because the Bonetaker wanted to face Ig without interference.

Whatever else he might have been, he was a wizard, and that implied a degree of ego. An ego that Ig had slapped in the face with a banana. And the only way for this necromancer to feel like a man again was to face the kobold that had slighted him.

Duck!

Ig had been well conditioned to obedience by now, and he hit the floor like a ton of bricks as the Plutonium blast sailed by overhead, setting another section of the carved cube room glowing.

As swiftly as he went down, Ig rolled to his feet again, in as close to fighting form as a kobold could get after our adventures together. The Bonetaker emerged from the shadows, the green glow of his magic giving his skin a sickly cast, and his teeth in particular shining out of his grin looking like he was in desperate need of some dentistry.

"Finally we have the chance to test ourselves fully, Archmage Absalom Scryne." He cackled. "If you were going to impersonate a real wizard, you probably shouldn't have chosen one of the most famous on the continent. Honestly, everyone and their mother knows that Scryne is the Imperator of the Invisible College of Arpanpholigon. It is like gluing horns to a rabbit, and skipping past pretending it's a goat to claiming it is a demon."

For future reference, a horned rabbit is a jackalope. Or a wolpentinger, if it has wings. This buffoon could not stop showing his ignorance.

"Is going to be future?" Ig asked, and I did not have so easy an answer to that as to matters of horned lagomorph taxonomy.

"Well, Archmage, my pet, since everyone knows what a stickler you are for tradition, let's have ourselves a very traditional wizard's duel. Look, I'll even curtsey." The Bonetaker bobbed, and despite himself, Ig bowed his head ever so slightly just to keep his eyes locked on the enemy. Cackling, the necromancer cried, "And away we go!"

They led with a Plutonium blast directly at Ig's face. Without lead to invoke, there was no defense, and with the speed that it traveled, there was no hope of avoiding it. Ig, panicking as always, threw up his hands, and flung raw Quintessence out.

A dead bunny landed on the floor between us and the Bonetaker.

Typically so musical and flamboyant, the necromancer's voice sounded particularly flat in comparison when he said, "What?"

Again, Ig, swiftly!

Another rabbit shot out from Ig's extended hands, then another, and another. He threw wild magic out into the world with all haste, before the necromancer could ready another spell. Each time, the poor little bundle of fluff soared through the air and struck the evil wizard, disrupting his concentration and preventing him from launching another killing spell our way.

Keep it up, Ig!

And the truly hilarious part of it all was, he could. Each tiny bunny took only a miniscule spark of Quintessence to create, and Ig was drawing it in now with such ease and frequency that he could have maintained a steady flow of tiny rabbits until the heat death of the universe.

They began to heap up on the ground in front of the Bonetaker, loping about and being adorable. Given enough time, they would continue to pile until they filled the entire chamber, and the Bonetaker would be smothered in tiny bunny fluff, but that did not seem like the most plausible way that a duel might be won.

Moments before, he had been so full of confidence that you might never have expected a backwards step from the Bonetaker, but now he struck a full-on retreat, yelping on occasion when a sharp bunny elbow or bucktooth impacted upon him.

It bought us the moment to glance around to Ildrit and Wyn.

Both of Wyn's blades were locked on opposite sides of Widowtaker, and they were straining with all the unholy strength of undeath to wrench the blade from Ildrit's hands. Throughout it all, in so soft a voice it almost brought a tear to Ig's eye, Ildrit was whispering. "I know that you're still in there, Wyn. I know this isn't you. Just stop. Please."

I didn't have the heart to tell him that Wyn was not in fact still in there, it truly wasn't him, and it was actually just the malevolent will of the necromancer animating the corpse of his friend.

All of the desperate pleading probably would have been rendered somewhat less tragic if it weren't for the fact that even the corpse was ignoring Ildrit entirely, eyes locked instead upon Ig. Who its master was likely now commanding it to attack in favor of the swordsman, since a steady flow of lagomorphs was unlikely to slow it in the same way.

The Golden Flames of Galgalagrin the Great, Ig. Behind the necromancer, quickly.

The bunny-tide ceased, Ig drew a deep breath, focusing his concentration, and unleashed his magic with a cry of "***Fragor!***"

Golden flames did not leap from his fingertips to seal off the necromancer's escape route—surprising absolutely nobody—but a banana did soar past him to land with a wet splat.

The necromancer may not have had time to get a spell out yet, but there was time enough for them to snort out a laugh at Ig's pathetic attempt at offensive magic. A snort that continued into a surprised wheeze as Bonetaker's heel came down on the banana and he slipped.

Quickly now, Ig, focus upon Carbon.

"That is one that not . . ."

The one that is not Potassium. Focus!

We would not have a repeat of the werewolf problem, because there was literally nothing else going on that he might get distracted by. All he had to do was focus on Carbon, say **Congelo**, and we'd have a petrified necromancer that we could just leave here to rot. Or . . . accumulate moss, as the case may be.

So of course when he opened his mouth, he instead yelled *"Fragor!"* again.

Thinking that this was the final blow in their duel, Ig had thrown what I'd have to describe as a frankly obscene amount of Quintessence into the spell. Far more than any sort of Carbon blast might have required, not that I could readily think of any spell in any legitimate spell-book that would have combined an inert element like Carbon with so destructive a word of Archaic. What luck for us then that Ig's famously razor-sharp focus had been diluted somewhat. While, to my mind, he had been taught only two elements, Ig, sifting back through his memories, had instead struck upon the other one that he had inadvertently tapped into. Sulfur.

I had expected another torrent of dust if he failed. A sandblast like he'd pelted the poor werewolves with earlier. Instead, heck was let loose. Flames burning yellow-green, so hot that every hair on Ig's body was crisped just being in their presence. They leapt out from his hands, swirled across the room to the Bonetaker, and collided with whatever frantic defense he had managed to raise.

Where it struck that barrier, the heckfire exploded. Not just a fireworks puff of sparks but the kind of solid concussion that could shake down mountains. A sound as hard as a rock. A heat as scorching as a year in the sun. Ig was knocked from his feet, and so too fell the Bonetaker.

Yet while Ig rose blinking and stunned, when the necromancer tried to right himself, he found all that he had left was the other arm. He had imperiously cast his shield with his right hand, and now it was missing from the elbow down. Seared away to nothing but ashes.

Ig blinked at the sudden delicious aroma of roasted meat, then promptly began retching.

Oh for the love of . . . It is a fight, Ig. People are going to get hurt. The goal is to make sure that they get hurt before they hurt us.

I was not certain if the kobold could hear me over the necromancer's girlish screams or his own vomiting, but I had to try to console him somehow.

Ig, you need to pay attention, you are going to get attacked while distracted.

How he could throw up so much having not eaten anything in the past day was beyond me.

When he finally rose back up to his full height, his eyes were bleary with tears, but there was enough clarity there to make out what was happening in the battle between the dead elf and Ildrit through the oily smoke.

Finally having overcome his initial desire to not desecrate his friend's corpse, at some point, Ildrit had gained the upper hand, dislocating the shoulder that was already loose in its socket from earlier. The knife was still held in a death grip, but the arm dangled uselessly, even though the corpse-elf would still sometimes attempt to flail it in the correct direction.

With only a single knife up against his greater reach, the tide of the battle had turned firmly in Ildrit's favor now. He launched a counter after each parry, and if Wyn's circulatory system were still functioning, they would have been bleeding from a half dozen lethal wounds. Instead, they went lumbering on, trying to break away from Ildrit and rush to their master's aid.

With a flash and a spin, the dangling, useless arm came off and sailed across the room to land with a splat beside Ig. That was two severed arms in this corner. We were starting to get a theme going here.

From there, the fight became ever more brutal instead of easing. The ex-elf slipped on one of the fleeing tides of bunnies and Ildrit sprang in to take advantage, separating the other arm from their torso with the same ease as the last. Entirely armless, but not entirely harmless, Wyn now charged in blindly, chomping their pearly white and perfectly straight teeth in preparation for biting out their dearest friend's throat.

With a sigh, Ildrit made one final cut.

Wyn's head spun free of their body, and at last, the desecration that the Bonetaker had inflicted was at its end.

Ig scampered over to the warrior, still standing with his blade bare, slick with the cold blood of his dearest friend, and he did something that it would never have occurred to me to do. He flung his arms around Ildrit's waist and crushed his face into the man's hip, and then he clung as though being parted from the warrior would be the end of all things.

For a moment, Ildrit stiffened, unaccustomed to such contact as I would have been, then his hand drifted down to rest on Ig's shoulder. "It's over now, little friend."

Ig mumbled something into his side that even I couldn't decipher despite being inside his head. Ildrit gave his shoulder a squeeze. I suppose that the words mattered less than the meaning. And in this moment, physical contact was all the meaning that was required.

When Ig drew back to look up at Ildrit, the man looked like he'd aged a decade in a day, all the exhaustion of our long flight through the wilds writ upon his face, all the horrors that he'd faced this day sunken into his eyes. But even so, he mustered a soft smile for the kobold.

Then the necromancer's spell hit him.

It was not a killing curse empowered by Plutonium—even pain-drunk as he was, Bonetaker was still smart enough to know that he needed the vagabond alive if he meant to claim the bounty—but it was something potent, possibly derived from Methane and Chlorine. His eyes rolled up into his head and he hit the ground hard before Ig was fully disentangled from him.

The Bonetaker rose again. His severed arm had been replaced with Wyn's, though clearly with some serious mistakes, given that the flesh was already sloughing off it, leaving only the glowing green bones behind, still animate. Staggering slightly, the necromancer tittered. "Oh, darling, you've just given me a whole new aesthetic."

Ig had no answer for that except for a terrified little chirp as he tried to retrieve his arm from under Ildrit's unconscious form and run.

"Heckfire! I never knew that you had it in you. I'm impressed. Of course, given that you've got that hat telling you how to do everything the rest of us scraped and studied and bled for, maybe that's what I should be impressed with rather than you? What do you think, pet? How do you think you'd manage without it?"

Ig scrambled backwards, trying to put distance between himself and the necromancer, as if the Bonetaker couldn't kill him at any distance.

Green light enveloped the Bonetaker now. He was invoking Plutonium without casting, simply radiating light and harm. "Where's all the funny business now? No more rabbits to pull out your hat? No more banana peels to make people slip on? Take away all your silly little tricks, and what is left?"

He sneered as he reached down and seized me by the point.

"Nothing but a stupid little rat, in a stolen little hat, darling."

Then he ripped me off.

CHAPTER TWENTY-SIX

THE RODENT DEFIANCE HYPOTHESIS

What happened while I was off Ig's head, I would only find out in retrospect. In the time between my removal from his scalp and my return to awareness, millennia may have passed entirely without my awareness. All that I knew was silence and darkness and a lingering sense that something had gone terribly wrong.

As Ig described it, "Bone man talked lots and lots, say me is dum-dum. But me is not dum-dum. Me is wizard. Me say me is wizard. Bone man got big mad. Says me is only wizard because hat. So me make bunny. Then he zap bunny dead. So me make more bunny and he get even more big mad and blast all bunnies. Then he make bunnies come back all bony and he chase me to wall. And then he say he going to show me what wizard can really do. Then he put on hat."

At which point my awareness of events resumed. There was Ig, pinned against the wall, the necromancer flooded with power, ready to cast the spell that would not only wipe the poor kobold from life, but also pulverize his every cell out of existence. To each side of Ig was a ravenous horde of reanimated lagomorphs of various sizes, their buck teeth quite terrifying-looking without the soft fur to hide them.

Leave that kobold alone! I bellowed it with every bit of will that I had, enough that it would have driven Ig to his knees, but I was no longer contending with the will of a kobold, I was atop a wizard, or at least the closest that this sordid region of the world could boast of, and I struck upon his mental defenses like I was the tide parting on a rock. The Bonetaker cackled, "At last I get to hear from the man with the organ grinder rather than the monkey. Tell me, oh fabulous hat, what lies did you tell this poor little cretin to get it to be so loyal? Did you promise it food, buxom kobold wenches, hirsute kobold gents, a robe and station of its very own when you got back to Arpanpholigon? However did you buy such loyalty from a creature so devoid of ambition and thought?"

Ig helps me, because I am in need of his help. Not that a blackguard like yourself could ever understand such noble intentions.

He was sobbing with amusement by this point. "Noble intentions?! It's a rat that learned to walk on two legs, you idiot of a hat!"

Ig's fur bristled, but he could not move to my aid without the skelebuns attacking.

That kobold knows more of kindness and nobility of spirit than you have failed to learn in your entire life, you pompous, arrogant upstart.

"It is a kobold!" The Bonetaker's uproarious laughter was beginning to grate on my nerves.

And you are supposed to be a human, yet here we all are.

That stung the necromancer more than I would have expected—a small jab on my part, but touching on some old hurt that we could exploit later. "And I suppose that as a piece of haberdashery, you are the best judge of one's humanity."

When a hat and a kobold can look upon you and see what a pathetic excuse for a man you are, I suspect that tells you all that you need to know.

It seemed that the Bonetaker had no clever comeback to that one. "Minions, take the kobold and the swordsman outside. We are heading to civilization."

Ig made several terrified meeping noises as the skeletal horde scooped him up and carried him off, and I imagine that Ildrit would have made some similar noises were he conscious for his own manhandling.

But the Bonetaker himself was silent. He had no friends to keep his mind off things, no allies with which to chatter. He was alone with his thoughts, as vulnerable as he was ever liable to be. *So why don't you tell me who it was that first told you that you were less than a man? They were right, of course, but probably not for the reasons they thought.*

"Be silent, hat, I will not be taken in by tricks." The necromancer hissed to himself. "You are a tool that I shall use to increase my power, not a confidante. Do not think that I will dally with fruitless conversation."

Sidestepping any jibes about the respective fruitiness of this little chat. You must realize that if any harm comes to Ig, I will never be anything but a hindrance to you.

"Really, you are trading your life, such as it is, for the safety of a kobold." He snorted. "Need I remind you that the average life expectancy of a kobold can be measured in minutes? You would not even need both hands to count the number of minutes. If you had hands."

If you let the kobold go free and unharmed, then I will grant you the same respect and deference that I'd give to any master. All that you are due.

He tapped one glowing, skeletal finger on his lip. "What a curious way of phrasing that, almost as if you didn't intend to help me regardless."

Whatever oath you want me to swear, I shall, just let Ig go.

"Or, alternatively, I can tear every scrap of knowledge out of you painfully, safe in the knowledge that nothing is being withheld or hidden out of malice."

The Bonetaker seemed to consider his options for a moment before nodding. "Yes, let's go with that one."

You shall gain nothing from me.

"And there you go again misunderstanding the situation. The kobold was your pet. I am your master. I own you. Whatever pleases me, you will do."

Actually, I'd rather if you didn't shove me right up your . . .

"Ron!?" Bonetaker cried out in despair. "Oh, you silly sausage, look at what they've done to you. What a waste."

I wasn't aware that the two of you were close.

"Oh, pet, you have no idea. We were as close as a man and an ogre can be. He was huge and strong and I . . . I was a little taste of decadent civilization." He lit up as he spoke, not with fond memories but with the sickly glow of Plutonium. **"Ortus."**

The flesh melted away from Sour Ron's remains, leaving only the dense skeleton behind. Skull and severed hand needed to roll back over to be rejoined, but at this point in the process it was less like healing and more like stacking blocks. The new skeletal minion, somewhat more impressive than the bunny swarm, took up the task of carrying Ildrit.

Ig was still hauled along, bouncing over the top of bony bunny backs. It seemed that the necromancer was more concerned with damaging his prize than the kobold he so detested.

As we emerged into the daylight, the Bonetaker came to a complete stop, looking out over the devastation that Ig had caused. "Oh my . . ."

I should probably have made some braggadocious statement about my true power and fearing me and all of that, but I just couldn't quite find the energy when poor Ig was looking green at the sight of all the dead bodies. He'd managed up until now to keep from doing any more vomiting, but if he puked on the Bonetaker's robes then all bets were off regarding his survival.

Once more the Bonetaker invoked Plutonium and whispered, **"Ortus,"** and abruptly we went from having to deal with a necromancer with a bad attitude and worse fashion sense to a small legion of ogre skeletons.

Ig looked ever so tiny from the outside. While I was seeing things through his eyes, he seemed to be the perfectly normal height and everything else far too large, but now that I was on the outside looking in, I was overwhelmed by how fragile he appeared.

He stared up at me, atop the necromancer's head, with a little glint in his eye that I did not like. Determination. If he made an attempt at snatching me back, he was liable to be clubbed to death with his own limbs, and that was assuming that the necromancer didn't just blast him into oblivion himself.

You know, master. There are probably many who would pay a great deal to see a kobold that can perform magic. You might sell him along to a circus or somesuch?

"Oh, do shut up about the rat, you are getting very boring." The Bonetaker scoffed. "Come now, surely after all this time with nobody of intellect to commune with, you must be desperate for some adult conversation."

Oh, wise master, what wonders you have performed with these skeletons. Will you modify them, as you did your servants back at the dungeon? Combining the rabbit bones with the ogres to make living weapons?

That gave him pause for a moment. "You know, that's not a terrible idea actually."

He began working through some rather complex incantations of Archaic, leaving me some time to concentrate. The longer that I could delay him, the more opportunities I would have to come up with some grand, cunning plan that would free me of his yoke, and the longer I kept him distracted from Ig, the more likely it was that his instincts might kick in and he'd run for his life like a sensible little kobold.

The Bonetaker's reserves of Quintessence were greater than Ig's as he'd had a lifetime of training, but they were only a fraction of what he might have achieved had he studied properly instead of going off galivanting. Yet while Ig's were constantly being refilled, it seemed that the Bonetaker needed to stop and focus to draw fresh power from the world. It wasn't much of an advantage, but it was something we could work with, I supposed.

Pray tell, master, how is it that one so learned in the arcane arts came to be banished like you? When the Invisible College would doubtless have snapped you up in a heartbeat?

"Hah." The necromancer scowled. "Those stuck-up fools took one look at my resume and rejected me outright. Absalom Scryne himself signed off on my rejection. A talent only for limited applications, he said. Unlikely to do well in an academic environment, he said. You should have chosen another name when you were trying to fake your transmogrification. The real Absalom Scryne would have remembered my name."

Except, of course, I didn't. I rejected more potential students each week than this fool had lovers. For him it had been a pivotal moment in his descent into madness, but for me it was just another day.

What a fool that Scryne was to turn you down when you are so obviously puissant and learned.

"Right!" the Bonetaker cried. "That's what I said!"

With a snap of his fingers, a pair of his lumbering skelebunny ogres stepped forward and lifted him into their arms, then the whole troop set off along the quarry to head for the Great Wall.

How he thought he'd get past the gates with a skeletal horde was not clear. Perhaps he meant to hide them in the bushes on arrival. Regardless, we would no doubt make good time being carried by tireless creatures with so broad a stride.

Ig was caught by the scruff of his neck and hauled up to be dangled along, while what remained of Ron still carried the sleeping Ildrit.

Conversation lapsed somewhat since it was now apparent that talking wasn't actually going to slow our progress, and what followed instead was a silent battle of wills. The Bonetaker was trying to burrow his mind into mine so that he could extract what I knew, while I was trying to push him out and burrow in the opposite direction so that I might find some psychological weakness that might be exploited.

Neither of us made much progress, what with both of us having to keep on focusing on protecting ourselves from the other, but just as he got little snippets of arcane knowledge out of me before I could cut him off, I received little motes of memory in return.

He had the expected sad childhood: Roadkill following him home as his powers began to manifest. Some very deliberate invitations not to attend funerals of friends and family. There was nothing unexpected there. It didn't help that the vast majority of his treasured memories that he let slip were of a carnal nature. Frankly, I was amazed that he had been able to walk the distances that he had in the past few days. It was as though he had thought there was some sort of award to be won for the most men ridden in a single lifetime.

No, you are not detecting any hint of jealousy. I devoted myself to higher pleasures than those of the flesh. And now, of course, I had no flesh with which to experience such things, even if I were so inclined. Not that I would have minded getting my point straightened and my felt brushed clean by an attractive young lady.

Each time that the Bonetaker grasped some new theorem or principle of magic that had previously eluded him, he made a satisfied little smacking of his lips, as though he were literally devouring the knowledge that he was wresting from me.

In many ways, he was the perfect antithesis of Ig. A creature of pure ego and indulgence, with all of his attentions turned inwards. This weirdly left all of his senses, which Ig fully occupied at all times in case of danger, completely unattended. So while he was technically hearing all of the same things as Ig, he was completely oblivious to them.

As such, he did not know what I knew now. If I had a face, I would have been grinning.

Ig knew; you could tell from the way he was suddenly, frantically scrambling and struggling to get away from the ogre skeleton that had him tucked under one arm. He knew, and he was terrified.

Rightly so, to be fair. If I had made a whole pack of werewolves absolutely furious at me then led them on a days-long hunt throughout the whole of the Badlands before they finally caught up to me to silence me, I probably would have been a little nervous too.

Even someone as self-involved as Bonetaker could not miss the howling when it began. All along the ridge of the quarry, lining both sides, there were wolves. Massive by regular wolf standards, pretty average if you were expecting a werewolf, and frankly, I had been expecting werewolves for quite a while now. You couldn't be the alpha of a pack like that if you let a kobold stroll in, blow snuff at you, and wander off again with your most dangerous secret. The only way to maintain control would have been to hunt down the threat, using werewolves' incredible sense of smell to track it over miles.

"What is this?" the Bonetaker snarled, head whipping from side to side. "What did you do, runt?!"

Poor Ig had no answer to the accusation beyond a little, "Weh?"

You made powerful enemies when you crossed Ig, master. We are only visitors to the Badlands, but this is his domain.

"He is a kobold! He has no domain! He has no allies! He has no power! He is barely sapient!" the Bonetaker ranted, but even as he spoke, you could tell that doubt was beginning to creep in. Ig had leveled New Orc City, he had slaughtered the ogres, he had conjured heckfire. Was a troop of obedient werewolves at his beck and call really so ridiculous in comparison to all that?

The wolves began their descent, pouring down the vertical surface of the quarry walls like a furry tide. Where the ogres had only two legs and a sense of balance only achievable by skipping leg day at the gym for decades, these were hunters built to traverse any terrain, from windswept mountains to gothic castles. It probably helped with their confidence that this was not a silver mine, so the fall couldn't actually kill them. Some did in fact lose their footing and tumble, but it mattered little. They lay in a hairy heap for but a moment before rising again. Growling.

The skeleton's progress along the quarry had come to an abrupt halt. The Bonetaker disembarked his ride with all haste, readying his magic and turning to point at Ig. "You! This is your doing! Call them off!"

"Me can'ts!" Ig wailed, eyes bulging in terror.

"You call them off or I'll kill you where you stand," he declared, invoking Plutonium for a killing curse.

Harm him and there will be no end to the wolves' fury.

Screaming with rage at victory being snatched from his hands, the Bonetaker spun back to the approaching wolves and barked out, "***Morior!***"

It was one of the young ones who bore the brunt of his fury. One of the ones clumsy enough to fall. A wolf that looked like it should have been hanging out, rebelling against its parents and ignoring everything adults said. She could not ignore the command in that ancient word of Archaic.

Green light washed out from the necromancer's hand and enveloped her. The teen wolf fell.

All at once, the other werewolves diverted from their course and went rushing to her aid, circling around the still and silent body of the werewolf where she lay upon the gravel.

Bonetaker cackled, "That's right, you fuzzy little brats! Fear me! The next of you to come my way gets the very same! And the next, and all the rest too. I can do this all day!"

It was a shame, really, that I had rejected the Bonetaker's college application, however many years ago that was. He really would have benefited from the kind of education that you could only receive at a top-notch institution like that found in Arpanpholigon. You could learn not only about yourself and the magic that you wielded, but all of the other magic in the world too. All of the magical creatures.

Then he might have known what I told Ig back when he was arsing around in the werewolves' herb garden. They are incredibly resistant to magic.

The crowd parted and the teen wolf rose to her feet once more, hackles raised, and a growl that I could feel vibrating right up to my pointy tip was emanating from somewhere within her.

You should have listened when you had the chance.

Ig was now in paroxysms of terror, bucking loose of his skeletal oppressor but having nowhere to run that wouldn't immediately put him in reach of either another skelebun monstrosity or one of the werewolves trying to hunt him down. He was paralyzed in fear, certain that he was the target of these werewolves after he had so mistreated them during our visit to their village.

Yet I knew what Ig did not.

When you take a wolf and combine its nature with that of man, you do not end up with some ravening beast drawn only to wicked violence. Since near the dawn of time, humans had been instilling their traits into a pack of wolves, breeding them deliberately to make them more like us. Infusing them with our values and expectations. We called those creatures dogs.

So consider the scenario not as one of massive wolves, but as of dogs. A whole load of dogs just had a nice long walk, and now they were confronted with a pile of bones.

The first of the ogre skeletons was down and being gnawed on faster than you could blink. The one standing guard over the Bonetaker had its leg hauled out from under it, and just beyond the ivory heap, a fluffy tail could be seen furiously wagging.

Enraged, defeated, humiliated, the Bonetaker turned on the only person in the world more powerless than him to take it all out on. Ig stared up at him with eyes the size of tea saucers.

Drawing all of his remaining power together, the Bonetaker invoked Plutonium one last time and readied his killing spell.

Ig was about to die.

I clamped the necromancer's mouth shut. He fought me, of course he did, his will against mine, all the home-field advantage going to him thanks to it being his body that I was trying to hijack. But what he had not counted upon was the simple fact that everyone had been overlooking more or less since the moment that I became a hat. The fact that I too had forgotten in all of the chaos. I was not some enchanted headgear, I was not a kobold, I was not any of the things that they had assumed I was. I was Absalom Scryne, greatest wizard in the world.

Whatever power he might have wielded over me, the Bonetaker could not contest that one undeniable reality, not now. I was Absalom Scryne, and just as I had rejected him before, now again I would crush all of his hopes, dreams, and will down, and maintain control over his mouth.

So long as he did not speak, he could not cast. So long as he could not cast, he could not kill Ig. The power that he had gathered was screaming to be released. The Plutonium he had invoked was searing him from the inside out. All of the power he'd meant to unleash was trapped behind his pursed lips, unable to escape.

And Ig himself, standing face-to-face with this warlock of incredible might, surrounded and cornered in a way that he had never faced before in his life, found something like courage buried deep within his heart.

To the kobold, fight or flight was not a question. There was only one good answer, and that was to run. Evolution had honed them to run screaming in terror from anything that approached, be it a bumblebee or a dragon. Everything could kill a kobold, so kobolds survived solely by running as fast as their little legs could carry them, and hoping that they outpaced whichever of their kin was the slowest.

Yet the dichotomy remained within Ig despite all of the refinement that nature had put the kobold through. Fight or flight. There was nowhere for him to run. No escape. No means of flight available to him. This left only option one.

They say that you should never corner a rat, because the normally peaceable and docile creature, which is always willing to run at the slightest provocation, is left with only one alternative.

In the case of Ig, that one alternative was charging headfirst into the man standing before him. And as a little reminder with regards to their respective heights, Ig's head was level to a certain area of the Bonetaker that he had cherished since his teenage years.

The necromancer's cheeks puffed out as he doubled over. Veins of noxious green began to trickle across his cheeks as the Plutonium struggled to escape. Then all it took was for Ig to reach up and pluck me off.

Then it was hello to darkness, my constant companion; hopefully this was to be only a passing visit.

To my immense shame, it felt like home when Ig returned me to his head. The dim eyes, the low-slung perspective, it all felt supremely familiar.

Much obliged, my friend.

The kobold grinned. "Me butt him."

Indeed you did, that's using your head.

"It was!" Ig concurred.

As the Bonetaker straightened up again, I was not sure what to expect. What I definitely did not expect was for him to manage to swallow all his power back down again. If he'd exploded, that would have been expected. If the Plutonium he'd invoked had turned him into a puddle, also within the realms of possibility. But the fact that he was able to regain control of his magic and crush it back down into his reserves, that was kind of impressive.

His bun-ogres were all gone now. Ildrit lay face down with his knees bent and his ass pointed directly up at the sky, just begging for a good kick. All that remained were a great many satisfied-looking werewolves gnawing on bones. All but one. The injured party in all of this. The obnoxious teen that had caused all of our problems with the wolves to begin with, who had tanked through the Bonetaker's death-spell, and who was now staring at him with the kind of focus you don't normally see in a wolf's eyes.

Panting, the Bonetaker paid her no mind. "You . . . little . . . runt."

"Me is normal size for kobold," Ig corrected, to no effect.

"I . . . am going to melt your bones. I'm going to turn you inside out. The things that I'm going to do to you . . ." He called on his magic once more, clearly not one to learn from his mistakes, and he pointed at Ig with one finger of his fleshless arm.

I caught fragments of the Archaic that he was chanting, some vast and complex torture invoking a half dozen elements to put Ig through a fairly comprehensive tour of every pain receptor in his body, as well as a fair few that he'd have to grow just to experience the incoming unpleasantness.

You need to run, Ig. I don't know how to stop this spell.

"Me no leave Ildrit," the stupid little bugger said.

The Bonetaker glowed with all of the gathered Quintessence, and in all likelihood, both Ig and I were about to discover what lay on the other side of the veil between the lands of the living and the dead.

Except that was the moment that the teen wolf chose to leap and latch onto the only bone that remained unchewed: the Bonetaker's replacement arm. She leapt, she bit, she yanked, and he lost his balance and his new arm in one sharp tug.

"No!" he managed to scream, before his tongue flew from his mouth like a slug being fired from a cannon.

With his concentration broken, the many already spoken parts of the spell began sucking Quintessence out of his reserves and manifesting their effects. His flesh began to bubble, his back arched as he was rolled backwards into a perfect sphere, both of his eyeballs shot out in opposite directions then bounced back and forth as though they were on elastic rather than thick cords of nerve. Various bodily fluids sprayed out in every which direction, narrowly avoiding Ig and I but entirely drenching Ildrit.

The warrior rolled over and sat up, startled out of his slumber by the splash of something viscous and green. Awake just in time to see his old friend completely lose all control over his magic and explode apart.

The raw Quintessence that the necromancer had been trying to wield was unleashed into the world. And as with all raw magic, it followed the natural laws.

Where a dead necromancer had stood, now there was a fountain, not of blood or any of those other horrid liquids that had been spraying out before, but of bunnies. Tiny, fluffy and adorable bunnies, sailing up and out in every direction. Emerging from behind every stone. Popping out of the thick fur of the werewolves and immediately regretting their existence.

If you had thought that chaos and pandemonium had been seen before when the wolf pack was confronted with a big heap of moving bones to chew on, imagine their delight to suddenly discover over seven hundred rabbits in their midst. As one, the whole pack's tails started wagging.

CHAPTER TWENTY-SEVEN

A PARTING OF WAYS

"We need run," Ig told Ildrit without prompting.

"Right." Ildrit turned back towards our cave and sprinted. "Yes."

"Need run fast," Ig called back as he overtook him, all the exhaustion of the day forgotten with the baying and yipping wolves at our heels.

Admittedly, those wolves were actually chasing after the unfortunate rabbits that were heading the same direction as us, but that was not the sort of knowledge that would get Ig where I needed him to be faster, so I chose not to share it.

"Where did all these wolves come from?" Ildrit panted as he finally caught up to Ig.

"Secret village," Ig managed to squeak out as we reached the base of the great gravel ramp and swerved away from the obvious route of escape towards the dwarf tunnel.

"Why . . . are we heading underground?"

That was something that I'd sort of hoped wouldn't come up until we were already safely inside the tunnels and I'd contrived some way to collapse the entrance behind us.

Ig also became immediately confused on that subject, his wild sprint slowing as he tried to pick a direction.

Because the woods are full of wolves and the tunnels aren't!

"No wolves!" Ig yelled, as if he'd known all along.

They ran for what I hoped would be the last time in a long time, for the questionable safety of the mines. Air burning in Ig's little kobold lungs. Exhaustion clinging to his little kobold limbs. If only the Bonetaker could have treated Ig to a nice magically induced nap in the midst of all this chaos then perhaps he'd have had the same renewed energy as Ildrit.

Ducking into the cuboid entrance, we lost the werewolves only very briefly. If their noses had carried them this far, then they'd be sure to lead them right to Ig as soon as their excitement over all the little loping fluffy things had worn out.

On we charged into the dark, never glancing back, until we collided with Ildrit. Who for some reason had decided to stop dead in front of us.

"Ow," Ig exclaimed, more out of habit than any actual pain.

"You must carry on, my friends. The dwarves are industrious and their reach is long. Through these tunnels you might traverse beneath the civilized lands that would shun you until you reach Arpanpholigon."

"Me knows that!" said Ig, who most assuredly had not known that. "But why you stopping?"

Reaching down, Ildrit found Widowtaker just where he had left it, or rather, where it had fallen from his numb, sleeping fingers as he was carried out by skeletal rabbits. "I shall hold them off while you make your escape."

Idiot.

"You thinks you is hero now?" Ig asked.

"You know as well as I do that I'll bring doom down on anyone that I travel with. The sins of my past have not yet caught up to me, though I try with all my might to outpace them." Ildrit had a sad smile on his face as he looked down at Ig. "There will be few times in my life that I have a chance to do something that could even border upon heroic. A chance to do some real good in this world. Please, friends, let me do this for you."

Ig weighed this for a moment, then answered, "No."

"What?" Ildrit seemed to be genuinely confused. Presumably he had grown up having heroic tales told to him too, that told him in moments like this there would be grateful tears instead of scowling kobolds.

"Me say no. Me needs you help," Ig clarified. "You no help if stay here and get chewed."

Ildrit clearly thought there was a communication problem, or possibly that Ig was too stupid to understand what was going on. Honestly, it was a fair assumption. More often than not it seemed there was nothing behind the kobold's glassy eyes but the gentle ping of his solitary brain cell bouncing from one side of his skull to the other. "Didn't you hear me before? I am cursed with a dreadful . . ."

"Yes, know all that." Ig cut him off. "Doom bad. Me no care. Need help. World scary, you strong."

Ildrit dropped to one knee and cupped Ig's cheek in his hand. He'd regret that later; I sincerely doubted we'd find any soap in this mine. "I am offering to die for you, here and now."

"No need die." Ig shook his little empty head. "Need live."

"You don't understand." The swordsman sighed. "If you knew the kind of man that I have been, the Bonetaker, he was just a lieutenant to me. I was truly on the path of evil."

Ig shrugged. "You good now."

"It is not so simple."

"Yes is," Ig assured him. "Me was kobold. Now me wizard. You was bad. Now you good."

Ildrit sounded truly anguished. "I cannot simply forget . . ."

"Then no forget." Ig spoke over him before he could descend into more of this maudlin nonsense. "No even forgive if not want. But you is dead, you do no goods. All you leave is bads."

Ildrit seemed to be wavering, until Ig said something so profoundly stupid that it sounded like wisdom. "Be brave. No run away from life."

For a moment, kobold and warrior were eye to eye, then Ildrit seized Ig by the shoulder and hauled him off his feet as he took off running deeper into the mines. Howls echoed in from behind us, possibly just the wolves reveling in their hunt, but just as likely an alert that their true quarry had gone into hiding over here.

We must seal the passage behind us. Examine the runemarks, Ig.

"Weh?"

The marks around the door. The scratches.

Ig tugged at Ildrit's sleeve, stopping their charge as they arrived at the door to the mining complex. "Need look at scritches."

"What?"

"The runemarks will tell us how to seal the way." I forced the words out through Ig's mouth, leaving the poor little bugger choking.

He swung Ig around like a lantern and pointed him at the square doorframe where it protruded from the rock. The original slab that had sealed the way had slid off somewhere out of sight, but if we could find the mechanism . . .

"I don't want to alarm you," Ildrit interrupted our attempts at deciphering the scribbles, "but I think the perfectly normal villagers with nothing to hide may have found us."

His eyes may not have been up to the task, but Ig could most assuredly smell that familiar wet-dog aroma of werewolves headed our way. Panic began mounting in his chest. His heart hammered away so fast I had some fear it might actually crack a rib or two. "Me no understand boon marks."

Runemarks, not . . . it doesn't matter. You do not need to understand them, you just need to look at them so I can understand them.

"You understand them?" Ig asked me with such sincere hope that I didn't have the heart to tell him that they'd been too worn away with time for them to be decipherable.

The way cannot be sealed by the dwarven arts. We must find an alternative.

"We needs make tunnel fall down," Ig announced to Ildrit.

That would not have been my first choice, but as we are short on time, I suppose that we must. Given but a few moments more, I could instruct you in the way of the archmage, which is to say, a wizard who is capable of constructing vaulted doorways through stonecraft, but it seems that such time eludes us once more, so we must rely upon what you already know.

"Me know how to make a 'splode!" Ig announced.

This time, instead of merely looking concerned, Ildrit took off running for the relative safety of one of the farthest tunnels branching out from the chamber beyond. He dragged Ig along with him, even though if we were being honest, he was likely the thing that he should have been running from.

Channeling his grievously incomplete knowledge of Sulfur, Ig prepared himself to cast the same explosive curse that had scorched an arm from the Bonetaker and left molten stone dripping from the ceiling where it had passed. Now that we had been returned to that same chamber, we could see the damage he'd dealt, and understand how he might deal it again.

Yet we did not have long for our contemplations. From the tunnel back to the quarry, there was the unmistakable sound of slavering hounds approaching. Yipping and barking and howling all the way. Death came for us on four paws, and we were all trusting in Ig to save us from it.

His heart was hammering in his chest already, and with the approach of the wolves, it now kicked into vibratory overdrive.

You must be cautious, Ig, the destructive possibilities of this spell put all of us at risk.

Ig laid a hand upon my brim and smiled. "Me gots this."

Then, at the top of his little ratty lungs, he bellowed, **"Fragor!"**

All of the Quintessence that he had gathered since his last casting was unleashed, but where before there had been a sudden eruption, instead, this time the swirling mass of yellow-green flame curled back around on itself before escaping to wreak havoc, stabilizing into the most common shape in the cosmos, the sphere.

My little baby wizard had just made his first fireball.

And now it was going to kill us all.

He did not know how to direct it away from us with a push of his will. He did not know how to craft a secondary spell from Nitrogen and Oxygen to push it towards its intended target. All he knew how to do was all that I had taught him, which was to draw in more Quintessence and pour it into a spell until it did what he wanted it to do.

The swirling sphere of heckfire blazed brighter and brighter as Ig fed it more magic. Getting larger and larger with every passing moment. Swelling until even the internal pull of the magic itself was no longer sufficient to contain it and flares began erupting from the surface of this tiny subterranean sun.

Run, you imbecile, run!

Ig shook his head once more, all the pride in his many victories this day giving birth to the world's first case of an overconfident kobold. He grinned as wide as he could and announced, "Me gots this!"

In the ensuing explosion, Ig's unconscious body was flung in the general direction of Ildrit. The roof of the chamber that we had all been occupying was ripped asunder by the lashing tendrils of flame, now looking distinctly more demonic once they'd been freed from the sphere, and all of the stone that the well-constructed ceiling had been holding up now fell directly down.

The chamber collapsed. The sudden arrival of all the stone drove the air out of it, launching anything light enough to be disturbed by a sudden gust in every which direction. Including, as it would turn out, hats.

I had only a fraction of a second's reassurance that Ig was still breathing before the concussive force of the exploding heckfire ball and the collapsing chamber jerked me off his head and sent me sailing off down one of the other corridors. Or at least, I assume that was what happened.

Wherever I ended up was completely dark and completely silent, just as it always was. And since I didn't feel like anything fundamental had been shredded, I had to assume that I made it outside of the blast radius of the collapse.

And so my journey back to humanity came to its end, in this most ignominious of places. Abandoned in some dark tunnel, sealed off from the outside world and doomed to an eternity of slow decline as the Quintessence that maintained my sapience slowly drained away. Who could guess how many millennia would pass with me trapped in such torment? Who could imagine a more terrible fate for one of the greatest minds to ever walk the world to be condemned to than this? To have all of my knowledge and no way to share it? To have such a thirst for learning, but no senses to absorb that which the world longed to show me? Forget the place with the flames of Sulfur and the dancing imps with pitchforks: this was heck. This was truly heck. An eternity of nothingness.

Needless to say, someone picked me up and put me on about half an hour after the explosion.

ABOUT THE AUTHORS

Luke Chmilenko is the author of the Ascend Online series, among others. He grew up in Mississauga, Ontario, and now lives in Burlington, Ontario, with his wife, daughter, and two cats. Visit his website at lukechmilenko.com.

G. D. Penman is the author of more books than you can shake a reasonable-size stick at. Before finally realizing that his guidance counselor had lied about one's not being able to make a living as an author, Penman worked as an editor, tabletop game designer, and literally every awful demeaning job that you can think of in between. Nowadays, he can mostly be found smoking a pipe in the sunshine and pretending that deadlines aren't lurking behind him with a club. He lives in Dundee, Scotland, with his menagerie.

DISCOVER
STORIES UNBOUND

PodiumAudio.com

Printed in France by Amazon
Brétigny-sur-Orge, FR

17578279R00161